David Cartwright w Golden Age of Satu that time and forev watcher and reader of Science-Fiction and Fantasy, encompassing the likes of The Hitchhikers Guide to the Galaxy, The Walking Dead and the works of J.R.R. Tolkien and Neil Gaiman.

David has been a Jack of many trades, but so far, a master of none, working mostly in manufacturing whilst studying in Media and Counselling.

He lives in Hampshire, England with his family, cat and untameable moustache.

You can follow the author via his social media profiles;
D.Cart-writer on Twitter and
David Cart-writer on Facebook

Black Knight

Camelot 2050
Book One

David Cartwright

Published by Ingramspark

First published in Great Britain in 2017 by Ingramspark

Printed and bound in Great Britain by Ingramspark

A catalogue record for this book is available from The British Library
ISBN 978 1 5272 1901 4

Foreword

My father did something he probably ought not to have when I was around 4 or 5, and that was let me watch *Excalibur*. You remember that film right? That wondrous, gleaming and sometimes quirky film about King Arthur and the Knights of Camelot, featuring the likes of Helen Mirren as Morgana, a loud Patrick Stewart being pretty much himself, and even a young Liam Neeson making an appearance. Knights on horseback riding out, banners all a-fluttering with *Carmina Burana* adding to the thunder of their charge. Let's not also forget the unabashed violence and gore. Which is fine. It didn't affect me in any detrimental way (he says, eye all atwitch). My father also constantly reminds me of when I was a wee lad and would strike out to the park proclaiming the immortal line of "Any man who would be a knight and follow a king, follow me!" From this film I progressed (again, dad you're totally to blame for this) to the Conan films and even Red Sonja, using the training scenes in them to get a better handle on the art of sword fighting than any of my peers (and yes, I am aware I said I was 5 at the time).

Out of *Excalibur* grew my love for fantasy and all things fantastical. Out of these sword-and-sorcery films came the fascination with finding any excuse to wave something vaguely sword-like in the air and make like an Arthurian knight (which incidentally proves a problem when you are neither all that tall and certainly not muscular in any way). So while casting around for ideas, imagine my delight when I realise that somewhere nearby in my green (and wet) homeland of Wales (which apparently might have been where Arthur, Merlin and even Camelot could well have been according to some historical sources), there were regular gatherings of people who camped out in a forest for a couple of days in the year, donned armour, costumes and weapons, and proceeded to play at being fantasy characters - trying to be all adult and serious about it, while really it was just a big excuse to dress up and hit people with fake weapons. *Perfect!* I thought.

Into this creative melee came Dave Cartwright – a bear of a man not unlike the character of Sir Dominic in the story you are about to read, albeit with less beard. Striking up a friendship with this gentle, though lewd giant was no hard task (see

Dave? I said *hard*). He came along to my wedding, and not to be outdone I went along to his. I was escorted from my wedding in a Rolls Royce, Dave in a TVR Chimera. I had *Nothing Else Matters* as the first dance, he had his sisters *sing* Metallica. So we're totally not in competition here.

One day he casually flings my way a little something he'd apparently been working on, and so I was one of the first to be treated to the very first draft of the book you are about to read. As I've already stated, Arthurian stories were very appealing to me, and to have a story based on a big "what if" like Arthur surviving the battle of Camlann intrigued me greatly. The *science* part of sci-fi had always been a problem for me to write, but not it seemed for Dave. Cyber-knights atop robotic steeds (with a "c" mind you, because annoyingly "cyborg" doesn't start with an "s") really helped me recapture that sense of wonder I had at seeing knights in gleaming armour riding out from Camelot in *Excalibur*. However it was a single, simple moment that tipped me over the edge and remained lodged in my head thereafter that this was something very special. Cassie the hacker is visited in her cell by Eric, her cyber-raven, who proceeds to transform himself so that his wings become a QWERTY keyboard, and his head projecting a holographic display. That was it, I was done. I *had* to have more of this in my life. In fact, since the story wasn't completely finished in that first draft, I actually wrote back an angry note, threatening to visit misfortune on him and his house if he didn't finish the damned story.

Here we are some years later (I guess my threats just weren't that good) and we finally have Camelot 2050 to wow us and thrill us and view Dave's scintillating take on what the good old British Isles would be like if our single greatest historical figure (whether or not he was just a fiction or an amalgamation of many figures) had gone on to forge that mighty bastion of honour, justice and valour that was Camelot. Just what kind of shining example could we have been to the world if we had that gleaming castle of silver and gold standing tall over Big Ben like it does in this book?

And that for me was another mark of this book's brilliance. When I was younger I read a few books which were sci-fi takes on established stories – one I particularly recall was basically Robin Hood with aliens as the enemy. But we're not talking about a remake of an old story here. We're talking about a "what if" story. We're not retelling the Arthur story and trying to put a different spin on it per se, not like those god-awful films that Hollywood keeps putting out. The Arthur story has happened, and in these pages it now continues. This is a *continuation* of the Arthur tale, and that's important to remember. The magic didn't stop, it carries on right here.

So sit back and let Dave Cartwright take you on a journey that captures the splendour of *Excalibur*, in all its thundering glory, shining brilliance and quirky characters. Let *Carmina Burana* sing out as the new knights of Camelot strike out against an old darkness. And then let's all get together and craft a really good threatening set of emails that make sure Dave writes the next one, and quickly. And let anyone, who would read about some knights, and follow a king, follow me!

MJ Bridger

Author of *Monk-son of Kunlun* and *Tales of the Ten Kingdoms*

This book is dedicated to those people who, by interest or inspiration, have encouraged, engaged or brow-beaten me to 'Get it done,' and in so doing, have become a part of the ongoing effort to see it published.

<u>Camelot 2050: Black Knight</u>

Prologue: The Battle of Camlann 537 AD.

The battle lines of destiny had long been drawn. Two armies waited in the high summer sun, that of the old King, and that of his bastard son and would-be heir. Thousands of armed men faced each other across the field as their Generals spoke in hopes of peace. In the open, halfway between the opposing forces they met, father and son. They spoke at length of things that had gone before, matters of fate and honour. Soon enough their talk turned to all that might come after. Finally, father embraced son, and a peace was struck.

Then the viper appeared, the snake in the grass. A man drew his sword and lopped off its head, too late realizing his mistake. The sun shimmered along the blade. Across the field came a dozen like reflections and then the cry of 'Treachery!' rose along both sides. The hard won peace was dashed aside, the generals swiftly withdrawn by their personal guards as, in an instant, battle was joined.

The sun beat down upon the chaos and dust, horses screamed and men died; the thirsty earth drank the blood of the dead and dying, as the battle pressed to and fro. The King rode out with his bodyguard into the sea of steel, searching for his son so that the slaughter might end. Finally, after a hot and dangerous search and with a trail of bodies in his wake, the old King gained sight of his son upon a rise, laying about with his sword and sundering men with each stroke. His expression grim and his bodyguard at his back, he dismounted and strode up to face his son, his enemy.

"Mordred!" cried Arthur "Let us stop this now!" Mordred turned and glared at his father from beneath a darkened brow.
"It's too late my father, my King!" He spat, bitterly. "It has gone too far, and we are but pawns of fate now!"
"Fate is what we make of it!" Arthur returned, but he knew the truth of his sons' words and held his sword aloft.
"Enough, father! One of our legends ends this day, and the other will be born anew in blood!" Mordred raised his own blade and charged.
Father and son were evenly matched, Mordred with youth, speed and endurance; against Arthur with experience, cunning and patience. Their swords met over and over as, above them, the sky darkened and the wind started to howl. A deathly cold crept from the earth and into the air over the battlefield. Time and again, their swords rang out as they turned, struck and circled each other upon the rise. Finally Mordred's' youthful impatience overcame him, and he struck out in frustration. Driven by years of

experience, Arthur's arm drove his sword out and in, deflecting the oncoming blade and parting armour and flesh. With a twist, he withdrew the fabled blade of Excalibur, now dripping crimson with his son's blood.

Mordred looked at his father's sword, then his hand touched the seeping gash in his own armour. He raised bloodied fingers as Arthur, stunned, lowered his blade and staggered back from his son in horror. Mordred chuckled weakly at the sight of his own life staining his fingers, and the laughter rose, echoing out over the rise to reach a hysterical crescendo. Suddenly, jaw locked and eyes aflame, he threw himself once more at his father. Arthur met his maddened eyes and resigned himself to his fate.

Time crystallized around them.

The wind stirred the old man's greying hair and tugged at his cloak. Around him, his bodyguard fought in the press. He felt he had time enough to gauge the effectiveness of their every sword-stroke, and all the while his son's sword point approached with the unstoppable inevitability of a glacier, and he could not bring himself to parry. He closed his eyes.

The thud of blade into body brought Arthur back to himself. The tip of the sword that scraped at his armoured chest didn't waver, but didn't pierce him. Lancelot, interposed between Arthur and Mordred, toppled to the ground like a discarded doll; his golden hair formed a halo around him as he fell, despite the darkened sky. Mordred, defeated and dying, slumped gasping beside Lancelot.

Arthur sheathed his sword and knelt between his son and his fallen friend. Gently, he raised Mordred to his lap. Discarding his mailed gloves and oblivious to the battle around him, he looked down into still defiant eyes.

"My son..." he began.

"It is how it should be, father." Mordred drew a shuddering breath. "I thought not to destroy Camelot, nor your memory, but Mother's desire for revenge was nigh irresistible. I'm sorry... Father" and with a final sigh, Mordred perished.

Arthur held his son close to him, and blinked back the tears that welled in his eyes. After a moment, he rested him on the bloodied ground, and turned to where one of his bodyguards now supported Lancelot.

Mordred's sword had pierced the gallant knight in a weakened spot on his breastplate, and now protruded grotesquely from his torso. Lancelot looked heavenward, but his eyes were glazed and unfocused. Cold sweat ran from his brow and plastered his hair to his pallid face as he licked at dry lips.

"M...my liege..." stammered Lancelot.

4

"Hush now, friend," Arthur drew his hand across the fallen man's brow, clearing the matted hair from his eyes, "you must conserve your strength."

"Surely you jest, sire?" Lancelot shivered, the movement jarring the sword that pierced his body making him cry out. "I have delivered enough death blows to recognize mine own."

"Lancelot..." Arthur began.

"Sire" the dying knight raised a trembling hand to take Arthur's. "Time is short, I must speak." He drew a ragged breath and, gathering his last strength, brought his eyes to focus on Arthur.

"My betrayal, my sin; let it die with me. Let my blood buy some forgiveness, not for myself nor for Guinevere, but for Camelot. One man's weakness may crumble walls built on faith, but surely a sacrifice for the sake of loyalty might shore them up?"

His words spoken, Lancelot seemed to shrink as his strength left him. Arthur gripped the fallen knights' hand in his and took hold of Lancelot's shoulder with his other.

"Lancelot; not for loyalty did you do this, but love. You have saved my life, and for that I will save Camelot. I cannot forget your weakness, but I can forgive you, and offer this for your sacrifice. When this day is done, I will mourn not one son, but two."

Lancelot smiled weakly and his last words were a whisper. "Thank you my friend, above all others I... loved you..."

The reign of Camelot has lasted over a thousand years. In the centuries following the battle of Camlann, the beacon of law and order that Camelot stood for has only blazed brighter and brighter.

Chapter 1

Rosalyn sat on the edge of her bed, her hands gripping the mattress. Her breathing was rapid and ragged, and a fine patina of cold sweat beaded her brow. The edges of her nightmare were fading; a storm-wracked sky, the smell of old death and the beat of terrible, leathery wings. Those wings buffeting her had awoken her, and now she sat in the stillness of her room, shaking.

With a deep, shuddering breath she tried to gain some composure. Taking the glass of water from the nightstand she drank, washing away the taste of dust and old tombs. She sat for a moment more before running a diagnostic. Cerebral implants functioning within recommended parameters: Physiological implants reporting status 'ready': Respiration and adrenaline levels elevated - returning to normal.

She listened to the beat of her heart as it slowed to a more even pace. Anxiety? She'd known anxiety before when waiting for a test result or embarking on a new scheme of her training. The physiological symptoms were not unknown to her, but this? The cold sensation in her mind that locked down any notion of action or response? This was new to her. Was it fear?

Unsettled, she looked at the clock. Five forty five in the morning, a quarter hour before her alarm. She glanced around the room; it was familiar to her and reassuring. A guest room in one of the executive suites at the Savoy, London. Her liege, Sir Phillip stayed here whenever he came to the city on business and, when she travelled with him, she stayed in this room. The plush carpets, soft bed and fine furniture attested to the affluence of the place, and she had used the ornate writing desk by the window so often in her studies that it might as well have been her own.

Still she couldn't help peering into the shadowed corners of the room, watching the dark gap of the barely open wardrobe door in case some shadowy creature launched itself forth. She closed her eyes and shook her head. Monsters? She hadn't been scared of monsters in the closet since... well, ever. As long as she could remember; almost as far back as the day she was delivered to Phillip's household as his new squire after her parents passed away, she had never been afraid... or angry, or (if it came to it) happy. She had journeyed through her life thus far knowing only anxiety toward an as yet untried task, satisfaction in its completion and the underlying bond of loyalty to her liege. That this should only occur to her now was even more unsettling.

A soft knock on her door shook her from her introspection. "Come in," she called softly.

Sir Phillip cracked the door and leaned in, he flipped the switch to the bedside lamps set on the wall just inside the door. Rosalyn flinched at the sudden light. "Is everything alright?" he asked, his voice quiet and measured.

"I'm fine, just a nightmare," she replied and smiled.

He paused in the doorway as the silence stretched out. "Is something wrong?" Rosalyn asked.

"Nothing," Phillip shook his head, "I just couldn't remember the last time I'd seen you smile. It looks good on you." He seemed to remember himself and stood up straight, all business and propriety. "Anyway," he cleared his throat a little, "It's good that you are awake early. We have a lot to do. We have to relocate to the Castle for the games."

"Yes my liege," Rosalyn responded automatically, then stopped herself before asking, "May I ask why? In the past few years I have attended and, even when I compete, we have stayed here. Why must we now take rooms at the castle?"

Phillip stared at her a moment before responding.

"Because you are growing up Rosalyn, and I don't want you growing up alone. It is time you made some friends." He turned to go, then stopped and called over his shoulder. "Oh, and you won't be 'taking rooms' as you put it. You'll be in the barracks, with the rest of the squires." He looked back at her over his shoulder. "I'm aware there may be some 'ruffled feathers' still lingering. I'd advise taking gifts."

Castle Camelot (relocated to the site of Old Londinium) 2050 AD.

On the eve of the King's tournament, the sun shone red as it sank toward the horizon. In the months of late spring, the white outer walls of the Castle took on a deep orange hue, radiating a reassuring image of warmth to all that might see them for miles around. This year, as the pennants and banners for the coming games fluttered in a gentle breeze, the wall had taken a deep red tone, the colour of fresh blood. An echo of days of violence past, or perhaps a fitting portent of the times to come.

The squires' barracks were alive with activity. Time was pressing on before the grand ball that would mark the start of the tournament. The King and his knights would be greeting visiting dignitaries and personalities, and it would be the duty of the squires to present themselves in a manner befitting their liege lords. In the basic quarters of the barracks hall, they set to preparing their personal gear and dressing in finery for the ball. Some sat at info-ports and picked their events for the coming competitions, while others compared new augmentations, and quietly attempted to sound out their masters' competition.

"Hey Swift!" a cheery, dark-skinned youth dangled upside-down from the bunk above to greet Geoffrey Mayland, Squire to the Baron of Stafford. Geoffrey recognised the boy before he'd uttered the first syllable of the greeting. His enhanced nervous system and higher brain function picked the name to match the face instantly, along with the memory of being dubbed 'Swift' by the other squires, after winning a bet involving a tech-familiar messenger swallow and ten miles of open fields. Geoffrey was well liked among the squires. His open and honest nature, quick wit and handsome features prompted many predictions of great things to come once he attained knighthood.

"Hello Royston."

Royston Glasbury was a young squire. This was only his second games, but he'd already made a name for himself on the archery scene. The chromed plate that covered his right temple was testament to his tech implants.

"Is that targeting array still giving you trouble? That was a shame last year."

"Oh no, no!" the young squire grinned sadly over the memory of his near victory in the previous year's archery event. Tipped as the youngest champion ever, Royston had suffered an augmentation glitch in the final round. With the targets set at three-hundred metres, his targeting monocle had jammed in its housing and he had been forced to shoot without his enhancement. Though his muscular refinements had let him make the distance, his perfect vision and natural ability couldn't copy the accuracy of his targeting implant, and he had narrowly missed out on the medal positions.

"The technicians fixed the stuck bearings and boosted the clarity. My liege thinks that with my natural abilities I can shoot accurately over any distance a bow can reach. This year I intend to prove him right," he finished with a warm smile.

A gentle change in the current of the rooms' hubbub alerted them to a new arrival.

"Uh-oh!" Royston exclaimed, and the chrome plate in his head opened, swinging the small silver targeting monocle over his lead eye. Geoffrey could hear the whine of micro-servos as the augmentation focused on the new arrival. "Grayson's here, and he's coming this way."

Belvarre Grayson, son of the Duke of Oxford (and squire to the same) swept into the room sparing little more than an aloof glance for the other occupants. His eyes lit upon Geoffrey, the only squire present whose liege-knight approached his father's standing, and he smiled coldly. No love was lost between the two; they shared the same chilly acquaintance as their Lords. Grayson's father had demanded the M.A.G.E.s genetic manipulation abilities be pushed to the limit for his squire and heir. Duke Jerome Grayson detested the 'cumbersome nature' of mechanical implants and the way they marred the natural form of the bearer. Baron Dominic, Geoffrey's knight, submitted to those implants that best suited his nature and helped him serve Camelot the better. He had little concern for the aesthetics.

Jerome's distaste had passed to his squire, alongside the advances in gene-therapy his exacting standards had born. The only sign of any form of procedure upon Belvarre's body were the penny-sized silver plates upon his joints, access points for chemical stimulant injections, bio-enhancement treatments, or diagnostic equipment. Belvarre himself held little regard for those events that weren't directly associated with a knight's station. Such events as foot races, swimming or weightlifting were beneath his notice. Belvarre craved the acclaim of more martial events.

"Hello Geoffrey." Grayson's voice insinuated itself into the room. He glanced disdainfully over the metaplast material woven into Geoffrey's body, visible now he was dressed only in shorts and undershirt to prepare his clothes and equipment.

"Still on those old Ulysses 442 exo-frames and the rigoplast tendon links I see."

Geoffrey spared a wry grin for his fellow squire. "I do find myself rather 'attached' to them, Bel."

A chuckle rippled around the room in response.

Belvarre sniffed dismissively. "Still acting the messenger-boy?" any interest he displayed was feigned; his manner clearly advertised that he was simply making his own opinions known to any of the year's newcomers.

Much as he disliked Grayson, Geoffrey couldn't help but admire him. Time and again they would spar like this, trading veiled barbs again and again and always before an audience. Grayson was arrogant and sure of himself, Geoffrey was more than aware of this. He lived to display his own superiority, but when he did find some measure of a challenge (as he did in Geoffrey's quick-witted banter) he couldn't help but come back again and again until he had proved himself its equal, or its better.

"Well now Bel," Geoffrey grinned around at the room, "It's just no good being the finest swordsman in the realm if the second finest finished the fight before you got there." His overdone display of humility tipped the scale in his favour and the chuckles and murmurs of approval his statement provoked drew a dark veil over Grayson's features before he could school them back into a disinterested mask.

Another arrival brought a sly smile to Belvarre's thin lips. "But I do declare that the sport just got more interesting." Grayson continued without acknowledging the barb.

"Here comes the delightful Rosalyn Juliet Taunton-Savant of Essex. I always did think her liege could afford as many names for her as he does implants, don't you think?"

Ros entered the noise and excitement of the bunk-room and the general chatter fell to a hushed murmur.

"Well look who it is," a mechanical voice grated through the room like the chains of a ship's anchor careering out of the hull. Sebastian Crown of Dorset unfolded from his bunk. Standing at close to six feet and ten inches he was almost as tall as some of the knights of the Table. He'd always been tall for his age and ungainly with it. Before he was chosen as a squire, he'd been ruthlessly teased about his clumsiness. After his selection his liege had, perhaps unwisely, allowed him to choose his own programme of enhancements, resulting in a gyro-stabilised micro-hydraulic framework that gave him the strength to lift two grown men in each hand. His optic implants (while dated and appearing as a pair of bulky brass opera glasses) protruded slightly from his face and allowed him to record and assess where he struck an opponent and what damage he had caused. The tech-collar that encompassed his neck and merged into his torso allowed him to speak any language on net records at volumes that could shake a building to pieces (albeit a poorly constructed one). It was no secret amongst the other squires that he enjoyed seeing just how much pain he could inflict in contest, and that he reckoned himself an engine of destruction in service to the Crown (though whether it was the Crown of Camelot or that of his own name was often discussed at length by his peers). It was an image he went to lengths to preserve.

The older squires knew to expect a confrontation whenever Ros and Sebastian met, though the intensity of the meetings could never be anticipated. Once, upon a wager, Ros had entered into a wrestling match, Sebastian's chosen event. To the surprise of all she had triumphed on a technicality. Her own augmentations and reflexes had kept her far enough ahead of Sebastian's attacks that he had lost his temper, knocked her down with a wild, back-handed swipe and made to crush her with a powerful foot-stamp. When Ros rolled out from under him, the ring floor had given way under Sebastian's attack and he had snapped a power-cable underneath. The resulting shock had knocked Sebastian out and awarded Ros the win. Though she had never wrestled in competition again, Sebastian still bore the embarrassment of his defeat.

"I thought your liege would have bought you your own place in the city, not let you slum with the rest of us." A soft murmur of agreement ran through some of the room while others just turned away. As squire to one of the richest households in the kingdom, Ros was often afforded augmentations and equipment that others could only dream of. She was often a figure for jealousy amongst her fellow squires.

The room fell silent as Sebastian awaited some response from Ros, even Grayson kept his mouth closed for the confrontation. Looking up into the big squire's crudely augmented eyes, Ros reached into her large carry bag, drew out several dark bottles and placed them on a foot-locker in front of him.

"Phelleson Hydroponic-Port," a nasal voice whined, and a lank-haired individual peered out from behind Crown's broad form, "And a '56 vintage at that, very good."

"Good enough that it might shut you up for a while, Raoul?" Ros stated boldly. Raoul Folkestone was a squire in his own right, but always seemed to be around Sebastian Crown. His nasal cavities were rumoured to be the most sensitive in the land, rather unfortunate when a botched metabolism enhancement had raised his core temperature and now caused him to sweat profusely.

Folkestone opened his mouth to reply but Sebastian rumbled on.

"Maybe, just for now. Though I might have expected you'd buy your way out of trouble."

Taking the bottles in his massive hands he headed for his bunk, a small crowd of followers tagging along behind.

Ros hefted her bag again and headed to an empty cot next to Geoffrey, pointedly ignoring the smug look Belvarre directed her way.

"Is this bunk taken?" she asked the question as if she expected a curt 'Yes'.

Geoffrey and Royston shared a grave look for as long as they could stand before both started to chuckle.

"Not at all, please, be our guest." Geoffrey supplied as he stood from his bed.

"Geoffrey Mayland, Squire to Stafford and this" he introduced himself as he reached up and took Royston by the collar, dragging him unceremoniously off his bunk with a yelp of surprise, "is Royston Glasbury, Squire to Tonbridge, and we are both deeply honoured to meet you." Geoffrey couldn't keep the mirth from his voice as Royston picked himself up from the floor, dusted himself down and jabbed Geoffrey in the ribs with his elbow.

"The honour is all mine then." Ros offered, the surprise in her voice giving way to warmth as she went on. Geoffrey held out a hand, sure of his own notoriety.

"Master Glasbury caused quite a stir at last year's games if I recall." She thrust her hand out to Royston who shook it readily, much to Geoffrey's bemusement. Ros rolled her eyes and allowed herself a chuckle.

"And who hasn't heard of Stafford's squire? I'm glad to finally meet you Geoffrey."

"Swift." prompted Geoffrey "All my friends call me Swift."

Ros turned away to set down her bag (and hide the slight flush that had crept to her cheeks) when she turned back she held another bottle.

"Rosalyn Taunton-Savant. You can call me Ros. I'm afraid those brutes cleared me out of port but I do still have a nice Chablis to my name."

"Maybe after the dinner," smiled Geoffrey "We should be wary. Sebastian may be put off for now but he's like a bad penny, he'll come back to you at some point."

Geoffrey considered a moment. "Royston, would you mind putting that eye of yours to use and see if you can find the Ox of York? Ask him to meet us back here after the opening ball. I owe him a drink and he's not bad company to have around."

"Sure thing, Swift." Royston threw a mock salute and moved off among the bunks, a knowing smile upon his face.

As he left Ros turned to Geoffrey "What's that about?" she questioned.

Geoffrey grinned hugely "A little insurance, you'll see. Now, shall we go to the ball?"

Chapter 2

The walls of Camelot soared over the surrounding city of London. They towered even above the nearby citizens' parliament building and its famous clock tower. The city bustled around the great, white edifice, but the moat and grass banks that ran around the massive castle gave Camelot an air of regal serenity through even the most boisterous public celebrations, and the King's Tournament was surely one of those.

The castle gates stood open as the evening drew on, as guests arrived from all corners of the kingdom and beyond. The main courtyard stood lined with men at arms in smart dress uniforms, as all manner of vehicles disgorged their passengers. Strings of elegant lights crisscrossed overhead, giving the impression under the darkening sky of a vast, vaulted ceiling over the courtyard. The main doors to the grand reception hall, old oak and the height of three grown men, funnelled the guests together as they passed through, and a good natured air permeated as greetings were exchanged and old acquaintances renewed.

All of the current knights of the Table were in attendance with their wives, children and squires in tow. The county nobles and their households, foreign dignitaries from the known world as well as prominent business, sport and entertainment figures were there. Even the secretive Guilds had sent high-ranking representatives. The richly-dressed members of the Engineers and Technicians Guild stood out against the background of the more mundane guests. Bedecked with technological trinkets, they moved like islands of light within the throng. Their personal entourages were also decked out with the products of their craft, the latest technologies showcased for the event. Light enhancing fibres (intended for camouflage garments) allowed for elegant displays of shifting, morphing patterns on broad shoulders and feminine curves alike. Holographic-projectors mounted in rings emitted tiny laser models of famous landmarks as they rested upon slender, nimble fingers. Each tech stood at the centre of their own small audience of admirers, smiling and displaying their treasures.

Almost in direct opposition, the representatives of the M.A.G.E.s Guild (Medical Augmentation and Genetic Engineering), heavily robed and cowled in fine materials, seemed to walk within their own bubble of personal space. Around the shadowy figures the conversation hushed, and people stared in awed silence at the passing members of Merlin's secretive cult.

The Knights themselves towered over the crowd. Each of them acted as a demi-host for the Castle of Camelot. Some moved gracefully, warmly greeting each person with impeccable manners, while others shook hands with gusto, traded loud greetings and roared with good-natured laughter. A few made sober salutations, extending the minimum acceptable courtesy under the circumstances. All were immediately recognisable by their stature. The least of them stood head and shoulders above the tallest of the other guests. Every knight wore, over fine clothes, a tabard in their house colours with their family crest resplendent on the right shoulder and the Royal crest of Camelot over their hearts. Even with their fine clothes, many proudly displayed the other physical marks of their status. Bared arms revealed splendid, gunmetal exo-skeletal lacings, polished and flexing with every movement. Heads and faces bore chromium plates which glinted under the lights like so much jewellery, each one housing a bio-mechanical marvel to augment one or more of the knights' senses. Many were accompanied by the whirr of micro-servos as they moved. Others leaned toward more organic augmentations, their hair and skin sharing the chameleonic abilities of the Tech's clothing, or artificial double-jointing allowing a range of movement that a contortionist would envy. Indeed, some of them could shake hands with guests at all points of the compass without turning away from a single conversation, and their flexibility let them perform wonderful displays in the dance hall. Some told the stories of the ancient tapestries that bedecked the hall's walls, tales of high adventure, great hunts and battles long won. They added to the tales with the implants in their throats allowing them to mimic voices, bird calls and a range of other sound effects to the joy of the listeners.

At the inner doors stood the four senior knights of the Round Table council. They greeting each guest as they passed through the inner portal, and each of them stood with their attendant squires.

Rosalyn stood slightly behind her knight, Phillip Christian-Dubois, the Earl-Adamant of Essex. He greeted guests with a ready hand and modest smile. Tall and sporting, with neatly cropped dark hair, he made an almost regal figure that commanded respect across the kingdom. Rosalyn knew that Phillip was considered an oddity amongst the knights of Camelot. He invested generously in commercial ventures within his lands (this in itself was a common practice) but Phillip also owned his own company and actively participated in matters of business. His easy charm made him popular amongst the knights, but his economic endeavours had made his household one of the richest in the land. His financial efforts even allowed him to afford the high guild-rates charged to allow his house a M.A.G.E. in residency.

Between shaking hands with guests he leaned down to her and spoke softly. "In every situation is a lesson. Let us review your knowledge of some of our comrades, shall we?"

Welcoming an opportunity to shift focus from the dazzling spectacle around her, Ros turned her mind to what she knew of the Knights and representatives in attendance.

"Well," she began, "Next to us is Baron Dominic Fairchild of Stafford, with his squire."

As if noticing the attention, Geoffrey winked at Ros as he caught her looking around. Ros smiled somewhat bashfully and looked again at Dominic.

The Baron stood tall (even for a knight) and was all the broader for the heavy mechanical implants laced into his legs, spine and shoulders. A great mane of red hair and beard framed a wide, toothy grin, and a face creased with lines from his perpetual smile and good nature.

"He's known as a siege engineer of unsurpassed skill. Opinions vary as to his character. Some members of the upper echelons often decry the low quality of his celebrations, however, those who know him, such as yourself my liege, realise that the events he hosts stretch across his lands and holdings to include every person. Few others mirror his generosity, even on the main public holidays." She shifted her focus to the next knight.

"Across from us is Dame Seraphine Feldon of Consett," Ros could barely keep the admiration from her voice as she considered the knight who stood serenely, the proud equal of any member of the Table. "She is known to be the better of any knight with sword, bow or rifle, and a favourite in the competitions to come. Currently she is unattended by a squire, but everyone knows that she has exacting standards, and has not yet found a suitable candidate for the position. Some question if she ever will."

Seraphine's cool blue eyes quickly assessed each member of the crowd, prompting Ros to continue. "Her irises are augmented, they phase through spectrums of light and heat to detect and identify the smallest power sources and possible threats."

'Even as her beauty and quietly spoken words reassure each person of their own important place at the ceremonies', Ros thought to herself. The squire deeply admired Dame Feldon, her chameleonic hair shared and accented the colours of her gown and tabard, highlights shifting through its full length. She drew envious glances from all quarters, not least from Ros who (perhaps unfairly) thought her own

26

cropped bob and velvet dress so utterly outclassed that she must seem as a peasant next to such a vision. She moved on, looking to the knight next to Dame Feldon.

The last senior knight of the council stood unnervingly still. He greeted each visiting delegate soberly and briskly with stiff formality. His pallid complexion and silver-white hair only served to enhance his cold, detached appearance.

"His Grace Jerome Grayson, the Duke of Oxford, the most gifted tactical mind of his generation, some would say the century. He possesses filter lenses built into a third, nictitating eyelid. These technological marvels complement Dame Feldon's ability by visually scanning for broadcast signals and their sources. The lenses' base function of sweeping the infrared band for heat signatures give the Duke's eyes a faint scarlet hue which, given the owner's pale colouring, often leads to the mistaken assumption that he is an albino. His passionate resentment of this frequent misunderstanding and his cold demeanour have failed to endear him to many of his brother and sister knights, but none could deny his skill in single combat or political acumen." He spared Ros a withering look as he caught her appraising him and muttered something to his son Belvarre, who just smiled that smug smile of his and said nothing. She could sense Phillip's amusement at the frank description.

Next in line to formally greet the guests stood the senior guild advisors to the Court of Camelot. Rosalyn considered them a moment as Philip shook a foreign dignitary's hand.

"Lady Teresa Mulholland, advisor to the King from the Tech Guild." The woman glittered under the function lighting, her dark skin complemented by the shimmering iridescence of her dress. The shining colours of the gown nearly matched the shine of her eyes, which were alight with the joy of the occasion. A slender 6' tall, she was a favourite with the palace residents and visitors alike. Her wit and charm were seemingly contagious, and she possessed an unaltered singing voice that was the joy of many an evening gathering. Rosalyn couldn't help but be warmed by Teresa's presence. On the few occasions she had visited the castle with Phillip, she had occasionally had cause to speak with the technical advisor, and found her to be a mine of useful information, castle gossip and simple good company (though Rosalyn kept this fact to herself).

"Lady Mulholland has served the Crown as advisor for three years, and shown herself to be as technically gifted as she is charming. Her opposite number is the castle's senior resident M.A.G.E. Arcady Mountbatten." Ros suppressed a shudder as she contemplated him. Hunched-over and concealed beneath a cowled robe, he seemed to remain as a matter of form alone. He shared greetings with few but those of his guild, and glanced constantly at the large clock high on the hall wall. A burgundy robe heavy with gold embroidery bedecked his shoulders, obscuring his form, but his stoop clearly advertised his advanced age, even while the shadows of his hood concealed his features. At his side, and rather more openly, stood his apprentice Nicholaeos Westbrook. Rosalyn had rarely seen the young mage outside of formal occasions (admittedly she only just remembered his name). Young, tall and slim, he sported a simple, unhooded robe of royal purple. Slick, black hair, and a fussy, triangular goatee were his only adornments. He stood uneasily among the high-status guests, avoided by squires, knights and nobles alike. Hardly privy to the conversations of his guild peers, he clearly awaited the end of the function with barely disguised eagerness.

"Lord Mountbatten has served Camelot for over seventy-five years, though I know little about him personally. He has, in his time, made great strides in the fields of cybernetics and gene-therapy, but seems only to attend formal events as a matter of obligation," she concluded.

"Concise and well put, my squire," Phillip smiled. "Perhaps you can discover more this evening."

29

Once the guests had dined, the evening turned to dancing and social chit chat. The attendant squires were released to enjoy the ball before they returned to their own duties, or the barracks rooms they would share for the duration of the games. Rosalyn was standing at the edge of the dance floor, enjoying the music and the movement of the dancers when she detected a polite cough behind her.

"May I have this dance?" drawled a grinning Geoffrey, bowing flamboyantly.

"Why, surely, m'lord," Ros affected a demure air and took Geoffrey's offered hand, "I hope your dancing shoes are as quick as you running ones." She smiled as a spirited beat took the orchestra, the dancers and Geoffrey and Ros along with them. They bobbed and turned, rather amateurishly compared to some others upon the floor, but with the honest enthusiasm of the moment.

The song came to an end and Ros and Geoffrey found themselves near the edge of the floor as the dancers broke, bowed to each other and gently applauded the musicians. A more traditional waltz started up and the pair prepared to dance once more.

"Master Mayland, I do hope you don't intend to monopolise this fine lady all night?" Belvarre Grayson smoothly imposed himself ever so slightly between them.

"That depends upon the lady," Geoffrey allowed a hint of annoyance to creep into his voice.

Rosalyn was caught. She couldn't simply refuse Belvarre without appearing rude, and she had already danced with Geoffrey. Even with all her training in social situations, courtly behaviour and etiquette, she found herself at a loss. So far in her life she'd faced such situations with cool detachment yet here, she paused. She didn't really want to dance with Belvarre. Thankfully the decision was taken out of her hands.

"Excuse me gentlemen, a moment with my squire if I may?" Sir Phillip stepped in and smoothly led Ros out into the dance. Try as she might to enjoy herself, every time they passed close to the edge of the dance floor she caught a glimpse of Belvarre watching her. Not wishing to cause a scene, she stepped off the floor as soon as she was able and sought out Geoffrey. Perhaps the company and the drink she had promised him would save the soured evening.

Chapter 3

Beneath the Castle walls lay a vast network of cavernous storage rooms, guards' quarters, kitchens and the workshops of the King's own technical division. Attached to the guild, but in service to the Crown, they laboured for long hours preparing, maintaining and repairing all the castle's equipment and, during the tournament, the equipment of all the competitors. The air was hot and the atmosphere cramped as technicians put in the overtime required on the newly arrived visitors' equipment. Voices shouted across the noise of power tools and rumbling loaders carts. Camelot's chief tech, Master at Arms Sidney Carter, stood at an outer doorway puffing a cheap, black cigar. Perspiration beaded his bald head and ran around the raised brass plates on either side of his skull, as the cherry end burned bright in the dark. His heavy leather apron hung from a broad neck and was weighed down by the numerous tools and measuring meters of his trade slung here and there about it. He reached up and wiped away the sweat with a cloth, the biomechanical bands that covered his forearms catching the red-glow of his cigar along the neat banks of micro-tools arrayed on them. Tutting to himself, he turned smartly, descended the stairs and made his way through the service areas.

In the outer rooms, crates stood piled high full of spares and equipment. Next, he strode past the garages, everything from high-end sports cars and luxurious state vehicles to military transports and urban pacification units inside them. Further on in the maintenance shops, guild seniors, juniors and apprentice technicians stood at all manner of bench tools fabricating, repairing and servicing kitchen appliances, info-net ports, comm's equipment and all manner of multimedia hardware. Soon after came the main armouries, each with a standing guard and accessible only to more senior techs, the duty officers of the castle guard and the knights themselves. All these areas bustled with life and activity as the Master walked into the central workshops. Here the rooms started to resemble operating theatres more that workshops. Bright lights hung from the ceiling, even though the walls themselves seemed to glow, illuminating every nook and crevice. Those working in these areas moved with quiet purpose on surgical-booted feet past the frequently spaced sterilizing stations and the doors of clean rooms. Only the most promising apprentices accompanied their masters in this area. None of them gave a second glance to the grubby chief tech; they all knew him as a master of the craft who would just as soon service a car engine as he would install a cybernetic eye or brain-link chip. Each one was also well aware of his numerous personal implants and the discrete force field generator on his belt that would not allow a single molecule of contaminant to leave his person until he left the sterile zone.

Alongside the theatres, where all cybernetic and mechanical augmentation in the castle took place, were the stables. Sterile white alcoves held racks lined with diagnostic screens and tools while bundles of fine cables snaked from the ceilings and plugged into the subject of each booth. The C.T.E.E.D.s (Cybernetic Transport, Engagement and Evasion Devices) stood like life-sized artists' mannequins of draught horses, their metallic flanks coloured to the requirements of the rider in gunmetal grey, cherry red, sky blue and sun-fire yellow; even themes of urban and forest camouflage were present. The units stood arranged according to the owner's rank and their A.I. generation.

No first gen units remained in service. The decision had been made to add A.I. personalities to the C.T.E.E.D. programme to give each unit greater flexibility on operations beyond specific, pre-programmed tactical responses. They were meant to learn the preferences of the rider and adapt their reactions appropriately if forced to make autonomous choices. The first gen had responded well in straight battle but became easily confused when faced with 'guerrilla' operations. They soon came to regard any spontaneous civilian action in favour of the knights as 'terrorist activity' rather than 'militia assistance'. They also developed a vicious killer instinct after a few engagements which (when coupled with their on-board weapons systems) resulted in unfavourable dead-to-wounded and collateral damage ratios. Attempts to improve their performance with addition software simply resulted in various forms of artificial-personality disorder or total positronic-psychosis. As such they were soon withdrawn and deactivated.

The second gen were welcomed when they first arrived, unarmed but with improved mobility and defensive capabilities. However, conflicting programming in the area of ally recognition often gave them an almost paranoid and downright dour outlook. They did, however, work, and became the initial transport of every new knight.

Third generation units followed in the second gens' unarmed footprints (knights had lost the desire for additional firepower in combat) but additional refinements appeared in the areas of communications and rider life-support functions. The A.I. was regarded as personality stable, but each unit tended to pick up a similar outlook to the knight who rode them, even as they learned their owner's tactical preferences. The C.T.E.E.D. programme had progressed past fourth and fifth generations with little true advancement, however each A.I. generation typically held itself above the others. Gradual improvements to on-board systems became incorporated as they were developed, though a programme peculiarity in the fives meant that they tended toward a sunnier disposition than any other model.

The horse-like heads swung to and fro as they monitored the passage of visitors to the stalls and turned toward one another as they occasionally communicated with each other via low intensity microwave bursts.

Sidney passed by all the stalls in turn, ignoring the stares of the cyborg horses as he raised his hand and touched a point behind his ear. A section of the brass plate in his head opened and a wire-thin microphone extended until it reached his lips.

"Apprentice," he stated gruffly, "I'm on my way and you'd better be working." With that, he signed off and strode purposefully until he reached the final stall. Larger than the others, this alcove was fully outfitted for any possible eventuality and housed the King's own mount. Here stood the peak of C.T.E.E.D. technology so far, the only fully functioning sixth gen outside of the Tech Guild itself, Centaur. Named for the mythological half-man half-horse because of its advanced higher brain functions, Centaur dominated the room. Even without its holographic-mane display active, the iridescent metallic finish of the units copper, red and gold paint job showed to marvellous effect within the sterile surroundings. The embossed royal seal on its shoulder was picked out in gleaming platinum. The luminous blue eyes brightened for an instant as Sydney strode into view while the cyborg ran a recognition match of the Master at Arms.

"How are you doing, old girl?" he seemed to ask of no-one in particular.

"I have occasionally wondered," sounded a clipped, male voice "given the human propensity for treating all machines as females, why my personality clearly displays masculine traits and, given those traits, why you persist in addressing me in the feminine form? Also, since I have seen barely two years, three months and five days service..." The voice sounded like a butler in a tin can "why you would address me as 'old'. I might be inclined to take offence."

"Call it force of habit," growled Sydney. "How's he doing?" the tech nodded at the other figure in the room. The young man was dressed in the leather apron of a junior tech and he crouched close to the rear end of the C.T.E.E.D. He seemed to be industriously applying himself, with magnifying goggles and a pen-like device, to shining a strip of laser-light three inches wide back and forth over the metal thigh-plate of the techno-mount.

"The apprentice is performing adequately, Master at Arms. I calculate eighty-three percent efficiency with the laser scrubber and the resulting light refraction should prove suitably aesthetically pleasing on the morrow."

The tech chief stroked the stubble on his chin with thumb and forefingers, "Eighty three eh?" he considered.

"Correct." trilled the horse; Sidney just crossed his arms over his chest and waited.

'I hate when he does this' thought Brandon Squires, the young tech polishing the King's mount. Traditionally the most promising student in the country, upon their second year of training, was appointed to the Master at Arms of Camelot as his apprentice until such time as they earned their place as a guildsman. Brandon had been fortunate to be finishing his second year when the choosing came around and skilled enough to catch the Master's eye. When Brandon averted a near disaster by diagnosing a potentially catastrophic flaw in an over-ambitious student's new fuel-injector system, the master thought he'd found his candidate. When Brandon recalibrated the system to function safely there and then, Sidney knew he had.

After three years, Brandon had swiftly mastered all the conventional maintenance practices of vehicles and appliances and started on the basics of tech arms and augmentations. He'd also worn the shine off of being the 'Master's apprentice' and realised that, for all the privileges he was allowed, the expectations upon him were elevated accordingly. However, every year of his apprenticeship, he was awarded the supreme honour of polishing the King's' horse for the tournament. And every year his master came and stood over his shoulder for those last moments as he finished the job. But it was worth it, just to spend time between the phases of cleaning studying the performance readouts and schematic scans. To Brandon, the mounts of the household knights were closer to art than tech, and the sixth gen was the Da Vinci that he aspired to improve on one day.

Eventually he stood back, switched off the laser and raised his goggles.

"Eighty three percent?" questioned his master.

"Thirsty work sir," replied Brandon, standing at a close approximation of 'attention' "Had a cup of tea, that and attention to detail I account for the loss." he glanced at his master's eyes before quoting the older man's own adage "Measure twice, cut once, sir."

Sidney met his apprentice's gaze and grinned "Teaching the old man to suck eggs, eh?"

Brandon straightened his expression and barked "No, sir!"

"Good!" Sidney clapped his hands together and rubbed them as he glanced about the stall.

"Doing a job fast isn't the same as doing it right. Well, you look done here so off you go. Get some food in you. But stay on your comms," he tapped his brass plate "if I need you I don't want to be waiting. And you'd better be first in to baby-sit the squires in the morning." With that, he allowed Brandon to leave and went back to his own duties.

Ros and Geoffrey were well into the Chablis when Royston sauntered into the room.

"Hey," he greeted them "I found him."

"So who is this 'Ox of York' you haven't told me about?" asked Ros.

Geoffrey finished his glass and looked sidelong at her.

"The Ox," he began "is something of a legend of his own making, I'm surprised you haven't heard of him." He put down his glass and turned to face Ros as the eager Royston settled down next to them.

"He used to be a man at arms for one of the minor nobles, Baronet of Easingwold or something like that. He was sold into it as a child to cover his father's' debts, so he says."

"But how come he's..." Ros interrupted.

"You remember the great fire at Berkeley castle?" Geoffrey asked, "Big accident, so many killed. The lord's' daughter only just got out?"

Rosalyn nodded.

"The Ox got her out. Easingwold was visiting Berkeley at the time and Ox was part of the baronets' retinue. He had just managed to get the baronet and his family out when he spots the lady in question in an upper window. So, with no thought to his own safely and, without any enhancements I might add, he just rushed back in to save her. Did a good job too, by all accounts; the girl was all right, but..." Geoffrey tailed off.

"What?" urged Ros.

Geoffrey sighed, "The fire reached an unsecured arms locker and there was a munitions explosion. He threw himself over the girl and took the brunt of it. Shrapnel chewed up his right arm, some of his back. A lot of damage and his liege lord couldn't or wouldn't afford the reconstruction."

"Oh, that's just awful," gasped Ros, "But then, how could he be a squire?" she asked, a little frustration creeping into her voice.

Geoffrey finally caught on to her urgent tone. "One of the other guests that night was Sir Andrew Sachs-Kholberg, Knight of the Round Table and Duke of York. He said that such bravery should not go unrewarded and, in order that the young guard receive the best of care, he took the Ox on as a squire."

Royston spoke up at this, "I saw him at last year's tournament. Sure, he's a little older than the rest of us and a little slower too, upstairs I mean, but my liege said he'd rarely seen such a noble soul. Not quite sure what he..."

"Ports gone!" announced Sebastian Crown. He'd approached unnoticed while Geoffrey told his story. "Now it's time to pay the piper, Savant."

Ros stood slowly, holding her hands up placatingly, but never wavering. "You're drunk Sebastian. Let's do this another time."

"Coward!" sneered Crown, the stolen port still pungent on his breath. "You're not fit to be a Knight!"

Ros felt her anger rising too late to stop the retort leaping from her lips. "That's rich coming from a drunken bully like you!"

"Now hold on," Geoffrey stood to interpose himself, just as Crown's meaty fist flew forward.

Geoffrey was struck a glancing blow which, nonetheless, threw him back to his bunk.

Ros let out an inarticulate cry and punched Crown squarely in the face, first with her left, then right fist. Strong and fast though she might be, she wasn't built for closed quarters brawling like the bigger squire. He shook off her blows and reached out, his right hand clamping about her throat, and lifted her from her feet. Slowly, with a smug grin he drew back his other arm, crooked to deliver a punishing blow.

"That ain't very friendly, Seb," came a deep voice over his shoulder, and an arm thicker than Geoffrey's thigh looped under Crown's cocked left arm, and hooked onto the back of his neck. Crown's face flushed with anger as another arm, a chunky construct of ferro-fibre muscles, hard edged ceramisteel bones and studded about with corroded, coppery neuro-receptor alloys, came down hard on the upturned elbow of the arm which gripped Ros. The augmented arm protested with a whine of servos, but the fully-mechanical aggressor forced the joint to buckle and Crown dropped Ros. A swift movement from his opponent, and both of Crown's arms were locked tightly behind him.

An honest, square jawed face looked over Sebastian's shoulder. "Won't be a minute, Geoff," he stated cheerfully.

The room stood quiet as shocked squires watched the struggle. Neither Sebastian nor his captor moved or spoke but it was clear that the contest was close. The newcomers' fully synthetic arm held Crown's augmented limb behind his back with no problem, but it was clear (from the lack of any metalwork) that his other arm, though heavily muscled, was entirely natural. Even with superior leverage and a firm half-nelson on his side, sweat was beginning to form on his brow.

Suddenly the artificial limb straightened, releasing Crown's arm and dropping his weight forward. As Crown leaned back toward his captor to steady himself he found a hand the size of a dinner plate transferred from his neck to his face and a powerful shove sent him careening back across the room. Before he could steady himself he hit a footlocker and fell sprawling to the floor with a heavy 'Smack!'

"Well, that was fun," announced the newcomer. "You a'right there, Geoff?"

Geoffrey dragged himself up from his sprawl on the mattress. "Seeing a few stars, but I'll be ok. How's Crown?"

"Sleeping it off!" the big squire called over his shoulder, just in case Crown hadn't got the message. Now that he stood clear and straight, Ros could make out just how big the newcomer was. He was maybe six foot six and change, shorter than Sebastian Crown but taller than anyone else in the room. He was also far bulkier than Crown, with broad shoulders and pronounced muscles showing across his chest even under the tabard bearing the crest of York. Unlike the other young men about the room, he sported a growth of dense stubble across his chin and upper lip, and his short dark hair was just a touch on the shaggy side. When he grinned again, Ros suddenly realised that his teeth were a steely grey in colour.

"The Ox of York, I presume?" she ventured.

"John Loxley, squire to Sir Andrew Sachs-Kholberg, at your service m'lady."

"See Ros, I told you he was good company!" Geoffrey chortled, "Well, the drink is gone but the night is still young. Who wants to go to a party?"

"We just came from a party" Ros stated apprehensively.

"No, we just went to 'The' party, now I think we ought to go to 'a' party."

"Where?" Uncertain of where this was taking her, Ros nonetheless felt compelled to see it through.

"Well," Geoff rubbed his chin, feigning deep concentration, "We're all dressed up, why don't we hit the town? I know a few clubs and such."

Ros was taken-aback, "I'm not sure. I mean, all my public appearances so-far have been pre-arranged."

"Relax, Ros," Geoffrey smiled, "This isn't a 'public appearance'. It's a few drinks out with friends, and we've even got a responsible adult!" he waved at John.

"Y'what now?" grunted the older squire.

Chapter 4

Toward the rear of Camelot keep lay the detention block. Political prisoners, those suspected of treason and the occasional heretic often found themselves within its thick beige walls.

Cassie sighed, and let her head rest on her knees as she sat on the sparse room's cot. Ten by ten cell, one cot, one desk, one chair and a toilet; terrific. She looked up at the fading evening light through the tiny, barred window set high in the wall. So she'd hacked the info-net, sold a little information here and there to jealous spouses for their divorce cases, dished a little dirt to the journalists about palace budgets, what of it? She let her head rest back on her knees. The question wasn't why she was here; it was how had they found her? She'd been so careful, fake trails, firewalls, intelligent counter measures, the whole nine yards. Well, found her they had, and since she was a hacker stealing from the info-net, and the info-net was the territory of the holy sect of Merlin, and that made her a heretic. She scratched absently at the laser-tattooed 'heretic' stamp on her arm. In days gone by the black sunburst would've been a true brand, not a tattoo. Cassie had never heard of heretics being transported specially from Bristol to

Camelot for trial. A mystery wrapped up in an enigma. Cassie left off contemplating the unfairness of it all when a flutter and a squawk drew her attention back to the window. A large black raven turned first one, then the other beady black eye on her. "Feeling sorry for one's self are we?" it declared. Looking closer, it was possible to see a faint green glow behind its eyes, and where its claws and beak were chipped or scratched, the trace glint of some metal alloy winked through. The voice it produced was quietly well spoken, but had a tinny quality that made it sound like a lawyer over a bad phone-line.

"Eric!" Cassie tried to keep her voice down, but her joy was evident. "Wings need lubricating old friend?"

"As well you know," the cultured voice responded peevishly, "I produce my own silicone alternative to oil from trace minerals in the air and any concentrated deposits I can..." it hesitated before continuing, "Scavenge," it declared distastefully. "If perchance you refer to the tardiness of my arrival then I shall just have to refer you to the Castle's cybernetic insurgence countermeasure. A worm programme that had me headed to East Anglia before my own internal monitor programmes found it and shut it down." The raven affected a testy sniff. "You're lucky I got here at all."

Cassie smiled and patted the cot beside her. "I assume your stealth measures are sufficient for a

48

quick systems check or you wouldn't have made direct contact."

"You know me," Eric shot back "Or you should, you programmed me. I'd advise against anything more than a local system check. This IS Camelot after all." With that, the cyber-familiar hopped down to the cot, lowered its head and tail and spread its wings. A QWERTY keyboard superimposed itself over the feathers of the ravens' wings and a faint blue screen projected as a small hologram over the creature's back. Cassie's fingers danced over the keyboard running diagnostics on her familiar's systems. The bird was cloaking to its full capacity. Rather than try to mask its presence entirely, it mimicked the raven it was built to emulate. Body heat, cardiac rhythm; as much as possible its systems made it seem like a raven to sight (even on the infrared spectrum), smell and even augmented hearing.

Cassie ceased typing and the bird straightened up, closed its wings and de-activated the holo-display.

"Well then." She took a deep breath. "Any suggestions?"

"To what purpose, my dear?" the raven replied quizzically.

Cassie's brow furrowed in annoyance. "To get me out? Hello? What else would I need suggestions for?"

"I regret to inform you Cassandra," The raven cocked its head, "that I can find no viable course of escape that will not result in either permanent, debilitating injury or swift and painful death. My best recommendation is that you sit it out, and see what lies in store for you. At the very least, we can wait for them to transfer you to a less secure facility and work from there."

"Well that's unhelpful," sighed Cassie.

"Well pardon me, I'm sure." The Raven affected a disinterested sniff. "That is as helpful as I can be given your circumstances."

The footsteps of an approaching guard rang hollow in the corridor.

"Make yourself scarce Eric," Cassie urged. "Go and be inconspicuous, but see if you can keep tabs on me. If I need you I'll stick a shoe on the window ledge."

"Charming," squawked the raven "summoned by a show of foot odour."

"Scram!" growled Cassie as Eric made a swift retreat through the bars.

Just then the guard appeared at the bars and the heavy door 'clanked' as the thick bolts were drawn and the guard entered with a tray. Cassie surveyed her meal and let out another sigh. "Wonderful," she murmured.

The limousine purred through the darkened city streets. Ros watched the yellow glare of streetlights whipping past the window. The others laughed and joked in the seats around her. Geoffrey had 'procured' the vehicle from the castle garage. It was part of the Stafford entourage, and the driver had received them with a knowing smirk. She leaned over to Geoffrey and spoke softly.

"You know that Royston and I aren't 'technically' old enough to go to an establishment that serves alcohol?"

He smiled, "Well, therein lies some of the fun." He saw her worried expression and his eyes softened. "Don't worry, I know the manager. He likes to have me in, but, if you don't want to go, we'll go back."

Ros glanced out the window again then turned back, "Let's have some fun."

The car pulled up in front of 'The Tilt', one of the upmarket venues named for competition jousting. Bright lights and flashing neon over lit the line extending around the building, even at this hour. The driver opened the door and Geoffrey stepped out before offering a hand back to Ros. She stepped out onto the red carpet of the VIP entrance. The people waiting in the queue turned and there was a barrage of flashes from camera phones. Geoff waved and smiled; 'worked the crowd' as Rosalyn's P.R. tutor had put it. For her own part she put on her 'press face' and walked with Geoff up to the velvet rope.

The bouncer, looking relaxed in his tuxedo, lifted the rope without hesitation and ushered the party through. A young man in the Tilt's signature uniform led them through the club where lights strobed, lasers cut through smoke on the dancefloor and music pulsed. Ros marvelled at the ease with which Geoffrey moved through the club exchanging smiles and handshakes. A kiss on the cheek here, a quick word and a wink there, spreading good feelings and fun with a few choice contacts.

They moved through the packed club to a balcony table overlooking the DJ booth and dancefloor. With a gesture, their guide brought over one of the bar staff and a round of drinks was ordered up. For an hour they drank, danced and talked, as the club seethed just a few feet below them.

Ros was halfway through an amaretto and cola when Geoff leaned over.

"So," he began, "How's your first unplanned public appearance?"

Ros had just returned from the dancefloor. Dance was part of her training scheme, as was gymnastics, although the movements in this place were more... primal, more to do with instinct than practice. "Surprisingly enjoyable," she admitted.

"I've got to say I didn't expect you to take to it so quickly. I mean, I've seen some of your interviews on Teen Screen and, to be frank, they all seemed kinda scripted to me."

She shrugged, recalling the times she'd been 'on camera' for the popular young people's programme, "That's because they were." He seemed confused so she went on, "Watching you here tonight, and from what I know of you, you're either well practiced or naturally charismatic." She let his grin at the complement subside, "I'm not. I know etiquette and protocol for the courts of Europe and the boardrooms of the far east, but the simplest interpersonal exchange has always been a little beyond me. So we put together a public persona whereby I would encourage my fans and social media followers in their academic pursuits. That I do understand."

Geoff nodded, slowly, then his ready smile returned as he regarded her critically for a moment.

"From where I'm sitting, you seem to be doing rather well."

At this point, one of the large, well-dressed door staff stepped up to the table and spoke quickly into Geoffrey's ear. He nodded quickly and downed his drink.

"Time to go." he said with a wink, pulling on his jacket.

"Why?" Ros questioned but downed her drink anyway. Her head was a little fuzzy from drink, so lessons about 'sipping' and 'pacing' went completely disregarded.

"The press have arrived." Geoff was waving at Royston who was down on the dancefloor. "I mean, Clive the manager, he'll drop a few hints that we were here and a few pictures will show up on the 'Net. Just as long as we're not actually caught on camera we'll be fine. We're just going to slip out the back, its fine, I've done it a hundred times."

And with that they headed down the stairs and toward the rear of the club. There were more winks and chuckles as the group passed through the service areas, Geoff greeted them with a wry smile and a 'what are you gonna do?' shrug. Still working the crowd, thought Ros.

The back door was opened for them and they emerged into a dark alley, which was suddenly lit by a barrage of flashbulbs.

"Ah, it would seem they have anticipated my cunning plan," Geoffrey growled, ruefully. "Well, shit."

The sun had barely crested the horizon, and the great field of Camelot was already alive with activity. The cool, crisp spring morning brought a soft breeze, alive with the scent of ornamental flower beds, and the clear light glistened off the morning dew as groundsmen bustled to make sure each competition field was clipped and every track clear. More staff strung final lines of bunting for the opening ceremony, and techs moved between stands and commentary booths checking wiring looms, lighting and P.A. systems. Everything stood ready.

The tech halls under the castle were oddly quiet as the visiting squires were led to the storage area allocated for their masters' equipment. Each squire was traditionally responsible for the final checking, polishing and additional maintenance of their knight's gear as well as their own before any tournament or battle.

Fresh from a joint dressing-down for their antics the previous night, and nursing a rather sore head, Rosalyn followed Geoffrey who followed a junior technician through the corridors under the castle. Their friends and fellow squires trooped quietly behind them. While Phillip had been angry, there were traces of pride in his demeanour. Baron Dominic, an imposing bear of a man, had seemed more frustrated that Geoffrey had allowed them to be corralled like that.

The squires were led to a spacious room where wheeled tables were burdened with all the equipment their knights would require for the tournament. Each table also had its own attendant tech standing silently by, ready to lend assistance should any problems arise. Over each table hung a household pennant, and underneath that the gear of the knight whose colours were displayed. Ros made for the table marked by the Essex coat of arms, and immediately gave the items on the table a swift mental check. Satisfied that nothing was obviously missing, she made polite introductions to the tech on station and glanced about to see who was near her. Geoffrey was stationed at a table in front of her; he gave her a cheery grin before turning back to the task before him.

Raoul Folkestone sweated at a table to her right despite the room's air-conditioned coolness. He shot her a black look, and she didn't doubt he would have made some crude remark except that to his right John Loxley flexed his mechanical arm with a sound like a gorilla cracking its knuckles. Loxley winked at her as he did this but when Raoul turned toward him his expression became a mask of thunder which, without Sebastian Crown's presence, had the perspiring Folkestone sweating uncontrollably.

Ros allowed herself a little smile, and turned to her task when someone spoke up behind her.

"Oh dear, dear Rosalyn. What interesting company you've been keeping lately?"

Ros didn't even turn to the speaker when she answered. "Belvarre, how nice to see you. How are you doing, oh good. Let's not do this again shall we?"

Belvarre Grayson continued as if she hadn't even spoken. "I mean, what would your liege say about their 'calibre'?"

It wasn't that anything Belvarre said was overtly insulting, but somehow the fact that he was squired to his father convinced him that he was somehow better, superior to the other squires. What was all the more frustrating was that his natural ability, commanding nature and the charm he could bring to bear when he wanted to went a long way to verifying his belief.

'If he didn't frequently act like a condescending prick he might even be the best of all of us,' mused Ros silently.

Dragging her attention back to the conversation she turned and scowled at Grayson.

"And what does that mean?" she asked, hostility evident in her voice.

"Well look at them," smirked Grayson. "Loxley, though the beneficiary of fortunate circumstance is basically a thug in that tabard, and the oldest squire in the room, though his progress through training is no more advanced than young Glasbury. And let's not overlook little Royston, just because he's only a child. A poor provincial knight is all he can ever really aspire to be, little better than a prominent sports figure really, no real use to the table. And of course, Mayland, how could I forget the promising squire of Stafford?" Grayson sneered at the name. "Mayland is a fine enough boy but that's all he'll ever really be, he doesn't have the gumption, the killer instinct for

57

politics that's needed to rule this country in the peoples' interests. Not like you or I Roslyn, not like us." Grayson leaned forward intently, awaiting Ros's response.

She didn't keep him waiting, her head hurt and Phillip's words that morning had been at odds with his demeanour. She was confused and grumpy and didn't have time for this elitist little shit. Ros lunged toward Belvarre, hands outstretched as if to throttle the pompous squire. Only the table between them stopped her.

"I hope you're man enough to make it in the sword competition Belvarre!" she spat.

Belvarre backed away rapidly, stunned by the sudden outburst. "W..why?" He stammered.

"Because, I'm going to kick your ARSE!" yelled Ros.

Chapter 5

Geoffrey turned at the outburst, and saw Ros reaching out as if to break Belvarre Grayson's neck. He chortled to himself and turned back to his own table.

"What was all that about?" the tech next to him inquired almost to himself, but Geoffrey answered him anyway.

"That," he indicated Grayson "Is the right 'honourable' Squire Belvarre Grayson of Oxford trying to charm the delightful Rosalyn Juliet Taunton-Savant of Essex, and getting a right old telling-off too by the look of it, the pompous bugger that he is."

The tech looked shocked and bowed his head. "I'm sorry sir, I spoke out of turn."

Geoffrey laughed aloud and clapped the tech on the shoulder. "Not at all, the more eyes on hand when Grayson cocks-up, the better." He lowered his voice in a faux-conspiratorial whisper, "Though I may need to call on you as a witness later. What's your name?"

The tech let a smile creep onto his face. "Brandon, sir, Brandon Squires, apprentice to the Master at Arms."

Geoffrey held out a hand. "That's enough of the 'sir' nonsense. Leave it until they knight me! Geoff

Mayland of Stafford, glad to meet you." The two young men shook hands.

"Now," announced Geoffrey, "Where were we?"

"Techno-sword, si... Geoff." Brandon lifted the jewelled scabbard and handed it to the squire.

Geoffrey touched his thumb to the small oval bio-pad at the mouth of the scabbard. It glowed briefly, then the hilt of the sword gave a 'click' and jumped slightly as the magna-lock released the blade from its secure grip. Drawing the sword, Geoffrey marvelled at the construction of it. Rather than a mundane straight-blade, the weapon appeared as only the offensive edges, with a nest of wire-work and pulsing diodes within its length that generated the different offensive fields that made the tech-sword such an awesome weapon.

Geoffrey held the sword and twisted the band set around the hilt, just below the crossbar. The field, which moments before had glowed a dull red, built to a bright yellow, spitting and crackling, giving off waves of heat and then subsiding to an even blue radiance.

"A-ok!" breathed Geoffrey, his voice quiet with reverence as he deactivated the blade and replaced it in the sheath.

All about them, different flashes of light, electronic whines, throbbing motors and the buzz of rotating blades signalled the other squires testing kinetic-maces, magna-flails, tech-swords, concussion-hammers and pulse-glaives. Every one doing all that they could to bring honourable victory to their liege knight in the coming tournament games.

Once all the checks and diagnostics had been completed, the attendant techs helped each squire wheel their tables down to the arming rooms where the squires would arm and equip each knight for the opening ceremonies and grand parade of the King's Royal Tournament.

Geoffrey bid Brandon farewell, and spent a few moments tweaking the arrangement of the items on the table before settling to await the arrival of the Baron of Stafford. Standing with his feet planted at shoulders width apart, hands clasped behind his back and chin held high he allowed himself a moment to consider the events of the tournament that were held for the squires.

He was entered in his speciality events, the foot race (five miles through the streets of London), the eight hundred metre freestyle swim, and the triathlon. Each of these optional events would take a day with a stage of the indoor events being held in the evenings. Then there were the mandatory events; target jousting from the saddle of a motorcycle, tactics (using a holographic battlefield and computer controlled elements of chance), and swordsmanship. He suppressed a shudder of trepidation at the thought of the competitions. He'd trained hard and long, his augmentations were tuned and ready, but still he felt nervous. In these peaceful times, the tournament took the place of open warfare as a chance to win honours in sight of the King.

If... No. When (he corrected himself) he won his events, he'd be proving the Baron's faith in him and taking another step towards full knighthood.

The door darkened as Baron Dominic eased his huge bulk into the arming chamber. He made an imposing figure with his mane of red hair and fierce grin, even dressed as he was in the simple, insulated gambeson that was the base garment for every suit of armour.

"Morning again, Geoffrey." The Baron's voice boomed in the confined space, still slightly reproving from necessity to see him earlier today. Geoffrey drew himself to a full stance of attention.

"Hear you set up Dorset's squire for a lesson in humility in the squire's barracks last night." The statement was level and did not hint at the Knight's opinion of the incident in the slightest.

Geoffrey had long ago learned that Sir Dominic of Stafford held truth and honesty highly among the knightly virtues, and would accept most any explanation of events as long as it was truthful.

"Yes my liege," he stated simply.

"Why?" again Sir Dominic asked flatly.

"Sir, Sebastian was going to start a fight with Ros no-matter what she did. He was going to fight her in the barracks where her speed and skill wouldn't count. He'd have his fight on his chosen ground. Basic tactics, sir. I simply helped her level the field."

Sir Dominic grunted and nodded sagely.

"I have, but one question squire Mayland..." he began gravely.

Geoffrey stood rigidly to attention.

"Ros?" Sir Dominic quirked an eyebrow and grinned wryly at his squire.

Geoffrey held out for a full ten seconds before he dissolved into fits of laughter.

Rosalyn tried to stand still and at attention as she awaited her knight in the cool arming room. Try though she might, she couldn't keep the smile off her face whenever she thought of the look on Belvarre's face when she'd lunged over that table.

"Something funny, squire?" Phillip of Essex swept into the room with barely a sound to warn of his approach. Ros set her face into a mask ready to weather the approaching storm.

"Because if it's funny that Dorset has another axe to grind with me, I'd dearly like to know why." Phillip fixed his squire with a hard stare as he awaited her answer.

Rosalyn tried to find the right words to explain the events of the previous night.

"My lord, Sebastian Crown…"

"I'm well aware of the situation with you and Crown," sighed Sir Phillip, "it is a situation I have left to you to resolve, that you may preserve your honour. However, if you cannot resolve the matter yourself, I will have no choice but to raise the matter with Dorset and we shall have the two of you settle it formally, in public." He let the weight of the words have their full effect upon Ros. A formal duel would have lifelong consequences for the loser. Worse, it would inevitably be a televised event, broadcast over the open network for the entertainment of the masses. More than personal honour would hinge upon the outcome.

"My lord," she began "I don't feel that it will come to that. Crown might have pressed the point while I was still perceived as a lone agent. However I seem to have found an ally in Squire Mayland of Stafford. In truth it was because of his actions that Dorset's squire was denied the brawl he so desired."

Sir Phillip looked thoughtful for a moment.

"Young Geoffrey?" Phillip brightened noticeably "Thought I saw you dancing with him at the ball. Dominic certainly speaks highly of his squire and he's widely accepted as having a promising future…" Sir

Phillip tailed off as he noticed his squire's exasperated expression.

"But, aside from the political benefits, it is good to see you finally making some personal ties with the other squires. 'No man is an island' as John Donne so famously wrote. You won't be a squire forever and, believe it or not, I'm not going to be around forever either. One of these days, you will need a friend to rely upon, and probably sooner than you'd think."

Rosalyn had long endured her knight's opinions upon her tendency to seek her own company before that of others. She couldn't explain it, but she knew something had changed this year. For reasons she couldn't fathom, she felt the need to impress the knights, and even some of her fellow squires, to earn their acceptance within the brotherhood of the Round Table.

Try as she might, she couldn't find the words to ask her knight about the strange feeling. It wasn't that she didn't want to but somehow, whenever she tried to raise it her thoughts betrayed her. In the past she'd been able to discuss anything with her knight, it was the basis of the knight/squire relationship, and a bond of trust that would endure as long as both parties lived, and it was rare to find any exception.

She turned the situation over in her head as she equipped Phillip, linking armour plates to the gambeson and connecting the on-board systems to the bio-ports dotted around his body. After a few moments, the assembly of the complicated battle armour required almost her full attention. The task, a practiced routine, took nearly two hours to complete and by the end of it the Earl-Adamant, a slender 8'4" in his stockinged feet, towered over his squire to such an extent she required steps to finish the construction. The time also allowed Ros to reach a conclusion, she would try talking to Geoffrey. As a squire and prospective knight, his discretion could be assured. Further to that, she realised it would be good to have a friend of about her own age and in a similar situation to talk to.

She lowered Phillip's helmet over his head and snapped shut the locking ring on the collar that would seal the armour from all external agents. The lenses of the great-helm flashed yellow as the internal filters and systems activated and the great, red construct came to life. The chest-piece seemed to expand as Phillip stretched out his arms, almost touching opposite walls of the wide cubicle, and the three Seaxes emblazoned upon his chest rose and fell as he again lowered them with a quiet hum of servos. "All systems register in the green." Ros was always disconcerted by the soft, crystal clarity of Phillip's voice from within the helm. She couldn't help but expect a booming report from the massive figure every time she was granted the honour of assembling it.

"I wish I could say the same," she breathed before she realised she was even speaking.

"I'm sorry?" Phillips armoured head dipped and turned to look down at Ros, the yellow eyes seeming to strip away the outer layers of her carefully maintained poise as she reeled at the idea of the thought she had given voice.

"I..it's nothing my lord," she stammered "just some pre-tournament anxiety."

It seemed to Rosalyn that there was a significant pause before Phillip straightened up and held out a hand for his sword.

"That's nothing to be ashamed of, squire. Fear is not the measure of a knight, how they deal with it is."

The opening day of the King's tournament was as fine a spring day as any in history. London itself buzzed with anticipation for the coming spectacle. But beneath all the excitement and activity a dark current ran, furtive and with haste toward a purpose that no-one would have dreamed was possible.

The Grand Parade marked the true opening of the games. Rows of sightseers from around the known world thronged the route, eager for a chance to glimpse the nation's heroes, the Knights of Camelot.

The parade route was marked by banners and bunting with the King's own guard, enhanced militiamen all, keeping the crowd at a respectful distance. Media crews broadcast the event far and wide while entertainers performed on stages built for the occasion, and in amongst the crowd itself. But even all this extravagant show could not detract from the main event.

Each knight, resplendent in full armour, sat atop a mighty C.T.E.E.D. and was flanked by their squire, similarly mounted upon a combat modified motorcycle. Each squire bore the pennant of their liege, projected as a hologram from the tip of a ceremonial lance. An honour guard of the knight's own militia trooped behind them, marking the success of each knight's holdings. The different dress-uniforms of each battalion caused a veritable rainbow of colours in the procession. Some counted barely a dozen men, while others could sport a whole battalion with marching band in tow. Every one present carried the arms and munitions of their daily duties as guards of the realms of England and defenders of the round table. Every watching citizen in the audience knew as much. This blatant show of force was no threat, nor the gesture of any oppressive regime or overlord. On this day, Camelot reassured its subjects that, even during a day of celebration and spectacle, the court stood ready in the nation's defence.

The King himself, mounted upon Centaur, led the procession. He cast a shining figure in golden armour, his head unburdened by a helm; noble features not betrayed by his apparent youth but, adorned by the crown of the King of Camelot, he seemed ageless, and carried with him the authority of Arthur Pendragon himself. He rode at the head of a full company of the red-coated Royal Guard, whose name stood as a byword for loyalty and discipline in military circles. He led the assembled knights and their retainers out through the gates of Camelot, past an assembly of the honoured guests and visiting personalities, down London's Mall before the gathered masses of the general public to Horse Guard's Parade. Here the King and his guard formed up to receive the rest of the column.

After the march-past at Horse Guard's, and flanked by his company, the King then followed the parade on its return to Camelot, symbolically the first man to ride out of Camelot in times of need and the last to return from the fray.

Rosalyn sat astride a gleaming motorcycle, holo-pennant held ramrod straight. The house of Essex was currently enjoying the well-earned favour of the court, and rode out as the second in-line to the throne's own troops. Now was not a time to be lax in her duties or performance.

Although a full company stood between them, Rosalyn's augmented vision could clearly pick out the features of her monarch as he turned and waved to the crowds, ever benevolent to the people he ruled and protected.

It seemed strange to her. She had been to the tournament before and competed, even seen the King from a distance. She had attended court occasions with her knight and stood not an arm's length from him, and all she'd thought of at the time had been to convey herself properly before the monarch. Again, she felt the sense of something changed, something within her own mind, as she looked again upon her King, Anthony Pendragon the First. He wasn't that tall, by the standards of the knights of Camelot, but even at this distance there was an aura about him that couldn't be ignored. He possessed boyish features, an easy smile and long, flowing hair not unlike the classical images of Lancelot. The golden crown almost seemed to grow from his head rather than sit upon it. The broad shoulders of his battle armour gleamed in the sun and the decorative flutings that adorned every visible piece sparkled magnificently. He seemed a giant figure at the head of the procession. She had always looked up to Sir Phillip as a father figure with the occasional bout of hero-worship. She could easily admit this to herself. Even in the past few days she had come to respect Geoffrey, Royston and Loxley for their camaraderie but here, now in the presence of the crowned King, the master of the Knights of the Round Table, for the first time in her life she felt... awed by his presence. She still wanted to speak with Geoffrey about the sudden change in her feelings, but it was going to be hard. The events would start soon after the opening ceremonies began and then there wasn't going to be much time for anything until after the games; but once they ended, everyone would head back to resume their training in their own households. Who knew when she'd be able to take some free time to travel to the Stafford holdings?

She stopped herself. 'Travel to Stafford's holdings?' From the time she'd become a squire she'd never ventured far from Essex unless accompanying Sir Phillip on matters of state or executing some small duty on his behalf, now she was thinking about taking time to visit another squire over some vague feeling that something was changing the very way she was thinking. The whole half-baked idea just firmed her determination to speak to someone about it. Possibly she could catch Geoff at the lists while she checked who she'd be facing in her initial events.

Chapter 6

The parade and the opening ceremony had succeeded in preoccupying Rosalyn's thoughts for the better part of the day. The column had formed up around the edge of the main arena while the King took his place in the Royal box. Then the knights and their squires had ridden a circuit, acknowledging the households of the other competitors and affirming the unity of the Round Table by turning toward the centre of the ring and saluting their brother knights, then turning and saluting the King himself.

From that point, Rosalyn had watched from her saddle as teams of gymnasts, techs and even M.A.G.E.s worked together to perform scenes from the grand history of Camelot, from the first King Arthur to the great deeds of knights like Drake, Wellesley and Churchill.

Now she rode to the main garage to begin her preparations for the coming events. She recognised the young tech that had assisted at Geoffrey's table waving her through the doors of the garage as she gunned the motorbike up the entrance ramp, closely followed by a line of other squires. The knights would return their mounts to the stables via another entrance, where teams of techs would help them out of their armour. She pulled into her bay, killed the engine, flicked out the kickstand and pulled off her stifling helmet.

Her earlier thoughts returned as she made her way to the lists, displayed on screens at the garage exit. She was so engrossed that, though her ears registered the next approaching squire she still jumped when Geoffrey clapped a hand on her shoulder.

"Easy there Ros," he jibed cheerfully "It can't be that bad."

"Swift," She gasped, "I didn't know you were augmented for stealth."

"Ooh, ouch," Geoffrey chuckled. The very idea of a knight as a stealth specialist was too dishonourable and therefore too ridiculous to be anything but a joke, "Where did an honourable squire like you get a tongue like that?"

"Why, I learned from a master milord." Rosalyn punched her friends shoulder playfully, "I've been hanging around with you, remember?"

Geoffrey nodded toward the screen, "So? How does it look for you?"

Ros allowed herself a smug smile, "Not too bad. By the looks of things I should be able to work my way to a swords bout against Grayson in three days' time."

"Wonderful!" crowed Geoffrey, "I should have run the squire's London streets footrace that very morning. I'll be on a rest turn for the evening and I'd dearly like to watch you humble the insufferable prick first-hand."

The sounds of more approaching squires led Ros to draw Geoffrey away from the screen.

"Listen, Geoff," She stated earnestly, dropping his nickname for emphasis "I need to talk to you about something."

"Can it wait?" he queried, "I want to catch the start of the household militia marathon."

Ros was caught off-guard by the statement, "But you haven't looked at the lists, you don't know who you're competing against, how will you prepare?"

Geoffrey tapped the side of his nose with a finger and winked, "I like surprises, and anyway I'm sure it'll be much the same line-up as last year. I can handle it."

Rosalyn quite forgot her reason for wanting to talk with Geoffrey. That he could be so flippant about his opponents for the most important tournament in the world railed against her ideals of honour. "Geoffrey, you can't be serious. You accord your opponents no honour by not even affording them the courtesy of your own honest preparation."

"Rosalyn," Geoffrey held up his hands disarmingly, "I am well aware that each and every squire is taught the value of preparation, that a knight must afford another knight the honour of proper preparation before pitting himself in contest." Here he looked her straight in the eye before continuing, "But not all contests in life are fair and a good knight must be prepared to face an opponent about whom he knows little or nothing. I merely prepare myself for the uncertainties of life to come and, I hope, make myself a more worthy opponent for others."

Rosalyn shook her head, "That's either a most noble philosophy, or monumentally stupid, and it will take a more experienced mind than mine to decide which."

They walked away from the garage in silence, through the corridors of Camelot toward the arena.

"So," Ros ventured, "How is your philosophy serving you to date?"

"I'm not sure if I've got it quite right," Geoffrey admitted, "I seem to keep winning." He grinned.

The days passed in a kaleidoscope of frenetic activity for the squires. When not attending to their knights in either a tournament or domestic facility, they worked hard to maintain their own equipment and attend their own events.

By the third day, Geoffrey was a finalist and predicted champion of the eight-hundred meter sprint, and Rosalyn was causing a stir in both the tactical events and the sword arena. They were both busy at their bunks when Royston scampered through the door.

"I did it!" he yelled without preamble.

Geoffrey looked about theatrically, "Did what?" he shrugged.

Royston flourished the gold medal that now hung about his neck, "I won!"

Rosalyn cleared her throat and pointed to the view screen on the wall beside where Royston stood, "We know," she smiled warmly, and moved from her bunk to grab the little squire up in a hug. "We may have been busy, but we couldn't have missed it." Royston managed to turn and see the replay on the screen, not only of the awarding of the medal, but the final round of shooting that had confirmed him as the youngest squire archery champion the tournament had seen in decades.

Geoffrey dropped a hand heavily on Royston's shoulder. "Well done that man," he shook his friend's hand vigorously, "but shouldn't you be telling Sir Leopold?"

Royston's enthusiasm subsided a little. "I did, but he's been a little preoccupied these last few days, like something's on his mind. I've never seen him like it before."

Geoffrey turned Royston back to the screen. "Well, don't worry son. It's you making history now."

"He's not the only one," a new voice sounded in the room.

"Belvarre," snapped Ros "what do you mean by that?"

"I mean," replied Belvarre Grayson as he leaned casually against the doorframe, "that you might want to get over to the wrestling arena. I think Sebastian Crown is trying to make history as the first squire to kill an opponent in the ring."

"Who's he fighting," Geoffrey felt his stomach lurch as he guessed the answer before the words left Grayson's lips.

"Why, who else? Crown is fighting John Loxley."

As the three friends raced toward the grand gymnasium which housed the wrestling ring, Geoffrey activated the sub-dermal transmitter that acted as his personal link with the Baron of Stafford.

"My lord, I believe there may be a situation arising at the squire's wrestling."

The baron's deep voice came back clearly in his ear, "How serious?"

"John Loxley is fighting Sebastian Crown, squire Grayson believes Crown is looking for revenge over the 'incident' a couple of nights ago."

The baron grunted, "I'll contact the ringside officials, make sure this isn't just some prank of Grayson's."

"Thank you my lord." Geoffrey killed the link and bent his attention back to navigating the corridors that led to the ring.

They'd almost reached the gym when they were opposed by a crush of people pushing back down the corridor. People screamed or sobbed, shouted and jostled one another. Geoffrey, Ros and Royston instinctively pushed to one side of the corridor, lest their enhanced strengths caused the fleeing spectators injury.

"It must be worse than we thought!" shouted Royston.

Rosalyn glanced about before responding, "Royston, take the stairs to the upper tier, you should be able to get up there and see what's happening before Geoff and I get into the ring."

The younger squire nodded an affirmative then forged off up a nearby staircase.

Rosalyn and Geoffrey pushed their way into the press of people, Geoffrey keyed his comm-link again.

"My lord, we have a stampede at the gymnasium. It must be worse than we feared."

The stress was evident in Dominic's voice as he responded. "Agreed, I can't raise the officials. I'm contacting Dorset and heading your way myself but it'll be a few minutes before I get there."

"Received and understood," Geoffrey acknowledged.

As they moved through the throng the two squires had to stop here and there to pull fallen spectators from the floor, passing them to others in the crowd as they pushed forward. They could hear men at arms shouting for calm from further down the corridor and calling for medical assistance. Both knew that the first priority of the palace guards would be the spectators, it would be up to them to save their friend.

Royston's voice crackled over the scene on a broadcast frequency, "You need to get in here!" he cried.

"What's going on Royston?" Ros demanded.

"There's a camera man in here," Royston explained, "He saw it all. The referee tried to stop the bout so Crown threw him into the officials table! He looks to be raged off his head on combat stimulants! The judges need medics. The assistant referee isn't enhanced, there's nothing he can do. John's in a bad way but he's still fighting. He can't hold out much longer, hurry!"

Geoffrey urged Ros onward as the press around the door lessened and the flow of escaping people thinned. They rushed into the gym and took in the scene. It was just as Royston had described. A mess of debris and tangled limbs marked the officials table. The referee, an enhanced guardsman, lay atop the heap groaning weakly. In the centre of the ring,

Crown roared with triumph, the tiers of seats rattled as his vocal augmentation kicked in. Loxley circled him warily, his cybernetic arm hung dead and broken, he was limping badly and his face was bruised and cut.

"Sebastian!" shouted Ros, a fierce tone of command in her voice, "What the hell do you think you're doing?"

Crown spun to face her, hands high, fists clenched and feet spread. His grin was stretched too wide and his pupils contracted to pin-pricks, Ros could see the signs of a man, not only under the influence of combat drugs, but lost in them and loving it.

"Ex..am..ple," Sebastian growled through clenched teeth, "make an example of you all!"

She had to keep him talking, fighting him would be suicide and any time he spent talking was time for the drugs to metabolise and help to arrive.

"An example for who, Seb?" she could see Geoffrey out of the corner of her eye, moving around the wrestling ring, flanking Crown. She looked to Loxley, he met her gaze and gave her a pained wink; she turned back to Crown.

"An example for Dorset? For the King?" she demanded.

The big squire laughed wildly, "You will know! You will see her triumph soon!" he roared defiantly.

Ros couldn't understand; Sebastian was bound to be stripped of his position, his implants and everything for this outrage. How could he speak of triumph?

Crown finished his display and turned to Loxley, raising his hands high for the final, crushing blow.

She knew she could never get into the ring in time but she had to try and, failing that, she would make Sebastian pay. As she made a sprint for the ring, Ros heard a sound like tearing plastic and then something spun through the air from the high seating tier.

Her keyed-up senses recognised it as one of the auditorium seats, torn free of its mountings. It arced through the air and struck Crown where the brass collar of his vocal implant met the flesh of his throat. Royston's keen aim and ballistic targeting must have helped him account for its odd weight and predict the trajectory to the target. His aim was faultless and Ros gave quick thanks for the split second it gave her to reach the ring as Crown recoiled from the blow.

Quick as she was, she wasn't as swift as Geoffrey. As soon as Crown made to strike Loxley, Geoffrey took a standing jump, his leg enhancements carrying him effortlessly over the ring ropes. As Crown staggered from the impact of the seat, Geoff dropped low, behind Crown and made to sweep the big squire's legs from under him. He might as well have tried to kick through a concrete support pillar, as his strike did nothing. Crown was already recovering from his momentary shock and turned to focus on this new attack, swinging hard with his giant hands. Geoffrey was up and stood ready as the meaty fists started to strike at him. He might not be as strong, but his speed was immeasurably superior. Trained in various forms of unarmed combat, he avoided what he could and deflected Crown's blows only when he had to. The impacts on his limbs cost him; even as he diverted the force of one blow, another staggered him; Crown seized upon this opportunity and surged forward, bowling Geoffrey over with his bulk and attempted to trample him under foot.

Ros didn't hesitate. Grabbing the top-rope, she pulled back with all her strength and vaulted onto Sebastian's back. Her weight, added to his, carried him over Geoffrey and into the rope on the other side of the ring. She kicked out at his legs and he dropped, draping his arms over the tightly sprung rope. To her amazement he also used the rope to his advantage, the return spring of the rope carrying him back to his feet. He reached up and grabbed her arm, hauling her from his back and simply dropping her over the ropes. She impacted on the ring-side and then fell to the floor.

Geoffrey was ready when Crown turned to face him, from his back he arched his body, kicked out with both powerful legs and struck Crown in his stomach. Crown doubled over for a moment as Geoff came once more to his feet and delivered a round-house kick to his head, spinning him, but Crown was more experienced in this kind of combat. He turned with the spin, straightened his arm and brought a clothesline blow into Geoffrey's chest, flinging him across the ring.

Another seat came spinning from the upper tier, but Crown batted it out of the air. Ros could see, from the ground outside the ring, that Sebastian was breathing hard, the combat drugs must be wearing down, taking their toll for the initial boost they gave to his body. She dragged herself back to her feet and, taking one of the folding chairs from ringside, scrambled back into the ring.

Geoff was curled up as Crown tried to kick the life from him, taking blows on his arms, legs and back rather than his head or chest. Ros swung the chair hard over Sebastian's back, using the flat side to get his attention. He stumbled, but still turned on her as she swung the thin edge with all her might at his stomach. He brought his big fist down on the chair, crushing it to the floor. The look in his eyes told Rosalyn that, unless the fight was stopped soon, someone would have to die.

She could hear the men at arms getting closer, but it didn't matter as Sebastian back-handed her across the ring.

Caught in the final throes of the combat stimulants, his foes strewn at his feet, Crown bellowed out his laughter. He took hold of Geoffrey's leg and swung him across the ring, next to Ros, stalking after his battered quarry like some huge lion as he prepared to finish them off.

He was completely unprepared when John Loxley, with a final effort, came to his feet. The battered squire swung his prosthetic arm, dead from the shoulder as it was, like a morning-star, and struck him squarely in the face. Crown staggered, stumbled and went down, Loxley falling next to him.

For a few moments there was nothing but the laboured breathing of the fallen combatants.

The next thing Ros knew was Royston vaulting into the ring, not knowing who to check first as he yelled for medics.

'Good man,' thought Ros as she passed out.

Chapter 7

Nicholaeos had to skip every couple of steps to keep up with his master. Although true flight was forbidden, the older M.A.G.E.s were often granted a limited levitation generator to save their frail bodies and speed their passage from place to place. Master Arcady Mountbatten tended to glide that little bit faster when he was annoyed, which was often.

"The rough-housing of the Knights is none of our concern, why should the King request our council now?"

"Master, a competitor in the squire's wrestling was almost killed during a live broadcast."

"Hah!" snapped the old man, "Squires even! Why must my important duties be interrupted over a squire's misconduct?"

"Master," Nicholaeos fought to keep a note of frustration from his voice, "this incident may affect us all. For such a thing to happen at the King's tournament throws a shadow over Camelot and all who serve in her name. I would have thought the Guild would want us to be there as a duty to show its solidarity with the throne."

The master slowed his progress before responding coldly, "Nicholaeos, you are but a young apprentice, promising I'll grant but not yet advanced enough to lecture ME on guild duty. I was a full guildsman during the last Great War, Squires would die in training before they even saw combat, and still the young people flocked to the call of Camelot. The world has gone soft, mark my words, boy."

The old mage held up a wrinkled hand to cut off any apology Nicholaeos might have ventured, faded guild tattoos almost obscured by liver spots.

"There may be more to this than you have known, but for now you are to attend me, being seen and not heard. Do you understand?" the old man's voice held an edge like a saw.

"Yes master." Nicholaeos bowed his head in submission. Where had this sudden tension come from? His master was a demanding teacher, but never before had he felt such ice in his words. This would require patient observation and maybe a little investigation.

"What of the prisoner?" the old man growled.

"The... the heretic you had transferred from Bristol?" the young acolyte stammered.

"What other prisoner would I be talking about!" snapped Mountbatten.

"She is still in the Castle cells. Your order to keep her in isolation has been upheld."

The hunched M.A.G.E. huffed through his beard, "Good, her interrogation will have to wait until after this self-important display of so-called skill."

"Master, perhaps you might delegate that task? It shouldn't be hard to discover how she gained access to the castle's data-net."

Mountbatten rounded upon his apprentice, "I know 'how' she gained access, idiot boy! What I wish to determine is 'how' she chanced upon the means to do so and what she discovered while she was inside."

Nicholaeos took a step back from his mentor's wrath, "We... we have the records of the files she accessed."

"Again, you completely miss the point! She is from the outside! What passes for a data network amongst the plebs is as a child's picture book compared to the Library of Alexandria! Now, do as I say. Be seen but not heard and remember, no-one see's the prisoner. I will deal with her."

The crash of steel doors being flung open woke Cassie from a fretful sleep. The lights in the detention block were never dimmed, so sleeping was a 'head under the pillow' affair. She lurched to the bars of her cell in time to see a gurney being wheeled down the corridor, flanked by armed guards and laden with equipment and a huge figure. Cassie had rarely seen an augmented knight outside of news feeds and then never without their official garb. The man on the gurney was easily over 7' tall and his limbs were, to Cassie's mind, a grotesque mix of metal and muscle. The strange brass collar and goggles at his head and neck and head must surely be attached since he wore no clothing save a towel covering his groin. Everywhere that showed metal was bristling with plugs and leads, hooked up to monitors and a drip ran from his huge arm. Cassie watched in awe as the gurney rolled past and on to what she knew was a maximum security holding area.

Once all the guards and staff had returned from dropping off their captive and exited the holding area, she waited for a few minutes, then took one of her shoes and placed it on the small windowsill of her cell. She didn't have long to wait before a rustle of wings heralded Eric's arrival.

"Eric, what's going on?" Cassie demanded.

"Charmed I'm sure," sniffed the raven haughtily, "If you're referring to the individual who was wheeled inside just moments ago, and I calculate an eighty-five percent chance that you are, then that was one Sebastian Crown, Squire of Dorset."

"That was a squire?" Cassie gawped at her familiar, "He looked like a monster!"

"Nevertheless," drawled Eric "seems he allowed a personal grievance to influence him in the wrestling event and nearly killed his opponent."

"Now hang on..." Cassie waved her hands urgently, "That doesn't figure and you know it, the knights are well known for the strictness of their training and upbringing. Their code is strict on such matters, if there was a matter and this Crown wanted blood all he had to do was initiate an honour trial. Killing during the tournament? Even a cynic like me knows they just won't do it."

I'm just relaying the media coverage, my dear. The bout was aired live. Something had to be said and too many people witnessed the 'fight' for it to be glossed over." From the way Eric dropped the inverted commas around the word (with the aid of his holographic projector) Cassie could tell that it had been one sided and brutal.

"Something isn't right, Eric," Cassie took to pacing as she turned the thought over in her mind. For weeks she'd been chasing a murmur, a ghost on the network, something about the tournament but not from any source, Camelot, media or industry that she recognised and, as an information broker, anything someone didn't want her to know surely meant that she wanted to know it all the more.

"Something's going on Eric," she announced. "Something's going to happen during the tournament. Whether Camelot knows it or not, some of their agents may be compromised and this is just the start of it."

"So what are we going to do about it?" croaked the raven petulantly.

"At best it'll be our chance to escape," Cassie bit her lip anxiously "at worst, who knows what could happen."

"Well, look on the bright side," Eric cocked his black head, the minute green light in his eyes throbbed gently, "Things couldn't get much worse, could they?"

Baron Dominic paced like a caged bear teetering between anger and outright rage.

"Of course there'll be a trial, but it will have to wait for the end of the games. Though it's really only a matter of protocol, the whole thing was broadcast over the public network, for God's sake!"

Geoffrey stood, somewhat uncomfortably given his bruises and his master's mood, in Dominic's plush chambers.

"What will happen to Sebastian, Sir?" he asked quietly.

"For now, he's being held in the castle cells," Dominic subsided a little and quit his pacing.

"Once the trial is done, no doubt he will be removed from any position of honour, stripped of rank and privilege, then they will take out his implants and send him to the prison colonies." The Baron slumped momentarily into the room's grand chair, "A dark day indeed."

Dominic clapped his hands suddenly, startling the downcast Geoffrey. His vast reservoir of good humour seemed to be refilling itself before Geoffrey's eyes as the Baron came to his feet with a great sigh.

"But that is yet to be. The video-feed has shown the bravery of yourself and your companions, it will bring honours upon you, be sure of that. But for now, many things have been thrown off-kilter by this incident, yet the great games continue apace!" he clapped a massive hand on Geoffrey's shoulder and led him from the room. Dominic turned his squire to face him, his beard rent asunder by a savage smile. "The squire's race through London. It has been delayed that you may still compete. It will now be run at the time of the evening's round of the sword competition. The draws have been rearranged so that the race entrants may still attend both. You will run as the lights of the city are activated, they will be turned on a street at a time radiating out from the castle, following the route of the race, and it's no secret that there are wagers on you not only to beat the other entrants, but also to beat the lights themselves. It will be a tremendous feat if you do and a marvellous spectacle to reinvigorate this tournament!"

The tiered seats of the sword arena buzzed with a low hum of expectation, and wild speculation over the previous evening's wrestling incident. Spotlights illuminated the area of competition, leaving the spectators shrouded in half-light so as not to distract the combatants.

Rosalyn checked the lacing on her long boots and the elbow-length gloves which made up part of the contest uniform. She was still a little stiff. The enhanced healing abilities bestowed upon all squires had done wonders for the majority of the bludgeoning damage she had taken, but there was no way she would be one hundred per cent fit for her bout against Grayson. She'd spent the night after her de-brief from Sir Phillip in the infirmary, been scanned and prodded, pumped full of anti-inflammatory drugs for the swelling, and her body had managed to repair a few torn muscles while she slept. The morning had brought some physiotherapy, steam-room treatment, massage (all supplied by Camelot and under supervision by the tournament officials) then a stern set of calisthenics to make sure she was fit to compete. The day had crawled past after that, minutes and hours stretching endlessly while she'd walked the underhalls of Camelot looking for some solitude away from the bustle and fuss of the tournament. She'd ended up back in the arming chamber allocated to her knight's household. There she'd set herself to work polishing and running checks to keep her mind clear and calm.

Now she sat in the arena, wearing the colours of her knight and awaiting the official's call. The audience seemed oblivious to her presence, and would be until she entered the spotlight. Even the additional guards posted unobtrusively around the hall only spared her a passing glance. Earl Phillip and Duke Grayson sat together above and behind the officials table. They exchanged few words, but watched the attendant crowd rather than the competitors. Only one pair of eyes in the entire arena seemed to register her presence; Belvarre Grayson. Her opponent sat on the opposite side of the ring, eyes fixed intently upon her. Both of them had bested others to get here, both had proved their command of the traditional weapon of the knights of the round table, and now they waited for the moment of truth, the final moment of honour to decide who would celebrate their victory and who would lament their failure.

Rosalyn flexed her stiff muscles. "Oh, bollocks." she sighed quietly.

Geoffrey eased into the starting blocks. In the fading light, the gates of Camelot stood open before him, his fellow runners to either side. Looking through the gates, he could see the self-illuminating cats-eyes of the race route. The first stretch of street lights would come on with the starter's pistol. 'Beat the lights, beat the lights' he repeated the mantra over and over in his head, tightening his focus until his world contained just himself, the road and the lights.

"On your marks!"

Geoffrey slowed his breathing taking deep, steady breaths.

"Get set!"

He tensed, head up, muscles tightened, sinews sang and trembled like steel cables, 'don't predict the gun, don't predict the gun,'

A light sweat beaded his brow as his metabolism surged in preparation for the effort to come.

The pistol rang out, and before the first echo sounded from the castle walls, the runners were up and away. Geoffrey flew through the dark gates and onto the drawbridge, the cheering of the spectators dying away with the distance almost as soon as it had begun. The nearest runner was a hair's breadth behind him; it might as well have been a mile. The lights along the drawbridge came to life, casting Geoffrey's shadow ahead of him.

'This might be possible after all,' he cheered himself as he raced on into the dark city.

Dressed from head to toe in ceremonial armour, a reproduction of a 15th century full plate harness wired to record strike impacts, engraved with scenes of victory and edged with delicate ornamentation, Rosalyn faced her opponent at the piste.

"En garde!" Came the call from the official referee. Rosalyn and Belvarre swept their swords, three feet of edged steel longsword each to a fencer's salute. The heavy weapons of the squire's tournament always drew a crowd. The fencing of the knights was often too fast, too bound by rule and tradition to follow with the naked eye. The armour, harking back to bygone ages of chivalry, added to the spectacle and the weight of ages the event carried with it.

The armour was thick, padded underneath, but the sharp blades could cause grievous injury. The skill of the event was to best your opponent without maiming them. Unlike true fencing, the squires were allowed a square arena to circle and could strike with fist and foot if they found themselves disarmed.

The official stepped back, drew breath to call 'Fence!' when the lights flickered, dimmed and died. All talk around the auditorium ceased, a woman screamed before the red hued emergency lights cut in. Ros lowered her sword and looked around. A humming filled the room, like some oversized electric motor starting up. She heard Phillip speaking into his comms, apparently to no avail. The humming became more intense, the people in the room started to chatter in panic as the guards called for silence. In the middle of the ring, Ros could feel the air itself begin to vibrate. The humming became a buzz which soon became a roar, the vibration in the air became a vortex of wind, screams were muffled by the maelstrom forming in the centre ring as Ros and Belvarre were forced to the edge of the arena.

Ros didn't have a clue what was happening and, from the hissing static in her comm's implant, neither did anyone else.

Chapter 8

Geoffrey was ahead of the pack and pacing the lights when it happened. He'd been running, back lit by the street lamps, the ambient light from the buildings and the cats-eyes more than sufficient for the track ahead. The crowd was gathered at the castle, though some spectators were lining the route. And then suddenly, they weren't. He'd turned a corner and the street ahead was empty. The light from the street lamps had gone too.

Geoffrey slowed, confused and then thought he heard the starter's pistol again, and again.

Gunfire. Geoffrey turned and saw the muzzle flashes coming from the alleyways, pouring into the oncoming pack of racers. Within seconds it was absolutely clear that there was, for all his speed and strength, nothing he could do. Shocked, chilled to his core by the slaughter before him, he tried to activate his comms implant. Static sputtered back at him. He glimpsed a figure emerging from an alley, saw the colours emblazoned upon its coat, then he turned and ran, he ran faster than he ever had in his life. If he could return to Camelot he could raise the alarm, the guard would be called out and these murderers could be caught. Couldn't they? He wasn't thinking clearly, the spectators, what if…?

Unknowingly he'd followed the race route, and found himself once again on a lit street, crowds on either side. It might have been a bad dream except… screaming, running, the crowd had heard the gunfire and now they were panicking. He made for the first Camelot tabard he saw.

"The runners," he panted "are under fire, I think they're all dead! Call the castle!"

"Would that I could," the guard looked as panicked as the spectators, "I can't raise them, I can't raise anyone!"

Geoffrey grabbed the guards' rifle, "Go, send the first six guards to me then start organising crowd control. I'm going back for the others."

"But you said they're all dead!" the fear in the guard's voice was clear and Geoffrey turned, looking at him for the first time. He was young, younger than Geoffrey, pale and shaking.

"I said I THINK they're dead," Geoffrey worked the action of the rifle and the 'snap-clack' of the bolt rang sharp, the fire in Geoffrey's eyes forging purpose out of fear, turned the guards doubt to duty.

"I pray that I'm wrong."

The thrumming was unbearable. Every man and woman in the auditorium was forced to their knees, teeth gritted and eyes streaming with pain. Only the knights and squires still stood, barely. Rosalyn gripped her sword's hilt, still looking for the source of the disturbance. Suddenly, like a mirage made real, a dozen black clad men stepped out of thin air in the main floor. Ros stared, stunned into inaction at the sight. The intruders were not so disoriented. With military discipline they fanned out, raised compact submachine guns and started shooting. The Camelot guards were quickly dispatched as the men took control of the room. The disturbance in the air died as the roaring gunfire took over.

Rosalyn came to her senses. She looked over to Sir Phillip as he vaulted the barrier between the seats and the arena, oblivious to the bullets that chased around him. Duke Jerome followed closely. Phillip drew his ceremonial blade smoothly and swept toward the intruders as Jerome followed suit, sword sliding easily from its sheath and into Phillip's unprotected back.

Rosalyn felt the blow, deep in the pit of her stomach, a cold leaden weight in her limbs. She watched her knight's face as he registered the impact. He looked down at the blade protruding from his flesh. She saw him watch as the blade withdrew, so slowly it seemed to Rosalyn, the disbelief on his face, the pain in his eyes. Phillip turned to his attacker and Jerome swept his blade down across Phillip's chest, the force of the blow knocking the noble Earl to the floor, where he stayed.

Rosalyn felt her sword slip from her grasp and clatter to the floor. The sound rang out in a sudden absence of gunfire.

Duke Sir Jerome Grayson swept forward as if he hadn't just gutted a brother knight of the round table. He stood before the two squires. Rosalyn knelt in despair upon the floor and Belvarre stunned and silent, his sword forgotten as it hung loosely in his hand. Two of the black insurgents moved to flank Jerome. Members of the crowd whimpered in the background as the rest of the intruders covered them with their guns.

"You have two choices," Jerome announced, "come with me now, no questions, or die right here." He tapped his foot impatiently "Quickly, please."

"Father," Belvarre's voice sounded choked with tears, he tore off his helmet and Ros could see the confusion and anger in his face, "Why father?"

"Not now boy, choose!" some emotion crept into Jerome's voice and it was impatience.

Belvarre's anger coalesced into rage, his hand gripped his sword and he stepped forward to strike out at his father. The men on either side of the Duke brought their weapons to bear. Belvarre would die before he could even swing and Ros felt powerless to stop it.

'No,' she thought 'not powerless.' She took up her sword and threw it hard.

As she raised her head she saw Phillip, bloodied and shaking, rise up behind the other guard.

By chance she had lashed out at the right man and her sword tumbled end over end. It struck true and carried the man with it as it flew across the room. Phillip swept his own sword down with the last of his strength, cleaving his target from shoulder to stomach, the weight of the weapon dragging him and the sundered body to the floor.

Belvarre ignored all this and swept his sword up in a clumsy arc against his father. Under any other circumstances, Jerome could have batted the sword away with a bare hand but, in his arrogance, he had never thought that his son would raise arms against him. The tip of the sword took him under the jaw and ripped through his cheek, throwing his head back and knocking him to the ground. Belvarre seemed surprised that the blow had landed too, and he didn't press his attack. The rest of the black clad guards turned their weapons on the squires but Jerome's voice rang out again.

"Wait!" He climbed to his feet, the ragged gash in his cheek dripping blood, "You wish to try me, boy?" he sneered.

Belvarre cried out in rage and swung his sword. Jerome stepped forward, caught his son's wrist and gave a vicious twist. Rosalyn heard the joints pop and the bones break. She was about to move to his aid, but Jerome tossed the fully armoured squire contemptuously into his one-time adversary.

"Fools," Jerome's voice came out wet with the blood in his mouth.

"You shall live and learn, and when you feel you are ready, I will seek you out and crush you anyway." He waved his hand and, all of a sudden the disturbance and noise that had heralded the intruder's arrival returned at full volume and the black clad men along with Duke Jerome vanished.

Rosalyn heaved and pushed Belvarre's unresisting form from on top of her. She scrambled over to Sir Phillip, shedding helmet and gauntlets as she went. As she reached out to take her knight's hands, the cold knot in her gut tightened, she fought for breath as she realised it was already too late.

"Cassie, darling? Time to wake up!" the insistent and tinny nature of the voice, combined with the artificial feathers whipping across her face brought Cassandra out of her slumber. She had barely opened her eyes, but she could see something was wrong. The lights were out. Emergency lighting cast a dull light in the cell and the corridor outside.

104

"What's going on Eric?" she demanded.

"There are large scale power outages across Camelot and parts of London. I'm picking up a well-co-ordinated software assault on multiple fronts. It seems to be targeting the Camelot cyber signature. That allows me to monitor it without being affected. The strange thing is, I can't isolate any source, or sources. The signal or signals just are, without being 'from' anywhere."

"That's very, very… impossible Eric. But apart from that, how does this help me? When the power is interrupted the magnetic deadlocks activate on the cells, so the door is still locked." Cassie managed a smug smile.

"Yes dear, however…" Eric turned his head to an unnatural degree to look at the cell door. Cassie watched him target a bright red data-beam from his eyes on the locking mechanism which 'thunked' encouragingly. "With the power out, the computer firewalls that protect the lock from tampering are offline, so I can influence the lock itself with a micro-magnetic frequency and open the door."

A screech of tearing metal and screams from down the corridor caused them both to pause.

"Of course, not everyone needs high technology and brain power to open their cell."

"Eric," Cassie breathed, her voice a whisper, uncertainty and fear clouding her thoughts, "What do I do?"

The cyber raven slumped a little, like he always did when performing priority calculations.

"Hide, under the bed." Cassie gawped at her familiar. "Follow the logic. You run ahead, we have to open the doors, the rogue squire catches us…" his pause was precisely measured.

"Second, we follow, let him open the doors. Either he sees us, or we run into a security patrol coming up behind him. Third, you hide under the bed. A limited, high-risk time-frame then we make a plan for a proper escape."

Cassie nodded, shaking as the screams from down the corridor died away. She crawled under the bed as Eric made for the window. The concrete floor was cold, and her breathing and heartbeat sounded loud in her ears. She fancied that she could feel the footsteps of the giant in max security as he apparently vented his anger at being confined. She could see the monster in her mind tearing up anything within reach. Maybe she could still run…

She couldn't mistake the next noise. Louder than anything so far, it was the sound of the security doors being pulled from their mountings. Cassie gasped in awe at the strength this indicated, then stifled her outburst with her hand. Heavy footsteps approached, Cassie wanted to scream. Instead she just bit down harder and tasted the coppery tang of her own blood. She could see the feet of the giant as he strode past her cell and then... stopped. He took a step back. The door, the door to the cell was unlocked, it must have swung ajar. The door opened slowly outward then, with a grunt of effort and the crack of the hinges, it was torn from its mountings and tossed away. Cassie closed her eyes and curled up on herself, biting hard on her hand to stop from sobbing aloud. A giant foot stepped into the cell then paused. A humming filled the air, followed by the air itself vibrating all around. The giant retreated and then, as the humming reached a painful peak, he vanished like a nightmare with the rising of the sun. When the air had settled once more, nothing moved except the trickle of blood from under the cell bed.

Geoffrey sat in the cold interview room. He still wore his running gear, and the chill of the bare walls wasn't helped by the lack of heating, which was still inactive after the attacks.

'The attacks'. He'd heard snippets of conversation when he returned to Camelot, every major event and every guard post in the city had suffered casualties from the unknown interlopers. In some cases those losses were total, such was the speed and savagery of the assaults. He was still reeling from the attack on the race when he'd been escorted to this interview room, this... cell.

He heard raised voices from outside.

"But sir, he was the only survivor. That gives us cause for suspicion!"

"Suspicion be damned, Sergeant!" There was no mistaking the roar of his own knight in full fury, "HE led a response team, swept for survivors and tried to locate the assailants! HE is MY squire and has acquitted himself with nothing but honour in my service and the service of Camelot. So, YOU let me in THERE before I break YOU in half!"

The door slid partially open and stuck halfway. Baron Dominic clamped a huge hand on the malfunctioning portal and slammed it back in its recess without any apparent effort. He bulled into the room like a storm front and tossed a bundle of clothing onto the rooms' solitary table.

"Bloody chilly in here," he growled.

Geoffrey nodded mutely, not moving to touch the clothing.

"I read your report, wanted to handle the interview myself but..." Sir Dominic let the words trail off.

"I heard sir, multiple attacks on targets throughout the city. You were needed elsewhere."

Dominic grunted and shrugged.

"The council... what's left of the council, convened some hours ago. I just came to confirm what you've reported before we go and re-join them." Dominic shuffled the papers he carried with him. "The crest you saw, you're certain of it?"

"Aye, my lord." Geoffrey saw that his master wasn't questioning his report, just enacting protocol for the benefit of others. "It was a purple dragon upon black, the ancient coat of arms of the forces of Morgana le Fay."

Baron Dominic knelt next to his squire. He was still taller than the seated Geoffrey as he rested a hand on the squire's shoulder. His next words came out reluctantly.

"Geoffrey, we're to go to the council room. You will have to confirm your statement before the King and then... then I fear you will learn some harsh truths," he held up a hand to quiet Geoffrey's protests. "Those are for the King to explain. For myself, I just sought to train you, to prepare you as best as I was able. As best as I was allowed."

The two men shared a silent moment of understanding. After what was to come, neither would emerge the same as they were. The very nature of the life they knew was about to change, and the long years of fellowship that they had served as knight and squire would end at this very moment.

Chapter 9

Rosalyn sat very still in the Great Council chamber. She sat at the very round table that had always accommodated the Knights of Camelot, but here she felt no awe, no weight of ages, no heightened sense of duty. She sat silently in her appointed place, a chair behind and to the left of the seat of Essex, the chair of her knight, now vacant.

Seated closest to her at the moment was Dame Seraphine Feldon. Far from the glamorous figure of the ball those few nights ago, she now sat with her hair pulled back practically, if severely, and her wonderful gown was replaced by comfortable battle fatigues. It was Dame Feldon who had brought the shell-shocked Rosalyn out of an interview chamber and into the round table room; who had reassured her that all was well at the Essex estate and that Lord Obermann, the resident M.A.G.E. had not defected like the others. She had said it was a tribute to Phillip's ability to command loyalty. The words came as cold comfort to Ros.

Next to Dame Feldon sat the King himself. They exchanged heated words and the King had to repeatedly throw the hard-line cable that was plugged into his skull, feeding tactical reports directly into his head, back over his shoulder like an unruly lock of hair. For a moment his eyes alighted on Ros and his face softened for a moment in something like concern, then Dame Feldon drew him back to their discourse and Rosalyn went un-regarded once more. Several other knights sat at their appointed places around the table. Now that limited communications had been re-established, they were co-ordinating national defence responses to the attacks. She looked past the King. Belvarre sat in a similar position to her behind the seat of Oxford, the only difference being the guard who stood behind him. If anyone in the room was feeling worse than Ros, it was Grayson. That much was evident. She wasn't sure how she knew it, but she knew that Belvarre Grayson had been broken into pieces by his father's betrayal. Somehow he would have to rebuild himself, and for that he would need help from somewhere.

An amount of time passed, Rosalyn was too lost in her own thoughts to know how much, but when she looked again more seats had been filled. The table was a long way from full. Sir Andrew sat at the seat of York, the space behind him conspicuously absent of John Loxley. Sir Roland (knight to Sebastian Crown and lord of Dorset) fidgeted under the watchful eyes of another guard, and Royston sat alone behind an empty knight's chair. Just then, Baron Dominic entered with Geoffrey in tow, and they took their seats on the far side of the King. This seemed to be the signal the monarch was waiting for as he stood, called the room to silence and looked around gravely.

"We are at war," he stated simply,

"We have been at war for quite some time it seems, however we have been sadly unaware of the scale of the threat." He paused for emphasis.

"Yesterday evening, the forces of Camelot across the country came under an unprecedented and well-coordinated attack from unidentified forces." Gesturing to the empty seats around the table he went on.

"From the reports we have had since the attacks yesterday evening, roughly a third of all the knights, knight-errants and squires of Camelot have defected to this unknown foe. A further ten percent of our brothers and sisters have been slain this past night, some by the very defectors they once called friends." He turned from the table, taking a breath to compose himself.

Rosalyn could barely believe what she was hearing. Knights of the table turning their backs upon oaths of honour which had held strong for generations in some cases. Before she could begin to take in the information the King was speaking again.

"So far, there appears to be no connection between those who have defected. As you can see, we now have many knights without squires and visa-versa.

How they have been recruited by our foe is also a mystery at this time."

Rosalyn felt the nervous energy in the room. It radiated from every knight, the need to do something, to raise arms against the enemy in defence of the realm, and the frustration that there was no clear target to rally against.

"However, these losses are not confined to the table alone." He gestured to Lady Teresa.

The palace technical advisor had been stood to one side of the chamber. She was flanked by the master at arms, Sidney Carter, still dressed in his leather apron.

"It would seem," the sombre note was out of place in her normally light voice, "That several members of the Technicians Guild hierarchy have absconded, along with their equipment, resources and some staff. There were no records, or any travel plans for the individuals in question. We have checked security records but all of them have been erased or corrupted. Once we bypassed the traps they set." Teresa looked sadly at the King, "We suffered some losses ourselves."

"A parting gift from our erstwhile colleagues." growled Master Sidney, chewing hard on the end of his cigar.

Teresa consulted a data-slate in her hand, "We've conducted a top down sweep of the castle for similar devices, we've found nothing, but we're performing another sweep and rotating the techs performing the search."

The King nodded silently, then beckoned with his hand. The doors of the chamber were swung open and a timid figure was ushered in, none too gently, by the guards.

"Apprentice Westbrook," the King's words rang with authority like hammer-blows, "where is your master, Arcady Mountbatten?"

The young mage couldn't meet the King's gaze or that of anyone in the room. He seemed curled inward, deeply withdrawn as he answered quietly, "I don't know your majesty."

The Kings expression hardened, "I ask you again, your master, Arcady Mountbatten, who served me, who served my father loyally, and who has served Camelot for the last seventy-five years, where is he?!" the King's voice rose to an infuriated roar.

The apprentice trembled. It was hard not to notice the tears in his eyes and tremor of fear in his voice. Rosalyn felt a pinch of compassion for him. Like Belvarre, it seemed he had been betrayed by his master, the only father figure he would have known for many years, but at the same time she could understand the King's' frustration. Mountbatten had been a stolid feature of the council of Camelot for such a long time, and to lose his expertise to an enemy was a colossal blow.

"I don't know, sire." The young man ventured.

The King slammed his fist down upon the round table in frustration. He turned to Dame Feldon, "I asked for the most senior mage in attendance at the tournament to be brought to me, and this is it?"

The knight nodded. "We searched everywhere, and it would seem that all the elder mages disappeared in the minutes after the attacks. We have a few apprentices left behind. Initial statements indicate the mages disappeared in the same manner as the insurgents."

The King was silent. His gaze bore into Nicholaeos until the young man was forced to look up, to see why such silence reigned in the chamber. His eyes met the King's and he was held, locked by the stern gaze as the King spoke in a measured tone.

"It is my belief that our enemy has not left us entirely, but, rather than subversive agents or saboteurs, they have left behind a veil of mistrust. They intend us to trip over ourselves, doubting our allies and our own agents. They wish to undermine the ties that bind the table and the guilds together, as much as the ties that bind brother knights or guild colleagues." He scanned the room looking for any hint of doubt before continuing.

"Before this day, I would have said that all those who served under Camelot's banner were worthy of my trust, completely and without exception or restriction." He took a breath, "Now I say this. Each and every person in this castle remains in my trust until such time as they prove me wrong." He let the words sink in while the room remained silent.

"Apprentice Westbrook," he barked suddenly, startling the young mage, "I wish you to contact the academy of mages post-haste. Our adversary wishes us to fumble around on our confusion. I say we take decisive action. I wish you to take account of those among your fellows who have been lost or defected. Then, from those that remain, I wish you to summon two suitable court advisors to take Lord Mountbatten's place. Speed is of the essence, so these guards will accompany you and a palace scribe will provide you with my authority in the matter. Go, now!" Summarily dismissed, the young mage with the fussy goatee scurried thankfully away.

Ros drifted away from the meeting. Tactics, security measures, code-phrases, all these details could be recalled from a neuro-buffer which had long ago been installed in her head. She'd have to 'watch it' to properly assimilate the information, but she couldn't bring herself to do that now. Right now, all she could see was Phillip's shocked face as the sword pierced his chest, the lack of any kind of animation as she rested his head in her lap after, as his blood pooled around them both. The man had been as much of a father to her as anyone could be, and he was gone. Ros wasn't accustomed to loss. She wasn't familiar with the shock, the pain and the overwhelming weight of emotion that went with it. She could see Geoffrey with Sir Dominic, still pale and not yet recovered from his ordeal, she could see Dame Feldon trying to disengage from a deep discussion of palace security with a senior Man-at-Arms, the Dame's quick glances showing that she intended to catch Ros once she finished. Ros left. She wandered the halls and corridors away from bustle and noise, across quadrangles and greens until she found a place of peace. In this quiet garden she sat beneath the clear sky that was untroubled by the events of the day.

A small sound broke her moment of stillness, someone drawing their breath in pain. Fearing that a casualty of the attack had been missed and might be lying hurt in the quad, or even worst, one of the attackers left after the withdrawal, Ros turned her head, listening. There was a stand of trimmed shrubs behind her bench and Ros edged silently around it scanning for movement. When she saw a girl sitting on another bench on the opposite side, she sighed in relief. She didn't seem obviously wounded, and didn't appear like one of the hostiles, but someone ought to check on her.

Ros skirted around to get a better look at the girl. She was maybe 20, her dark hair shot-through with coloured streaks. Ros sniffed the coppery tang of blood and saw red stains on the girls smock, she hurried forward.

"Are you alright?" Ros knelt before the girl, she was rather dishevelled and dirty too, wide eyes turned up, shocked at her approach.

"Umm.. I'm f-fine," came the stammered reply.

"Here, let me see that hand," Ros urged, "What's your name?"

The girl winced as Ros took her hand and drew it toward her to inspect it,

"Umm, Cassie." The wound was obscured with clotted, scabbed blood but it looked like...

"CAW!" Ros turned at the sudden croak of the raven sat on the far end of the bench as she turned back she caught a glimpse of something. Where she'd cradled Cassie's' elbow her sleeve had ridden up and Ros had seen the edge of something. She scowled and roughly pushed the sleeve up, showing the prisoners 'Heretic' brand clear and new on her arm.

Ros and Cassie shared a look, Ros fierce and angry, Cassie wide-eyed and lip quivering. In desperation, Cassie swung a shabby punch at the squire, but Ros didn't even have to see it coming. She caught

Cassie's' wrist, stopping the incoming swing and then squeezed the girl's injured hand eliciting a yelp of pain. Ros pulled Cassie's hands together when suddenly she was buffeted with frantic, flapping wings.

"Eric, go!" shouted her prisoner and the buffeting ceased, the raven flapping off into the spires of the castle.

Ros turned Cassie around and held the girl's wrists behind her. She looked at the heretics' shabby smock, tousled hair and slumped shoulders which started to shudder as her captive began to cry. Ros sighed, "Come on," she said quietly "let's go get that hand seen to," and started the walk to the infirmary.

Ros walked in silence but eventually the constant blubbering of her captive got to her. "Please stop crying... what was your name again?"

"Cassie," whimpered the prisoner.

"Short for Cassandra I take it?" Ros returned stiffly. Cassie nodded. "What did you do to get that brand?"

"Hacking," Cassie ventured hesitantly, "I used to sell information."

Ros allowed herself a small smile, "I didn't think you were a terrorist, you almost wet yourself when I came upon you in the quad. And you hit like a girl."

Cassie muttered under her breath.

"Well yes, not everyone CAN be a genetically modified 'super-freak', was that the term? But not, I feel, for the reasons you might think."

Even with her enhanced hearing Ros nearly missed what Cassie said next.

"What will happen to me?"

Ros heard the pain and uncertainty in Cassie's voice and felt a pain of her own.

"I do not know, usually heretics are handed over to the Mages, though that might not be possible for some time. I simply cannot say."

Their exchange ended when Ros spied Dame Feldon walking toward them with a squad of palace guard in tow.

"Squire Savant, there you are, and who have you found?"

"M'lady Feldon. This is Cassandra, a prisoner from the detention block. I was escorting her to the infirmary, she is wounded."

Dame Feldon beckoned two guards forward who took her charge, while Ros was addressed by the knight herself. "You disappeared after the council."

"I needed some space m'lady," Ros supplied.

"You may call me Seraphine, Rosalyn, since we are to be working close together in the coming days."

"Then I am to be your squire now?" Ros would once have been honoured by the proposition, conflicted surely by her loyalty to Phillip; but still. Now it was simply another reminder that he was gone.

"Squire? You are not so lucky my dear. The King has announced that you, among others, will be elevated to full Knight and take the seat of Essex, Sir Phillip," Seraphine was silent a moment, and just for that second the lustre in her hair was dulled.

"Sir Phillip had no issue, his business assets are passed to his wife but his seat was to be passed to you."

Ros was about to object but Seraphine carried on, "Of course you are not ready, but there is an old precedent for such times. I will serve as your mentor and counsel should you wish, until such time as you feel ready to assume your duties upon your own authority."

Ros was staggered. Essex was a big holding, and such a seat falling upon a new knight was beyond recalled memory and, to be a Knight! Suddenly the world was cast aside, troubles and pains gone for an instant as the goal for which she had worked so hard was presented before her, and then it all came back in a rush when she remembered the man who had taught her so much was gone and would not see her elevation.

"Come now, Rosalyn," Seraphine placed a hand on her shoulder "Anthony would speak with you, there is much to be done and few of us to do it."

Chapter 10

Rather than leading her back to the round table, Lady Seraphine walked Ros through winding corridors down into Camelot's heart. In a small, nondescript room, Baron Dominic waited with Geoffrey and the Chief Tech, Master Carter. Dominic looked ill at ease and Carter dragged, distractedly, at a stubby cigar. Furtive glances were exchanged before the King himself swept into the chamber.

"Savant, Mayland?" They stepped forward "Both of you have now been elevated to knighthood, but we have little time for ceremony. You will be formally appointed upon your return."

The two friends looked at each other. "Return my lord? Where are we going?"

The King nodded to the master at arms, who stroked his bald pate and touched the brass plate on his temple. The plate slid back, and he ran a calloused finger along the ridge it left, pressing a barely noticeable button on the rim.

The King stared hard at Ros and Geoffrey in turn. "What follows is of utmost secrecy, 'pon your honour, you are sworn to this in the name of Camelot."

The new knights nodded.

"Then follow me." A slide in the wall had opened to reveal a palm-print scanner, and the King laid his hand upon it. Two doors parted in a previously blank wall and slid back to reveal a staircase. London was built upon blue clay, with no rock for hundreds of metres down, but the passage they descended from that innocuous basement room was hewn granite, completely out of place.

The air was cool and damp, and minute crystals sparkled to provide illumination. The King spoke as they descended.

"The founding of Camelot has been told as history. Arthur united the Anglo-Saxons under the values of truth, justice and honour and eventually led them in battle against the Normans who followed his son Mordred. We all know the facets that are regarded as fairy-tale, Merlin the wise counsellor was a wizard, Excalibur the magical sword and Morgana le Fay the dark sorceress..." he paused briefly before going on, "The Lady of the Lake."

They walked down a few more steps in the glittering light and the cool silence.

"What if I told you that the story, fairy-tale and all, was true?"

Ros and Geoffrey stopped in their tracks, the King just continued down the stairs so they hurried to catch him.

"I can tell you do not believe me. That is understandable, so I offer you proof."

The staircase ended and a sheet of granite blocked their path, "Behind this wall is The Lake and within resides The Lady, but this treasure is guarded by one of our most precious relics, the sword of Uther Pendragon. The Sword in the Stone."

The king stood aside to reveal a sword, embedded in stone, hilt toward the ceiling of the cave.

"All one must do to access the Lady's demesne is bear this sword before them. So I invite you now, Mayland?"

Geoffrey stood forward, half smiling in uncertainty at the situation. He wrapped a hand around the hilt of the sword and tugged. Then he put both hands on the hilt, he tugged and pulled at the cross-guard, braced and strained until sweat broke out on his brow. He looked to the King in confusion and stood back.

Ros, entranced, took a step past Geoff and reached for the hilt herself. She could see the gold lettering, ancient Saxon runes, unfamiliar to her, but still she knew what they said; "Whosoever Pulleth This Sword From This Stone Is Rightwise King Of England". The gold etching swam in her vision becoming familiar, she could almost read those runes as she reached out until the King laid a hand on hers, "We have precious little time I'm afraid." he said.

The sound of his voice broke her out of her daze. She glanced up at his face and saw... something. She couldn't tell, but for a moment his gaze caught hers intently before he looked away.

Letting her stand quietly to one side, he gripped the hilt himself and pulled. The blade slid free with a faintly ringing note of steel on stone and little apparent resistance. The runes inscribed along its length caught the subtle illumination of the passage and seemed to glow. The blade held the soft, clear tone as Anthony presented it to the glittering granite wall before him. The light from the runes cast the image of the sword upon the wall and the stone grated as the huge slab pulled back, revealing a vast chamber.

A lip of stone like a jetty ran out some twenty feet into a subterranean lake. The water was dark, casting reflections like glass and just as smooth. At its edge it glowed with a strange blue light, which was caught up by the rows of massive crystal growths which lined the cavernous, vaulted ceiling, and cast back the light of the lake, giving the whole cavern an ethereal quality like something from a barely remembered dream.

Ros felt she was in a cathedral, a holy place, hallowed and ancient. Sounds echoed off into the darkness, her first shocked gasp rebounded around the cavern even now. King Anthony placed the sword in the

126

empty scabbard at his hip with a whisper of steel, and the tone it had held since he pulled it from the stone stopped. He bowed his head as if in prayer then strode out along the jetty.

"Lady, I call to thee. Anthony, King of Camelot, descended of Arthur who was son of Uther Pendragon calls to thee!"

The words rolled around the cavern, and the crystals on the ceiling chimed as it passed them, making the cavern sing. The waters of the lake stirred and reached upward like a stalagmite, the blue light becoming white as the water formed a glowing figure that solidified into a woman, dressed in a white shift with skin like alabaster and hair like snow. She turned to them, standing upon the water, as if it were solid, and smiled. "Greetings to thee Anthony, descendant of Uther Pendragon. What need hast thou of the Lady of the Lake?"

The King bowed low at the waist, and as he spoke the lady approached and circled him. Where her feet touched the water, rings spread from her feet, and as she passed from water to stone, wet footprints marked her passage.

"An old enemy has reared its head, one you told us would return some day. The colours of Morgana le Fay fly once more and bring fire and death to Camelot."

The lady reached out and ran her delicate fingers through the King's golden hair. Ros couldn't help but notice a twinkle of mischief in her eye, betraying her demure smile as she did so. Geoffrey just stared in open mouthed amazement.

"You have the look of your namesake 'tis true. Fitting that it comes now. What would you have of me?"

The King took the lady's wandering hand gently in his own and looked her in the eye. "If your predictions hold true, then we need Merlin. These are the ones I choose to seek him…"

When the lady turned eyes on Ros for the first time, it felt like someone was looking through her, reading her like a book. Unlike everything else about the woman, her eyes were a piercing pale blue and reflected humour as well as wisdom. "What are you?" Ros breathed.

The lady looked to the King who nodded slightly.

"I am one of few who now call this world home, and have done so for a thousand years. Far from a fairy-tale, I am one who is tied to the element of life, water. I come from a culture far advanced of your own. In the early days of Camelot it was easier to explain my abilities as magic, but I gather now that you might grasp the term 'sub-molecular manipulation'. Why mortals must distinguish betwixt magic and science does escape me." To illustrate her point, the lady brought a thin strand of water up from

128

the lake and, before the astonished eyes of the watchers, the water coalesced into a perfect red rose.

"Alas, there are those who can threaten even me, so with Merlin's assistance, we helped Arthur build Camelot as a moral beacon and allied ourselves to it for mutual protection."

"Where are you from?" Geoffrey offered.

"That is difficult to explain, I am from here and at the same time not." She rolled her eyes and smiled even wider "The difficulties of a multi-dimensional existence."

"Where is Merlin?" the King asked softly.

"Merlin is where Morgana left him," the lady supplied "Entombed in stone upon an island she called Avalon. However, all is not lost, as I am bound to water Merlin is bound to stone. He is simply sleeping."

"So, Merlin is like you?" Ros ventured. The lady smiled.

"Not quite. Merlin was human a long time ago, before your Christ walked the Earth even, but he had promise, and I liked him, so I extended a gift to him that I might enjoy the experience of his company just a while longer."

She smiled again but sadly. "It has been a long time, even for me. Morgana took Merlin to a Crystal cave, an immense geode, which is not just a place of astounding beauty but a focus of natural energies, and the land she called Avalon, you call Greenland."

"Wait, wait!" Geoffrey held out his hands. "My liege, you mean to send us to Greenland in search of 'The' Merlin? The figure of legend we learned of as children and who, if he really existed, has been lost for a thousand years or more?"

The King turned stern eyes upon Geoffrey. "Yes," he said simply.

"What makes you think we'll find him?" Geoff pressed.

The King stared hard at him, then his eyes softened as he replied, "Faith."

Ros shook her head, the enormity of what she had just heard and witnessed staggered her. A million questions assailed her mind, and in the face of this revelation she had but one option; practicality.

"My liege, the stories say Merlin turned to stone when Morgana interred him in the cave. How are we meant to awaken him?"

The King gestured to the Lady and she smiled. "There are but two ways to rouse Merlin from his slumber. One would be to force Morgana herself to release him," she laughed at the shocked expressions Ros and Geoffrey couldn't begin to hide. "The other is far simpler. One touched by the Lady of the Lake might wake him." And with that she beckoned them both forward.

"If you will allow me, I will anoint you both to this purpose."

Rosalyn and Geoffrey took halting steps forward.

"Please, close your eyes and calm yourselves." The Lady's words were soft and soothing as she extended her hands to touch the knights' foreheads. Since she had her eyes closed, Rosalyn didn't see the brief look of surprise that quickly became an accusing glare the Lady levelled at the King as her hand touched Rosalyn's skin.

"It is done," said the Lady, her features once again serene but far from amused.

"If it please you, brave knights. I would speak with the King awhile, alone."

The emphasis on the last word left Ros and Geoff with little doubt that they had been dismissed.

Ros and Geoffrey left the King with the Lady and headed back up the stairway.

"I'm not sure I believe what I just saw." Geoffrey admitted. "Was it a validation of all Camelot stands for or...? I don't know."

Ros touched his arm "Not now Swift, we have a mission, remember?"

He stopped and turned to look at her. "We're at war, at war Ros. How can you be so calm?"

She avoided his gaze. "I don't know, I don't know if I can. These past few days I've had feelings, my emotions have affected me like never before and then..." she trailed off.

Geoffrey took in her pained expression and the way she hugged herself as she spoke.

"And then Phillip was killed. Oh God, Ros, I can't begin to imagine..." he took her in his arms and held her. Ros for her part was finally overcome by her grief and her breathing came ragged.

"I feel more, more than I ever have Geoff, and it hurts." Her words dissolved into shuddering sobs as he held her on the glittering stone stairway deep beneath Camelot.

In the darkness, Sebastian Crown heaved in a ragged breath and slowly raised his head. It felt as if he'd been fighting forever in this damp cavern who knew where under the world. He'd slain armed men, unarmed men, beasts and monstrosities by the dozen in this place.

He was caked in the filth of his victories. His hair hung lank and matted with blood, his shredded clothes were little more than rags hanging from his exo-frame. Dozens of wounds oozed his blood into the wretched, brutalized remains of his victims. Dimly he was aware of the cracks in his sanity, but that mattered little. His mistress demanded he fight and kill, so he fought, and he killed.

A small door opened and his next victims were shoved roughly into the charnel pit. The women looked so scared, so fragile. Sebastian licked his lips and stalked forward. He was going to enjoy this.

Chapter 11

Winds whipped over the deck of the ship. Geoffrey stared out over the wind-tossed seas, and recounted the preparations for the journey. First, he and Ros had been through what little tactical intelligence they had with Baron Dominic. The mission, to find and release Merlin from the Crystal cave and return him to Camelot. The way was dangerous, flight was never an option, (it was forbidden technology) so they sailed.

Some of their companions they'd chosen themselves, Royston, Belvarre and Loxley were on board. Geoff had gone to see the Ox himself in the infirmary. Seeing the man's face swollen with bruises under the stark, sterile infirmary lights, he'd almost regretted the decision to ask him along, but when the Ox's face split in a stiff but earnest grin, Geoffrey was heartened.

"The medics don't think you're up to operational strength, I'll understand if you say no," he'd offered.

"Don't talk daft Geoff, I've had loads worse than this. I'll be fine."

"I know you will John, I just..." Geoff struggled to finish but his friend stepped in for him.

"You don't want to see more of your friends hurt?"

Geoffrey nodded. Not for the first time, Loxley's affable demeanour belied his age and greater experience.

"Well tough, 'cause it's not your call, kid. I'm goin' with you and that's that. 'Sides, I'm more likely to get some use of this where you're goin' than I am laid up in bed." John bared his gunmetal teeth and raised his artificial arm. "The Master at Arms hisself built and attached it for me, whaddya think?"

Geoff was impressed. The new limb was a construct of creamy white poly-ceramic bones over-layered with bundles of steely ferro-fibre muscles, and banded with coppery neuro-receptor alloys. John flexed the supple looking fingers. "And with some luck we'll meet up with that bastard Crown again and I can shove this down his bloody throat!"

Geoff smirked as he recalled the conversation, some nights ago now. They'd ridden out two days after it, and been aboard ship since.

Some of their party had been assigned. Brandon Squires was a welcome addition. He'd spent much of his time on the ship ensuring that the gear was correctly and securely stowed and wasn't going to be affected by damp or cold. One of the few times Geoffrey had caught him above decks, he'd been trying to smoke a damp roll-up in the lea of a bulkhead and failing miserably. When he'd seen

Geoffrey watching him he'd gasped so hard he nearly swallowed it.

"My Lord, Sir Geoffrey!" he'd choked out, trying to stand to attention.

"At ease, soldier," Geoff had joked. "And I told you, it's Geoff."

"Yes Sir... Geoff." Geoffrey had stared out into the grey drizzle and Brandon seemed to relax after a time.

"Um, Geoff?" Brandon asked after more silence.

"Yes master Squires?" Geoffrey thought he heard a hint of a tremor in Brandon's voice.

"On this mission, is there going to be... I mean, will I..." he took a deep breath and blew in out. "Will there be fighting?"

Geoff turned square on to Brandon who just looked straight out to sea, "It's likely, Brandon."

"What do I do? I mean, I've never had any combat training or anything," the young tech asked.

"A student of all arms and master of none," Geoffrey supplied philosophically.

"Please sir, don't joke." Brandon looked as downcast as the weather.

"Worst comes to the worst, you can hide," Geoff had replied. Seeing Brandon's' affronted reaction he held up his hands. "Or I can show you how to use one of the SMGs we have below deck. But I warn you, a little knowledge is a dangerous thing, especially in combat."

Brandon looked thoughtful then set his jaw, "Thank you Sir, I'd like that."

That was only yesterday, Geoffrey realised, and already they'd gone through some basics. He'd probably bring Brandon on deck to let off some rounds over the dark water of the ocean this afternoon.

As well as Brandon were two odd additions. Neither particularly welcome, but for entirely different reasons.

In the bowels of the ship Cassie regarded her new 'Master'. After she'd been taken from Ros, she was ushered to the infirmary where a harassed looking nurse had cleaned and bound her hand, before being presented to the fussy looking young man she now stood before, Acolyte Nicholaeos Westbrook. He'd tried to be mysterious and threatening, but with his stuttering, uncertain manner it was almost comical. However, he was one of the cult of Merlin, and she had no idea of his abilities. The conversation they'd had (it couldn't be called an interrogation, not really) had been as stilted as he was, until they started discussing tech. How Cassie broke the castle security programmes, what measures she used to cover her tracks, how she communicated with her customers. As soon as they started, he became more animated, more certain of himself. He'd asked questions and she'd answered, and soon it was like they were old friends discussing techniques, then (she cursed herself for her stupidity) she'd called Eric. She'd forgotten herself in the moment and summoned her familiar in through a tower window and given up her one chance of escape.

Of course, Nicholaeos had been fascinated by the Raven and more questions flowed from him aimed to her and Eric both. They'd talked for hours, food had been brought and Cassie had started trying to think of ways she could use the Acolyte to get her out of Camelot, when he'd come out with a proposition that almost made her choke on her food.

"I want you to join the Cult of Merlin." Nicholaeos offered the dark-haired, dishevelled young girl.

"What?" she blurted through a mouthful of bread and cheese.

"I know, I know. Everyone thinks that we in the cult burn heretics, or do horrible experiments on them, and while we encourage the rumour, more often than not we induct them into the cult and make use of their expertise to further our knowledge. If we stifle creativity, we will simply stagnate and make no progress, yes?"

Cassie stared at him agog.

"Of course," he continued, leaning across the table "Some think they can accept and then flee. It never ends well for them... ever." To illustrate his point, he held his hands a small distance apart and a bright electric spark jumped suddenly from hand to hand, startling Cassie, and she had dropped her knife and fork with a clatter.

"But there's really no need for any of that Cassandra, just think. Access to our technology, our resources and freedom to use them for the good of everyone, what more could you want?"

"What's the catch?" Cassie said quietly.

"Not so much a catch," Nicholaeos admitted. "You start as my bondsman, my apprentice, until I am certain of your loyalty, then you work up through the ranks like everyone else." His voice was quiet when next he spoke, sad. "We have many spaces now to fill."

"What if I refuse?" Cassie ventured.

Nicholaeos looked her in the eye, still saddened but steady. "With the threat we face now, I will have no choice but to recommend to the King that you hang. I'm sorry."

Cassie was shocked, this seemingly mild-mannered man, slight and hesitant as he was with his fussy black goatee, would have her killed unless she joined the cult?

She thought for a moment. He seemed genuinely saddened by the prospect, perhaps he might let her loose or perhaps it was all a trick? All she could do at this point was buy time and see what there was to see.

"I'll do it. I'll join."

Nicholaeos smiled at that. "Good" he stood and came around the table "I would hate for such talent to go to waste."

"Is there some oath or ceremony?" Cassie asked.

"For initiates, yes," Nicholaeos nodded "But for bondsmen, there is this." He placed his hand over her bandaged hand, the same arm that still bore the heretic brand and Cassie felt heat. The bandage smouldered, became brittle and crumbled and the heat increased, Cassie gasped as a feeling like a thousand tiny needles piercing her skin shot through her arm, and then the Mage removed his hand from hers.

She held up her hand, the skin wasn't blistered or burned but whole. The bite which had marred her palm and knuckles was gone entirely and replaced by another mark, the mark of the Cult on the back of her hand. She looked to Nicholaeos questioningly.

"That is a nano-tat," he answered her unspoken question, and rolled up his own sleeve, showing her

141

his own mark mid forearm. "Thousands of tiny machines now exist in your system, they will allow you to use Cult tech and tell me where you are at all times. As you learn and advance, the mark will rise up your arm until it obliterates the Heretic brand and you are cleansed fully of that stain."

"Of course" he indicated his own mark, "that is some way off."

Cassie looked at the mark, then back at her 'master'. "What else can they do?" she asked eagerly.

Nicholaeos rubbed his hands together, "Let me show you."

Somewhere under the world, Sebastian Crown lurked in his pit. No food or water was presented to him, so he'd taken to feasting on his victims. The door opened and he crouched, ready to pounce.

"Be still." A cool voice came from the dark doorway, a rolling scots drawl that promised so much.

It was her, she was here! His limbs trembled with excitement as she paced around him, taking in the carnage of the pit. Her red hair fell in luxurious waves down to the small of her back and framed a face that engendered so many hungers in the corrupted warrior.

"My dear boy, my warrior," she spoke softly, her full red lips shaping the words like whispers of unimaginable pleasures yet to come. "The feeble trappings of Camelot have been shed I see, you have done well. Now you are a predator, now you are my wolf, and that is the nobility I shall teach you. The supremacy of the hunter. You'd like that, would you not?" she asked coyly, sensually tracing a finger across his hunched, greasy and blood caked shoulders.

"Hurrr, yesss mistresss," he slurred.

"Good!" she smiled, and her joy was almost childish. "Then let us begin by removing those atrocious 'implants' shall we?" she clapped delicate hands, and robed men entered with knives.

"Hold still, my child," she drawled stroking his chin, "and this will be over much quicker."

It was not long before the screaming started, and it was a long time before it faded to silence.

Most of the 'expeditionary force' was in the ship's mess when Nicholaeos entered nervously. It was quite clear to some that he been attempting to hurry, yet still seem unruffled as he came into the room. Shuffling up to Ros and Geoffrey's table, he sat anxiously and cleared his throat.

The young Knights were still somewhat wary of the acolyte, he kept apart and alone and at least tried (and sometimes comically failed) to cultivate an aura of mysterious power but, he still carried the authority

143

of the cult whose technologies could be wondrous or devastatingly destructive. For all that, the young man wasn't much older than them, and had been thrust into a role that was, like their own, far too big for him to properly fill.

After a moment's uncomfortable silence Ros spoke. "What can we do for you, Master Westbrook?"

The mage recoiled slightly at the address. "I, umm. I don't want to concern anyone but I think... something is following us."

Ros and Geoffrey traded a sceptical look and then glanced around the mess-room.

Nicholaeos frowned. "Not here, out there," he gestured toward a porthole.

"No offense, master Magus" Geoffrey held up a hand "but this Corvette is outfitted with state of the art warning systems. If something was out there we would know."

"Good Sir knight, if only it were simply the instruments we need rely upon." Nicholaeos pinched the bridge of his nose, "We don't know how much of our tech has been handed to our enemy, nor what agents they have yet amongst our number," he sighed deeply before continuing. "While we have been in transit, I have been meditating and monitoring radio frequencies,"

"At the same time?" ventured Ros.

"Well, since you ask... yes," replied Nicholaeos "But I have noted... inconsistencies. We are travelling under radio silence, but our encrypted beacon has been transmitting our location for Camelot Operations, or so we had been told."

"So we had been told?" Ros chimed in sceptically.

"Yes, the signal has been going out, but during my meditations I have detected something."

"What? What has brought such concern to you?" Ros pressed.

"I don't think it's getting out," Nicholaeos said bluntly. "I feel there is a barrier, some kind of cloak around this vessel which is bouncing the signal and someone closer is receiving it instead."

"Surely the ships comms officer would have realized," Geoffrey reasoned. "Someone would have informed us."

"But they haven't." Nicholaeos wrung his hands, his apprehensions clear. "I feel we are in grave danger."

Ros and Geoffrey watched the young man, he was clearly nervous but his resolve seemed genuine.

Ros stood up and walked to the ship's intercom. She opened the channel to the bridge and spoke swiftly, "Savant to bridge. Captain, take us to alert status and call all hands to combat stations."

The channel burbled but remained silent.

"Savant to bridge, do you acknowledge?" She waited a moment, silence.

"Answer me, dammit!" she thumped the box and the line stuttered for a moment before a response came back "We are ready for you, Knights of Camelot."

Ros stared at the intercom in surprise then jumped as the main bulkhead doors to the mess were slammed and secured.

"To arms!" she cried, as five black clad figures swept in from the kitchen with sub-machine guns at the ready.

Geoffrey responded instantly, diving over his table and bearing the acolyte to the floor as a burst of fire ripped over their heads. Royston saw another of the figures swing his gun toward the tech, Brandon, who sat there stunned into immobility. The squire scooped up his tin plate and whipped it across the room. It impacted in the assailant's throat and he dropped, gurgling, to the deck. There was a screaming of steel as Loxley tore up one of the steel tables that were bolted to the floor and turned it over for cover. He was joined by Belvarre Grayson, and the two of them hoisted the table and charged their attackers. Three of the remaining men were caught and, as their guns rattled off random bullets they were smashed into the mess' serving range by the two enhanced squires.

The last man out of the kitchen dived aside toward Ros who swung a short-arm clothesline which, when met with the man's own momentum, flipped him clean off his feet. Before he could recover she wrapped her arms around his head. In her mind she saw Sir Phillip, rent by the blade of a man he once called 'brother,' and felt nothing but cold as she pulled, hard.

The rattle of fire died and everyone looked around, stunned, until Ros took charge.

"Belvarre, Royston! Grab weapons and cover the kitchen door. John, police these men for weapons and ammo, secure anyone still breathing. Squires! Secure the mess door and make sure no-one comes in." She made a quick, visual assessment of each of them as she spoke. A few bullet grazes seemed to be the worst of their injuries. She went to Nicholaeos and offered him a hand up.

"That was... fast," he gasped.

"Combat is. Luckily we're trained for it," she reassured him.

He swallowed and grimaced at the prone men around them "What now?"

"Tactical evaluation," Ros let out a shuddering breath, "the ship's complement is eighty-five, they couldn't have that many agents aboard."

"Why not?" ventured Nicholaeos.

"Because they just couldn't!" Ros snapped. "I can't believe they could have infiltrated us so thoroughly." Nicholaeos said nothing, but nodded.

"Could they have teleported onto the ship?" Ros asked, a hint of desperation in her voice.

"No," the acolyte responded. "Even if they had our exact location there's no way they could account for the movement of the vessel. Their men are no good if they are fused with the walls."

"So," Ros thought hard. "The Bridge could be taken with three men, the engine room with five and five to secure us and lock down the crew. Then they rendezvous with another ship to take on crew, or to pick them up after they scuttle this one." She caught the mage's questioning look. "It's how I would do it," she said simply.

Nicholaeos scowled and closed his eyes, he seemed to listen to something far away for a moment then opened his eyes again. He seemed to stare through the wall as he spoke. "You're correct, they are meeting another vessel. We don't have much time."

The pair moved over to where Loxley was disarming the three men he'd near crushed with the table. Ros glanced at Nicholaeos. "What can you do for us in this situation, Master Westbrook?"

Nicholaeos was about to speak when one of the bound men pulled a knife from an ankle sheath. The mage raised his hand and blue-white sparks leapt into the blade and its wielder. The unfortunate man shuddered and writhed and the air started to smell of cooked meat. The sparks died when the blackened and burned man stopped moving. The mage turned sheepishly to Ros, looking fairly sick. "I have a few unpleasant surprises," he managed, before he rushed into the kitchen, and Ros heard him heaving into a sink.

"Wonderful," she mused wryly, then saw the Ox staring at her. "What?" she asked.

"Later," he shot back then tossed her one of their assailant's tac-vests. "Mags in the left, grenades and pistol rounds on the right," he reported tersely as Ros shrugged into the rig.

She took a pistol and shoved it in her belt-band, then picked up one of the SMG's from the table.

"You, me and Geoff are going to the bridge, Belvarre, Royston and the others are going to lock down the engine room and try to free the crew." she released the magazine from the compact weapon, checked the rounds and slapped it back into place before working the action with a decisive 'Ka-Chack!'.

"Any thoughts?"

"Just one," Loxley grinned, his easy nature reasserting itself. "I always had a thing for girls with guns."

Chapter 12

The sound of gunfire rattled through the ship, and Cassie found herself alone and under a bed once again. 'A girl could get sick of this,' she mused. Several black clad men had come rushing down the corridor a few minutes ago, so she'd ducked into the nearest room. Then the doors had shut and locked, but this time she wasn't in a Camelot dungeon, and she was determined to do something. Once she was sure that they weren't coming back anytime soon, she crawled out from under the bed. A brief search of the door revealed an access panel to the electrical motor, and a search of the bunk room provided a pocket knife. Cassie rushed the screws out and surveyed the wires. She quickly bypassed the switch and jacked the motor to a live wire. The lock released and the door swung open. Slowly, she crept out into the corridor. Shots had echoed from the direction of the mess so she shouldn't go that way, should she? She started to head away from the mess toward the engine room when footsteps sounded ahead of her. The corridor she was in had one of the steel bulkhead doors at immediately leading to one of the steep, naval ladders at the end. She started hurrying forward. If she could close and secure the door, anyone coming would have to go around.

When she saw a head wearing a black balaclava coming up the stairs she broke into a sprint. The head whipped up at the sound of her footsteps but couldn't raise a gun without letting go of the ladder rungs and falling off. The big man started hauling himself up the ladder. Cassie let out a strangled yell and threw herself at the bulkhead, both her and the door slamming into the man as he crested the ladder and went for his gun. There was a jarring impact, a meaty "Thunch!" and Cassie's would-be attacker tumbled back down the ladder. Cassie herself rebounded off the door and went sprawling to the deck. She scrambled to her feet and lunged for the door again, slamming it shut properly and spinning the wheel that secured it against water and anyone beyond who might want to hurt her.

Rubbing at her now throbbing shoulder, she turned back up the corridor, back toward the gunfire.

'Rather that than back under the bed' she thought grimly, and crept back down the hall. When she came to the corner, she stopped. She wasn't sure why, but she thought someone was coming toward her. Cassie cast around for a weapon and found a foot of steel pipe. She gripped it hard and pressed herself to the wall, waiting and listening. She heard the soft ring of careful feet on the steel floor, and held her breath so as not to gasp. She judged that whoever it was close, nearly upon her. She screwed up her eyes, took a firm grip on her improvised weapon, then she stepped around the corner, swinging.

A firm hand caught her wrists and twisted her clean around, and in an instant she was being held firmly enough that she couldn't draw breath to shout with her hands trapped above her head. She jerked her head to one side in a panic and found herself staring into the steely grey eyes of the white-haired squire, Belvarre.

"M'lady," he spoke softly, "I'm going to release you now. Do not scream."

His hands released her and she stepped away. Behind him were Royston, Brandon the tech and Nicholaeos. She went to him and, in sheer relief, threw her arms around him.

He stood there stiffly and, after a moment, gently cleared his throat and pushed her away.

"Cassandra, we're going to try and release the crew, but unless Lady Rosalyn and her team secure the bridge we can't over-ride the bunk room lockdown."

"Maybe we can," Cassie replied. "If we can get to your quarters, I can use Eric to get into the ship's systems."

Nicholaeos glanced ahead to Royston and Belvarre. They shared a look and then both nodded assent.

"Alright, let's go," he said.

Ros, Geoff and Loxley moved swiftly down the ship's corridors and up the stairs toward the bridge. They approached cautiously and lined up behind the bulkhead to the bridge. With a series of swift hand gestures, Ros outlined how they would proceed. She held up three fingers then dropped them one by one. Geoffrey pulled the pin on a concussion grenade, Loxley put his shoulder to the door and heaved it open, Geoff tossed in the grenade and there was a violent 'Bang' and a flash of light. Ros swept in, weapon held up, and took in the room.

Bullets had ripped up the bridge at shoulder height; blood spattered the cracked glass and instruments. Three figures in black were stumbling from their places at the helm, comms and sonar stations but, disoriented as they were, they still had guns.

Ros drew a bead on the target in front of her and the cold feeling descended as she fired a short burst from her weapon. The compact machine gun bucked and the rounds took the man high in his chest. John and Geoffrey followed suit, and more gunfire echoed around the bridge.

A quick sweep confirmed that they had cleared all the hostiles, and that the bodies of the bridge crew had been dragged and dumped to one side.

"What now?" Geoffrey asked, gun still held at the ready.

"We need to check for incoming," Ros swore quietly. "We should have brought Brandon. I don't know how to operate half of this equipment."

"Well," Loxley chimed in, "I'm not a sonar operator but there's someone out there, about a thousand yards and closing."

"How can you tell?" asked Geoffrey.

"I looked out the window. We gotta do something."

Ros turned to the window, and sure enough there was a vessel approaching; she could make out the shapes of smaller craft too, dinghies carrying assault troops. She focused on the larger craft, saw the serpentine figurehead and the colours flying high on the mast.

"Damn!" she spat, "The Norse have thrown in with Morgana, and we're in trouble. We need to get the crew free now!" she kinked her head to one side and engaged her internal frequency to Royston, "Status!" she barked. Gunfire stuttered over the link before Royston's voice (carrying a hint of nervousness) came back.

"Acolyte Westbrook and Cassandra went to override the lock-down with her cyber-familiar. Belvarre, Squires and I have hostiles pinned down in the engine-room but we could use a hand!"

"Hold them," Ros returned. "We have inbound hostiles. Someone needs to free our people!"

Just then, the klaxons blared and red lights started flashing around the room. Geoffrey turned to a computer console near him and barked out a startled laugh. "I think somebody just did!" he spun the screen and showed the overlaid image of crossbones under a skull; a raven's skull.

The ship burst into life, shouts and footsteps echoed all around. Ros snatched down the intercom from the captain's position and turned the dial to ship-wide announcement.

"Now hear this, all crew to stations! We have hostiles in the engine-room and inbound Norse raiders. Battle stations!" she hung the microphone back up and turned to Geoffrey.

"Go, help Royston and then get our gear. We need to be ready to repel boarders!"

Geoff nodded. "I'm gone," was all he said before he leapt out into the corridor.

Geoff hurtled down the corridors, he rebounded off walls and vaulted stunned crewmen. Ladders were ignored as he dropped straight down to the decks below and slipped through open doors. The engine room was cramped. Geoff swept past Brandon and hit cover behind Royston.

"What's the hold-up?" he barked, and sprayed a volley through the machinery at a dark shape.

"Oh y'know Swift, four hostile contacts with submachine guns and a lot of cover! Nothing special!" Royston barked back.

"Won't do, Royston, we have raiders inbound. We're going to have to wrap this up fast!"

"I'm out!" called Belvarre from across the narrow walkway.

"Magazine!" shouted Geoff and tossed one of his over, "right, you and Belvarre suppress them. I'll go down the middle and shake things up!"

"No, you won't," Belvarre called over. "I'll go."

"Not going to argue!" Geoff shot back, "Go!" he and Royston broke cover and laid overlapping bursts of fire down the corridor.

With an uncharacteristic snarl, Belvarre broke cover and dashed down the spanning corridor firing, he was arguably as fast as Geoffrey and closed the gap in an instant. Their opponents were staggered in cover. When Belvarre reached the first, he simply pointed his gun into the alcove and emptied the clip. The next startled combatant was hauled out to meet the sudden return fire of his colleagues. The body twitched as rounds thumped into it, and then the squire tossed it ahead like so much meat. Bullets ricocheted around him as he reached the next man, he planted a hand over the balaclava-clad face and pushed him violently back. With Belvarre's augmented strength and speed, the man was shoved back into the machine housing behind him with a sickening 'crack!'

Belvarre swept into cover and ripped a grenade from his vest before throwing it hard. It flew straight and smacked into the last enemy's face before detonating, the flash and thump of its concussion payload eliciting agonized screams from the man. Without hesitation, he rushed out from cover with a yell and piled into the thrashing man, hammering him against the deck plates. The man struggled weakly as Belvarre hauled him up and slammed him down again and again.

Geoffrey saw the shock on Royston's face as he approached Belvarre. What he was pounding into the floor couldn't even be easily described as a 'man' anymore.

"Bel, stop!" he shouted to no avail, "He's dead, Bel!" Geoff laid a hand on his comrade's shoulder.

Belvarre swept around with his fists held high, violence and death in his eyes... and stopped.

Geoffrey stared him straight in the eye, unflinching and spoke quietly, "We don't have time. More are coming."

Belvarre glared at him with a frightening intensity before visibly shaking the rage off.

Turning, Geoff called down the corridor. "Brandon, we need our gear. Show us where it is then get Ros and John's arms up to the bridge."

Ros watched the approaching vessel and addressed her comrades on her comms.

"They'll try to cripple us first. Royston, Brandon, assist the deck gunners as soon as you're ready. Then they'll try to board. Geoffrey, Belvarre, John and I will repel boarders. Norse raiders regularly use high concentration steroids and stims so put them down hard, any other observations?"

Nicholaeos' voice sounded reedy over the radio. "M'lady, the aggressors' Skald will likely try to breach the ship's systems with technomancy. Cassandra and myself will block their attempts and try to counter them."

The reply was muted by a thunderous report from the deck cannon. The ship shuddered with the recoil. A clattering outside the bridge marked the arrival of Brandon, laden down with arms cases. Without a word he commandeered the large map table and started releasing catches.

Ros and John discarded their TAC vests and weapons in favour of their own gear.

Ros' personal armour was a shirt of polarised chainmail (each ring magnetized to repel the next for maximum kinetic energy absorption) over a Kevlar jack. She strapped on her rapier and duelling dagger (both of which oscillated at a high rate when triggered, giving them the cutting power of chainsaws) then retrieved the submachine gun she had claimed in the mess hall.

Across from her, John had hauled a half-coat of carbon-fibre split armour onto his broad torso and was locating the magna-links of his prosthetic arms battle plates. His weapons of choice were a matching set of kinetic maul and shield. A field of energy produced by each weapon reduced and redirected incoming kinetic energy and maximised the transfer of inertial energy outward. When used in concert they could be devastating. He nodded to her as a sign of readiness and they headed out on deck.

The Raiders were coming closer now and the deck gun thundered again. Ros' audio filters cut in and muffled the sound to a bearable level. The small boats flanking the main vessel scattered, and a plume of water fountained from the roiling sea. Smaller guns on the Camelot vessel opened up alongside the crew's small-arms. Streams of automatic fire tore down, toward and into one of the Norse outriders. The half dozen assault troops in the boat jerked and spasmed as they were riddled with bullets, then the boat itself was engulfed with a dull 'Whumpf!" as a fireball consumed it.

Ros stared, startled for a second, then cast about for another of the small boats. Royston appeared beside her and she grabbed the young man's shoulder. "Look closely at that boat, what do you see?"

Royston's monocle was already over his eye and the servo's whined as it focused.

"The boats are packed with explosives, and the troops are wearing suicide vests," he reported flatly. "They probably intend to get below decks and destroy our engines or clear out the crew and offensive capabilities, then blow the hull with the boats."

"That is if they don't simply intend to ram us and detonate!" Ros spat an oath, "Dammit! We can't let them close, Royston."

"Understood" the younger man looked a little pale but his face was grim as he acknowledged her and headed for the bow. As he ran he drew one of the arrows from the quiver on his back and knocked it into his compound bow. The arrow flew out over the water and impacted a trooper on one of the closing boats, there was a dull 'Thump!' and a small explosion which soon became bigger as the exploding arrowhead triggered the soldiers bomb-vest and the rest of the dinghy's payload.

Hollering and whooping, Loxley had commandeered one of the .60cal machine guns which a crew-man had set on the side-rail, and was joyously sending streams of burning phosphor tracers at the incoming boats.

The deck gun finally found its range, and a plume of fire erupted from the Raiders' main vessel. Screams and black smoke drifted out over the water, but the hulking, mismatched and rusted warship ploughed on through the waves, straight for them.

Ros ducked back through the bridge door. "Status!" she barked.

"They're not turning, ma'am," the helmsman and acting Ex-O reported. "If we keep this heading they'll ram us amidships and cut us in half, if we turn we'll lose speed and they'll draw up alongside."

The rattle of gunfire and boom of the deck-gun sounded from outside, along with the whoosh of spray and occasional screams.

"Turn," Ros stated, "We'll deal with them."

"Yes ma'am," the sailor said crisply and span the ship's wheel.

Ros looked back outside, she could see individual figures on the Raider now, whooping and jeering, waving guns and axes.

The ship finished its turn and there was a sensation of acceleration as the engines returned to full power. They hadn't been caught on the turn, and now they were pulling away from their pursuers. Ros started to smile when suddenly there was a thumping explosion and a rain of sea-water from the rear of the ship. A curtain of water fell, then black smoke came billowing from aft. Ros dashed toward the smoke as a klaxon started shrieking. Belvarre appeared beside her, his white hair and pale skin stark against the dull grey of the ship and the dark smoke.

"What happened?" she shouted.

"One of the outriders caught us, I don't have a damage report but it seems the engine is disabled at least. If we're not taking water it'll be the most luck we'll have today." There was a gleam in his eye as he watched the Norse hulk gaining on them.

"'Bout time we dealt with these bastards," he growled.

"Well it looks like we're going to have to now," Ros shot back.

A cheer went up from the Norse warriors as one of the men on their prow pulled a tarpaulin off a massive harpoon cannon. Ros dragged Belvarre back through a bulkhead as the cannon roared, and the massive, barbed projectile howled past them and ripped through the decking. The snaking cable that trailed after it snapped tight, and their vessel came to a full stop with a shudder and a shriek of torn metal.

The Camelot crew swarmed to the deck armed with a mix of SMGs, assault rifles and shotguns. The squires were interspersed amongst them, shining metal amongst black Kevlar and grey naval fatigues.

Chapter 13

The hulk roared past, belching smoke and casting its shadow over the sleeker Camelot ship. Ros had plenty of time to consider it. Clearly it had once been a small passenger liner, but its front hull was covered in rusting sheet metal welded on as an extra layer of armour and daubed with crude symbols. The white sides were stained with filth, blood and soot, while the smoke from the stacks was much darker than it should have been.

All the training, all the drills and exercises Phillip had taught her ran through her mind. Phillip; the very thought of him caused her heart to cramp with emotion and she froze for a moment before a wash of adrenaline and combat conditioning shunted those thoughts away and locked them up tightly for later.

She leaned out from the door and sent a chattering spray from her machine gun into the warriors crowding the rail. The Camelot crew took this as their cue, and sent a withering hail of fire into the raiders. The raiders, in return, cast grappling hooks in amongst the sailors of Camelot, trying to hook either the men or the rails. Several of the hooks found marks among the Camelot sailors, and their screams were piercing as they were hauled from their feet. The lines hauled the ships closer, and frothing Norsemen hurled themselves from the rails of the hulk toward the Camelot vessel. The first few fell screaming into the sea. One warrior's piercing shriek was cut short as the hulls clanged together. Roaring warriors poured off the hulk's deck into the massed fire of the Camelot sailors. Ros watched as Loxley caught a falling warrior with his bionic arm, then slammed the berserker onto the ship's rail, snapping his spine before dropping him over the side.

Ros herself emptied her magazine, reloaded, and resumed firing with Belvarre beside her. The Raiders kept coming and, by sheer volume, drove a wedge onto the smaller vessel. Gunfire started from above, not the automatic fire of machine guns but the stuttering fire of a group of bolt action rifles. Nevertheless, the Camelot crew were forced to seek cover, and yet more of the Norse warriors leapt onto the deck. Ros saw lines being dropped for more warriors to shin down as she rattled her last clip into the mass. Now that the lines were in place, more heavily armoured warriors were boarding, and the little 9mm rounds rattled off Kevlar-backed plates and shields. The Norsemen bellowed in challenge and charged, furs and chainmail interspersed with Kevlar, long-knives, axes and swords alongside heavy revolvers, 9mm automatics and SMGs. The Camelot sailors went to cover, and tried to lay down an ordered pattern of fire, but the Norsemen paid little heed to tactics or discipline and simply charged, firing wildly and bellowing. Suddenly the exchanges of gunfire were interspersed with frantic melee combat, and discipline dissolved.

Ros thrust her sword into the first warrior to rush the bulkhead, and slashed her dagger across his throat while he was still surprised, then kicked him back into his fellows. Beside her, Belvarre swept upward with his shock-sword, and the electric discharge it generated threw the unfortunate Norseman backward even as the blade carved and blackened his flesh. Ros saw the feral joy on Bel's face and knew that if she didn't stick close he'd probably get himself killed; and if she did, he might get entirely caught up in the thrill of combat and accidentally kill her.

"Dammit!" she hissed under her breath and pressed up behind him as he advanced.

Below decks, a strange ritual was taking place. Cassie could barely believe it, but it was happening all the same. She'd always treated tech like a tool, and regarded the disciples of Merlin as more scientists than anything else, but here, now, she was seeing Nicholaeos practice his religion. Synapses and circuits married into something greater, something magical. Her new 'Master' had

167

connected to Eric the Raven by leads which he had plugged directly into the base of his skull. As he closed his eyes in meditation, she could feel the building charge hanging heavy in the air, and her hair stood on end. Static discharges leapt from Nicholaeos into the tables and deck plates. Together he and Eric had joined with the ship's computers, and the combined processing power had staggered Cassie. She herself was typing frantically at Eric's feather keyboard to counter cyber-attacks on the ship's systems, and listening for prompts from Nicholaeos of weaknesses through which to counter-attack the Skald and his followers.

Cassie struck at the keys even as she flinched at another shudder from the ship around her. Nicholaeos sat across from her, quietly chanting in between occasional terse commands. His eyes darted around the room, viewing things only he could see; systems codes, surveillance feeds and comms channels, and as he identified a threat his hands would sweep around in front of him, illustrating his mental actions with physical movements.

Sweat beaded his brow and his brow furrowed in frustration.

"It's no good," he spat, "They are too numerous. Instigate transmitter firewall and lock-out all ships systems."

Cassie's eyes never left the holo-screen as she responded desperately. "But we won't be able to access anything, we won't be able to drive or steer!"

"We cannot do those things in any case," Nicholaeos thundered "Do it now!"

Cassie's fingers flew over the keys, barring all access to the ship's computers, engines and weapons. Once she was done, she breathed deeply. "What do we do now?"

The air stilled around her master. Static dispersing, he schooled his features to a calm mask.

"Now we find Dame Savant. We need to get to the Skald and kill him."

"We?" Cassandra gulped, apprehensively.

Geoffrey bit back a curse and swept his shield up in front of him, as the brutish Norse raider smashed a massive two-handed hammer down in an overhead arc. Geoffrey braced, and grinned a feral grin at what was about to happen. Little did the barbarian know that Geoffrey's shield had a kinetic repulsor engine inside, and as the hammer met its face, it was deflected with such force the head swept straight back, snapping the thumbs of its wielder and smashing the head back up into his face; it was messy. As the Norseman staggered back, dead but too belligerent to accept it, Geoffrey swept the flat of the shield into him, and the repulsor engine kicked his sagging body over the side. Geoffrey whipped his pistol round and snapped off shots into the Norsemen as Loxley came up beside him. The .60 was empty, and John now swung it like a club, unable to find pause to draw his own, technically-superior weaponry. A volley of fire from the crewmen behind him pressed the Norse back momentarily. When the hatch besides them swung open, Geoffrey immediately raised his weapon to it.

When he saw Acolyte Westbrook, he immediately turned the pistol back toward the Norse. If Nicholaeos even saw the danger he gave no sign.

"We must find Dame Savant," the mage offered quickly.

"Chances are she's a mite busy, Nick!" Geoffrey ducked behind his shield as a spray of bullets tore through the air at him, then rattled away harmlessly throwing up some sparks.

"All the same," Nicholaeos continued, "we must find the Skald and stop him and his followers attacking the ship's systems. Even if we repel the attack, he could gut the ship's OS from inside and strand us!"

"Chances are the War-leader is with the Skald, Geoff," Loxley chimed in. "If we wanna finish this without hacking our way through every bloody Norseman on the ship, we gotta take him out." The butt of the .60 clanged off a helmeted head and John punched it forward into the snarling face underneath.

"We'll have to hack our way through every Norseman on the ship just to reach him!" Geoffrey shot back with a smile. "*Ce la vie*; I guess we have to find Ros in any case."

He hunkered down and touched the call button on his comms.

"Royston, where are you? Do you have eyes on Ros? Over."

"Do I ever," came the reply "I'm halfway up the sensor array and have a pretty good view. Ros and Bel are just forward of your position, behind that pack of hostiles. You've got them between you, but more are coming off the hulk behind them, they're gonna be trapped and hard pressed in about twenty seconds. Over."

"Received and understood, meet at their position in fifteen. Over and out."

Geoffrey shot a serious look at Loxley, "Ready to stop playing with these swine?"

"Just say the word, Geoff," John replied.

"Well drop that pig-iron and get some muscle behind this." Geoffrey hefted his shield to illustrate his point.

"You know that'll burn out the power unit," John offered.

"Such is life," replied Geoff, unstrapping his shield and tossing it to his comrade. John dropped the

171

machine-gun that had been his makeshift club and caught the shield.

"On three. Stay close" he called over his shoulder.

"One!" called Geoff, pistol-whipping an opponent and dragging his longsword from its sheath.

"Two!" bellowed John, deflecting an incoming strike with his bionic arm and then hammering his hand down on the Norseman's shoulder with an audible cracking of bone.

"Three!" They yelled together and, with a furious battle-cry, Loxley put all his mass behind the repulsor shield and charged forward.

Full grown men were scattered like bowling pins before a cannonball, battle cries became shouts of confusion and alarm as men were smashed against bulkheads, steel railings, or just plain thrown overboard. The shield itself began to smoke and spark as its purpose was thoroughly abused.

Geoffrey followed in Loxley's bull-rush like a whirlwind, his sword struck out at the veins and arteries of staggered opponents, his feet landing savage kicks that smashed ribs and cracked sternums.

In the wake of the violence, Nicholaeos and Cassie followed, flanked by honest Camelot sailors, looking for all the world like a diplomat and his assistant simply strolling along the avenue with their bodyguards.

As John neared the reported position he slowed, and laid about with the rapidly failing shield. Geoffrey was beside him now, his blade flickering into spaces and gaps. With a final, scraping whine, the repulsor engine failed, its power cells discharging the last of their energy through the shield's own grips and up Loxley's un-enhanced arm. He flinched and dropped the ruined item, reaching desperately for his own weapon at his belt. A Norseman surged forward, longsword intent on the big squire's throat. Geoffrey blocked a strike at his own flank and knew, even with his superior speed, that he couldn't save his friends life.

With a whistle from above, an arrow pierced the barbarian perfectly through both wrists. The force carried the swing of the sword short of its intended target, and with arms fixed together, the blade cut deep into the attacker's own leg. Blood sprayed, and Royston dropped down behind his shot. He might not have been as fast as Geoffrey Mayland or as strong as John Loxley, but his augmentations allowed him to read the combat like a book. Wherever there was a blade aimed at him, Royston wasn't there anymore, and the sinews of his arms (which allowed him to pull the tremendous draw of his combat bow) could, combined with his targeting abilities, deliver pinpoint strikes to crush a larynx or disable a knee, shoulder or elbow.

The remaining barbarians lost their nerve and turned to flee, only to find more swords behind them. Belvarre's anger had passed through berserk fury and was now a deep, cold rage. His strikes were clean and measured, but without mercy or pity, as he maimed and killed his foes. Ros covered his rear, fighting desperately against a new flood of Norse warriors.

Though they'd only been fighting for minutes, even the enhanced stamina of a Squire couldn't carry on forever. Ros breathed heavily and sweat ran down her brow. She was relieved when other bodies pressed in beside her and forced the berserkers back. She was more relieved when a hand on her shoulder drew her back from the front. Bullets started whipping past into the massed ranks, and the Squires drew back for a moment's reprieve.

Ros found herself hunkered down with Geoffrey, Nicholaeos and Cassie. The girl was white-faced but seemed determined, a pistol held awkwardly in her small hands. Nicholaeos seemed tense and grim while Geoffrey, though breathing heavily, grinned fiercely.

"We have to board them," Geoffrey said simply. "If we can take out the War-leader we can rout them, but Nick says we have to take out the Skald, and I think it would be a good idea to sink that floating obscenity they're riding too."

"Oh," Ros nodded, "nothing too hard then?"

"Just another day in the life." Geoff winked.

"And how do you suggest we go about it?"

"Don't look at me." Geoff said shaking his head. "I'm just the ideas man, plans are your department."

Ros couldn't help but smile at Geoffrey's good humour. She looked up at the overbearing hulk and scowled.

"If we can take out the commanders and hit the bridge, we can get that ship to pull away from us, then we can use the main guns to hole her and send her down."

"I can signal track the Skald, I shouldn't imagine he or the War-leader will be far from the bridge," Nicholaeos offered.

"So all we have to do is fight our way up the boarding ropes, clear the deck, get to the bridge and kill two powerful Norse pirates on the way," Geoffrey sighed sardonically. "Sounds good, let's go!"

Ros spotted Royston sending arrows into the Norse from his covered position, and she tapped her ear bead to signal him.

"Royston, get as many grenades as you can from the crew nearest you. Get them on the deck of that wreck near the boarding ropes and clear us some space, over."

"Acknowledged. Thirty seconds," came the reply.

"John, Belvarre?" Ros comm'd, "We go for the ropes in twenty."

"Understood," the Squires responded.

Ros settled down to catch her breath for the longest twenty seconds of her life.

Chapter 14

A volley of automatic fire cleared the deck for them, and the warriors of Camelot broke from cover and dashed for the ropes, which had so recently allowed their enemies' access to the ship.

Several small, dark shapes sailed overhead, and clattered as they hit the deck of the hulk above.

'Five, four, three,' Geoffrey counted in his head as he jogged toward the ropes. He allowed John to get in place first, the big Squire hunkering down with his bionic hand flat and outstretched.

'Two, one!' Putting on a sudden burst of speed, Swift stepped on the offered hand and gathered himself for a tremendous leap upwards. The grenades Royston had thrown detonated in a chain of concussive noise, fire and shrapnel, as Geoffrey himself exploded upward through the smoke and flame.

He landed lightly on the deck and swept his gaze around looking for threats. Ros, Belvarre and Royston surged up the ropes and soon gained the deck behind him.

"Catch!" came a bellow from below, and Geoff glanced back over the rail to see Loxley, partway up the rope himself, reach down and grab the girl,

Cassandra, by the material of her jacket and heave her upward. The raven that seemed to accompany her everywhere croaked in protest and took off from her shoulder. Cassie screamed, and Geoff reached down and grabbed her lapels as she crested the rail, depositing her safely on the steel plates next to him. Loxley reached back for Nicholaeos, but the mage, who had shown little aptitude for such physical pursuits, suddenly became a blur. Despite his robes, he scaled the side of the ship like a lizard on a wall, disdaining the ropes entirely. Geoffrey stared in shock as Nicholaeos regained his feet and settled his clothing.

The mage caught his astonished look and shrugged, somewhat sheepishly, holding up his bare hands. "Electromagnetic implants, usually for holding delicate pieces but they have... other uses," he ventured.

"Any more surprises?" Geoff asked.

"One or two," came the reply.

The mage concentrated briefly as John hauled himself over the side, then pointed.

"There," he said quietly. "Two levels up, roughly central."

The Norse warriors who hadn't been killed or heavily injured by the grenades were coming back to themselves. Filthy hands grasped brutal weapons as they started swaying, unsteadily to their feet.

"Minimal contact!" barked Ros, "Conserve ammo and go, go, go!"

The Camelot strike team raced for the nearest hatchway, taking out any Norsemen who had recovered too swiftly, but maintaining momentum. Ros and Geoff ran point, leap-frogging each other as they engaged targets. John and Belvarre guarded the flanks, with Royston running behind Nicholaeos and Cassie, keeping them at pace with the others.

They moved into dark corridors, fluorescent lighting patchy and unmaintained. The windows which should have let in natural light had been sprayed black with paint and other, less tasteful fluids.

The squires were blackened from soot and cordite and splashed with blood and gore. Those Norse who did see them had to look twice to see that they didn't belong; but a second look was more than Ros and her fellows allowed them.

They swept quietly up the stairwells to the level Nicholaeos had identified, and Ros peered through the doorway.

The space beyond had once been a leisure promenade for passengers. It was wide and open with the remains of shopfronts and restaurants in evidence. The floors had been cleared of seats and tables, and the surfaces daubed with ritual symbols, runes and sigils. Ros didn't want to guess what they had been painted with. At the centre of the space stood an altar of sorts. It looked like parts of the ship's various instruments, radio, radar and others, had been conjoined by a maniac and adorned with animal bones and more sigils and various rich trinkets of gold and jewels. Before the altar stood the Skald, draped in animal furs and circuit-boards, wires running over and into her. Deer antlers crowned her head along with a radio aerial, and black war paint wound its symbols over every inch of exposed skin on her face, arms and breasts. Around her, crudely wired together, huddled a gaggle of men and women. Some wore the garments of the Norse raiders while others wore chains and manacles.

"Slaves," hissed Ros.

"Not slaves, servitors." Nicholaeos voice came calmly, "Their minds are consumed to increase the Skald's processing abilities. You cannot save them," he added sadly.

Ros looked again, and true enough, the servitors knelt, staring blankly upward. Foam came from their mouths and filth coated their emaciated bodies.

"Those others are cultists," Nicholaeos pressed on. "They might have some ability to disrupt your arms and armour. I will try to lock them down to mere physical means, but the faster you dispatch them, the quicker I can deal with the Skald."

"You're going to..?" Ros returned sceptically.

"It's my duty," he replied, soberly. "I'll distract them."

Before Ros could stop him, Nicholaeos swept past her and marched, with more confidence than he felt, into the cult's ritual circle. He closed quickly on a servitor and placed his hands on the frail man before he spoke.

"In the name of Merlin, desist!" he thundered and released electricity from his hands. There was a scream of feedback and the whole circuit reacted. Servitors went into convulsions while cultists jerked and scrabbled at their connections.

In her mind, Cassie heard Nicholaeos' voice say "Broadcast white noise now!"

The squires had seen Mages accompanied by tech-familiars, and were familiar with C.T.E.E.D.s, but it was still a surprise to see the raven emitting its holo-screen and keyboard.

"Royston, covering fire and look out for Cassandra," Ros ordered before marching into the ceremony chamber.

The Skald barely flinched at the electrical interruption; she gripped an ornate staff which sparked as it earthed the discharge. Ripping out her own connection to the ritual, she growled something harshly at Nicholaeos and then shouted orders to her writhing followers.

There was little time before re-enforcements came, so Ros intended to make full use of the opportunity. The Skald had maybe twenty followers interspersed among the servitors, but they were recovering quickly and bringing arms to bear.

Geoffrey had never seen such a strange sight, but he was familiar with the principles and necessities of an ambush, so when one of the swiftly recovered cultists made a run for a doorway he rushed to intercept. He went into a slide and scissor-kicked the filthy wretch's legs from under him. The momentum dropped the cultist onto Geoff and they slid across the floor, each struggling for an advantage.

Ros and Bel rushed to flank Nicholaeos. Belvarre swept his sword around and cut the cultist before him; it didn't discharge its lethal voltage.

"My sword!" he bellowed angrily.

"I know!" Nicholaeos hissed through gritted teeth.

Ros felt a strange buzzing at the edge of her hearing, and sudden realisation of the true danger they were in dawned.

"He's trying to keep the Skald out of our neuro-links!" Ros shouted. "If that feral bitch gets to us we'll become just like the servitors!"

"Get me closer," Nicholaeos hissed, "Just one chance..."

"Just shoot her!" Bel sneered drawing his pistol and snapping off three quick shots.

As the gun barked one of the 'dead' servitors jumped to its feet and intercepted the rounds. It jerked with the impacts and dropped, lifeless once more.

A wicked grin crossed the Skald's face and the buzzing in Ros's head ceased.

"This is bad!" she shouted, blocking an incoming blade. Her forward momentum was halted as a hand grabbed her ankle, another of the 'dead' servitors held her in a grip like iron.

Geoffrey grappled with the wiry man on top of him. The cultist wasn't skilled, but he was greasy, frantic and possessed of a deranged strength, and Geoff hadn't thought to pull a short blade. The man got both hands around Geoffrey's wrist, the hand holding his sword, and ripped at it, slamming the hand down on the floor. Geoffrey tightened his grip and swung at the fanatic's head with the butt of his pistol. The strike glanced off his opponent's shoulders to little effect. The man changed tack and raked at Geoff's eyes. The knight released his sword and grabbed for the matted hair of the man's head and bit savagely at the offending fingers trying to blind him. Blood filled his mouth as the hand was ripped away with a startled scream. Geoff kicked his powerful legs up and the pair rolled with the knight now on top. From this position Geoffrey could use the grip of the pistol to better effect, and he pounded on the dirty face until the cultist lay still. As he reached for his sword, a weight hit his back, and something solid smacked him hard enough in the head to blur his vision. As images of being bludgeoned to death raced through his mind, the weight was suddenly gone and, rolling over, he saw Loxley lift his new attacker high and throw the shrieking cultist bodily away. Loxley offered Geoff his meaty paw and, scooping up his sword, Geoffrey was hauled to his feet.

A high, cackling laugh filled the chamber along with the crack and snap of electrical discharges. Energy crawled over the filthy technomancer, arching from her crude implants and running over her body. Where the sparks and static ran the Skald traced her fingers over her skin, her laughter interspersed with sighs and shudders. Around her the slack-jawed servitors twitched to their feet and turned toward the interloping squires, dead eyes filling with rage and foam coming to dry, cracked lips. The withered and emaciated slaves surged forward in a frenzied wave, unconcerned with pain or death, intent only on serving the Skald and rending flesh with their bare hands.

"Oh balls," sighed Geoffrey.

The fighting became close, frenzied and dirty, as the servitors threw themselves forward, heedless to blades and bullets. Geoffrey span and ducked, thrust and cut his way through the crowd but, even with his superior reactions the press of bodies soon began to tell. Hammer-blows from fists that no-longer felt pain started to land on his back. Servitors hung from Loxley's arms and legs, worrying at his armour with their teeth and dragging him down by their sheer weight. Rosalyn and Bel kept Nicholaeos between them, blades whirling and guns barking, pressing closer to the witch. From the doorway came the rapid report of an assault rifle. Bullets pounded the servitors, smashing joints and pulping heads as Royston took advantage of any target that presented itself.

Ros, working hard to advance, cast a glance toward Geoffrey and Loxley over the heads of the throng, only to see Loxley disappear under a press of bodies, and Geoffrey slip on the bloody floor as three of the crazed servitors descended upon him. Spitting curses she kicked out at the servitor in front of her and snapped over her shoulder, "Are we close enough?"

"We'll have to be!" Nicholaeos responded, "Step aside!"

Ros ducked aside as the Mage thrust his arms forward.

"Dodge this!" he smirked to himself, as twin blasts of fire jetted from his palms and lapped over the servitors and Skald alike. The servitors were eerily silent as they burned, but the witch shrieked and convulsed under the flame. As she burned, her control over her meat puppets lapsed, and they dropped to the floor like marionettes whose strings had been suddenly cut. Ros stared at the mage acolyte aghast, new respect for his abilities dawning upon her. The slight, prim looking young man looked back with a slight smile (and fast deepening shadows under his eyes). "Napalm jets. I can only do it once and it takes a lot out of me."

Ros nodded slowly, still shocked as the shrieks of the Skald died away to the sound of crackling flames and spitting fat.

"We haven't got much time," Bel chimed in, "someone must have heard that."

"Someone did," said Geoffrey, pointing down the hall. A large figure in furs and a horned helm approached them, flanked by a dozen armed guards. They strode confidently toward the squires with weapons held steady and level.

"How do we play this?" Royston had brought Cassie up and stood beside his comrades.

The squires slowly fanned out into a line. "Looks like a stand-off," Geoff offered quietly.

"Until they get back-up, and even if we're lucky, we won't all make it out of this," Ros said levelly.

The Norse chieftain and his bodyguard swept around the biggest pile of bodies and lined up facing the Squires. The chieftain grinned a crook-toothed grin full of malice, patiently savouring the moments before the inevitable violence. The only sounds were the distant chatter of gunfire and the rumble of the engines.

"I wouldn't worry about us," Geoff smirked, carefully not looking at the silently shifting pile of corpses.

Bloodied, bruised and rising like a wrathful mountain, John Loxley emerged from the pulped bodies. His huge hands reached out and, even as the movement registered in the peripheral vision of the nearest guards, he seized the chieftain's horns and twisted savagely. The 'grunch' of torn tendons and ripped cartilage was loud enough to catch the attention of everyone. The big Norse war-leader toppled forward without a sound of protest, clattering to the floor. No-one moved for what seemed like an age, then the Raiders' weapons sank, and they began a keening wail, before discarding their arms completely and running from the scene.

Geoffrey holstered his pistol and smirked at John, "Well thank God you didn't make that look too easy or anything."

Loxley rolled his eyes and chuckled.

Ros scanned around to make sure no threats remained. As her eyes ran over the group, she quickly assessed them for wounds. The squires reloaded and watched the entrances, Nicholaeos was studying the 'altar' and its symbols. When she came to Cassie she stopped; the girl was white as a sheet, trembling and near panic as her gaze wandered between the dead chieftain and John.

Moving beside her, Ros touched the young hacker's arm.

"What's wrong?" she asked gently.

Cassie jumped slightly at the soft sound and, swallowing hard, she spoke softly.

"It's just that, I know that we have to fight and I'm okay with the shooting and the swords I suppose but that... that was so cold, so callous and brutal and John's usually just this big, funny guy, I just..." she tailed off.

Ros thought for a moment, back to the galley and the man who she'd killed. She could have disarmed him, could have spared him and interrogated him; but right then she'd just wanted to hurt him like she'd been hurt by Phillip's death, and to kill him. She recalled how John had looked at her for just that instant after she'd broken the man's neck.

"We do what we must," she said quietly. "Now come on, there's more to do."

Ros went over to where Nicholaeos was studying the 'altar'. The acolyte had cleared many of the bones, skulls and trinkets from the heap of mismatched instruments. He 'tutted' to himself critically as he viewed the violated machinery.

"Don't know how they even keep it working, heathen savages..." he was saying as Ros approached.

"Shall we make for the bridge?" she asked.

"We might not need to." The Mage held up a hand to indicate the altar. "All the basic ship's systems are here, if Cassie can reroute a few wires and identify the correct systems in this mish-mash, we can re task the hulk's engines and pull it away from our ship."

"Can't you do that remotely?" Ros ventured.

"No," Nicholaeos looked disdainfully at the heap, "I would have to connect via hard-line to this system and, as much as it might save a little time, I feel I need a tetanus shot just looking at this contraption, let alone plugging myself into it," he finished ruefully.

Chapter 15

Ros watched the listing and smoking hulk as it disappeared into the distance. The sea was smooth, and the Corvette was making good pace away from the battle despite the damage to one of its propeller shafts. The losses to the ship's complement were regrettable, but not overly telling to the crew's performance. She looked down at her hands, studying them intently, but they didn't look any different for the blood and soot that caked them. They didn't suddenly look like the hands of a cold-hearted killer; but she knew what they'd done. What she'd done.

Heavy footsteps behind her signalled the approach of John Loxley. The squire was taking a long pull on a bottle of rum as he edged up next to her at the railing and offered her the bottle.

"Wanted to talk to you, Ros." He stifled a belch with his hand as she took a swig of the rum.

"Is this going to be a talk about revenge and how it won't bring Phillip back and won't stop the pain, filled with tired clichés and heart-warming assurances of how I won't be alone?"

John looked at her for a moment before leaning back on the railing.

"Bugger that," sniffed the squire "kill as many of the bastards as you can, and good luck to you."

Now it was Ros's turn to stare at John.

"But you watch yourself; I seen that cold look. I seen what happens when you make that decision one time too many."

"I made that decision many times today." Ros interjected.

"That was different. That was combat," John replied. "Listen; I've been around, and I've seen some things I'd rather I hadn't, and I've done some things I ain't proud of."

He looked out into the distance and heaved a big sigh.

"In the thick of it, killin' is one thing. You gotta look out for yourself and your mates and when that red mist descends 'cause you're angry or someone's done you wrong, then that's different too. That's hot killin,' and for whatever reason, that heat protects you inside. I'm not sayin' it doesn't stay with you, just puts a bit of distance on it, if you get what I mean?"

Ros nodded slowly.

"But cold killin' is another matter; cold killin' when your hands are around the other fella's throat and he's stopped beating back at you and there's that moment where you can let it go, let it be and know you'll both see the sunrise tomorrow, or you can squeeze just that little bit longer and feel the life go out of him. That's the moment when it gets to you, no fire to protect you, and when that light fades from his eyes it takes a piece of your soul with it. After a time there's so little soul left to go that you don't care anyways, and one day it don't matter whose throat you got your hands around."

Ros had a moment to regard the big, genial man in a new light. His scarred face looked somehow darker now, and his shoulders bore a weight that had nothing to do with the day's exertions.

"I haven't been able to tell anyone, but I've been feeling strange even since before Phillip..." she let the name hang for a moment.

"I never really 'felt', not that I remember," she began. "I was always so concerned with training and learning, I didn't have the time or the inclination to make friends, it didn't seem important. Then, back at the beginning of the tournament, it started to become important that I did. Something changed inside me, something changed the way I think. And then when Phillip was killed, I didn't know how to cope, or how I would have coped without Geoffrey or the rest of you."

Tears welled in her eyes and she made no effort to hold them back.

A large hand laid on her shoulder and shook her gently. "Seems to me like you done just as well as any of us could've under the circumstances, but your mind changin'? That might warrant a little investigating for sure."

Ros took a deeper pull of the strong spirit, wincing at its harshness before handing it back.

"In the meantime, I'd appreciate it if you didn't tell the others that I'm losing my mind." She smiled, weakly.

"I wasn't here, this didn't happen, and I certainly didn't hear you sniffin' an' bawlin' in such an unladylike manner." John winked.

Ros punched him in the arm, not too lightly. "You certainly didn't, you great oaf." And her smile took on a glimmer of its former radiance.

The coastline of Avalon loomed majestically out of the morning mist, and the whole group gathered on the foredeck to greet it. Snowy cliffs reflected the light of the sun, and the water was a deep, lustrous green beneath the ship.

"So what's waiting for us?" Royston voiced the question on all their minds.

"Didn't you read the holiday brochure, sorry, the mission brief?" Geoff shot back with his customary grin.

"Oh aye, topography, climate, survival briefing, all very useful. But, what's out there?"

"Squire Glasbury," Nicholaeos interrupted in one of his rare addresses to the group as a whole. "If you are expecting trolls and dragons, then let me assure you there are none, despite what folklore might suggest. The indigenous people, the Inuk, are semi-nomadic hunters who have been largely ignored by European expansionist culture, and only rarely encountered at all since we have little interest this far west of Ireland and the Northern oil fields. The Inuk are loosely tied to the larger Inuit nation of what we call Canada, a collection of the native nations who resisted the initial attempts of Europeans to colonize and who declared their sovereignty and were recognized during the 15th century, much as the American nations were after Columbus found their shores."

"Alright, alright, enough history professor." Geoff chortled, "What he means is, what we can expect is a quick hike and then a fast voyage home where we'll be hailed as heroes."

"I wouldn't be so sure, Swift," Ros interposed. "Let's not forget that Morgana left Merlin here, and if her cult has emerged after all this time, the likelihood is that they know he's here and that we'll come looking for him."

"Now that I don't get," Belvarre piped up. "Aside from the fact that we're talking about 'The' Merlin and 'The' Morgana le Fay, if they knew he was here, why not just use the same tech they used to get into Camelot, take the mage and leave again?"

"Perhaps the same reason they staged their initial attack during the games?" Loxley said slowly. "Seems to me the only reason to attack us when we had all those cameras and people about to witness it is clear." The others looked at him quizzically until he continued.

"Whoever's behind all this is a giant tart; a show-off of monumental proportions who is going to take every opportunity to show us up and rub our noses in it."

Royston sniggered and Belvarre 'harrumphed!' at John's simplistic explanation, but Nicholaeos cleared his throat to quiet them.

"Actually that does make sense." He looked each member of the party straight in the face before continuing. "I've been theorizing on the technology behind the teleportation, and although I can't begin to actualize the process, I have come to the conclusion that, relativistically speaking, if you could move a man a foot you could send him to the other side of the world. In fact, sending him that one foot is theoretically sending him around the globe in any case..."

"I'll take your word for it," John interrupted.

"So what are we doing?"

"Well," Ros spoke levelly, "Once we've landed we'll have to locate some of the Inuk and hope their elders have some information on Merlin they'll willingly give us."

"That's if they even speak English," Belvarre noted dourly.

"Oh I think we've got that covered." Ros looked at Nicholaeos and they shared a wink.

In the darkness, Crown drifted in and out of consciousness. Blood loss and fever from the infections caused by the filth in his wounds had brought him to the brink of death, but he fought, he fought with the will of a mad man to cling to life. She had promised him power, power like none of those fools at Camelot would ever know, and he intended to have it all.

When she came to him, she placed a cool hand on his burning brow, and he let out a shuddering sigh. Her hair caressed his face, and he could feel the warmth of her body close to his. "Oh my child," she purred, her voice a seductive scots drawl washing over him like a balm. "My beautiful, beautiful child. It is time, time you were remade as you ought always have been, as you were destined to be." She trailed off into a quiet chant, nonsense syllables to Sebastian's ears. Her body moved against his in the soft, yielding morass of the cavern floor. Even through his fever and delirium he could feel the building of energy in the room, beyond the sensations her writhing engendered in him.

"For those you have slain shall now protect you, for those whom you have proved weak will make you strong," she cooed in his ear, her lips brushing his bleeding and befouled face.

Had his eyes not been plucked out with his implants, Sebastian would have seen black ichor crawl from the bloated, corrupting corpses that lay strewn about the room. The stuff pooled about both him and his lady with the consistency of pitch and a smell as noxious.

"Do you swear, my knight? Do you swear to love me, honour me, cherish and keep me? For as long as I allow you to live?" she demanded, sudden iron in her voice.

"Yes my lady," he managed to croak from his ruined throat.

"Then," Morgana began, stretching and purring like a contented cat, her hands gathering the pooling, black poison, "let us remake you."

Hands dripping ichor, she trailed them over every part of the ruined man on the floor.

The Corvette deployed its landing craft, and the flat-bottomed boat lurched through the surf to the gravel beach the Ex-O had identified as their landing point. The ship would wait and make repairs in this narrow cove, out of sight and hopefully safe.

The lander reached the shallows and its entire front end dropped to make a ramp to the shore. Five powerful dirt bikes and a land rover laden with equipment surged through the shallow water and onto the coarse, dark stone.

Ros spoke into her radio as she guided her bike over the loose stone. "Keep your eyes out, I expect there will be opposition forces searching for us here, but we don't want to get paranoid and pop a local by mistake."

"And how do we find them?" Belvarre queried again.

"They'll find us. Once we get away from the coastline we'll park-up and wait."

After riding for more than an hour, Ros called a halt and the group dismounted. The knights wore their personal armour, additional thermal and wind-resistant layers beneath the only concession to the cold. Cassie, Nicholaeos and Brandon wore more conventional arctic gear, and the wind tugged at their parka hoods.

The group settled into a rhythm. Ros took shelter by the Rover to check the map out of the piercing wind, while Loxley used the same shelter to heat a kettle on a chemical block burner. Royston, Bel and Geoff took a three point watch, and Brandon went to each vehicle in turn checking tires, fuel lines, and the measures to protect the various systems from the cold.

Hours passed, and the group activities became setting up tents and setting watches.

When a flurry of snow started to obscure visibility, Ros pulled the sentries in and they secured the bikes, settling in for the wait.

In the morning they were there, about a dozen men standing silently as if they had always been there and the knights had simply failed to see them. Weathered faces watched the group as they emerged blearily into the light, and silence washed over the scene as the two groups observed each other. The Inuk gestured to the Camelot crest on the knight's tent and vehicles, and conversed almost serenely in their own rolling language.

Before long, it seemed they reached a consensus, and they beckoned Ros and her comrades to follow them. Breaking camp as quickly as they could, the group uncovered their bikes and mounted the rover, rolling through the receding unseasonal snowfall that had driven them inside before the Inuk approached their camp.

"Does anyone know what they were saying? Because I don't want to say 'I told you so' at this point," Belvarre drawled.

"I'm patchy, but I think they want us to follow them to their elders," Nicholaeos supplied.

"Before our 'snowy skin becomes icy with frostbite' I think one of them said," Ros finished.

"Okay, I'm officially impressed. How did you two do that?" Geoffrey was genuinely surprised.

"Whilst the rest of you were enhancing your bodies, some of us were looking at the more cerebral end of the catalogue," Ros teased.

"And the cult requires that initiates past a certain level are installed with polyglot implants to speed the learning of classical languages," Nicholaeos added.

"Thankfully our hosts were quite chatty with one another, the implant got a good sample of morphology, syntax and grammar from them."

Royston chuckled over the comm-link and the rest of the group joined him for a moment's mirth.

Their new guides took to a number of dog sleds and headed out over the snowy plains. After nearly a full day's travel through the bleak but beautiful terrain, they came to a collection of yurts huddled in a large hollow. The group stopped, and Ros was beckoned forward. Her Polyglot implant had had time to interpret the patterns of the Inuk language, and she followed what was said without too much trouble.

"Wait here, we will let the elders know you are coming and we will beckon you if they agree to see you."

Ros nodded her assent, and re-joined her friends on the ridge. After a few minutes, a figure waved at them from the village, and they drove their convoy down into the hollow. Children ran between the small semi-permanent dwellings, and people young and old stared at the newcomers before returning to their tasks.

Without ceremony, Ros and Nicholaeos were brought into a yurt. The last thing Ros saw as she entered was Geoffrey waving to a young child who seemed overawed by the newcomers.

Inside, the smell of wood smoke and dried fish permeated the air, and a group of older men sat in a semicircle around a central stove.

"Sit," one of them offered the knight and M.A.G.E. The man was clearly the oldest, and his grey hair bristled from under a brightly beaded hat.

"I am Asasaq, and I have seen your coming."

"Thank you for seeing us Asasaq," Ros and Nicholaeos chorused.

"I must help you, you seek a great wise man to help you against the shadow that follows behind you," the old man continued doggedly. "If I help you, the shadow will fall on my people."

Ros glanced worriedly at her companion and spoke. "We do not wish to endanger you, we will leave."

Asasaq held up a hand, "If I do not help you, then the shadow will fall over my entire nation, this is what the spirits have told me."

Nicholaeos leaned forward intently and spoke clearly. "Tell us what we need, and we will leave directly."

Asasaq leaned over a bowl of gently smouldering leaves and inhaled deeply, while the others in the tent took up a rolling chant. "Go north to the mountains and follow them toward the sun until the path you seek is written in the walls. Go now, they come."

Ros and Nicholaeos shared a troubled glance and headed out into the day again. As Ros ducked into the sunlight, her eyes took a second to adjust. She could see the child again, carefully approaching Geoffrey who now held a sugar bar outstretched. Then, split-seconds before the report, divots of stone erupted from the ground tracing a line toward the child and Geoffrey. It took Ros another split-second to realise they were under fire.

Chapter 16

Geoffrey held the snack bar out and wiggled it in front of the child, who watched it intently before ambling cautiously forward. The 'plink' of ricochets and the line of eruptions triggered an instant reaction and, before he realised it fully himself, Geoffrey was racing the bullets meant for him to the child who merely stood between the shooter and his target.

Again that feeling of time slowing, adrenaline poured through his system as his mind caught up with his body and he sprang forward, grabbing the child with a prayer on his lips as he expected at any moment to be riddled with bullets.

It may have been his imagination, but Geoff fancied that he felt the turbulence as the bullets passed by his body as he shielded the child and ran for cover.

A whooping holler went up from the Inuks, and bolt action rifles began appearing even as the attacker's rounds started to find their marks and the tribe's people started to die.

Geoffrey ushered the child into a yurt and scanned around. He heard the fizz of fuses and realised that Loxley, Belvarre and Royston were trying to provide the cover of smoke grenades even as white stinking clouds engulfed the village. More fire came down into the smoke and Ros crouched behind her team's land rover. She keyed her comms.

"We have to get up there and get them off the high ground."

"Agreed," Belvarre returned.

"They might be all around, this could be intended to push us up the far side into an ambush."

Royston chimed in.

"But these people are dying!" Geoffrey hissed as more bullets rained down on his position.

"We ride," Ros decided, "Bel, Royston and I will go left, John and Geoff right. When you crest the ridge swing clockwise and engage at speed, okay?"

"Received and understood." A chorus of similar responses came back to Ros.

The Inuk were returning sporadic fire, but no-one could see much in the smoke and the attackers were firing into a bowl. Every shot fired out drew a withering hail of fire in response, and indiscriminate bursts tore into buildings as women and children sobbed and screamed.

Ros gritted her teeth and ran to her bike as she thumbed the starter and gunned the engine, the bike leaping forward even as bullets tried to find it. Royston and Bel joined her after mere moments, their tyres spraying gravel and engines roaring.

Cassie stood stunned as bullets ripped into the tribespeople gathered around her. Moments before they had been drawn to her. They'd chattered, she'd guessed about Eric, as the raven perched quietly on her shoulder. Suddenly blood sprayed and chaos and smoke consumed them. One of the women took her arm and pulled the little hacker into a crouch, as rounds impacted in her own back and she fell, sprawled on the ground. Cassie stared into the tribeswoman's dead eyes for a second as Eric tugged at her jacket. "Cover, get to cover!" squawked the familiar and Cassie crawled for the nearest solid object, the land rover. She fumbled her gun from its holster, the black metal still unfamiliar to her, and she looked around for a target. As she raised it toward the ridge, a slender hand pushed the barrel back down. Nicholaeos stood in the smoke, flinching ever so slightly as the report of rifles sounded around them.

"What are you doing?" hissed Cassie, "Get down!"

"I have a protective field," the acolyte replied distantly. Even as he spoke, ripples of light moved over his body where bullets struck him and fell harmlessly to the ground. "It won't last long but while they are shooting me they aren't shooting anyone else. By the way, they are also aiming for anyone shooting back so I wouldn't do that if I were you."

Cassie nodded, dumbstruck, as the door to the vehicle opened beside her, "Get in!" shouted Brandon, "We need to go, now!"

Cassie scrambled in, followed by her Master, as Brandon threw the car into gear and mashed the accelerator. "M'lady Savant!" he called into his comm, "I have Cassie and Nicholaeos and we're mobile. Which way?"

Ros' voice came back with the stress of the situation clearly evident. "Head north, we'll inconvenience these bastards and triangulate on this comms frequency as soon as we... what the hell is that?!" The radio link stuttered and broke off.

"What's happening? What's going on!" shouted Cassie as bullets 'spanged' off the fleeing land rover.

"She switched frequencies, that's all." Brandon reassured her, 'I hope.' he added to himself.

"What the hell IS that?" Ros blurted into the comm. Ahead of her she saw the nearest of the enemy forces, and it was like nothing she'd ever seen before. Vaguely humanoid, its hulking form was bigger than most knights as it stood, still firing down into the Inuk village. Its limbs, while clearly effective, were misshapen and lop-sided, and it was dressed in an approximation of black battle fatigues to suit its ill-formed frame. Ros gunned her engine and drew a pistol from her hip, aiming and firing at the brute on the move. Round after round thudded into the beast who simply turned to her and roared. Its face was heavy-browed and thickset, oversized teeth protruded randomly from a square set jaw. The thing was like some caricature of a Neanderthal with elements of gorilla and bear mixed in. Ros roared past on her bike making sure Bel and Royston were still mobile.

"Did you see that?" the younger knight called out.

"It didn't seem affected by small arms fire," Bel noted, "looks like we'll have to do it the old fashioned way."

"Negative," Ros answered, "We need to gauge their force strength and draw them off before we engage, understood?"

"Understood," came the reply.

"Geoff, John," Ros called.

"Go Ros." the answers came a second later.

"Circle the village, count aggressors and head out north, okay?"

"But what about the village?" John shot back.

"These things aren't here for the locals, they're here for us," Ros reasoned. "They'll follow us out."

Ros holstered her pistol. She had fired at every one of the 'things' she'd seen to get their attention, and was nearly at the northern edge of the hollow. She spied at least one more, laid in a sniper's stance and concerned only with what was in front of its sights.

Ros gritted her teeth and dropped a gear, the engine howled as the revs rose and the beast turned briefly toward her. Ros stood on the bike's stirrups and bounced with her powerful legs lifting the front wheel just in time to run the bike over the monstrous sniper's face.

The bike lurched under her and stopped with a jolt as the beast hollered in pain. Ros was catapulted over the handlebars. Rolling when she hit the ground, she came to her feet to see what had happened. As the beast had raised a hand to defend its face, its fingers had tangled in the rear wheel and, rather than be sheared off or dragged, the monster had dead stopped the rushing motorcycle.

Though its face was ripped and bleeding from the front wheel, and the hand which had stopped the bike was a ruined mess, still caught in the spokes, the monster lurched to its feet with a howl and cast the bike overarm at Ros, ripping free its mangled appendage as it did. She ducked and spun, whipping her helmet off, throwing that back at the creature's head and, as it dodged she closed, drawing her sword. Bullets tugged at the beast as Bel sped by firing and started a sweeping turn. Ros took advantage and swept her sword across the broad chest, the oscillating blade ripping deeply and spraying dark blood. The monster recoiled from the weapon, but not without spinning a devastating kick toward Ros. She swept under the massive limb, blade raised to rend once more as the creature, with agility that shouldn't have been possible for a beast that size, carried through its turn, dragging its good hand over Ros, gripping her tabard and throwing her bodily away.

Royston appeared then, turning his bike in a skidding arc that sprayed stone and dust at the recoiling beast. "Get on, now!"

Stunned though she was, Ros sheathed her blade and climbed aboard. The two of them sped out, joined by Bel, and headed north.

"What was that?" Royston called over his shoulder, "You ran it over and sliced it to ribbons, Bel put half a dozen rounds in it and it kept coming!" Ros glanced back over her shoulder and set her features hard.

"It still IS coming, and so are its friends."

True enough, the huge beasts came loping along behind them, about a dozen all told, using all four of their mis-matched limbs to achieve startling speed.

Two more Camelot bikes roared through the brutes, dodging flailing limbs intent on shattering the bikes and breaking the riders themselves.

Ros watched closely. Even though the things were fast in a straight line and agile in static combat, once they began to move she could see that, due to their bulk, they were committed, slow to stop and unstable to manoeuvre.

"Keep going!" she ordered and reached around Royston. As well as his favoured bow, he had a backup weapon on the bike; a high calibre rifle.

Although she knew she wasn't as good a shot as her friend, the brutes were close and presented large targets. She twisted herself to bring the monsters into sight and worked the action of the rifle, raised it to her shoulder and focussed.

Silicon pathways laced into her brain were flooded with adrenaline, and a short lived coolant that vastly increased their transmission speed. She'd have a headache for the rest of the day, but right now everything slowed. The rush of wind, the jouncing of the bike and the irresistible approach of the foe all flowed in the sudden clarity of her mind as she pulled the trigger, worked the bolt and pulled the trigger again and again.

Ros snapped off three quick shots and the bullets smashed into the two front-running beasts' lower limbs. Ankles and knees suddenly unable to support them, the pursuers collapsed, and those directly behind ploughed into them with frustrated bellows.

"Let's get out of here." She comm'd tersely.

The outriders caught up with the land rover in a wide riverbed some time later. Ros jumped off the bike and strode purposefully to where the others were exiting the rover.

"What the hell were those, and how in God's name did they find us?" she shouted.

Nicholaeos was taken aback at the naked aggression in the knight's voice.

"M'lady, what do you mean?" he ventured uncertainly.

"I mean that I saw no sign of vehicles and I'm sure someone would have seen those big bastards coming, so they must have arrived by other means, and if that is the case then they had to know where we were!" Ros glared about her at each of the team in turn.

"We've supposedly been running silent, no beacons, no transmissions beyond our short-wave comms, and yet they've triangulated us after a day and attacked us and the innocent people helping us!" Ros raged as tears came to her eyes. "Those people did nothing! They didn't wear our colours, they weren't our allies but now they're dead because of us, because of me!"

Geoffrey moved to support her as she sagged, but recoiled as she pulled her pistol and aimed it at his forehead.

"C'mon Ros, calm down." Geoffrey held up his hands placatingly, "We'll work it out."

"Damned right we will!" Ros reeled drunkenly as the other knights held up empty hands, their movements exaggerated and slow.

"I swear, if one of you has betrayed me I'll blow your fucking head off!" her voice had raised to a hysterical pitch, in the back of her mind she struggled against waves of paranoia, grief and rage, trying to exert logic over the rising tide of madness that sought to consume her. Her mind reeled at the emotions surging through her, anger, fear and frustration. In the aftermath of the battle, they paralysed her logic and unhinged her mind.

"I'll find you, we'll find you, traitor!" she snarled, ready for another fight.

"I think we already have," Brandon called from the rover he and Cassie were standing beside. He flinched as the pistol pointed his way, but the barrel wasn't steady any longer, and he beckoned gently for Ros to approach.

"When you said about the frequencies, I got Cass to sweep with Eric," he started slowly, his hands slightly raised. "You're right, there is a signal. It was cloaked, but once we knew we were looking for one it wasn't hard to find. We're just tracing the source."

Ros blinked back the tears as the pistol wavered in her hand. After scanning Eric's holo-screen for a moment, Brandon crossed to the far side of the car and reached under the wheel arch pulling out a small electronic device.

"I can't be sure, but I'd guess it was planted as a backup by the traitors on the ship, and set with a timer so our pre-sweeps wouldn't find it. It was just bad luck they came upon us in the village milady, the fortunes of war I'm afraid."

Ros lowered her gun and took the bug, her fingers closed around it until the plastic cracked and connections parted before hurling it away with a shout of frustration. The gun swept upward once more, and this time it stayed steadily pointed at Brandon's temple.

"Ever so convenient," she growled/ "You checked everything yourself, you can't tell me you didn't see that down there!" she spat. Brandon glanced about for help and held his hands out. "I didn't know it was there, I didn't plant it. I'm not a traitor!" he babbled frantically.

"Can't take that chance," she breathed and started to squeeze the trigger.

"That's quite enough of that," a cool voice hissed in her ear as a hand laid itself over her wrist and fire shot through her body. The spasms depressed the trigger, but allowed her assailant to redirect the muzzle safely skyward. Her vision faded and Rosalyn passed out.

Nicholaeos released her wrist with a flash of blue sparks, and caught her before she could fall.

"Ah, a little help please?" he said weakly.

"Let's get her in the rover," Geoffrey suggested. "We better move on before they trace us here, and I think we should follow the river. I have a hunch those monsters have pretty keen senses."

The others let out the breaths they'd been holding through the confrontation before answering, "Agreed."

Geoffrey stepped forward and took one of Ros' arms, as little Royston came forward to take the other. "I reckon you'll want to rethink that 'No trolls' statement eh?" he joked lightly, "Ah well, at least there aren't any dragons," he winked, as they loaded Ros into the Rover and mounted up.

None of them saw a large, dark figure watch them leave.

Chapter 17

Nicholaeos was sitting with the recumbent Ros when John Loxley approached him.

"How is she?" the big squire said softly.

"Not so well I fear," Nicholaeos replied as gently as he could. "The apparent mental trauma aside, her body temperature has risen to nearly feverish, she appears to be in shock and her pulse is uneven and irregular." As they spoke, Nicholaeos beckoned over both Cassie and Brandon, who came somewhat sullenly, but reacted with shock at Rosalyn's pallor and the occasional convulsions that wracked her.

"I've never known the mind affect a body so completely."

"Well you were the one who tasered her, professor," John spoke wryly.

"Yes, but a calculated discharge to incapacitate her, not this. If I had to guess, I'd say she was rejecting one of her implants, but as far as I know she hasn't had any so recently as to be at risk."

John thought a moment before speaking. "Nick, back on the boat, she said something to me. Something about not being herself, her mind changing, something like that. You don't think that's something to do with it, do you?"

Nicholaeos' brow furrowed in thought, and he looked at Brandon. "Well I suppose, if something in the artificial implants was in conflict with her natural impulses, it could produce such psychosis."

Brandon perked up. "But that doesn't happen anymore, implants aren't made to influence active thought. Back in the early days they tried it, enhanced aggression, suppressing fear, all that bollocks, but even with extensive profiling, setting the implants to the individual was just too much. The slightest error and the programming broke down and damn near took the subject's mind with it."

Nicholaeos was studying Ros carefully. He looked at both Cassie and Brandon. "We have to make sure."

Brandon recoiled at the suggestion. "Whoa! We don't have the equipment for that, no clean room, and neither of us has the experience to go fiddling with cerebral implants."

Nicholaeos closed his eyes and took a deep breath. "Nevertheless, if we don't try, then Lady Rosalyn might die."

"And if we do, she might end up a frigging vegetable!" Brandon protested.

Cassie cleared her throat, "We have to try," she said softly. "Both of you were apprenticed to masters in their respective fields, you both have the promise and the capacity to do this, and we can use Eric as well."

Both Brandon and Nicholaeos gave that pause for thought.

"Okay," stated Brandon, finally. "We jack in the familiar, it navigates the software and we find the problem part."

"We can't risk an extraction unless we have no other choice, and I doubt we have a spare anywhere, so we close off the problem until we can get back to Camelot, agreed?" offered Nicholaeos.

"Agreed," sighed Brandon. "My master's gonna have my arse for this."

"Well, at least you have a plan," chuckled Loxley.

"How are the others doing?" Nicholaeos enquired.

"Shaken," John admitted. "Bel's still coming back to himself after the business with his father; he won't be right 'til he deals with that one way or the other. Royston's coping after a fashion, good lad that he is," John sighed and looked into the distance. "It's Geoff I'm worried about, he's taken a right shine to Ros and for her to crack like that... he's drawn into himself. Only time and your efforts will bring him out."

Brandon gulped. "But what if we're attacked again?"

"Oh if we're lucky," John winked. "Bit more action would do us all good, and worse comes to the worst I wouldn't have to put up with Bel's gallows humour anymore. Come on," he grinned, "work to be done eh?"

Ros was cast upon a roiling sea. Tossed and turned in the tempest she floundered, unable to find up or down. Images bombarded her, dead faces hounded her for her failings even as familiar friends voiced shocked concern, her parents (what little she remembered) appeared for a moment before they shattered and were gone. When was the last time she'd thought of them?

She tried to recall when she'd last thought of them, to find a rock in the maelstrom of her mind. She rolled on through the waves of powerful emotions, directionless and lost, when a lance of pain drove into her skull. She bucked and writhed with the pain, her limbs thrashing in agony.

"Hold her, HOLD HER!" cried Nicholaeos, as Ros convulsed beneath them.

John placed two big hands on Ros' chest and pressed down hard.

"I don't understand, all I did was plug her in." Cassie was ashen faced.

Brandon quickly applied a voltmeter to the plug in the girl's hand, and then to the port behind Ros' ear. "Dammit," he swore, "It's not the usual frequency. Cass, can you reset Eric for this transfer rate?"

Cassie read the meter readout and her fingers flickered over the Raven's 'keys.' "Shouldn't be a problem," she replied.

"We have to get him back in if we want to regulate her neural responses, otherwise she's going to die." Nicholaeos voice was crisp with tension as he attached his own leads, ready to plug into the cyber-familiar.

"There we go," Cass called, hammering out a final key sequence and flipping an unseen switch under Eric's feathers; "plug him back in!"

Brandon muttered a quick prayer, and slid the jack back in place.

The convulsions subsided and Ros went back to drifting. The lightning in her head subsided to a dull throbbing and, though she still moved through the roiling sea, she felt her passage somewhat more level and less random. After a time, a beating of wings descended upon her, and pinprick claws alighted on her shoulder.

"This is most irregular," came the voice of the cyber raven. Unlike other times when Ros had heard him speak, the voice wasn't high and tinny, but a strange electronic basso rumble. "Your synapses are the very devil to navigate. Not at all like proper electronics, but that's where random evolution gets you I suppose."

Ros batted absently at the familiar. "What are you doing here, Raven?" she slurred.

"Eric, if you please," the bird supplied, "I'm afraid you're suffering some kind of psychotic breakdown which may or may not be linked to a rather odd piece of hardware in your brain. Currently you are comatose, and I am regulating your body's functions, as unpleasant as that might be for both of us."

"And how are you talking to me, or is this just a fever dream?"

The Raven cocked its head and regarded her in what might have been a very serious way.

"My dear, as complicated as your brain might be, it is still a computer, after a fashion. Synapses respond to electronic pulses, and in this way communication is achieved. Now," the bird looked around, "I am leading Acolyte Westbrook here to help you, and I think it favourable that we establish some order before he arrives, don't you?"

"He's in," Cassie breathed in relief. "We can mediate her base-line biologics for a time, but the sooner we fix whatever's wrong the better. He's established contact with her frontal cortex, her personality centres, and he's attempting to stabilise her. It's time, Nicholaeos."

The acolyte had several plugs embedded in his scalp and the top of his spine, and he held the terminal ends in a shaking hand. "Once we are connected, you must not unplug us. I will be conscious and, I hope, lucid, and I will keep you appraised of the situation, but once I am in, there will be a certain amount of overlap. I will have to actively disengage from Lady Rosalyn before we disconnect. Do you understand?"

Cassie and Brandon nodded.

"Then let us begin," Nicholaeos voice was almost a whisper as he handed his plugs to Cassie to attach to her familiar.

He felt a sense of resistance, and then he was almost in two places at once. He could still see Cassie and Brandon, with John standing by should he be needed again, and yet he also stood on a simple jetty amongst a maelstrom of colours. Ros stood at the far end with Eric the Raven on her shoulder.

"What are you doing here?" she sighed wearily.

"Milady, I am here to try and save you," he answered.

"Why?" she demanded. "Why not just let me die and go on with the mission without me? Instead you risk us both and the familiar, why?"

Nicholaeos nodded, "I can see the logic in that, but I cannot simply abandon you without pursuing every possible means to save you. That is the way of Camelot. Fellowship, loyalty and duty to one another, is it not lady knight?"

Ros turned away. "What's happening?" she asked after a moment.

"I'm unsure," Nicholaeos admitted, "but it would seem that your reason and logic centres have been

223

overwhelmed by your emotions. If I knew no better, I would venture that you have never learned to deal with them, and the stress of this sudden outpouring has brought you to the brink of a breakdown of massive proportions."

"So what do we do?" Ros asked.

"I am going to attempt to imprint some meditation techniques I have learned into your consciousness to begin with."

"But won't that create the same fault as the artificial behaviour reprogramming?" Cassie blurted.

"I don't think so," Nicholaeos replied calmly, "the nature of the programmed implants is rigid and resistant to change; by sharing my organic patterns, Rosalyn's brain will be able to restructure and absorb them over time."

"Sorry?" Rosalyn frowned, "Who are you talking too?"

"Forgive me," Nicholaeos, apologised, "I will attempt to keep my attention here for the time-being. Now it would help if you accepted the wave patterns I am about to share of your own free will. Here." A sheaf of sheet music appeared in his hand and he offered it to her.

"Sing this,"

"I don't usually sing," Ros stated flatly.

"If it helps, it isn't really music, but a construct by which your mind can accept the patterns of thought I am offering you and I... like music..." the acolyte shrugged sheepishly.

Ros took the papers sceptically and, at the mage's urging, she started to sing.

At first, it was like reading music, but soon tones, tempo and rhythm entered her, flowed through her, and she felt it influencing her. Her sense of purpose returned, her strength and clarity of mind came back to her. The colours and currents surrounding them all began to ease, to soften and take on an almost structured pattern.

"Well done," Nicholaeos breathed in admiration.

"Something's happening, Eric." Cassie scanned lines of code and patterns of waves on the Raven's screen.

"Would you care to elucidate, my dear?" The Raven's voice was slightly slurred, "My processors are running near capacity."

"The rogue chip, it's drawing power and starting some sort of cycle. I can't really tell why, but I have a bad feeling about it."

Nicholaeos raised a hand to his temple as sudden pressure started to build, "I can feel it too. I think the chip was some kind of emotion buffer, it allowed Rosalyn to learn without the distraction of overwhelming emotions. But why is it breaking down now?"

Cassie scanned the codes, thinking furiously.

"Before the first attacks there was something in the 'net, rumours and ghosts, but a couple of times I nearly caught something, some kind of surveillance programme I think. It usually fragmented and dispersed before I could confirm, but this looks like..." she tailed off.

"Looks like what?" Nicholaeos hissed, the pain in his head building.

"It's the same kind of thing, but in reverse. The codes are aligning, building up. The enemy is in Ros' head!"

Rosalyn turned to look out at the becalmed sea of her emotions as it turned to black granite, the 'sky' above became like thunder clouds and a giant shape came forward out of the gloom. It resembled an armoured spider, and it was approaching with astounding speed.

"What the hell is in my head?" Ros screamed at Nicholaeos.

The mage was on his knees now in the vision, hands clutched to his head, and Ros could see where a smaller spider-creature had climbed his back and was trying to drill into his temples with its fore-limbs.

"It's the chip!" he gasped, "Some kind of embedded programme to destroy your psyche, and with us linked, mine too!"

"What can I do, how can I help?" Ros looked around for an idea or a weapon.

"There's nothing you can do, I can't teach you in time," Nicholaeos cried out as the creature on his back bit into him and redoubled its efforts to drill into his head.

"Excuse Me," interrupted Eric the raven, "But I think you can help."

"What!" cried Ros, "What can I do?"

"Take back your base functions, keep calm and stand clear." The raven seemed quite chipper under the circumstances. "You're very lucky I'm here, you know."

The Raven hopped off Ros's shoulder and erupted in a tornado of black feathers which surged toward the oncoming spider-beast, until a new shape emerged from its depths; a giant with a Raven's head in a white toga, a wreath of gold laurel adorning it's feathered brow. Giant and spider met with a peal of thunder which shook Ros's mindscape. She turned to Nicholaeos and tried to pry the smaller spider-beast from his back.

"It is possessed of a very fluid code engram," Eric reported to Cassie. "I am able to hold it, but it doesn't afford me the processing capacity to assess and deconstruct it if I do."

"Hold in there, old bird," Cassie was trying furiously to read the new, unfamiliar code on Eric's screen. "We'll find something."

The two titans struggled in Ros's peripheral vision. The spider struck out with its various limbs but the Raven giant weaved and twisted, avoiding the strikes and keeping the spider at bay. She turned back to Nicholaeos and tried to lift the smaller spider off him. Its sharp shell cut her hands and soon it was slick with her blood, too slick to grasp. She tried to kick it, but it shifted and shook, dragging its victim away from her attacks. Ros spat a curse and went after it again.

"It's using some of Ros's own brain as back-up memory, increasing its own speed." Cassie was staggered by the realisation; the technology involved was as far advanced of anything she had dreamed as it was monstrous in its application. "The only way to beat it is to match like for like. I might be able to pick a weak code line if you can get Ros on-board."

Eric clucked, "I shall see what can be done."

A sudden movement caught Ros's attention. The Raven giant stepped back from the spider, dragging the beast and hurling it away across the landscape. As the creature writhed, trying to right itself, Eric the colossus dissolved into feathers and became the Raven once more.

"I require your assistance," he said briskly. "The programme is using your untapped cognitive ability against you; if we are to destroy it, we must link your higher functions with mine to succeed."

"But, Nicholaeos!" Ros gestured helplessly.

"A small part of the whole," the Raven jabbered, "Destroy the whole and save the mage," he insisted.

Ros grimaced, she felt helpless and she hated the feeling. This wasn't her chosen battlefield, but she'd be damned if she would just stand by and watch this thing tear both her and her friend's minds apart.

"What do you need, raven?" she asked.

"For the purpose of this particular interpretation of the situation? I believe I shall need a gunner."

Ros was about to question why when Eric changed again, feathers shuffled as he hunkered down before an impossible amount of black steel slid, panel over panel, out of the bird. Steel grated and cogs engaged as massive tracks snaked around heavy drive wheels, and finally, with an echoing 'K'thunk!' the turret emerged and settled in place.

"You've got to be kidding me!" Ros gasped, "You're a bloody tank!"

"No I'm not," the raven's voice came from the massive machine. "You're the one interpreting the source code, I simply manifest in your lucid dreaming as a tank. Now," he said, and as his engine rumbled and roared he sounded almost smug, "Get in, and let's kill this thing."

Real or not, Ros felt a feral grin split her lips as she dragged Nicholaeos, spider and all, into the hulking metal monster.

"I've always wanted to do this," roared Ros as she traversed the turret, "Now, get out of my head!" she screamed furiously and pulled the trigger on the massive gun.

Chapter 18

Sometime later, the warriors of Camelot sat around a small campfire.

"You are kidding," Royston marvelled. "A tank?"

"Upon my very life," Ros had a silver survival blanket draped around her shoulders and a cup of soup in her hands, "A chieftain tank, as I live and breathe."

Royston turned to Cassie "Really?"

Cassie ruffled the feathers of the bird in her lap affectionately. "Eric has some serious software fire-power. I should know, I wrote it."

Belvarre nodded to John as he joined them. "How's Westbrook?"

John sniffed and settled on a large rock. "One hell of a migraine, but I think he'll survive."

"And Squires?" the white-haired squire enquired.

"Bel, though this sudden concern for your fellow man is endearing, it wouldn't kill you to use first names y'know." John chuckled and punched Belvarre playfully on the shoulder.

"How is Brandon," asked Belvarre somewhat meekly.

"Still frothing about what the tech-heads did, I swear I can't understand one in three words the lad's speaking, so I gave him some schnapps and sat him in the Rover. I wouldn't be surprised if he's asleep inside ten minutes."

"Do you always have booze, Ox?" Royston cut in.

"Well someone's got to," John shot back, playfully.

"What about those monsters following us?" Cassie asked, suddenly worried.

"Never fear love," John reassured, "we got lucky with this valley system we're in. We're secluded, hidden from sight and sound as long as we keep the fire low and our voices down. The wind's gusty and it's picking up, so scent's gonna be unreliable. We'll post sentries, but my guess is we'll be fine 'til morning."

"Oh good," Cassie yawned, "then I might just close my eyes for a..." she never finished the sentence but fell asleep where she sat. John clucked his tongue, "I don't recall volunteerin' to play mother but, oh well." He sighed, and rose once more to go kneel beside the little hacker. As he lifted her, Ros was struck by just how young she really was, and how much like a child she seemed in his arms.

Belvarre followed suite. "I'm going to check the perimeter, Glasbu... Royston? Care to join me?"

Royston hopped to his feet and they wandered out into the night.

Ros looked over at Geoffrey; he'd been silent the whole time. He was sat facing outward with his back to the fire.

"Swift?" she ventured, and when he didn't answer, "Geoffrey?" Still he would not answer her.

She sat down next to him. "Geoffrey," she urged, "What's wrong?"

Geoff was lost in his own thoughts when Ros came to sit with him, it seemed she had been trying to get his attention as he emerged from the fog of his contemplations.

"What's wrong?" she urged him.

Geoffrey shrugged. "Just thinking. It's been quite a day, you know?"

"Tell me about it." Ros smirked, "computer viruses in my head, a complete psychotic breakdown and a running battle with monsters."

"We're calling them O.R.C.s," Geoff offered, "Organic Re-sequenced Commandos. Nick said they were men who someone's been messing around with, after he sampled some of the blood and tissue from your tunic."

"But he has no equipment," Ros was puzzled, "how did he analyse it?"

"He didn't analyse it, he sampled it," Geoff made a face. "With his mouth."

"Oh, well that's... disgusting." Ros felt a little sick. After a moment she frowned, "Hang on, orcs?" she asked.

"Yup," Geoffrey confirmed.

Ros sighed. "I bet he played those fantasy roleplay games growing up, didn't he? I'd bet my rations on it." Geoff grinned for a moment then looked away.

Ros and Geoffrey sat in silence for a time.

"I, uh, I thought we'd lost you there for a minute," Geoff finally managed.

"Or you hoped you had" Ros joked. The look of sudden horror Geoff shot her before he realised she was joking gave her pause for a moment. Geoffrey recovered himself and looked away again, Ros almost missed what he said next his voice was so uncharacteristically soft.

"I thought I'd lost you."

She looked at him puzzled, "I know it would have been a blow to the mission but..."

"No!" Geoffrey insisted, "I... I thought I'd lost you!" and he turned to her, his eyes intent.

"Geoffrey I, I'm not sure I understand," Ros stammered.

"It's not that hard a concept to grasp Ros," Geoffrey flushed with sudden annoyance. Dammit, he was trying to tell her he loved her and she was looking at him like he was an idiot.

"You could've died, and there was nothing I could do to help and all I could think was that I... didn't want to lose you," he finished weakly.

Rosalyn was stunned that Geoffrey was doing this now. She knew she ought to be flattered, part of her

234

even shared his sentiment, but right now all she felt was annoyed that he'd waited so long and chosen this circumstance. Fatigued and cold as she was, fire filled her belly and animated her tired limbs.

"You have to do this now?"

Now it was Geoffrey's turn to be stunned.

"Well, when should I have done it?"

Ros cast her arms to the sky. "How about a week ago before the raiders tried to sink us?"

Geoffrey came to his feet, suddenly angry. "Well *Jesus* Ros! Next time I try to tell you I love you I'll be sure to check it against your diary!"

Ros surged to her feet and stood nose to nose with Geoffrey. "Perhaps you should, that way I could tell you it was okay, or if it conflicted with a mission to save our *Goddamned* home, you insufferable prat!"

They stood there for a moment, eyes locked and chests heaving, snorting their breaths like wrestling stag.

Geoffrey eventually subsided, taking a deep breath and blowing it out into the cold air.

"I guess I could have chosen a more appropriate moment," he conceded.

"Damned right, you could've," Ros chided with a mock pout, "but I wasn't joking about you being insufferable."

Geoffrey managed a wry grin. "I am what I am," he admitted, with exaggerated modesty.

235

"And what you are is insufferable," Ros returned, punching him on the arm for good measure. "Come on, let's get some sleep."

After another day's hard riding, they reached the foot of the mountains that had been looming ahead of them since early that day. The granite giants seemed to erupt out of the sparse greenery that dotted the retreating snow. They turned roughly west and followed the base of the steep peaks, keeping a wary eye out for any pursuers.

They camped another night and had travelled another half day; they were almost sure they had shaken all signs of pursuit, when Royston's keen eyes picked out black shapes to the south.

"We were going to have to deal with these freaks at some point," he called out over his radio.

"But now we have an advantage," Ros sent back. "We can see them coming and we have a lead on them. Let's just find a nice choke point and set up a friendly little ambush, shall we?"

They found a canyon with a convenient bend in it, and Brandon was driving away with Cassie and Nicholaeos, over-revving the engine as far as he dared to draw the orcs in. With a final series of swift hand gestures, Ros signalled the plan and they waited to spring their trap.

The first the orcs knew of the danger was a couple of hastily rigged grenade 'mines'. The explosions echoed through the confined rock space as a couple of the monsters were taken off their feet, shrapnel tearing chunks out of the beasts. Into the smoke and dust swept the knights of Camelot, their enemy was disoriented and blinded, so Ros and her team used the opening to full effect. Even as one of the victims of the 'mines' wavered stubbornly to its feet, Loxley caved its head in with his mace. Another had its throat ripped open by Ros's blade, and Belvarre dispatched another with a cleaving blow that left its head very nearly severed.

Royston moved behind, slinging arrows into the foe. His first headshot simply glanced off an orc's thick skull, and a follow-up shot through the neck failed to kill the beast, so he set to targeting knees and shoulders to disable and debilitate, to weaken the foe for his comrades.

Between them, the knights managed to swiftly dispatch five of the dozen or so malformed beasts in short order, but the orcs recovered quickly, and brought the tight space of the canyon, cruel long-knives and sheer mass to their advantage. Though they could barely fit three abreast into the passage, the orcs' sheer resilience worked in their favour, and soon the fight was starting to tell on the knights. They shook off discharges from Bel's shock-blade, Loxley's concussion mace staggered them but couldn't fell or throw them, Ros's own vibro-blade ripped into the beasts, but it took a tremendous amount of blood loss before they would fall. Then they started climbing.

Like monkeys, the rearmost orcs took to the craggy walls to try and climb over to outflank the knights. Geoffrey, breathing heavily, took stock of the situation and nearly laughed in exultation.

"You've gone and done it now, you bastards!" he roared and, sheathing his sword, he leapt into the air like a cricket.

With little apparent effort, he sailed to one side of the canyon, then twisted in mid-air and pushed off the rock wall to fly back and into his first target. He heel-kicked the orc in the jaw, crushing the monster's head against the rocks, and the stunned creature fell back into its fellows. Below, Belvarre saw his opening and renewed his attacks, hewing strokes opening great gashes in the staggered foes.

Geoff launched straight up from that attack and landed feet first on the next orc, again dropping it into reach of both Belvarre and Ros's blades. With all his strength, he pushed off a final time and, shield held firmly before him, crossed the canyon again into the last resourceful beast. Although this one saw the attack coming, it was unprepared for Geoff's repaired and renewed tech-weapon. The orc raised an arm to bat Geoffrey away, but the kinetic repulsor engine on his shield, driven by the knight's shear velocity, snapped the offending limb at the elbow and drove the orc into the canyon wall as if it had been hit by a car. Geoffrey grabbed at a handhold and hung there, taking stock of the situation.

Ros and Bel had cut a bloody swathe in their staggered opponents and Royston's arrows had clearly added injury to insult, but beneath him, John was in trouble. A big orc rolled forward and, as it dashed John's mace aside, it wrenched the shield off the man's arm and tossed it away. Using its bulk it bulled the big squire against the rock wall and wrapped its misshapen hands around his throat. Lifting him bodily from the ground, it started to squeeze the life out of him. John gasped and kicked and grabbed the monster's wrist with his hand.

His mechanical hand.

Suddenly, instead of John gasping and the orc bellowing, John was bellowing and the orc was screaming in pain as its wrist was simply crushed. Releasing the pulverized joint, John hammered the orc's head and neck with his shining bronze fist, driving it back and back. Dark blood flowed and spurted as the squire ruined the orc's face. It took a good dozen blows, but eventually the orc dropped and gurgled its last breath out of its shattered mouth.

Glancing about her Ros could see that, though they had taken a few cuts and bruises, the element of surprise had served them well. She shuddered to think of what would've happened in a straight fight on open ground.

The dust was settling now, and as the sun once more reached into the canyon, Ros noticed something she hadn't seen as they were setting up their ambush.

"Boys, take a look at this," she called, stepping forward and reaching out to brush some dust from the rock face.

"That?" Royston was puzzled. "Looks like a quartz vein, so what?"

True enough, streaks of white quartz slashed through the rock, caught the sun and glittered all around them.

"So, who's been polishing it all, genius?" Geoff winked. "I don't think naturally occurring seams would be so shiny."

"Fun as the geology lesson is," Belvarre interjected "Why is it relevant now?"

"Because Asasaq said our path would be written in the walls," Ros smiled softly, remembering the old Inuk.

"What?" Belvarre asked, puzzled.

Ros looked about at each of her friends. "Where did the legend say that Merlin was left?" she asked.

"In a crystal cave!" Royston chirped, proudly.

"That's right," Ros gestured around, "and these aren't just quartz, they're quartz crystals."

Once they'd caught up with the others, Ros and company moved on in convoy, Ros taking over driving the land rover. After a couple of hours, the twisting canyon became a labyrinth of cracks and crevasses. Calling a halt, Ros got out of the vehicle and opened the rear compartment.

"What's the plan, boss?" Geoff called as he pulled up and tugged off his helmet.

"We camouflage the rover and go in on foot," she called back, pulling a rucksack and a coil of rope out of the equipment stowed in the back.

"We'll have to carry what we need, and I'm guessing climbing and caving gear."

The others pulled up and gathered around.

"Do we know what we're doing when we find Merlin?" Belvarre asked.

"Not a clue," Ros shook her head, "we'll just have to work it out when we get there. Likewise, we don't know what to expect when we do get there, so keep your weapons to hand, alright?"

Loading up, they set out into the labyrinth.

"How do we know which way to go?" Brandon asked Geoffrey.

"We follow the crystals in the canyon walls." Geoff shrugged.

"Sounds a bit random to me," the tech muttered.

"I'm not arguing with that," Geoff grinned, "but things seem to be getting a little bit mythical on us so I'm willing to go on faith."

"Sounds a bit 'hit and myth' to me," Brandon winked.

"Hey," Geoff feigned annoyance, "I do the jokes around here!"

The two were silent a moment. Geoffrey shot a sly look at Brandon. "Why we're doing this is a 'myth-tery to me," he chuckled.

"I'm sure it's all a big myth-take," Brandon shot back.

Big arms draped over the chuckling pair's shoulders and dragged them together.

"If you two don't knock off the puns I'm gonna brain the pair o' ya and leave you behind," John threatened, light-heartedly.

Geoffrey was thoughtful for a moment then laughed, "I guess they'd have to list us as 'myth-ing in action' then?"

John threw up his hands in despair as the others laughed.

Chapter 19

The mouth of the cave was little more than a dark crack in the wall. Above them the grey rock soared skyward and ahead the crevasse snaked on, noticeably devoid of crystal seams. The wind howled overhead as the party eased themselves into the dark. Inside they fixed shoulder lamps and started to take in their surroundings.

The space was large with a high ceiling and a rock-strewn floor. Apart from a few stalactites, there seemed little remarkable about the cave.

"How do we know this is the place?" Royston whispered, the sound carrying through the cave.

"We're in the right place," Ros breathed and held her hand-lamp to the wall.

The light poured through the crystals like blood through veins, and the floor and ceiling glowed with astonishing radiance.

"Most definitely," Nicholaeos added studying the walls. Far from bare, the walls were smooth and adorned with intricate carvings.

"What are they?" Cassie breathed, awestruck.

"Early Breton scenes with accompanying Latin," the Acolyte mused. "One would've thought it would have degraded more." He studied the carvings. "It's the history," he announced, "Look, see here, Merlin helps Uther Pendragon bed Lady Igraine by disguising him as her husband Gorlois, at Tintagel. Here, Merlin steals away with Arthur, get of Uther, when Uther is killed in battle by the Saxons. Here Arthur, squired to a knight, pulls the sword from the stone and is crowned 'the boy king'. Here, he leads the army and drives out the Saxons. The round table, Excalibur shattering in the duel with Lancelot, Merlin takes Arthur to the Lady of the lake to reforge it, Arthur siring Mordred by his half-sister Morgan le Fay, it's all here!"

"Wait, what?" Cassie was confused. "Explain that, that wasn't in history class at school."

"Well, the common account is..." Nicholaeos shrugged, "sanitized for the masses."

"So, un-sanitize it." Cassie frowned.

Ros shared a glance with the mage and nodded, turning to the others she said, "Spread out, there has to be a way to go deeper."

Once they were alone, Nicholaeos turned to Cassie and sighed.

"Arthur was the get of King Uther Pendragon who coveted Igraine, the wife of a lord of his court, Gorlois. Such was his lust that he had Merlin give him the appearance of Gorlois so he could visit her in the night. Merlin agreed, but told Uther that there would be a price to pay. Uther agreed but the price wasn't his, it was Arthur's. At times in his life, Arthur was overcome by Uther's lusts. When he first met Lancelot, Lancelot sought a lord who could best him in combat, one who was worthy of his sword and service. Arthur was overcome with pride when Lancelot bested him and attempted to strike the valiant knight in the back, but Excalibur was a sword of law, and shattered as the unjust blow landed. Lancelot was convinced by Merlin to help Arthur return Excalibur to the Lady of the Lake to be remade and to teach him something of humility along the way and, once the sword was remade, he agreed to join Arthur's court."

"And that bit about Morgana le Fay?" Cassie tapped her foot, impatiently.

"Another part of the curse." Nicholaeos shook his head sadly. "Morgana was Arthur's half-sister, the child of Igraine and Gorlois, sired before Gorlois died and Uther took Igraine as his wife proper. Fearing for the life of her child at the hands of Uther, Morgana was sent away to who knows where. What we do know is, when she reappeared as the wife of King Lot of Orcadia, Arthur's curse raised its head once more. As with Uther, Arthur had to have her, not knowing she was his sister. Instead of asking Merlin to disguise him however, Arthur simply crept into her chambers one night when her husband was away and she mistook Arthur for Lot. When Merlin found out, he was furious. It was the first, but not the last time Mordred would come close to breaking Camelot apart, even before he was born."

"Oh." Cassie breathed, stunned. "I can kinda see why that bit was taken out."

"Um...'Sanitized' is the preferred term," Nicholaeos corrected, sadly. "Heroes rarely work when they are seen to be mere fallible mortals."

"You said he was cursed," Cassie said accusingly.

"Cursed by his genetics and an unstable upbringing maybe," Nicholaeos wagged a finger. "Not by magic. Magic is a fairy tale."

"Or a technology so far advanced as it seems like magic," Geoffrey butted in.

"What?" the acolyte was taken aback.

The knight waved away his protest, "C'mon," he beckoned, "We found a passage."

The group moved quietly down the narrow corridor. Rosalyn and Belvarre in the lead, Geoffrey, John and Brandon behind them and Royston, Nicholaeos and Cassie bringing up the rear. The veins of light continued to glow along their path, but it only illuminated maybe fifteen feet ahead, and it moved at a slow walking pace.

"That's not possible," Cassie whispered, her voice tinged with awe.

"Well, theoretically..." Brandon whispered, "if the light is refracted by the crystals to create the illumination, then all you'd have to do is focus it into a tight enough beam that the distance it has to travel through the prism is great enough that it takes the desired time to reach a certain point; that is, taking into account that light takes eight minutes to reach the earth from the sun."

Cassie stared at him blankly.

"Um, the light goes around and around inside the crystals very fast but only travels down the corridor at walking pace." He shrugged "It's only a theory though."

Cassie smiled at the tech. "It's a good theory," she said softly.

"I don't like this," Bel spoke softly to Ros, "If this is Merlin's resting place, surely someone would have found it by now."

"What are you thinking, Bel?" Ros raised a questioning eyebrow.

"Traps." Belvarre spat the word as if it tasted foul. "Tests to prove the worth of those that seek the wizard."

"Nonsense, Bel," Ros returned calmly. "It's simply the case that this land is far enough removed to dissuade treasure seekers, and the locals have no interest in the legend." She felt a brief pang of sorrow for Asasaq and his village.

The sound of stone grating reverberated through the tunnel, and the walls shook as a lilting voice rang in the air.

"Tástálacha a iarrtar, dúshlán glacadh."

"What is that?" Loxley bellowed.

"Gaelic," called Nicholaeos.

"But what does it mean?" the squire called as the floor trembled, staggering the group.

"It means challenge accepted!" Ros shouted glaring at Belvarre as stone walls shifted, closing them off from the others.

"Well that's just great!" Cassie spat, but she was trembling despite herself.

"Remain calm, apprentice," Nicholaeos spoke, levelly, "all will be well."

"Ummm, yeah." Brandon stood back from the walls he'd been examining for a few moments. "I can't tell you how, but there's not even a seam here at the join." He thumped on the stone where there had been a tunnel only a few minutes before. "Hello!" he called, "can anyone hear me?"

"Don't trouble yourself, master Squires." Nicholaeos sat on the floor and crossed his legs as if meditating, "Merlin was not one to take a life without reason. We must wait and see what is in store for us."

Cassie had accessed Eric's systems and was frantically tapping through sequences. "I can't stay here, I can't stay here," she repeated breathlessly, "I can't breathe!"

Nicholaeos frowned and closed his eyes, muttering softly. A faint aura of static grew around him, and Cassie's hands slowed on her familiars keys whilst her breathing eased. "What did you do?" she asked, quietly.

"Your brand," the mage stated simply. "I used it to stimulate endorphin production in your body in the face of your evident claustrophobia."

"You what?" Cassie, stunned, found herself shocked and angry at this revelation. "You never told me you could control the brand!"

"It's a failsafe, in case a bondsman ever went rogue. It allows me limited physical control."

Cassie was beside herself with rage. "Don't you ever do that to me again, I don't care if it's to save my life! Never violate me like that again!"

"Ummm, now might not be the best time..." Brandon cleared his throat, the tension between the hacker and the mage was palpable, "but it seems our way out has presented itself."

Cassie and Nicholaeos turned to the passage that had just opened beside them.

Geoffrey, Loxley and Royston traded worried looks in the cramped confines of their piece of tunnel. The shaking had thrown them together and some universal sense of humour had decided to give them the bare minimum of space.

"Well gee, I knew we were close guys, but this is ridiculous," Royston joked.

"Royston, the secret of comedy is timing, and now is not the time," Geoffrey said, deadpan. He craned his neck around trying to see any kind of escape route.

"Well gentlemen, I guess we wait."

"I hope we don't have to wait long," John grunted. "Those ration bars give me terrible gas."

All Geoffrey and Royston could do in response was groan in protest.

"I said there would be traps," Belvarre said flatly.

Ros fumed. "No, you told the Crystal Cave that there SHOULD be traps. Of all the idiot things to do!" she stormed away from him as far as their 'cell' would let her.

"You are just angry because I was right," Belvarre returned.

Ros let out a cry of pure frustration. "Of all the stubborn, arrogant, churlish! I swear, in your own way, you're as bad a Geoffrey!"

"Well, that was hurtful." Bel's voice dripped sarcasm. He surveyed the space that the sliding walls had left them. "Assuming we don't asphyxiate first, we won't escape this space unless whoever is in control allows us to leave."

"And what makes you say that?" Ros asked testily.

"I cannot reach the others on the comms, nor can I detect anything past the immediate space."

"Well it's a good thing I don't have to rely solely on you then, isn't it?" Ros turned and blustered past Belvarre to the wall nearest where she presumed her comrades to be. Placing her ear to the wall she closed her eyes and concentrated. Drawing her dagger she rapped the pommel on the wall.

"What are you doing?" Bel asked, genuinely perplexed.

"This place might be capable of doing some astounding things with physics, but it can't negate it." Ros said cryptically.

"Meaning?" Bel pushed, now it was his turn to be frustrated.

"Meaning shut up while I echo sound the chamber," she hissed.

"Why would you even have that modification?" Bel sneered.

Ros sighed. "It's more like a side effect of several others, so it's not precisely calibrated, nor is it one-hundred percent accurate, so shush!"

Belvarre frowned but remained quiet as Ros moved around tapping and occasionally striking the wall.

With each firm strike, she flinched away, paused, and shook her head, then resumed tapping.

Eventually Ros stepped away from the wall, sheathed her dagger and sighed, "Well, maybe they can break the laws of physics." She scowled at Belvarre. "When you're right Bel, you're right," she conceded.

"I told you there would be traps." Bel smirked.

Ros threw up her hands and screamed in exasperation.

"Well this looks promising," Cassie muttered darkly. The chamber they had found was a dead end, square and scribed like a chess board, but with only nine squares, each about three feet across. As the party moved hesitantly forward, the tunnel behind them grated shut, leaving an additional square space open.

"Were I capable of emotion, I might suggest it looked positively ominous," Eric rasped in his tinny voice.

"What's it all about?" Brandon whispered, "From one locked room to another."

"Merlin was known as a trickster, an illusionist with a love of games and puzzles. This is a test of some sort. Give me some time and I shall soon discover its purpose."

"Right." Brandon sighed and started pacing the walls. Nicholaeos stood silently in the middle of the room. Cassie huffed and folded her arms, leaning against a wall. Brandon was inspecting their 'entrance' when she felt a tremor. Glancing about, she noted a slight trace of dust fall from the ceiling right above where Brandon was inspecting the wall.

"Brandon!" she cried, hurrying toward him. As she moved the section of ceiling above the tech, marked in a pattern mirroring the floor, started to rapidly descend. She grabbed his hood and dragged him out from under the block. It struck the floor with a very final 'boom'.

Nicholaeos cocked an eyebrow, "Interesting," he murmured.

"Interesting?!" Brandon gasped, "That nearly killed me!"

"I think you should both come and stand with me," Nicholaeos suggested. "And watch the ceiling." He gestured primly upward.

"Yeah, no fear there." Brandon climbed to his feet and brushed himself off.

They stood in wary silence until, a short time later one of the room's corner blocks descended with another loud 'Boom'!

"So?" Cassie asked, "What's the test?"

"I don't know, yet." Nicholaeos shrugged.

"Well you better work on that." Brandon urged, "Cause that's a pretty big incentive right there, and this isn't a big room! We can't have much time."

"I think you're right." Nicholaeos frowned, "But I need to confirm something."

"What?" insisted Cassie, "What do you need to confirm?"

Nicholaeos held up a hand for silence, after a short time the block immediately in front of them crashed down.

"Three minutes," the Mage said. "From the time the door closed to the first block, then again to the second and again to the third." Cassie and Brandon stood in silence for a moment.

"So it's a numbers puzzle?" Cassie blurted. "We've got, like, twenty one minutes to solve it?"

"Maybe." Nicholaeos frowned deeply.

"Maybe?" Brandon looked about desperately. "We're stuck in a number puzzle in a mystic maze and we have to take it on faith that you can get us out!"

Nicholaeos grinned suddenly as another block crashed down. They now had only six tiles to stand on.

"Not me, master Squires, you! You have gotten us out." He took them both by the shoulder and pulled them back to the last row of tiles, "I simply have to identify how the sequence progresses from this point."

"What are you talking about Nick?" Brandon felt panic starting to rise in his chest.

"Wait, wait," Nicholaeos simply stated calmly.

Cassie and Brandon stood in anxious silence, hearts beating fast in their chests as the acolyte simply stood with a quiet smile on his face.

Another block crashed down against the wall right in front of them making the tech and the hacker jump.

"Can you tell us what's going on now?" Cassie begged, frantically.

Nicholaeos turned on them then, suddenly intense. "Merlin was an illusionist, a trickster and a genius. Why expend your own energies confronting an enemy when you can employ his own strengths against him? Merlin was a master of misdirection, here we are confronted with a trap that appears to rely upon breaking some mysterious numeric code, sequence or pattern when..." he stopped and listened, "It's speeding up." He said simply, and dragged his compatriots into the corner. The centre most block dropped, kicking up dust, making them all cough and rub at their eyes. Nicholaeos faced Cassie and Brandon something manic in his eyes.

"It isn't a puzzle, it is a test and it isn't mathematical, it's theological... it's a test of faith."

He dragged Brandon from the corner into the back centre tile then stood on the tile farthest from Cassie, "Stand in the centre of the tiles and don't move. Merlin didn't kill unless he absolutely had to, indiscriminate traps like this aren't his style, if you have faith."

"How do you know? How can you possibly be sure?" Cassie shouted.

Eric the raven, perched on Cassie's shoulder, spoke up then. "The descent is a simple systematic progression with limited interpretations. There is no apparent way to interact with the test and, were it simply a trap why not an instantaneous effect? The sequence accelerated when Master Westerbrook showed sign of having interpreted the nature of the test. I cannot fault the logic, however..." the Raven paused. "The percentages aren't a certain proposition, I have insufficient data."

The last block of the centre row slammed down with grim finality and Cassie let out an involuntary shout.

"So what do we do?" she screamed.

"Accept that this is the challenge and try to remain calm. If I'm wrong... it will be quick." Nicholaeos folded his arms and closed his eyes. Brandon glanced from Nicholaeos to Cassie and back again. He shook as adrenaline impotently flushed his system. Nothing to fight, nowhere to run.

Chapter 20

Geoffrey, Royston and Loxley lay in a groaning heap. The floor had opened beneath them, and after a roller-coaster slide through pitch blackness, they had been deposited in an undignified heap of tangled limbs.

Geoff dragged himself from the pile. "Everyone alright?" he gasped.

"I think so," came Royston's voice in the dark.

"Yeah, landed on my head, so no damage there." John's voice held a note of tension despite the lightness of his words.

A faint glow gradually cut through the darkness around them, revealing a tunnel stretching out ahead.

"No idea where we are," Royston muttered. "Something's dampening my internal gyro."

"Same with my Chrono," Geoff supplied. "Can't say how long we were out."

"Comm's are off too," Loxley added, "I'm only getting signal from you two."

They stood in silence for a while.

"Well, the only way appears to be forward," Geoffrey observed, and set off into the gloom. They moved quietly and cautiously down the corridor until it broadened out. The ceiling rose up into darkness and their footsteps became echoes. Royston hesitated. "I don't like this," he murmured.

Almost in response to his statement a loud grating noise obliterated the quiet and a stone pendulum roared through the air directly in front of the little squire. He leapt back with an involuntary shout and bumped into Geoffrey who stumbled back into Loxley, who simply held out a massive hand to steady his friend.

"This is no time for slapstick, boys." The big squire grinned mockingly, but his brow creased as he looked down the passage and saw the entire length now filled with seemingly randomly swinging pendulums.

"Some kind of obstacle?" Royston murmured.

"Obstacle? Hardly!" Geoffrey blustered. "There must be a brake mechanism at the far end, won't be a sec' boys," he announced, and leapt into a sprint.

"Geoff wait!" Loxley bellowed and grabbed for his friend, but too late. Geoffrey accelerated down the hall and into the mess of swinging stone. He dodged and weaved, and was about to throw a cocky look over his shoulder, when a stone beam scythed through the pendulums like a giant baseball bat, missing each in turn and walloping him square across the chest. Geoffrey flew back the entire length of the corridor, conveniently missing every swinging pendulum he had passed on the way.

"Down!" Loxley put a hand on Royston's shoulder and pushed him to his knees before bracing to catch the flying Geoffrey. There was a loud 'clang' and a 'whuff!' of expelled breath as Geoffrey knocked John from his feet and both were carried to the floor.

"Are you two okay?" Royston gasped leaning over them.

"Never... better..." Geoffrey choked, winded.

"Hold still, let me check you over." Royston gave Geoffrey a cursive examination and stood back scratching his head. "I don't understand, you ought to have at least a few broken ribs... Well, shattered ribs actually, not to mention possible dislocations and such, but I can't even find a serious sprain."

"Well then, I guess I'm fine to go again." Geoffrey sighed.

"Hang on Geoff." Loxley laid a hand on his friend's shoulder.

"I get a feeling that was your one and only break. Not only should that thing have broken you in half, but you should have hit something on the return journey. This 'obstacle' gave you a chance. It might not do that again."

Geoffrey thought about that for a second. "So what do you suggest John? Are you going to give it a go?"

"Nah, I don't fancy trying to muscle it through those things," Loxley snorted derisively.

"What?" Royston looked up suddenly.

"I said I don't wanna be clobbered myself" John chuckled.

"No, you said 'muscle' like you'd try to force your way through. Swift tried speed. Don't you see it?"

The other two stared at Royston blankly.

"They're both physical approaches, speed and strength. What if this isn't an obstacle? What if it's a puzzle?"

"You've lost me," Geoffrey admitted.

"I remember my history better than you, I see." Royston sighed. "Merlin, he taught Arthur that a good warrior is skilled, but a great leader is smart. He taught Arthur things like maths and language and how to avoid a fight with diplomacy or cunning. You still don't get it, do you?" He held up his hands, exasperated.

"You mean this is a lesson? We've got to try to be more than what we're perceived to be, and think our way through this?" Loxley ventured.

"Exactly." Royston grinned.

"So how do we do that? It looks simple enough, I just have to time my run right and pay attention."

"And get your head taken off by another beam and crushed to a pulp. C'mon Geoff, think," Royston pleaded. "At least hold off for a few minutes and try this my way."

"Okay," Geoffrey conceded, "So what do we do?"

Royston sat cross-legged staring straight through the swinging pillars. "We wait and observe," he said simply.

Ros sat opposite Bel in the small dark room. A faint illumination allowed them to see each other vaguely although they were only a few feet apart. They had been silent for what seemed like an age before Bel spoke.

"I thought I loved you, you know." He didn't look at her as he spoke, just stared into the shadows.

Ros was quite startled at the admission but held back for a moment, "You 'thought'? What does that mean?"

"I don't know. I suppose I didn't know what love was. I'm not sure I do yet." His voice was quiet, measured, but not devoid of emotion. Ros felt a weight in her chest, like her heart was suddenly made of lead.

"I, I hated you," she started. "Right up until the point your Father..." she trailed off. Belvarre's shoulders began to shake and it was a moment before Ros realized that he was laughing. He laughed and laughed, an edge of hysteria creeping in at some points as Ros watched him warily until, gasping for breath, he subsided.

"Well, I suppose I was a tad arrogant," he chuckled.

"Are you..." Ros took a breath. "Are you alright, Bel?" she asked.

261

He looked at her then, confused. "What do you mean?"

Rosalyn picked her way through her words like they were a minefield. "You've been... quiet of late. Then when it comes to a fight? It's like there's nothing else in the world but the fight. Seriously, at times, I thought the only reason you weren't fighting me was because you weren't facing that way!" The last came out in an unbidden burst and Ros clapped her hands over her mouth.

Belvarre was quiet for a long time, still like a statue or a cat ready to pounce.

"You're afraid of me." He spoke at last, "Not afraid I'd get hurt or cause one of the others to be hurt. You are afraid of me, like I'm a gun about to go off and you don't know who I'm aimed at." His voice was cold enough to cause Ros a shiver.

"Yes," she admitted, her voice barely a whisper.

Belvarre nodded. "Well you can take your hand off your gun, Ros, I'm not psychotic. Not yet." Ros realised she had placed her hand on her pistol's grip without even thinking about it.

"The truth is," Belvarre went on, "that I see a road. I'm at one end, and my bastard father is at the other, and every step I take on that road must be bought in blood."

"I hate to say it," Ros ventured tentatively "but it looks like this is the end of the road."

As he sat across from her, Rosalyn would have sworn Belvarre looked serene, almost content. A strange smile played on his lips when he spoke next.

"No, the Universe would not be so... cruel. I was born to privilege, raised in luxury, and had the world served to me upon a silver platter. But all I wanted was my father's approval, his recognition for my efforts. This small thing was denied to me. Then everything was swept away the day my father betrayed all I had been raised to believe in." He paused for only a moment. "But I have been granted a rare and precious gift. My father owes a debt of honour, a debt I intend to make him repay in full, and upon the day I bring justice upon him I will prove that I am the better man."

A low rumble started as Belvarre finished speaking and one of the walls confining them drew back to reveal a corridor.

"As I said," Belvarre said smugly "the Universe would not be so cruel. Our exit presents itself"

Ros stood. "Bel', don't confuse vengeance with justice," she said, as she began down the newly revealed corridor. After only a short walk, she turned back to Belvarre "And don't confuse an exit with a way out."

Belvarre came to the end of the corridor, barely wide enough to permit them to stand shoulder to shoulder, and looked out at a chasm nearly fifty feet across. The blue glow from the walls illuminated the gap and showed them an opening in the far wall but, to their left and right, above and below, the chasm disappeared into darkness.

Belvarre shrugged, "It shouldn't be too hard to traverse, and we have the climbing gear in our packs back..." Before he could finish, a familiar grating of stone on stone echoed down the corridor, ending in a rather definite boom.

"Correction" Ros commented dryly, "We had climbing gear back there."

Both knights stood at the lip of the tunnel, staring across the crevasse. After what seemed like an age, Belvarre spoke, "One of us will have to jump."

Ros looked at him, amazed. He was frowning but his eyes were fierce and eager looking at the challenge to be overcome.

"Jump? You can't be serious. Even with the run up, neither of us could make it."

"Not on our own," Belvarre returned, "but, if we timed it right, one of us could sling the other over the gap. Give them the extra push needed. I'll jump."

Ros squinted over at the other side, the opening in the rock face seemed so far away. "No," she said finally. "You're stronger, I'm lighter. I should jump." She sounded reluctant. Neither of them spoke for another long moment.

"This is going to take," Ros began, but Belvarre finished for her "Trust? I know you don't trust me. You wonder whether my father's betrayal has stained me. You wonder how I could serve him all my life and not know he was a traitor, so you suspect I did know, that I am a deeper part of it. Or you just wonder whether I am broken, insane or headed that way. I understand." He seemed saddened by the thought.

"I was going to say 'perfect timing,' but you're right. I don't completely trust you." She sighed. "But that doesn't matter. We help each other now, or neither of us will leave this place. I have to trust that you don't want to die here, alone in this gloomy hole." She stared straight at him until his gaze met hers, "And perhaps then I can trust you with other things. I selected you for this mission, Bel. I chose to have you along, because I thought you were broken, and by giving you a purpose you might be able to fix yourself. I've had my doubts, seeing you in combat, seeing the lust for blood in your eyes, but..." she grimaced as she searched for words, finally throwing up her hands in exasperation. "Forget it, Bel, let's just get this done and, if we survive, we'll talk about it then."

Bel nodded his assent, "Alright, once this mission is done." He looked sidelong at her, and added, "You can trust me. Just don't get between me and my father."

Ros stared hard at Bel, then walked back down the corridor. As she gazed along its length, her perspective seemed to shift; the run up shortened and the space beyond grew in her mind. Why couldn't she articulate her thoughts to Bel? It was true she didn't entirely trust him, but she wanted to, and that feeling, that desire to trust in him was hers and *that* she had faith in. That she could trust. Her doubts clouded around her, but that thought cut through them like a sword. She knew what she had to do. Ros shrugged her shoulders to settle her armour, leaned on her back foot and threw herself into a full sprint. 'Purpose, Duty, Honour...' she thought as she hurtled toward infinity. At the last moment she reached for Belvarre's outstretched hand and he hauled her past and flung her out into the void. The final thought to join Ros in her flight was 'Trust'.

Cassie felt hopeless. Nicholaeos was gone. Moments before the ceiling above him had dropped, she'd watched it happen. One moment he stood there serene, with his arms folded as if he was praying, and the next there was a grinding of stone and an echoing crash as the column dropped and he was gone. Brendan was pale and sweating, but he stood ramrod straight, muttering continuously under his breath. Cassie looked at the bottom of the pillar and part of her thought 'It's strange that there's no blood' and that very thought calmed her some. Pulling herself up, though still trembling and deathly afraid, she managed a weak smile as she reached out to touch Brendan's hand. As he looked to her she said weakly, "It's going to be alright." And then he was gone. The stone hit the ground with a thunderous 'Crash!' and Cassie was alone, any confidence she might have clung to fled and tears filled her eyes. 'This can't be', she thought, 'those stones must weigh thirty tonnes, there's no way anyone could survive!' She looked about frantically, trapped in a three foot square space with tons of stone about to crush her. In that place, deep underground, she wept and screamed and dropped to her knees when, just as the grinding of stone sounded above her she whispered three words in vain appeal to the universe. "Merlin protect me!" as the darkness engulfed her.

Geoffrey was growing impatient. Royston sat, cross-legged, watching the swinging mechanisms with infinite patience. Loxley leaned against the cavern wall rubbing at spots on his prosthetic arm and humming a bawdy tune to himself, leaving Geoffrey to pace impotently up and down the corridor.

"How much longer?" he cried in frustration.

Royston sighed. "It was almost there, there was a pattern emerging. Now it's just random again."

"What?" Geoffrey said questioningly.

"As we waited," Royston began, "I thought I saw a pattern emerging, a rhythm. It's something you learn in archery, if you pay attention," he said pointedly.

"I still don't get it." Geoff shrugged.

"Because you always go at things like a bull at a gate!" Royston snapped back, his own patience waning. "Look, when you draw a bow, slight movements in your body like breathing affect your aim. You can either hold your breath, or tune in to the motion to put your shot where you want it." He gestured to the pendulums. "These didn't have any predictable pattern at first but I think one was forming."

"How is that possible?" John rumbled, "Any mechanism like this ought to have a pattern to it. It can't really be truly random, the mechanism would be too complex."

"John, think about where we are," Royston sighed.

"Oh, yeah... right," Loxley murmured.

"If even one of us could get to the end of the corridor, there must be a kill switch," Geoffrey ventured.

"I don't think so," Royston mused. "Patience is a virtue. Camelot was built on virtue, and Loyalty is also a virtue. We all go, or none of us do."

"But Courage is also a virtue, so is Selflessness," Geoff countered. "If it means getting us through and finishing our quest I'll throw myself at this thing a hundred times."

"Wisdom is also a virtue," John replied. "And if we set Wisdom alongside Patience and Loyalty we get three to two," he finished, proudly.

"Also, Selflessness is a part of Courage," Royston went on. "The Courage to put others before one's self. So really it's three to one."

"You really think that patience is the answer?" Geoffrey sighed.

Royston put a friendly hand on his shoulder. "I know it is. Let go of your frustrations, calm your mind and," here Royston had a flash of inspiration, "wait for the starter's pistol. Think of it like you're in the starting blocks. If you rush on impatiently, you only have to go back and start again."

Geoffrey took a moment to re-evaluate the little squire. "You're smarter than I look, Royston Glasbury," he admitted finally.

And so they waited, and waited. Each man lost in thought about what had been and what was to come until the stone pendulums ground into a rhythm, a perfect wave pattern. Royston rose to his feet and beckoned.

"Now comes courage. We walk, don't run, and don't panic. Stay close and follow me."

Geoffrey and John exchanged a look. Royston's tone brooked no question but that they follow his instruction, a commanding tone the likes of which they had never heard from Royston before.

"By your command, my Lord," Geoffrey threw a mock salute as Royston grinned back at them, sheepishly.

Chapter 21

Ros hurtled toward the far wall, her mind racing. The line was good, but she was falling short and wouldn't make the lip of the opening. Panic started to rise in her chest, her already hammering heart starting to flutter. She gritted her teeth as she flew across the opening and dragged her daggers from their sheaths. As she hit the wall, she tried to find any crack or crevice to jam the blades into, even as the breath was driven from her lungs and her head was sent into a spin by the impact. One of her blades shattered on impact, and she started to slide into the vast, dark gulf beneath her. With a jolt, the second blade caught in a slim crack in the rock and held. Ros grasped the hilt with both hands, and scrabbled desperately with her feet until she found purchase. For a moment she sat there, clinging to the dagger's hilt and panting while her head stopped swimming. She spare a brief glance over her shoulder, first down into the hungry blackness she had so narrowly avoided, and then to Bel who was hanging as far forward as the smooth rock would allow him. "Are you okay?" he called earnestly.

Ros panted. "Yes, but if I never have to do that again, I won't be awfully disappointed."

She looked around at the rock face seeking hand-holds, and a route up the six or so feet to the ledge. Finding nothing, she gritted her teeth and swore. "Looks like I'm going to have to jump!" she called back.

"Take your time and get it right!" Belvarre shouted back.

"Well, shit. I never would have thought of that," Ros mumbled sarcastically. Briefly checking the daggers' hold in the rock face, Ros let the weapon support her weight as she sought higher footholds. Bunching her legs beneath her, she hung from her arms so that she could push off with her legs and pull up at the same time.

"Okay Ros, on the count of three." She took several deep breaths and steeled herself for the jump. With a defiant shout she launched herself upward, dimly realising that the dagger which had saved her life had pulled free at the last minute. Her shout became a startled shriek as she scrambled for the ledge. Her first hand caught but slipped and, as she reached the apex of her jump, she reached out with her other hand and grabbed desperately at the unforgiving stone. Her grip caught and then held. Scrambling and struggling, she pulled herself upward and came to rest, on her back, panting and sweating and swearing her frustrations at the cave roof above her. Eventually she regained her feet and stared back across the gap. "Well, that's me. Your turn!" She called.

"I don't think so," Bel called back. "Look around for a switch or mechanism, even an abandoned rope. There must be something."

Ros sniffed dismissively and glanced about. Sure enough, part of the light emitting crystal was formed in the shape of a hand. Tentatively she placed her hand over the shape and, from both sides, a thin bridge of stone extended, finally meeting in the middle. As Belvarre strode confidently across the gap, Ros muttered her disgust at the unfairness of it all. When he finally arrived at her side she held out a hand, "Come on, hand it over," she demanded.

"What?" Belvarre was genuinely confused.

"One of your daggers. I've lost both of mine and this was your hair-brained scheme. So... give!"

Bel eyed her, then smiled and handed her a dagger. As she took it he held the blade for a moment. "Thank you," he said.

"What for?" Ros asked, her turn to be confused.

"For trusting me," he ventured.

"I wasn't so much trusting you," Ros admitted. "I mean, I want to trust you, and it's that which I'm trusting in. If that makes any sense at all," she finished weakly.

Bel nodded. "Trust in yourself." He was thoughtful for a moment as they walked on. "For surely, if you

273

do not trust your own judgment, how can you trust another?"

"Quite," was all Ros could think to say.

After a time they entered a cavernous room. Here the glowing crystal veins split into a web-work of illumination, tracing through stalactites and revealing that they stood in a dome shaped structure. Even as they glanced around, three familiar figures emerged from another corridor across the broad chamber from them.

Rosalyn breathed a deep sigh of relief as Geoffrey, like a bolt of lightning, crossed the space between them and swept her up in a frantic hug. Pretty soon they were all gathered around clapping shoulders and grinning. Geoffrey released Ros with an embarrassed smile and cleared his throat. "So, any sign of the others?" he asked.

Ros shook her head. "No, and if they had to go through anything like we did, I fear for their safety."

"Then we'd better find them," John rumbled.

"But where do we start?" Royston asked.

"Well, we came from that tunnel," Geoffrey indicated with a wave, "and you came from that one. So where does that leave?"

Belvarre had walked a short distance away, but he called back over his shoulder. "Well, there's always that one."

Ahead of the group, the crystal light illuminated an arch that wouldn't have been out of place in a cathedral. The ceiling soared above them, and their footsteps rang out on the bare stone floor. As they passed under the arch, the lights revealed that the structure of tunnels and caverns they'd encountered so far had ended. Here was a network of chaotic walkways spanning an abyss. Ledges and walkways interlocked and swept past one another at different heights and angles. As the group entered, there was a rumble of deep, foreboding laughter.

"Looking for these?" a harsh voice bellowed, the sound echoing around the cavern.

Rosalyn and her companions scanned around; the space was vast and the voice echoed around, making locating the source difficult. Royston saw them first; Cassie and Brandon knelt at the lip of a precipice, a straight fall into the darkness. Nicholaeos was sprawled on the floor beside them, unconscious. Behind their comrades stood a hulking figure, clad in dark armour and studded with spikes, vicious horns sprouting from his helm. Rosalyn stared at the unearthly figure, the armour was bulky and uneven but the wearer moved with grace and surety. She squinted and pushed her visual augments. Where the crystal light of the cave touched the armour it seemed to writhe in protest, the whole figure seemed like a living oil-slick, comprised of shifting hues of black, purple, blue and gold. He looked like a stain walking free upon the earth, an unholy smear upon creation.

"Who are you, and what are you doing here?" Ros challenged.

"I'm hurt, Essex, you don't recognize your old pal?" the stranger roared. His faceplate withdrew, melting back into the helm. With her augmented vision Ros could just make out, "Sebastian?" she gasped. Gone were his crude visual implants and bulky exo-frame. His features were unmarked, smooth and pale as marble. The armour he wore looked antiquated but, between the black plates, Ros could just make out a glow of purple light. At his hip was a long-sword and in his hand a broad-headed axe.

"What happened to you? You went crazy during the games and then you just disappeared."

Crown laughed, "You still have no idea, Savant. Morgana herself reached out to me."

"You're deluded, Crown!" Geoffrey cried, "Morgana le Fay has been dead for an age!"

"And yet here you are, seeking the self-same wizard who so betrayed her!" foam flecked Sebastian's mouth and venom filled his words. "Well, I accepted, I had the courage to accept her gift of power, and together with the others we will remake this stale, decrepit world into a place without limits or boundaries, where the strong prosper and the mighty are recognised!"

"And the weak are trodden into the ground!" Loxley bellowed. "I know you, Crown, I know your type. No matter how big and shiny you get, you'll always be a bully, always be a coward!"

"A coward, am I?" Crown raged. "At least I have the courage to know when the flock must be thinned!" and with that he picked Cassie up, one giant hand clamped around the back of her neck. With a startled cry, the girl struggled against the giant who meant to toss her into the abyss, but to no avail.

"No!" This desperate cry came from Brandon as he pulled the first weapon he could lay hands on, and jammed it into the knee-joint of Crown's armour. Dark blood sprayed, and Sebastian howled in startled outrage, dropping Cassie to the stone. Reaching down, his massive hand clamped over the young tech's face and drove his head back into unyielding stone once, twice and a third and final time with sickening force. Lifting the limp body high, Crown let out a feral snarl and threw it far to land at Rosalyn's feet.

"Brandon!" Ros screamed, "No!"

But it wasn't the young tech she saw any more. In her mind it was Phillip lying limp and broken on the ground before her. Once again she was powerless to stop the ravages of the unrighteous.

'You could not prevent his death, but you are not powerless to avenge him.'

The thought crept into her mind, and although it wasn't her own, it galvanized her.

Geoffrey watched as Crown smashed Brandon's skull against the rock, frozen for an instant by the mindlessness of the act.

"Crown! Why?" he cried, almost pleading with the deranged giant.

"Because I can, you pathetic prick!" came the bellowed reply.

Ros seemed frozen. Belvarre, Royston and Loxley stood stunned, but Geoffrey was suddenly enraged. With a cry of "Bastard!" fire filled his veins and he launched himself forward, sprinting across the stone and launched himself toward Crown with a mighty thrust of his powerful legs. Sailing through the air, he drew his sword with every intention of beheading the hateful giant where he stood; in truth, Sebastian Crown was even bigger that Geoff remembered. He was faster too. With a triumphant howl, Crown launched himself into the air straight at Geoff and impacted with him, shoulder first. With a gasp of lost breath, Geoffrey went cartwheeling off his intended course and slammed into the rock floor.

Right then, Ros came to her senses. Turning briefly, she addressed her friends.

"John, get Royston to high ground then come get stuck in. Royston, circle round and check on Nick and Cassie and see if Crown's alone. Bel, on me!"

Without even looking, Royston leapt into the air. John thrust out his augmetic arm and, as Royston landed on it, he heaved and Royston pushed off. The little squire sailed up to a rock ledge above the group and took off at a dead run, all the time keeping eyes out for other enemies.

Rosalyn and Belvarre dived forward, trying to engage Crown before he could round on the fallen Geoffrey. Bel swung his shock-sword with a ferocious battle cry, only to have it batted aside by Crown's axe, which he followed with a mailed fist to the face that sent Belvarre sprawling. Rosalyn lashed out with her rapier; the keen blade danced across Crown's armour, but couldn't penetrate the thick, black substance. He turned on her with a derisive sneer, and struck out with his boot. Ros ducked under the blow, but Crown was turning and caught her with an open-handed slap as she regained her stance. She was cast down, shocked and stunned. Since when had Sebastian Crown been so fast and graceful? He was about to land a crushing kick to Ros' head when John Loxley hit him full-on like a battering ram. Crown staggered but recovered, and swept his axe overhead as if to cleave Loxley in two. John brought up his own weapon, and axe and mace met with a sound like thunder.

Loxley held his mace braced like a staff as Crown pushed down with both hands, and then brought his shoulder to the weapon. Leaning hard, he sneered "Guess who's got the leverage now, Ox!"

Loxley strained, sweat beading his brow, but grinned suddenly "You got the leverage, I got the brains!" and he slipped sideways, disengaging, and letting Crown's own effort carry him forward. As his opponent stumbled, John looped the haft of his mace under his opponent's chin. Grabbing both ends, he hauled him up. Crown roared as Loxley tried to choke the life from him, swinging him around into an on-rushing Geoffrey who came in low and planted a devastating somersault kick to Crown's jaw. The giant howled again and, with a mighty heave, threw John forward and onto Geoffrey, the two friends falling to the ground but rolling quickly away.

A rapid trio of arrows peppered Crown's armour but failed to penetrate. He glared up in the direction of Royston who winked at him, and fired a fourth arrow which exploded into a phosphor-bright star as it flew through the air. Sebastian bellowed and clutched at his eyes, and Belvarre took the opportunity to attack. Snarling, he hammered on Crown, blow after savage blow sending blue-white electrical sparks flying.

"No. matter. How much. Power you have!" he screamed between blows, "You will. Always be. An ignorant beast, Sebastian!"

Crown had hunkered down and his shoulders shuddered with each blow. Belvarre took it to be a sign of his impending victory, and he slowed his strikes. It was only then that he realized Crown was laughing. The big brute's hand shot out and clamped around Bel's wrists, pinning them, sword and all. Crown lifted Belvarre until the two were eye-to-eye.

"Look at you," he sneered, "so arrogant, so blind. A proper little daddy's boy. But daddy don't want you no more. Now you're just another poor, pitiful little bastard." And with that, he hurled Belvarre over-arm into the cave wall.

Ros rolled to her feet, but Geoffrey rushed past her. This time, Crown didn't dodge or even move to strike until the last possible second, when he look two long, loping steps forward, and Geoffrey simply crashed into him and dropped, pole-axed to the floor.

More arrows came down from above. Crown growled in frustration and hurled his broad-axe back in return. Royston ducked, but the long, heavy haft caught him across the shoulder and he screamed as bones cracked under the glancing blow.

Catching Loxley's eye, Ros nodded, and John went forward swinging. Crown hadn't had time to pull his sword, so he grabbed for John's wrists, when Ros came hurdling over Loxley's back and planted both feet in Crown's sneering face. Springing back over John, she landed and ducked low, while the bigger squire carried on with another series of measured swings. Again, Crown applied his fearsome bulk and surged forward. He barged Loxley aside and, grabbing Ros by the throat, he drove her into the ground. Startled, Ros couldn't resist the avalanche that was Sebastian Crown, and her senses were dashed aside by the impact.

Crown spared a split second to regard her as she lay on the floor before turning back to Loxley. The big squire was shaking with the adrenaline charging through him. Crown straightened slowly and held his empty hands out. "Let's finish what we started in the ring, eh?"

John looked at Sebastian, then around at his fallen friends. His eyes narrowed, and he dropped his mace with a 'clang!'

"Alright, let's do it," he growled.

Crown grinned evilly. "Fucking idiot," he chuckled and lunged. His black faceplate reformed as his hands clamped around John's head and he landed a savage head-butt. John staggered as Crown followed up, raining blow after blow until his opponent fell to his knees.

"You never really had that killer streak, did you?" he asked the fallen squire as he grabbed a handful of

Loxley's thick, dark hair and hauled him up, so he was half standing but still unable to fully support himself. "Don't worry, I got time now. I'll teach you." And with that, he landed a crushing overhand blow that laid John out on his back.

Pacing like a caged animal, Crown surveyed his fallen victims until he stood over Ros. She could feel his eyes wandering up and down her body as she lay gathering her wits. 'Keep him talking,' she thought, 'He loves to boast, buy time.' drawing a shaky breath she spoke.

"How--- how did you know we were looking for Merlin?"

Sebastian sneered. "What my mistress knows would boggle your mind. She knows who you are for a start. Knows who you are, and where you came from, you over-privileged bitch."

Ros swallowed, "What? But..." She thought, feverishly. What did he mean by that? "How did you find us?"

He actually laughed at that. "You're here to find Merlin, and I'm in the service of Morgana le Fay, so let me give you two answers. First, magic, you dumb bitch, and second, who put Merlin to bed in the first place? My mistress built this tomb!"

"Sebastian?" Ros began, but the corrupted knight cut her off in a furious rage. "Don't call me that! That boy was weak and stupid, and I am so much more! I am Morgana's Black Knight, I am Launde the Black!"

Crown/Launde let his face-plate withdraw and he leaned down, his body pressing over Ros and his rank breath hot in her face. Ros felt her fingers flex.

"They all thought you were the smartest, but here you are, on your back asking dumb fucking questions." He grabbed her then, hauling her body up close to his, pawing at her.

"What would you think were I to say we ditch this armour, and I'll show you what I showed my lady?" he leered. Ros found what she was searching for and wrapped her hand around the hilt.

Sebastian feigned a moment's thought. "Oh yeah, I don't care what you think," he spat and reached for the neck of her tabard, tearing at the material. With a hissed curse, Ros pulled out the simple screwdriver that Brandon had stabbed into the black knight's knee-joint. Shock and pain registered on his face for a moment before she rammed it upward into his groin. He howled and tried to push Ros away, but this time she held him and drew back her weapon once more, jamming it into his eye. He managed to throw her to the ground, then staggered to his feet, sobbing and cursing.

"I'll kill you, Savant! Mark my words, I'm gonna fucking kill you!" and then, with a surge of static, he was gone.

Rosalyn slumped back to the ground as feeling returned to the rest of her body.

Chapter 22

Cassie groaned and sat up. The world spun a little, and her skull ached where the massive knight had held her up by it. She looked around and spied Nicholaeos lying near where she was sat. She tried to stand, but everything started to spin again, so she settled for crawling to her teacher.

"How did someone so big move so fast?" she mused to herself. Reaching Nicholaeos, she checked him quickly. "He overpowered us before we even knew he was there." Gently, she shook the mage by the shoulders until he started to stir. "Eric!" she called out, "Where the hell are you, you useless bird?" With a flutter of wings, the cyber-familiar landed beside her.

"I could make commentary about 'workmen' and 'tools' but now I fear is not the time," he squawked reproachfully. "Where are the others? I thought I saw them." Cassie asked, ignoring him.

Eric hopped to the edge of the outcrop. "Your more martial comrades are currently dusting themselves off down there," he flapped a wing in the direction of Ros and the others. "Some minor injuries, but they will endure." He hopped in the direction of a sudden groan. "Master Glasbury is just behind you. I fear his shoulder is dislocated."

Cassie glanced around, "Where's Brandon? I heard his shouting and then..."

The Raven's wings drooped. "The attacker was going to throw you into the ravine. Master Squires... intervened most bravely upon your behalf. I'm afraid his bravery has cost him dearly."

Cassie stared at the little construct, even as Nicholaeos finally stirred, so that he too heard it when Eric said simply, "Master Brandon is dead."

Royston was pushing himself up on his three functional limbs, and made his way painfully over to them, "It's true. The coward struck him down, but he saved your life."

Cassie looked up at the young man, who looked considerably older for the news he had just imparted, and tears came to her eyes. "No," she whispered.

Geoffrey accepted John's outstretched hand, and allowed himself to be hauled to his feet. He winced at the pains in his body, then winced again when he saw John's bloodied and bruised face. "Thanks," John rumbled, sarcastically.

"What did I hit?" Geoff murmured. "And what hit you?" he grinned. The humour was shallow, but beneath it was brotherly concern, relief at their survival, and regret in the knowledge that one of their number hadn't been so lucky. Geoff stepped past his friend to see where Ros was cradling the body of the tech. Bel was already with her, standing looking down at the body, his features a mask hiding any emotion he felt.

Geoffrey was about to go to her, when Ros laid the body gently to the floor and stood. Wiping tears from her face with her hands, she straightened her shoulders and set to the task.

"Bel, you and John check on Royston and Cassandra. I'm taking Geoffrey and Nicholaeos and we're going to find Merlin and get out of here. Make sure Brandon is ready to move when we get back."

Not too long after (and accompanied by Eric the cyber-raven), the trio left their comrades and headed deeper into the caves. They moved in silence, each one lost in his or her own melancholy until Nicholaeos cleared his throat.

"Lady Rosalyn, I am sorry about Master Squires. It was my fault, I..." Ros cut in before he could finish.

"Don't, don't you dare, Westbrook. The only person to blame for Brandon's death is the son of a bitch who killed him!" The venom in her words convinced Nicholaeos to hold his own counsel for the time being.

It wasn't long before they entered another large, round cavern. As they crossed the threshold, the crystal veins in the walls seemed to flow with light, so that instead of a murky gloom, they were bathed in a blue-white radiance. The floor was patterned with concentric circles, like the sand of a beach as the waves recede. The walls were patterned with carvings and scenes from legend, and a ring of standing stones surrounded a flat-topped dais upon which was, what appeared to be, a carving of an old man.

"Welcome." The word had no source, but appeared in their minds like a stray thought. Geoffrey's hand went to the hilt of his sword, and he glared about the room looking for the source. Nicholaeos (with Eric perched upon his shoulder) cocked a sceptical eyebrow. He held out his arm and Eric hopped down, spreading his wings. Nicholaeos activated the familiar's screen. "Scanning for the frequency and attempting to locate the source," he said levelly.

Ros sighed. "Don't bother. It's coming from him," and she gestured to the figure on the dais.

"Well done, my dear," the thought-voice declared. "Welcome, children. I know that you are fatigued, so if you will release me, we can all return to Camelot, post-haste."

"Merlin?" Nicholaeos breathed.

"Yes dear boy, it is I." The voice sounded quite amused by the young mage's sudden awe. Nicholaeos clasped his hands to his chest and dropped to his knees, causing Eric to clumsily launch himself into the air.

"I hadn't really thought... I, I felt we were going to recover some lost piece of technology or..." he trailed off, dumbfounded.

Ros and Geoffrey traded a guilty look. Though they had shared the goal of the mission with their comrades, they maybe hadn't emphasised it well enough, and they certainly hadn't been specific about the existence of the Lady of the Lake.

"How do we release him?" Nicholaeos voice had taken on a desperate tone.

Ros and Geoff shared another look, but before they could speak, the voice intruded again.

"Yes, it is long past time. Those touched by the Lady lay a hand upon the dais."

"How is that supposed to help?" Geoffrey questioned but he stepped forward anyway.

The voice sounded somewhat impatient when it replied, "The touch of the Lady imparted a key code. A biological algorithm that will undo the matter transmutation that holds me here."

"What Lady?" Nicholaeos rose to his feet, there was a hard note in his voice.

Ros held out her hand to the stone table and replied over her shoulder, "The Lady of the Lake, alright? She resides in a stone cavern beneath Camelot."

"But," the Mage stammered, "I never knew. How could I not know?"

Geoffrey tried to keep his voice steady as he went to lay his hand upon the stone. "Because up until a couple of weeks ago, you were still a junior acolyte, not one of the highest ranking mages left in Camelot's service. Look, we'll get you fully briefed when we get back, heck I'm sure Merlin himself will tell you as we return."

"But Merlin has been encased in stone for centuries," Nicholaeos countered.

"Just because I have been sleeping, doesn't mean I haven't been listening," the voice declared smugly. "Now, release me," he tutted impatiently.

Rosalyn and Geoffrey placed their hands upon the cool stone. At first it seemed as though nothing would happen, until both noticed that the other's flesh had started to glow. It began as a simple fingertip point upon the temple growing in intensity, and then traced a pattern, halfway between Celtic knot work and circuit board pattern down their arms into the hands, which touched the dais where it spread from flesh to stone, crawling across the recumbent figure, and growing steadily brighter until Ros, Geoff and Nick all had to avert their eyes.

They were brought back by a wracking, rattling cough from the table. They opened their eyes to see the 'carving' of an old man sit up in a cloud of fine dust and cough in a less-than-healthy manner. Apparently undeterred by this, he hopped off the stone table, his ragged clothing becoming even more so as he went and, knees trembling, made to scuttle off back down the tunnel.

"Wait!" cried Ros. "Don't you want to take a moment?"

"My dear," he called back in a crackling voice that grew stronger with each syllable. "I've been lain in state for centuries. Another moment's inaction and I fear I will go quite insane."

Watching the retreating figure and how well it embodied the common, mythic image of a 'ragged, maddened, cave-dwelling hermit,' Ros couldn't help but catch Geoffrey's eye and whisper "It's a little late for that."

As they followed behind him, he talked almost constantly. "You have no-idea what it's like to be petrified. It's like being buried alive, and I have done that as well. Of course, Morgana tricked me and took me after Arthur's death, so that Camelot would no longer benefit of my counsel. Well, she meant to punish me for my part in her pains," he huffed a derisive snort. "Her pains! Had she not taken the road of vengeance, but paid heed of a higher calling, she would not have heaped such misfortunes upon herself."

He huffed along for a full three steps grumbling to himself before starting again. "So she turned my body to stone, but allowed my mind to remain, which brings a new definition to the word 'tedium,' I can assure you."

Rosalyn and Geoffrey walked behind the mumbling Merlin with Nicholaeos and Eric in tow. As they followed, they watched his gait grow surer, his posture grow straighter. The rags that had transmuted with him still flaked, cracked and fell from him in strips and pieces, but this didn't seem to concern him at all.

"But the mind is a tool, and there is none finer; I spent an age refining mine, overcoming Morgana's bonds a bit at a time. Given another thousand years, I might have freed myself, but as I chipped away I listened, and I was not disappointed. I heard the first radio broadcast, and I have listened to the majority of wireless broadcasts since, though I confess, that's been rather difficult of late." Here he half turned back to them. "How do you think I know how to speak modern English?"

"Ever heard the term 'Stark-bollock naked'?" Geoffrey mused absently.

Merlin stopped, cocked his head and raised a hand to his chin, feeling the crazed growth there he withdrew it and ran his fingers through the rampant white growth on his head.

"Well that will never do," he mused and, flexing his fingers, he passed them through his hair once more and the ragged mane was gone. In its place was a neat, swept-back cut of salt and pepper grey hair, perfectly styled. He ran a hand across his chin and, to their amazement, his flowing beard became a close cropped goatee and moustache. Even more amazingly he ran his hands then over the stone wall. It flowed and rippled, coming away as a sheet which he swathed himself in, and then cast away, revealing a stone-grey suit which fitted perfectly. The wizard spread his arms and turned on the spot to display his 'tailoring'. "I've waited years to try my hand at Savile Row. What do you think?"

They were astounded. The figure carved in the stone had looked like they'd always imagined the great wizard might, bearded, robed and wise. Then he'd 'awakened,' and he was some scampering mad-man clad in rags. Yet now, mere moments later, here he stood as if he'd stepped out of any high-end legal firm in London.

"I can't take this!" Geoffrey cried, "We've fought and bled and died to get here, and he's more concerned about his wardrobe!" In two quick steps, Geoffrey was on Merlin and shaking him by his lapels; or he would have been.

As he reached toward the wizard, Merlin waved his hand between them and, with a flash of discharged energy, Geoffrey was thrown back.

"Do you doubt me?" Merlin raged, suddenly imposing and not-at-all comical. "You doubt me? Who has walked the world since before the Christ-child? Who helped lay the foundations of Camelot itself?"

Just as suddenly as it had come the anger was gone, replaced by a look of fatherly concern, as Merlin stepped over to Geoffrey and helped the stunned boy to his feet.

"Destiny demands heroes, and heroes must be forged upon the anvil of hardship," he explained. "I can see that your emotions are still raw, so your loss was recent, yes? Within the cave even?" Ros nodded mutely. Merlin dusted Geoffrey down and went on. "Well, then perhaps there is something we can do about that, hmm?"

Cassie was sitting with Brandon's body. It wasn't that she had never seen death. God knew there had been plenty so far on their journey, but she had never been so intimate with it. The others she had seen had been faces, but Brandon had been a colleague, a friend, and she had never before had time to study the difference that death brought. He was so still, so pale, and it diminished him, made him

296

seem smaller. It was as if what had made him Brandon had been wrung out of him, so that he was now... someone else. She knew the stress was making her delusional, but the body next to her might almost not be Brandon, she thought.

When the others returned, they were accompanied by a man who looked like a slick executive, and Cassie began to wonder if she really had gone mad. He made his way over to her and knelt, laying a hand upon the recumbent body's forehead.

"What are you doing? Who are you?" she demanded.

"Merlin the Magician, nice to meet you," the newcomer stated briefly. Cassie stared, open-mouthed.

"What? Were you expecting a shaggy lunatic clad in rags?" he tutted, before standing and beckoning to Ros, Geoffrey and Nicholaeos. When they joined him, he spoke in hushed tones, but Cassie could still hear. "He is not so dead that a resuscitation is impossible, but it is a costly process. He may not be the man you knew before, if it works at all."

Ros traded hesitant, anxious glances with her comrades.

"What are you talking about?" Cassie demanded.

Ros looked to her. "Merlin may be able to restore Brandon, not fully, but to an extent." Cassie could tell Ros was unsure, perhaps she didn't believe it could be done, perhaps her doubts lay deeper.

297

"Where there is energy there is life, and where there is life there is hope. Many of his core cells are still respiring, but that won't last long. I can repair some of the damage, but not all. Whether he recovers all of himself is a slim chance, but it is a chance," Merlin continued.

The small group gathered around Brandon, exchanging more anxious glances.

"No," said Cassie, she stared each of them down in turn. "Why would you even consider it? Brandon wouldn't want this!"

"I doubt he wanted to get his head caved in either," Geoffrey said, sadly.

"But to be returned to life? Possibly brain-damaged?" Here she rounded on Merlin, "that's what you're saying, isn't it?"

"Look, who are we to deny Brandon a second chance?" Ros almost pleaded with the little hacker.

"Who are we to grant it either?" Cassie rose to her feet, her hands balled into fists. "He died to save me! I'd be the first to say 'take it back' if it was for sure. But it was his choice. He could have refused the mission, it was his choice. He could have stayed with the boat, it was His Choice!" she was shouting now and tears filled her eyes. "What he did was brave and honourable, and I wish he hadn't died for it, but he did. He died a hero and you want to bring him back when there's a good chance he'll be..." she stammered and grasped for words, "Less than he was? No, a 'slim chance' isn't good enough. Not when he has a chance to live forever," she almost whispered the last.

"What do you mean?" Ros reached out and laid a hand on her trembling shoulder.

"Brandon told me," Cassie began, "He said he always wanted to be a knight. It was his dream. But without the breeding, he had to play to his strengths, so he studied engineering and became a tech so he could help the knights." She wiped at the tears in her eyes. "What he did, with your help, he would be a hero. Perhaps a posthumous knighthood." She glared at Merlin. "I just, I can't explain it, but I feel it's better."

Ros nodded, "It's not our call to make, Merlin. It's unnatural and I think it's better that we don't..." she choked back a sob, "don't risk it."

Merlin nodded, solemnly. "You're right, there are things in the natural order which should not be challenged. Besides, I couldn't do it anyway."

The friends rounded upon the magician, shocked and angry. "Then why even suggest it!" Geoffrey roared.

"Because you had to learn." Merlin spoke calmly. "Even in circumstances such as these, especially in circumstances such as these. What I can do, what I can teach, it is a tool. It is not an answer."

"You know what?" Geoffrey held up his hands, "I don't even care anymore. Anthony wants you back in

Camelot, and we're charged to get you there, so let's do it and be done." And with that, he stalked off.

Chapter 23

It was dark as they left the fading light of the cave, but someone had built a fire just outside the entrance. The group approached cautiously, silently, but they found only a lone figure poking at the stuttering flames with a stick. White teeth showed against weathered, leathery skin as Asasaq turned to greet them with a smile.

Rosalyn breathed a sigh of relief and went to the old man. She took him up in a fierce hug. After everything that had happened, it just seemed so important he was alive. "It is good to see you, Asasaq," she greeted him. "Though we only left you a short while ago, it seems like an age."

"I can see that much has occurred," he wheezed, trying to disengage himself from Rosalyn's enhanced hug (or even just get his feet back on the ground). With an embarrassed cough, Ros set him back on his feet. It hadn't occurred to her in the elders' tent just how much taller she was than the wise-man.

"How are your people?" she asked softly.

"We have seen worse from the North-men!" the Inuit pounded his fist against his chest and stuck out his chin proudly. "We lost some, but not so many as we might, had you not drawn the 'qualupalik' away. How went your quest? Did you find what you were looking for?"

Rosalyn stared at Merlin for a moment, her expression intense. Finally she sighed and shook her head. "I don't know," she admitted quietly.

While the others sat by the fire, Rosalyn and Asasaq stepped away to speak.

"You carry a great burden and I hear pain in your words. Speak, Rosalyn."

She looked out into the dark skies and counted stars for a minute, collecting her thoughts.

"I don't know if I can keep doing this," she whispered.

"Doing what?" the old Inuk laid a hand on her arm.

"Leading," she shrugged. "We're headed into a war. Not all of us are going to survive. I don't know if I can go on, knowing my decisions might get more of my friends killed."

Asasaq nodded. "None of us can know the future. None can be sure of the choices we make. Some winters ago, the snow was fierce. I advised my people to make camp in a ravine to protect us from the worst of the wind and the cold."

Ros cocked her head questioningly. "That seems wise."

"It did," Asasaq nodded sadly, "until the snow overhang grew so heavy it fell upon two of our yurts and killed a family." He held up a hand to forestall her sympathy.

302

"It was my choice, my decision and my responsibility, but it was not my fault."

"What do you mean?" Ros was very confused.

"I made my best choice upon where we made camp, but I could not foresee the events of that night. I accept the burden of my choice, but I do not find fault in it. Yes, a family died, but the winter itself was out to kill. Your enemies will want to kill too. You cannot predict their every action. Yes, maybe your people will die, and it will be your responsibility, but it will not be your fault. You will not be the one to pull the trigger."

Ros shrugged, "I suppose..."

Asasaq smiled at her. "You have already shouldered the burden. You may set it aside, or you may hand it to another, but you cannot leave it behind."

She gestured toward the group. "Is it even worth it? This man we were sent for, Merlin, he's not like I imagined at all. He's callous and egocentric and..."

Asasaq held up a hand. "He is a powerful spirit-speaker. Power is a burden all of its own. Resisting the temptation of one's own power, especially when others place their expectations upon you, can be wearing."

"And being confined to your own brain for a couple of thousand years can't help either," Ros snorted.

The old man smiled. "You will grow into command," he reassured her. "Until then, carry this."

He removed a carved bone pendant from around his neck. Rosalyn took the delicate piece. It portrayed a dolphin in mid-jump. The edges of the carving were worn smooth with age, but the piece was still vibrant, almost alive to Ros' eyes. "The dolphin is a symbol of wisdom, fellowship and family among my people. I hope its guidance helps you in the times to come."

"Thank you Asasaq," Ros smiled. "For everything. Now we really ought to rest, I want to make the coast tomorrow and get Merlin back to Camelot as soon as possible."

"My people will walk with yours until we reach the coast, and though I remain here, I shall walk with you wherever you might go."

Launde the Black appeared in the great black castle's throne-room, where he collapsed, bleeding red upon red into the thick carpet and surrounded by servants and knights of all kinds. The crowd swiftly parted around him, presenting him directly before his queen. Sat upon a silver throne which dwarfed her slight form and clad in the simplest of silken shifts Morgana raised an amused eyebrow. "Why did you not take yourself first for treatment, my knight?" She knew well his infatuation, his obsession with her, but it entertained her so much to feign ignorance even as she cultivated that hunger.

"I had to... report," Launde panted, dragging himself unsteadily to his knees. "I pray your forgiveness my lady, I failed to secure the wizard."

Morgana threw back her scarlet locks and laughed in surprise. Launde stared at her in confusion as her laughter carried to the high ceiling where the rooms' acoustics twisted it into something dark and feral. Her mirth settled eventually, and she placed a finger to her rich, red lips and grinned impishly.

"Why, my brave knight, I did not send you to abduct Merlin. In fact, you have done much better than I could have anticipated."

Launde, wavering and near unconsciousness from blood-loss, could barely believe what he was hearing, "My lady?" he questioned.

"You have beaten them, shown that they cannot protect those that rely upon them, and it was only through luck that they were able to best you at all." Here she stood up and, like a naughty schoolgirl, pressed her finger again to her lips and batted her eyelashes. "How long will that luck hold, do you think?" she drawled, drunk with the pleasure of it.

"Now," she purred, reaching up to the single silver shoulder-clasp holding her flimsy dress in place. "Let us see to your wounds my knight." As she descended the stairs, her simple dress adorned nothing but the red-carpeted floor.

She was interrupted by Arkady Mountbatten, his hunched frame drifting rapidly across the floor, broadcasting his clear irritation.

"I do not know how you can tolerate this animal's continued failure!" he rasped.

Morgana placed her hand over the seeping wound in Launde's groin, and watched as the dark blood seeped through her fine fingers. "I don't reward failure. He has not failed me."

"Yet he returns here empty handed again!" screeched the old man.

"And what, pray, should he have brought back?"

"The girl! The heretic girl. He was supposed to bring her after we revealed ourselves to Camelot! Instead he pursued his petty vendetta, which I admit got him closer to her, but also got him so brain-addled with sedatives that he forgot to bring her with him!"

The slight, pale woman removed her hand. The wound was closed and Launde breathed deeply and regularly. She rubbed the blood between her fingertips, watching the play of light from the torches on her fingertips.

"As I said, he hasn't. Failed. Me. If you wish to take the matter up with my Black Knight? Do it yourself."

The journey back was far less celebratory than any of them might have anticipated. Cassie spent a great deal of her time in the hold with

Brandon's tools and belongings. Nicholaeos was ensconced with Merlin, listening with rapt attention to everything the old magician might say. Rosalyn, Geoffrey and the others were kept busy taking watches on the bridge, engine room and communications, in case of more insurgents. Between shifts, they largely kept their own counsel in the days following their departure from the island, until Ros walked in on Geoffrey drinking in the mess hall. She was about to turn and leave when, by chance, she put her hand in her pocket and touched the pendant Asasaq had given her. Taking a deep breath, she went to sit opposite Geoff. Though normally cheerful, he simply topped up his glass and stared hard at the liquor, twisting the glass this way and that under the galley lights. After watching him stare at the glass a while Rosalyn reached over, lifted the bottle from his grip and took a long pull.

"So?" She said.

"So" Geoffrey returned, noncommittally.

"What are you thinking?" Ros asked taking another pull and wincing at the harsh aftertaste.

"Right now, I'm thinking a lady shouldn't be swigging whisky from a bottle." Geoffrey managed a slight grin. "It's just a lot to take in. I mean, I know what we were trained for but, after the last real war, I guess I didn't want to believe it could happen in our lifetime. Add in the orcs, the magic, Merlin...it's a lot to take in."

"And Brandon?" Ros said simply.

"It would have been better if Crown had taken one of us. It's what we were bred for." Geoffrey took a long swig from his glass.

"He's going by 'Launde' now, not that it matters." Ros went to the counter and pulled another bottle from the shelf beneath before sitting down. "And he knew what he was doing, he always was a vindictive bastard. 'Show them that they can't protect their own, then that they can't protect themselves' he used to say."

Geoffrey rolled his glass between his hands. "I didn't quite believe it, you know." He couldn't meet her eye as he spoke. "That they'd betrayed us; that they'd turned." There was a long silence before he spoke again. "So many went, were seduced by this dark power. Launde wiped the floor with all of us, and if the others are even half as powerful..."

He rose suddenly and hurled the glass across the mess. It shattered against the bulkhead and sprayed whiskey over the white paint. Geoffrey slumped back into his seat. Ros had already pulled another glass and poured him a generous measure.

"I just didn't want to believe it. How can we win?"

Ros shrugged and gestured with the bottle. "Because we have Merlin?"

Geoff laughed derisively. "Him? I wouldn't get your hopes up. I wouldn't trust that egotistical asshole with a calculator, let alone Camelot."

Ros couldn't help but smirk. The whisky was making her head swim just a little, but her judgment was clear when she said, "We have each other."

Geoffrey clasped his hands together, rested his elbows on the table and pressed his forehead against them. "Is it enough?" he sighed.

Ros placed a hand over his, pulling them away from his face so he could see her expression as she said softly, "It has to be."

He stared at her for a second before his brain visibly 'clicked' and he let out a startled "Wait, what!?"

Now it was Ros' turn to laugh. "Gods you can be dense," she chuckled. "Come on, we can finish this in my berth or yours, your choice."

As they made their way down to the bunks, someone watched them. As they closed the door, he seethed with cold rage and went back to his own room.

As they neared the coast, plumes of smoke could be seen across the horizon. When they docked in Bristol they could see signs of fighting on the docks, and a pall of smoke hung over the city. Baron Dominic was waiting for them in his battle armour. As he removed his helmet they could see that, instead of his usual boisterous nature, he looked grim.

"It is good to see you all." He spoke swiftly and to the point. "A lot has happened in your absence. Follow me to the transport, I'll debrief you on the way."

The group was escorted by armed guards. Ros noticed that Merlin seemed unfazed by the city-scape or the trundling emergency vehicles passing by, and no-one who passed gave him a second look. 'Why should they' she thought, 'He looks like just another dignitary.'

Dominic continued speaking as they walked.

"Shortly after you left, forces wearing the colours of le Fay started... 'Appearing' and attacking targets all over the country. Military bases, factories, but not just sites of strategic interest." His eyes hardened. "They've attacked schools, hospitals, and even a music festival in your absence. We're still no closer to discovering how they appear and disappear, seemingly at will, but all stations are on high alert." He sighed. "Strong as we are, even we cannot keep this up. The strain is beginning to tell." Here he addressed Merlin directly. "I hope you can aid us, my lord."

Merlin waved a hand dismissively, "We shall see," he said calmly.

The big red-maned knight stopped, and turned slowly to face the wizard. Geoffrey could read Dominic well, and knew that his knight was on the verge of a furious outburst.

"And what does that mean, my lord?" He growled the last through gritted teeth.

Merlin turned to face Dominic, though he was more than a head shorter and maybe weighed a quarter of Dominic's unarmoured bulk, there was a tremor in the air around him and, quite suddenly he seemed that much bigger.

"We shall see, sir knight." The wizard's voice was measured, dangerous. "If there is anything left worth aiding."

Dominic scowled but said nothing. "The transport is this way," he gestured toward a number of luxury vehicles, all black with tinted windows. Dominic's C.T.E.E.D. stood near them, flanked by police motorcycles; the convoy's outriders.

Geoffrey, Rosalyn and Belvarre sat in the lead car, Nicholaeos, Cassie and Merlin rode in the car behind them, and Royston and John got in the rearmost vehicle. At a wave from Dominic, now astride his mount, the convoy rolled out toward London. As they drew level with him, Cassie watched as Merlin wound down the electric window and waved regally to Dominic. "Send word forward to Camelot, I would meet with Anthony and the assembled knights as soon as we arrive."

Cassie could feel the knight's anger as he simply nodded his assent. 'This is going to be a long trip' she thought to herself.

Chapter 24

All along the road back to London, they saw signs of Morgana's 'hit and run' tactics. Black smoke hung over every city and most of the towns that flanked the motorway. Regardless the roads were still busy, more-so because of the police and military checkpoints at major junctions. The traffic parted before the convoy and they made good time back to London. The great city was reeling. Armed police, soldiers and reservists were spread throughout the city, guarding any building of strategic significance or large concentrations of the general public. But here and there, Ros and her companions saw the signs. Scorched buildings still smouldering, civil engineers making good unstable structures, the signs above Piccadilly Circus announced a state of emergency instead of their usual commercial advertising, and every newspaper carried a headline about 'The War'. Ros saw police stopping civilians for random searches, and it hit home just how little they knew about their enemy. There was no pattern to the recruitment of the insurgents, anyone could be swayed by a promise of power, and the most dangerous of those were the ones you least expected. 'How many?' she wondered, 'How many, if any, of these people are just awaiting the order?' it was a sobering thought.

Soon she could see the walls of Camelot itself and, despite the various defences the castle boasted, the walls showed signs of detonations. It was clear that RPG's or IED's had impacted the cool white stone, blackening and staining it in places.

As they passed through the security point at the main gate, Ros could see the fatigue on the faces of the guards, the dark circles under their eyes. She could only imagine what they must be going through, standing ready against a foe that could appear and disappear at will, seeing the city torn apart around them, unable to stop it.

The cars crunched over the gravel to the grand hall doors, where King Anthony himself stood waiting. Even as they rolled to a halt, Merlin stepped smoothly out of the car, looking for all the world like some narcissistic industrialist, a stark contrast to his legend as the master of the mystical arts. He strode right past Anthony, barely even acknowledging the monarch and headed straight into the castle, tutting to himself all the way.

Ros saw the surprise on her King's face turn quickly to annoyance. He beckoned her over and she hurried forward and took a knee. He waved her to stand, "Is that..?" he asked tersely, indicating the wizard.

"Yes my liege," Ros answered.

"And he is…" Anthony was at a loss for words.

"Rather difficult, your highness," she finished for him. It quickly dawned upon her that, as much as they needed Merlin to counter Morgana's abilities, they had no idea how to treat him. Powerful as he was, he could act as he wished. Who was going to stop him?

The King set his jaw and, with a frown, beckoned them all to follow, as he turned and headed into the castle, to the Round Table room and the assembled council of knights.

As they filed into the council chamber and took their seats, Merlin was circling the table sneering. "Look at you, Knights of the Round Table! Hah! It's been a hundred years since any of you were truly tested, and look at you. Look at what you've become."

The King settled himself in his seat and steepled his fingers. "And what have we become, my lord wizard?"

Merlin rounded upon the King, "Agents of convenience!" he pointed a triumphant finger. "You are brave when it is convenient. You are just when it is convenient. You are honourable… when it is convenient!" he raged. "I thought I left a brotherhood, a fellowship born of honour, founded in indomitable stone that would carry the virtues I imparted upon Arthur Pendragon for eternity! But it would seem I over-estimated the strength of mortal mettle, because what do I find upon my return but cowering children? Begging me to save them from a legacy of betrayal that I warned against at the time! I find you here, more concerned with your public image, your celebrity status, and your thrice accursed stock portfolio's than you are about standing as a moral example to mankind! That is why this table was born! To bring unity to a divided nation and to serve as an example of just and fair rule to all!"

Ros glanced around. Many of the knights looked crestfallen, some bristled with barely contained anger. Why weren't they challenging him? Why wouldn't any of them stand up in the face of his tirade? And just as suddenly the answer came to her, it was uncertainty. This was the mighty Merlin of legend. They had read the reports she had sent ahead, they were cowed by his apparent power but... it was the cave all over again; a test of courage, of character. Merlin wasn't going to take it on faith that what he saw here was as he had left it, he wanted proof. But still he raged. "How else could the promise of power achieve such effect were it not for the moral decay that your own quests for personal recognition, fame and power had wrought over the bonds of fellowship that ought to unite this table! You are not knights. You are sportsmen, celebrities and industrialists. You should all be ashamed."

Here Rosalyn stood, she cleared her throat and spoke quietly so that every enhanced ear was focused upon her words.

"My teacher, Sir Phillip, was a man of business and a knight. He taught me that, in absence of war, finance was a lesson in strategy, and building a healthy company was of benefit to every community who had dealings with it. His practice's brought prosperity to his employees, his partners, suppliers and distributors and, through them, their families. He accorded himself with honour in all things, and brought the tenets of the table with him for the benefit of those who had not been afforded his station."

A slow clap started after she had finished. It was Merlin. His mocking applause done, he held out a hand toward her. "Such an eloquent speech; your liege taught you well. But who are you to stand in defence of this table?"

Ros was caught off-guard, "What? I don't know what you mean?"

Merlin pressed her, "Who are you, to stand in defence of this table?"

Ros scrabbled for an answer as uncertain glances were cast her way. "I am Rosalyn Taunton-Savant, Knight of Essex."

Merlin swiped a hand to cast that answer away, dismissing it, "WHO ARE YOU?"

She looked around, her eyes pleading with all present for aid. "I don't know what you mean!" she cried. All of a sudden, Merlin rounded upon the King again. "But you do, don't you, your majesty? Did you think I wouldn't notice?" He shoved his hands in his pockets and thrust out his chest in smug satisfaction, "I can smell the stink of it upon her, and you sent her, HER, to retrieve me from the cave."

Ros looked between her King and the wizard. "What does he mean, my lord?" Emotional as her words were, Anthony would not meet her eye.

"I mean," Merlin leered, "That the blood that runs in your veins is the same as that in his, just a much older vintage."

Now it was Anthony's turn to speak. "I had hoped... I wanted to redeem him, redeem his name. There were rumours from the east, and I thought it might be a way to avoid this war. But she came, Morgana came before we were ready."

Ros thought she knew what was coming but she wanted to hear it. "Who am I, my king?"

Anthony let out a deep sigh. "Excalibur held traces of blood from the last foe to die at its blade. I felt, I felt that I could undo the wrongs of the past and avoid a war if..."

"What his majesty is trying to say," Merlin butted in, "Is 'Congratulations! You are a clone of Mordred le

Fay, ne' Pendragon!" He rounded on the King as Ros slumped back into her chair, stunned beyond reason. "What were you thinking? The church forbids the study of flight, a technology that could have unfathomable benefits for mankind, and you say 'okay,' but think it's alright to recreate an entire human being from a genetic code stored in an ancient relic?!"

The wizard paced a circle and ran his hands through his hair. "So here she sits, the scion of your immortal enemy, and you didn't even take responsibility and train her yourself; you handed her off to a peon!"

She didn't even realize she had moved, but Rosalyn was on her feet and her sword sang as she pulled it from her scabbard and pointed it at the obnoxious wizard. "My lord was no simple peon. You dishonour him again and I will end you, regardless of your power."

Merlin actually laughed. "And if I were to strike you down right now, who would stop me?"

The room was silent until a chair scraped and Geoffrey, with steel in his words said, "I would."

More chairs sounded on the stone, some fell over as their occupants rose so quickly. At the last, Anthony himself stood and interposed himself mere inches away from the wizard, the whole table behind him. "You want any one of my knights? You must first best me," he said levelly.

The wizard held up his hands and stepped back from the King.

I had to be sure," he said simply. "I had to know that the table was still strong, still united."

As the riled knights settled, he went down to one knee before the King and spoke, his voice resonating with power so that it shook the very walls.

"I, Merlin, Archmage of the Secret Order, Keeper of the Holy Grail, Merlin of the Two Dragons, do herewith renew my fealty to the line of Arthur Pendragon. To serve the Round Table with all the power I command until my dying breath. I do so swear upon my word and upon my power, your Majesty."

As the assembled knights cheered and whooped. No-one noticed Rosalyn slip out of the room, well... almost no-one.

Rosalyn left the 'briefing' and hurried away down the corridors. She didn't stop until she had passed through a dozen doors and suddenly found herself outside. It was dark and rain was falling. She stood in a large alcove across from one of the vehicle sheds. Although she hadn't exerted herself, her chest was heaving, and as she laid her back to the cool stone wall of the castle her sobs finally escaped her throat. Looking to the sky, she searched the dark clouds for answers. Finding none, she sank to the ground and wrapped her arms around her knees.

Across from her there was a 'click,' and a light sparked in the shadowed alcove. The light glimmered for a second off brass plating before it was extinguished to leave a deep red ember. Master Sidney took a long pull on his cigar and blew out a leisurely cloud of smoke.

Ros watched the small, stocky engineer through red-rimmed eyes.

"All getting a bit much for you?" he asked evenly.

"I... uh, I just found out..." she began hesitantly.

"That you're not who you thought you were?" Sidney finished for her.

"You knew?" she asked.

Sidney took another long pull on his cigar. The cherry end burned brightly and the reflections cast his cerebral plates in a grim light. "Anthony sent me down, something about that windbag Merlin shooting his bloody mouth off and outing you in front of the whole table."

For a moment, simple questions seemed the easiest route. "Why you?"

The tech' chewed at a fingernail before spitting it away. "I'm not just the Master-at-arms here, lass. I served Anthony's father, and I watched him grow up here in these very walls. Since his parents passed, there's not many who know him better."

"So you were...?" Ros let the question hang, unspoken in the air.

"I've been the chief tech here for a long time, girl. I was personally involved, on the tech' side of things at least."

"Why?" Ros implored him, "What was I supposed to be?"

Sidney stepped forward and placed a grubby hand on the knight's shoulder to still the shaking. "Walk with me, lass. We need to run some diagnostics. I'll explain on the way."

Ros wiped her nose on the back of her hand and let the old tech drag her to her feet. She followed him with shuffling, miserable steps.

"Anthony told you there were rumours, right?" Sidney began as they retraced their steps into the castle.

"Yes," Ros muttered.

"Aye, well. He was telling the truth. Rumours of Morgana's continued existence have persisted since the days of the table itself. In fact, several notable faces from history are said to have been Morgana in disguise. Elizabeth Bathory the Blood Countess for one, Joan of Arc, Maid of Orleans, Catherine De Medici, Grace O'Malley the Pirate Queen of Connaught, Madame de Pompadour and a few others. She'd do anything to stir up trouble and strife in Europe, you understand, though she was proper busy in the 16th Century taking revenge on France for the whole 'Joan of Arc' affair. Then she disappears, but our information indicates that she headed out to Russia. Merlin's already filled in a few holes from this point for us. She became Catherine the Great, leading Russia in a vigorous expansion and enlightenment. Seems to me she was kicking back for a bit, consolidating her power-base and gathering her resources."

The technician clapped his hands before continuing. "But enough of the history lesson, time enough for that bollocks later. So, there have been rumours for a long time about Morgana, and then the east went quiet, so Anthony thought we should have a plan besides war, so he asks the Lady of the Lake and they come up with the idea of taking the blood of Mordred from Excalibur and 'resurrecting' him as a peace ambassador." He let that hang for a moment as their paces echoed in the corridor.

"That's why he wouldn't let me touch the Sword in the Stone," she ventured, "because it would have recognised me as a Pendragon."

"Aye," the Master acknowledged, "and, bein' a purer sample, it'd probably have locked him out too."

"So how did it work? How was it done?" Ros couldn't keep the edge of resentment from her voice.

"I'll not lie," Sydney shook his head sadly. "There were failures, a number of failures before we got you." He ran a hand over his bald head. "Anthony was uneasy enough about the process, so we tried to keep it as natural as possible. You were implanted in a volunteer and brought to term the old-fashioned way. You were taught in a secure location with a 'mother' and 'father' who were..." he considered his next words carefully. "Surrogates, for want of a better term. You went to Phillip as soon as it was feasible, but then there were the enhancements." A dark look came across his face.

"Mountbatten, that two-faced, traitorous bastard. He had to be involved of course and it was his idea to fit the cerebral implants to suppress your emotions." He glanced over to gauge her reaction to this but she simply walked beside him.

"He convinced Anthony that by teaching you to work from logic at an early age we could avoid any volatility that might be predisposed by your genetics." He spat the last in a mocking imitation of the old mage. "I called it horse-shit, but he wouldn't relent. Now I see what he was up to."

"And what was that?" Ros asked.

"To keep you malleable. Maybe he thought your loyalties could be swayed with logic at a later date so you'd go with the turn-coats. Looks like Morgana's schedule came forward a bit sooner than he expected, eh?"

"Or maybe he was hoping the realisation of who I am would break me and I'd seek Morgana out myself," Ros almost whispered.

Sydney shot her an uneasy glance. "No chance of that happening though, is there," he stated firmly.

"How do you know that?" she asked, the edge creeping back.

"Because you're more than just a genetic code." the tech' grunted. "Listen, make a sword and what have you got? A piece of steel, no more, no less. But put that sword in the hands of master of the art and it becomes liquid, grace and beauty all wrapped up in a dangerous package."

Ros frowned and looked questioningly at Sydney.

"What I'm saying is the human element won't be denied. You come from Mordred's blood, but you're not Mordred. You got your own life to live, and I've watched you too. You're a true knight, Rosalyn Savant, one of the brightest and best I've seen."

Despite her mood, that brought a small smile to Rosalyn's lips. Through his short, stocky and gruff exterior, she could see that the Master at Arms too, was more than the sum of his parts.

Something that had been nagging at her thoughts throughout the conversation chose this time to march to the front of her thoughts and wave itself guiltily in front of her mind's eye.

"I'm sorry," she said softly, "About Brandon."

Sidney stiffened momentarily, then turned his face away from her. "He knew what he was getting into," he said gruffly.

Ros hung her head. Sidney had been Brandon's master, the loss... she mentally chastised herself for not seeking him out sooner.

"He... he didn't die well, but he did die bravely. It was my fault..." she began.

"Just you stop right there," he said firmly. "The only one to blame is the bastard who killed him. And that's all I'll hear on the matter," he said, and stalked off.

After a moment, Ros followed.

Chapter 25

Geoffrey trod the quiet corridors of Camelot, his mind alight with questions. Even the fact that he now had time to ponder these questions gave him cause to wonder. Merlin, the egotistical old fart, had made a big song and dance about how he had erected a 'biometric electrostatic warding' around the country that would 'catch incoming organic transmissions (such as teleporting soldiers) and scatter their charred remains to the four winds'. He'd set it to broadcasting from the various dishes and antennas maintained by his cult shortly after arriving, so his meeting with the King would not be disturbed (though he had dropped a little line about 'protecting the innocent populace' in as well). Someone had asked how he had known to do this, and the old goat had just chortled and said, 'My dear boy, who do you think taught Morgana teleportation in the first place?' in that condescending tone of his. Geoffrey had watched and taken note at that. There had been a tightness in the wizard's eye, forced levity in his tone. Was it regret? Pain even? But beyond that, Rosalyn?! Was she as Merlin had said, a clone of Mordred? A product of forbidden alchemy, and a direct link to the line of Pendragon? He could barely comprehend the implications. Of course, he had stood in her defence, they were comrades, friends... or had been.

What was that? Why had he thought that? Geoff walked on confused, angry and (though he might not admit it) more than a little scared. He'd been taught to deride Mordred, the man had tried to kill the first King Arthur, tried to tear down Camelot itself and here, now his best friend and the girl he thought he'd fallen in love with was a scion of the very monster he'd been taught to hate. He couldn't think. He needed space, speed and the feel of the wind as his legs carried him wherever they may. Running always helped him think. He was headed for the running track when he was stopped by a familiar voice.

"Wouldn't have thought to find you alone, Geoffrey. Shouldn't you be comforting Lady Rosalyn?"

Belvarre stepped out of a doorway in front of Geoffrey, blocking his path.

"Ros can look after herself. I just need a little time..."
But Bel cut in before he could finish.

"To decide whether or not she's a traitor? Come now Geoff, you don't think I haven't seen that look before? I saw it myself on nearly everyone's face after my father defected. You know who didn't give me that look?"

Geoffrey shook his head.

"Rosalyn, that's who. She didn't label me for my father's treachery, so why should you label her for the treachery of a man who has nothing in common with her but blood?"

Geoffrey knew Belvarre was right, and that galled him. He was being stupid and he knew it, but to have it laid out in flashing neon didn't help, neither did the condescending tone to Bel's words. It was like an echo of the spoilt brat Geoffrey had always known. Taking a deep breath he tried to be reasonable.

"I just need a little time to clear my head Bel, just give me that."

Belvarre sneered at him. "You need time? Her world has just been obliterated and you need time? I'd never have thought you so callous, Geoffrey. Perhaps you're more like me than I thought?"

Geoffrey snarled and rushed Belvarre, pinning him to the wall, "I'm not, I'm nothing like you! I just need some space!"

"And Ros needs her friends by her!" Belvarre spat back. "You were happy enough to go to her on the ship, why not know?"

"What?" Geoffrey was stunned, "What's that to you?" and he shook Bel by his lapels this gave Belvarre some room to bring his legs up and push Geoffrey away across the corridor and into the opposite wall. He charged after, and now it was his turn to pin Geoffrey in place.

"I saw that you took Ros for a little 'victory lap' back on the ship, but now you're what? Ashamed? Sleeping with the enemy, is that how you think of it? You're absurd."

Bel dragged Geoffrey away from the wall and cast him to the floor. Geoffrey bounced to his feet and brought his fists up.

"So you want to do this here? Now?"

"And just what am I doing, Geoffrey? Am I making you angry? Didn't you want anyone to know about your little tryst? Oh, too bad, so sad," Belvarre pouted mockingly.

"You're pushing your luck, Grayson!" Geoffrey shouted.

"So what do you intend to do about it?" Belvarre challenged. "Oh it's all fun and games as long as no-one knew, but now it's an inconvenience, am I right?"

"You're way out of line!" Geoffrey fumed, he could barely hold himself in check.

"Oh, well forgive me for taking offense at your treating Rosalyn like a common whore!" Bel leaned into the insult, and Geoffrey snapped and swung a vicious hook that knocked Belvarre sprawling.

Belvarre stood slowly, and wiped a smear of blood from his split lip. "Alright then," he grinned dangerously, "I accept."

It was only then that Geoff realized; by striking a fellow knight, he had challenged Belvarre to a duel.

Striding purposefully away from his encounter with Geoffrey, a knowing smile on his lips, Belvarre was entirely unprepared when he rounded a corner and nearly walked into Merlin. The wizard leaned against the corridor wall casually smoking a cigarette.

"And what are you doing, young knight?" he inquired.

"None of your business," Belvarre snapped, "And I'm not a knight... yet."

"My inquiry was purely a courtesy, I know what you are doing, but I'm curious as to why? Why would you cause another knight to strike you and thus instigate a duel?"

"And what is it to you, the mighty Merlin?" Bel returned mockingly.

"Because young 'squire,' in all my long life I have learned to observe the minutiae. It's like the theory of the butterfly flapping its wing in Edinburgh and causing a typhoon in the Philippines, only much more complex. I doubt you would comprehend the specifics."

Belvarre glanced back down the corridor. He couldn't go back in case Geoffrey was still there, it would ruin the moment.

"I suppose you won't let me pass unless I tell you?" he asked.

Merlin smiled, "My, my. You *are* perceptive," he said with relish evident in his voice.

Belvarre frowned, weighing up his options. Finally he sighed. "Rosalyn and Geoffrey make an excellent team. If my instincts are correct, and I have no reason to distrust them, their partnership could be of great benefit to Camelot. I wasn't going to allow that to be jeopardized over some idiotic detail of genetics flaunted for all by an overbearing, drama queen of a wizard," he finished with a trite smile.

Merlin inclined his head in acknowledgment of the insult. "But why the duel, and why not simply challenge him yourself?"

Now Belvarre's smile turned cunning "I could not simply sit him down and explain it to him, he can be rather dense. So I have to teach him this lesson in a way that will make it stick. The castle has a healthy grapevine and I am confident it will relish the thought of a duel between myself and Geoffrey with Rosalyn as the catalyst. Given my reputation and a little misinformation from myself, it will be common opinion that I slandered the lady and Geoffrey stood in her defence. My house is dishonoured already, I can bear a little more." Bel had settled into his rhetoric, and was actually enjoying outlining his scheme to someone. "This appearance would not withstand examination if I challenged Geoffrey, he had to be the instigator. Also, as the challenged party, it is my honour to pick the terms and weapons of the duel. I can pick something that poses risk of injury and thus raise the stakes and make the lesson that much more," he chuckled "Pointed."

Merlin was nodding, "But what if you win?"

Belvarre shrugged. "I shall not, but know this. Geoffrey cannot afford to lose, but I shall not let him win easily."

Merlin rose from his relaxed position and flicked his cigarette away, gleefully. "An excellent plan, young man. I laud your effort. I will of course assist, the venture is doomed to fail without my help."

Belvarre gave the wizard an incredulous look but remained silent.

"Once this matter is over, I would like to talk with you further. You seem a driven and honourable young man, and one not overly obsessed with recognition."

Bel kept pace with Merlin as they walked. "I think I've had enough of 'recognition' after my father's betrayal," he growled.

"Excellent," Merlin clapped his hands with glee. "Tell me, what do you know of the Black Knight?"

Belvarre frowned, "Sebastian Crown called himself Morgana's 'Black Knight'. It is in keeping with the villainous heritage of the title."

Merlin laughed, "And thus you display your ignorance. The 'Black Knight' was not evil, he was merely a man who did what was necessary and sought no honour, nor reward for the deed. But that is for later, now! Onward, the game is afoot!"

333

Sidney led Ros into one of the clean white suites which dealt with biometrics and implants. An upright chair in the centre of the room was upholstered in white leather, which didn't quite conceal the numerous Velcro restraint straps attached to it. A couple of friendly faces waited within. Teresa Mulholland beamed at her as she entered the room. Her natural charm filled the room as she swiftly rose to give Ros an enthusiastic hug.

"Rosalyn, my dear. I heard all about it. How awful it must have been!" she sympathized as she broke the hug and held Ros at arm's length, looking her intently up and down. "Just give me the nod and I'll kick that oaf Merlin squarely, and I mean squarely, in the balls, dear!"

Ros smiled back and nodded a quick thank you. Also in the room were Cassie and Eric. Sydney gestured vaguely around. "Given your team's report, this lass has as much experience reading synapse coding as any of the other mages we have left, and I thought if someone were gonna monitor you during the diagnostic, it'd be better if it was someone familiar." Cassie stroked her familiar, and said softly, "I volunteered. Nick's shacked up with Merlin in the 'inner sanctum' for the time being, and I wanted to make myself useful. I thought you could use a friend right now"

334

"Thank you Cassie." Rosalyn allowed herself to be led to the chair where she reclined in the comfortable leather. Teresa brought over a skullcap that trailed a dozen wires, and fitted it over barely perceptible electrodes embedded in Ros's skull. The electrodes were no bigger than pin heads, and most lay hidden beneath her hair, although she bore a pair on each temple that allowed for the diagnostic cap to be easily located during tests such as these. She allowed her mind to wander as Sidney, Teresa and Cassie recorded her synaptic responses to a number of set questions, and compared them to previous tests. The two technicians and the hacker then reviewed Eric's data following the mind-hack, and set a diagnostic routine running to see if there had been any damage to the hardware installed in Rosalyn's brain. She sat there, eyes half closed, listening to the murmur of techno-chatter and the occasional sounds from the diagnostic consoles, and thought about what she'd learned. Did it make a difference? She'd accomplished some extraordinary things in the past few weeks, and the knowledge of her heritage didn't change that. Did it change her? No, she was as she'd ever been, and this little revelation meant nothing to her; her allegiance to Camelot was still unwavering. If anyone chose to take issue with her 'issue,' then she'd allow her actions to speak for themselves.

She was lightly dozing when an exclamation from Teresa started her awake. Glancing at the wall clock, she could see that the techs had worked late into the night and it was approaching morning. Suddenly, Teresa was in front of her with a look of pure excitement on her face.

"Oh my god, Rosalyn, you are not going believe this!" Rosalyn rubbed at sleepy eyes and mumbled "What?"

"Well," Teresa took a deep breath, "I just heard from my friend Janey in housekeeping, who heard from her friend Ronnie in the garage, who got it from Danni in the kitchens..."

"I've just woken up Terri," Ros pressed a finger to her temple. "Give me the short version, please."

"A duel!" Teresa near screamed in delight. "Two knights fighting a duel! Over you!"

Rosalyn jumped to full wakefulness, "Who?" she demanded.

"Geoffrey and Belvarre," Teresa supplied the astounded Ros.

Chapter 26

Geoffrey sat in his cell. The rules for duelling were rigorous, and once word got out about the fight there was nothing he could do about it. He had been taken for a full diagnostic scan and the medics were, even now, doing blood tests to ensure he wasn't on any kind if stimulants. He pondered for a moment how Sebastian had managed to get combat drugs into himself before the wrestling match all those weeks ago. He chuckled at the thought of simply punching Belvarre out at the go, but the memory of the wrestling ring and the rage he'd witnessed sobered him.

He'd had to think hard over who to ask as his second. Of course, he could have asked Ros, had she accepted it would have been proof positive that they were still firm friends, and maybe even ended the duel before it started. But still... He sighed. He couldn't ask her. What if she said no? What if, in his ignorance and selfishness, he really had hurt her? No, he'd failed to stand by his friend when it really mattered, how could he ask her to second him? So he'd asked Royston, and had quickly learned that Royston was seconding Belvarre, which had surprised him. So, finally, he'd turned to John. Loxley had given him a hard time over it, but it was mostly jokes and bluster. They'd sat for a while and talked over what had happened, why the duel was being called, and John had told Geoff the rumours that had quickly surfaced following the challenge.

"But why would Bel allow that to be the record?" he asked. "I was the one being an idiot, and Bel called me on it, he got me to throw the punch. Why would he accept the blame?"

"I dunno, Geoff, but until we know why, I suggest we just keep schtum for the time being." John had a twinkle in his eye as he said it.

"You know something," Geoff ventured. "C'mon John, truth and honesty are part of what it means to be a knight. I can't lie about this."

"You're taking a very shallow view of it there, mate." The big squire lowered his voice conspiratorially. "The truth of the matter is that you and Ros are good for each other, and you stopped being honest with yourself when you let this little revelation about her origins cloud that."

Geoffrey threw his arms up, "You've been talking to Bel!" he cried.

John held a finger to his lips. "Took you long enough," he grinned.

"And Royston?" Geoffrey asked, John just nodded.

"I've been hoodwinked," Geoff pouted.

"All the way, hook, line and sinker," John grinned. "But I'm in agreement with Bel, you dropped the ball and have to pay the piper. We can't allow ourselves to flake on each other, not now, and you need to learn that the hard way it seems. Plus, you've always wanted to test yourself against Bel. Now's your chance."

"But why all this? Why the deception? Why the spectacle?"

"Oh, I wouldn't call it a deception." John put his hands behind his head and relaxed against the wall. "In a minute I'm going to go have a 'chat' with Royston and we're going to agree on longswords, at dawn, first to three blood drawn from the torso. Think of it as a bonding exercise, but instead of you and Bel, you'll be reaffirming the bonds of Camelot. Showing everyone the lengths we ought to go for our brothers and sisters."

"The ends justify the means eh?" Geoff shot, accusingly.

"In this case, most assuredly." John turned to look Geoffrey straight in the eye. "I would've gone to see Ros myself, but she needed to see you and you weren't there for her."

They sat in silence, for a long time it seemed to Geoff, before John clapped his hands together and rose to his feet

"Right, I'm off to see Royston. Hammer out the details, do you want a cuppa when I come back?"

"Well, it's not like I'm going to be sleeping," Geoff grumbled. As John opened the door, Rosalyn was stood poised to knock on it.

"Hi Ros," John greeted her cheerfully.

"Hello John," Ros sounded uncertain and shy, as she returned his greeting. "The official said I could have a few minutes with Geoffrey?"

John nodded and let her in. He gave Geoffrey a stern look as he closed the door, and motioned him to keep his mouth shut.

Geoffrey ran a hand through his hair; though she'd said 'official,' what she meant was 'guard'. A duel was a serious matter, and she would have been searched for any kind of performance enhancing substances. Given the recent expose, Geoff was sure the guard would have been extra 'thorough' in his examination. Ros pushed the door to, and stood there for a moment. "Hey," she said finally.

"Hey," Geoff returned weakly. "Look, I just wanted to..." they said together and stopped, embarrassed.

Geoffrey held up his hand and said, "Please, let me go first? I know it's not how this kind of thing usually goes, but if I don't tell you now I'm probably going to bottle it."

"Okay," Ros said.

Taking a deep breath, Geoff blew it out and rubbed his hands together anxiously. "I'm sorry I wasn't there. I'm sorry I didn't come to see you after the table meeting. It was selfish of me. I should have been there for you."

"From what I'm hearing you were, in a way," Ros said cautiously. "You stood up for me at the table, you challenged Bel to a duel over my honour. From where I stand you've had my interests in mind all along."

"But I should have been there for you in person and I wasn't, and I'm sorry." He stayed staring at the floor for a while until the cot springs bounced, and he realised Ros was now sitting next to him. Her fingers found his chin and raised his eyes to hers.

"I forgive you. For a minute there I was doubting myself, but with a little unexpected help, I was reminded... I'm still me. I'm not any different, but..." she paused. "If I start to doubt myself again, I might need that help."

Geoffrey held her gaze. "You can count on me," he said and meant it.

"So, what are the terms?" Ros asked.

Geoffrey grimaced. "Longswords, three touches, blood drawn from the torso."

Ros hisses a breath through her teeth. "Bel's serious then. That could be very nasty."

"At least it isn't 'to the death', eh?" Geoff winked.

"Try to take it seriously, Geoffrey, and..." Ros leant in close.

Her kiss was short, chaste and lifted Geoffrey from his mood. "Good luck," she said, and hurried out leaving him stunned, but happy. Just then John returned with two steaming cups of tea, to find his friend grinning stupidly.

"All right, lover-boy, that's enough of that," John chided. "Get your head on. Terms are as we said, an hour or two to set up and then we go."

"Why do we have to go through with this, John?" Geoffrey pleaded. "I heard what Bel said, we don't need to hurt one another over this?"

"That's good," John nodded.

"What?" Geoffrey was confused.

"You accept that he's going to hurt you," John said levelly. "Every action has consequence, Geoff, you don't get to walk away from that. At least he's not out to kill you."

"Thanks John, that's very comforting," Geoff shot back, sarcastically, "Why longswords? Why not rapiers or sabres?"

"Why would you even want sabres?" John was shocked. "Trade a quick prod in the ribs for a slicing edge? No thanks."

"If Bel's satisfied with a quick prod in the ribs," Geoff snapped. "This is what he wanted, this is why he

342

drew me into punching him; so he could choose weapons and conditions."

"But it's only one weapon, Geoff, you got an arsenal more. You're fast, smart, and you kick like a mule. This isn't some fancy fencing match, it's a duel. Once you get out there, you fight like your life depends on it, you hear me?"

Geoffrey took a deep breath. "Okay," he sighed.

"Now remember, you go 'enguarde', you touch blades and you go. When you think you've scored a hit, you raise your point and withdraw. The official will verify the hit and you'll go again. If you fake it, or they think you're faking for a breather, they will let Bel score on you and leave it to his discretion how hard he does it. Okay?"

Geoff nodded and shrugged. "And here I thought 'the war' would make my life more interesting."

John punched his friend lightly on the arm, "Hey, with friends like us who needs enemies? Am I right?"

Geoffrey just smiled weakly. After all, Belvarre just wanted to make a point. Didn't he?

The sky was clear and the grass damp with dew. Although still technically summer, the distinct bite of autumn was creeping into the wind. The square for the duel was fenced, dictating the boundaries of retreat for the contest, with chest high white bars. Someone had tastelessly draped a leftover string of bunting from the games around the bar itself.

Geoffrey squinted into the morning sun as his breath misted faintly before him.

"Remember that," John urged. "Get the sun at your back, let it work in your favour."

"Thank you for that very basic lesson in tactics, John," Geoff chided.

"Hey, just 'cause it's Bel doesn't mean the basics aren't important," the big squire growled. "He's reckoned to be one of the best, but that don't mean he's gonna fight all fancy. He's as likely to punch you in the face as the next guy."

"Ah, the grace and decorum of the longsword." Geoffrey rolled his eyes. "Remind me why we don't just beat on each other with iron bars?"

"Because that's mace fighting, and you can still use the pommel for that," John joked. "See cutting, stabbing and bludgeoning. Not to mention the option to kick, punch, gouge and grapple. What's not to like?"

"So reassuring." Geoff shook his head.

"Right, head up and best foot forward. Here we go," John grinned.

Belvarre and Royston were approaching from the other side of the field, and the small group of onlookers was more a reflection of the early hour than the state of emergency currently in force. There were cameras, but there was also Ros. She was accompanied by Cassie and Teresa Mulholland. Sir Dominic was in discussion with Dame Seraphine, but broke off when he saw Geoffrey. He hustled over, his broad frame moving with surprising speed and grace. "I know I didn't come to see you last night, lad," Dominic started, "but we all have our responsibilities these days, haven't we?"

Geoffrey recognized that this was a statement of fact rather than a question. Dominic was annoyed that Geoffrey would bring something like this on himself at a time like this; that much was clear. Geoffrey couldn't explain the situation without revealing the superficial truth of the matter and rendering the whole exercise a farce (not to mention the additional trouble they would all be in for being a part of it). No, he would have to see it through.

"This is my doing sir, my responsibility."

"Well, deal with it, we have bigger matters at hand. Oh, and good luck," he tossed gruffly over his shoulder as he walked away.

John's meaty paw landed heavily on his shoulder and squeezed reassuringly. "You're not about to chicken out and send me in in your place are you?" he asked, jokingly.

"Is that still an option?" Geoff sighed.

"Only if you want me to kick your arse afterward," John grinned. "Right, off we go."

They set off at a sedate walk across the grass, arriving at the same time as Belvarre and Royston. The castle's appointed official (one of the martial arts instructors from the palace guard) stepped forward and addressed both parties in a firm, authoritative voice.

"You are both familiar with the rules of this duel. Bear in mind, this is a contest of honour not a grudge-match. I will hold you both to conduct yourselves accordingly. That said, this contest will continue until honour is satisfied. Am I clear?"

Both combatants nodded their assent and the official turned away to collect the weapons. As he did so, Bel leaned forward and said, just so Geoffrey could hear. "You can't afford to lose."

Geoffrey responded, just for Belvarre's ears, "And you won't 'let' me win."

Belvarre smiled, real pleasure showing in his expression. He even winked at Geoffrey.

Their referee turned back with a long black case in his hands. He opened the case so both men could examine the contents, a pair of steel longswords, identical in length and complimentary in dressing.

Heavy pommels of inlaid enamel had been set with the crest of Camelot. The grips (instead of the more traditional bound leather) were formed of a synthetic rubber compound, textured to improve grip, and designed to absorb blood or sweat so that they

346

would not slip from the combatant's grasp. They were also long enough to be held in one or both hands. One sat discreetly against the dark foam lining the box, black on black. The other a contrast of white, like a lone piano key of polished ivory set in an ebony surround. The cross guard or hilt of each sword was simple, unfussy and without engraving or detail, but flared slightly at the end to lend a striking surface if the wielder chose to employ the weapon as a war-hammer. And finally the blades, each sword fully three feet of polished steel capable of cutting flesh, crushing bone or piercing armour. Geoffrey considered the uniform for this duel as he shrugged off his jacket and handed it to his second.

Black combat boots and trousers and a white Lycra shirt, to make identifying hits that much easier. Both Geoffrey and Belvarre wore sashes with their house coat-of-arms emblazoned at the hip. So much for 'piercing armour,' Geoff thought ruefully.

As the 'offended' party, Belvarre got first choice of weapon. Once again, Geoffrey was reminded of how biased the rules were toward the challenged as opposed to the challenger. Bel let his hand hover over the white hilted sword for just a second, a small smirk on his lips, before taking the black grip firmly in hand and drawing the sword from the case. Geoffrey didn't miss the message, the truth of this matter was between them and them alone. He took up the white

347

hilted sword for the benefit of the audience. He briefly examined the blade, making sure it was straight, though he wouldn't have expected any less. Then he measured the balance and swung the blade around to get a feel for its heft, before bringing it to rest, both hands on the grip with the point aimed to the sky.

They stepped into the ring, accompanied by the referee who turned to address the crowd.

"This duel, to be fought between Geoffrey Mayland of Stafford and Belvarre Grayson of Oxford, over a slight against the honour of Rosalyn Taunton-Savant of Essex. The contest is to three strikes, blood must be drawn from the torso. Any infractions, time wasting or dishonourable conduct will result in a free strike being awarded against the offender." His piece said, the official stepped back and gestured to Geoffrey and Belvarre. Both men came forward, Belvarre pulling on a pair of black gloves. At a signal from the referee, they took their marks and saluted each other, blades held in front of them, points to the sky. The referee drew a short blade from his belt and held it out straight. Bel lowered his blade until it rested across the referee's, and Geoffrey lowered his likewise, touching his sword against his opponent's.

He barely had time to think 'No backing out now,' when the referee raised his blade, separating the swords and the bout was on.

Chapter 27

Belvarre came at Geoffrey hard, his sword describing a shining, overhead arc. Geoffrey had to grip his sword like a staff to counter and push back. Bel rebounded from that, taking his sword around and low toward Geoff's crotch. With a yelp, Geoffrey brought his sword down, but Belvarre dropped to his knees, changing the angle of his sword and thrust forward nearly parting Geoffrey's trousers at the seam.

"What the hell, Bel? Blood from the torso, remember!" Geoffrey cried and tried to push down on his blade to get the sharp sword away from his balls.

Belvarre just laughed and rolled away, taking the offending edge with him. He rolled to his feet and swung his sword hard at head height. Geoffrey countered again, but as their blades collided, a quick flip of the wrists again changed the angle of Bels attack and this thrust cut into Geoffrey's cheek. With a cry of pain Geoffrey pushed back and kicked out at Bel's chest, sending him staggering back. Raising a hand to his cheek he felt the raw cut and the wetness of blood on his fingers.

"God dammit, Belvarre! The torso!" he shouted angrily.

"Nothing to say I can't strike you elsewhere first," Bel shot back and attacked with another overhead swing, but this time he let the weight carry both swords down, turned and stepped into his opponent and brought his elbow up to strike Geoffrey in the other cheek.

Geoffrey fell back, and Bel brought his sword point to rest lightly against his fallen opponent's ribcage. With a slight effort, the steel slid slowly forward, cutting Geoffrey between his second and third rib.

Bel stepped away and let the official come in to confirm the strike. Geoffrey just lay there for a moment. Fast as he was, Belvarre was his equal when it came to combat reflexes. The space for the duel wasn't huge, mobility wasn't so much of an advantage in this ring. He gritted his teeth against the pain in his face and chest and sprang to his feet. The referee had them return to position, held up a hand on Belvarre's side to indicate the score, and raised his sword to start the next round. This time Geoffrey rushed forward, his sword sang as he swung it and Bel had to counter or be cut in half. As he batted Bel's sword away, Geoffrey launched into a somersault kick that threw his opponent to the ground. Regaining his feet, Geoff rushed Belvarre, but Bel had already rolled to his feet. Their swords locked and both struggled for an advantage, until Bel brought a knee up into Geoff's ribs and, grabbing a handful of hair, rammed his face into the rail next to them. Geoff recoiled, staggered and went down to one knee. As Bel attacked again, Geoff used his bunched legs and leapt forward. Swords met and Bel had to struggle to keep his balance as Geoffrey's momentum carried them back. Geoff used his body to hold the swords pinned between them. To give himself a little room to breathe, he head-butted Bel in the nose causing a spray of blood and a hissed curse. This let Geoff free up one of his hands to punch Bel first in the ribs and then in his bloodied nose. As Bel staggered, swearing, from this assault, Geoffrey simply let the weight of his sword rest against Bel's collar bone, and the red bloom against his white shirt was clear for all to see.

Geoff touched at the wound on his ribs while his point was confirmed and breathed deep. It hurt and, given time, it would hamper his movement, but right now with adrenaline pouring through him he could cope. They stood again in the starting position and Belvarre was smirking. Geoffrey knew it was a psychological ploy. Bel wasn't about to just let Geoff win. He wasn't going to make it quick or easy but, by dragging it out, he raised the stakes. Fatigue from blood loss would make them clumsy, and that was a dangerous gamble. Geoff knew he needed to win, but with each passing moment the risk of serious injury increased.

As the swords raised for the third time, Bel started to circle. Geoff had to move to keep Bel in front of him, and so they circled each other. Geoff lashed out with his sword once or twice but Bel just deflected or stepped aside without countering, and his intention became painfully clear. It was a little early for Bel to be counting on Geoff's wounds to slow him but, with his increased metabolism, it was a valid tactic, Geoff realised, and so he attacked in earnest. He swung his sword in a sweeping pattern, letting its own weight carry it through a vicious figure of eight. It was showy, but it gave the blade an incredible amount of momentum. He brought the sword down hard, hoping the force of the blow would let him nick Belvarre even if he blocked it but, at the last minute, Bel turned and let the sword sail past him. Now with his back to Geoffrey, Bel lashed out with an elbow to Geoff's face and, when he staggered back, donkey-kicked at his opponent's knee. The blow connected with a 'crunch' which elicited a true cry of pain from Geoffrey and, reversing his grip on his sword, Belvarre thrust the blade back under his arm. This time it was no glancing blow, no simple flesh wound. The sword sank into Geoffrey's gut just below the rib cage.

Geoffrey fell back to the ground, the steel dripping crimson as it emerged from his body.

Bel swaggered over to Geoff. "Do you yield?" he said, waving the bloodied tip of his sword just at the nape of Geoffrey's neck.

"You know I can't," Geoffrey snarled.

"Yes, yes I do," Bel smirked and turned away.

Geoff's mind raced. Bel was taking away his advantages one at a time. Endurance, speed, mobility. As he struggled to his feet, he grimaced as the knee Bel had kicked protested. The only thing Bel couldn't take was Geoff's wits (not without severing his head, and Geoff was sure that was against the rules) and so he thought hard as they returned to starting positions. He couldn't rely on his leg to carry him to Belvarre, so he'd have to bring Belvarre to him. It was risky, but it was legal. He had to provoke his opponent to attack and there was only one sure way to do that.

Bel was smirking as the ref raised his blade again, but that stopped when Geoff said quietly,

"Daddy's Boy..."

Belvarre's eyes hardened. The smirk faded away. 'Uh oh,' thought Geoffrey.

Cassie winced as she saw the steel bite into Geoffrey's gut. "Why are they doing this again?" she asked Ros.

"I honestly don't know." Ros replied. "I mean, I think I know why they're having the duel, I just don't know why they're punishing each other like this." She shook her head at the brutality on display.

"What do you mean?" Cassie asked.

"They could have used foils and sensors to record the touches, they could have shot at targets. They could have played chess for heaven's sake, but no." Ros gestured toward the steel blades flashing in the morning sun. "Longswords are one of the most brutal weapons available for duelling. They cut, they crush, and you're not limited to using the sword itself. You can kick, punch and use all manner of holds and throws, and it looks like they're going through all of them."

"So, why?" Cassie said again.

Dame Seraphine took a step toward them, "Politics, as ever, is to blame."

"What?" Ros frowned.

"Young Belvarre is in disgrace, his father's treachery leaves him as suspect." She glanced at them to make sure they understood before turning back to the combatants.

"He slandered you to elicit a duel like this, to reaffirm his dedication to the table. I doubt he meant anything by it, but he has to make a public show of standing for the table. If wins or if he loses makes no difference. He has made a show of defending the table and, by his choice of weapon, proven his dedication in doing so. You yourself, Rosalyn, are blameless either way."

"But what if one of them is killed?" Cassie blurted.

Seraphine just shrugged. "That is the price of honour."

"And I believe someone is about to get paid," Ros whispered as the ring of steel sounded out again.

With a snarl, Belvarre leapt at Geoffrey, swinging ferocious strikes as fast and hard as he could. Steel rang out as the blades clashed again and again. Geoffrey parried desperately as Belvarre leant all his weight into the blows. As the sword swept in from the side, Geoff saw his opportunity. He blocked the blade and grabbed Belvarre's hands, dragging him forward. With a quick turn of his body, he brought the pommel of his sword up to smash Belvarre in the jaw. With Belvarre reeling, Geoffrey swung his sword across Bels midriff, but he was too slow. Bel lurched away, out of range and Geoff was hard pressed to parry his next assault. Every stretch and swing was tugging at Geoffrey's wounds. Every time he shifted his weight, his knee protested, and he knew he couldn't keep up the pace, he had to do something soon. Bel came in again, a heavy overhead strike that was sloppy with the fatigue they were both feeling. Again, Bel leant into the strike trying to force Geoff to his knees. So Geoff resisted for a moment, before rabbit punching Bel in his swiftly bruising jaw, then he grabbed Bel's shirt and fell back. Getting his feet under Belvarre, he tossed him over, and fire erupted in his stomach. Bel landed heavily and Geoff felt the impact. Gasping for breath amid the pain in his body, he rolled over as fast as his wounds would allow. Seeing his plan was working, he tugged on his sword, tilting it ever so slightly as it came out from under Belvarre's prone body.

Belvarre cried out and rolled away, but it was too late. A long gash ran down his shoulder blade, bleeding profusely.

"Two all Bel, sure you don't want to call this off?" Geoff panted.

"What's the matter, Geoffrey?" Belvarre shot back, stepping close "Don't have the guts to see it through?" As he spoke he punched Geoffrey in his stomach, right where he'd stabbed him.

Geoff dropped to his knees gasping at the pain, and the official stepped in and pushed Belvarre away.

"Any more conduct like that and I'll call the duel!" he shouted, then turned to Geoffrey. "Sir, are you alright to proceed?" he asked.

Geoffrey raised his head, pale and sweating. "I have to be," he choked out through gritted teeth.

The official nodded, and beckoned for the combatants to return to their marks. Geoffrey swayed to his feet and took shaking steps to the centre of the duelling arena. Belvarre's eyes were dead, emotionless, and his face was set in a grim expression. Blood had streamed from his broken nose and the cut on his collarbone, and the front of his shirt was red. He held one arm close to his body. The gash on his shoulder must be pretty bad, Geoffrey thought. He spared a moment to consider his own wounds. He could barely support himself on his injured knee, and raising his arms pulled at the wounds on his torso, causing his head to swim with pain. His cheeks throbbed, one from the shallow cut and the other from the bruise that was swiftly forming. Still, he managed to bring his sword to rest beside Belvarre's on the official's blade. The sword raised and the final bout was on.

Rosalyn slipped through the watching crowd to John. Still watching the fight, she leaned in close. "Stop this!" she hissed. "You're the second, throw in the towel!"

"I can't," he growled, sparing her a troubled glance. "I mean, I would if I could. But I can't."

"The hell you can't!" Ros spat. "They're killing each other!" She grabbed for the towel in John's meaty hand. "I'll bloody do it!"

With a swiftness she'd never have credited him with before, John whipped the towel around her wrist and

357

pulled her irresistibly until she stood just in front of him and whispered rapidly in her ear.

"This isn't just about you, Ros. It's about Geoff. About living up to his potential, about responsibility and duty. Not just in the face of the enemy, but with your friends too."

Ros gasped as John twisted the towel hard enough to hurt.

"Ask Geoff after, I won't be the one to explain it, but it ain't just for you. It's for all of us." And with that, he released the towel into her hand. She turned to him and saw the look in his eyes. He wasn't happy, he hadn't wanted to hurt her, but there was a steely determination there; she had to understand. She rubbed at her wrist, but held the towel in hand as she turned back to the duel.

Belvarre circled Geoff. Limping, Geoffrey turned to follow his opponent's movements. Quick as a snake, Bel darted in and out, slashing at Geoff, who tried to follow and defend himself as best he could. Again and again, Belvarre attacked, and again and again, Geoffrey tried to counter, but suddenly the blade caught him across his arm. Hot pain flared against the cold steel, and as he recoiled Belvarre pressed in, opening shallow cuts on Geoffrey's arms and then, as Bel circled him like a shark, fire erupted in the thigh above his injured knee. Geoffrey faltered and fell, clutching a hand over his wounded stomach and trying to support himself on his sword but, with a sharp blow to the round pommel, Belvarre knocked it to the ground.

His mind racing, Geoffrey sought for a plan.

"Is this what you want?" He hissed, "Me on my knees? Humiliated and beaten?"

Belvarre faltered in his step. "All I wanted," he whispered so Geoffrey alone would hear, "is for you to be better, better than me and better than you. Be. Better," he finished.

Geoffrey saw something in his face, heard something in his voice and then he understood. It wasn't enough to do his best, not now, he had to go beyond that. For the sake of his friends, for their fallen comrades, for Camelot and the people it protected. He'd fought for his life, but they were in a war for their future. His friends saw something in him, and he had to prove them right.

His mind raced through this as Belvarre drew back to strike the winning blow, and Geoffrey noticed where his friend was standing. Sucking in a breath, he jabbed his fingers into his wound. Pain and adrenaline flooded his system and time slowed down. He saw everything, smelled the morning air, the grass and the blood. He felt the soft breeze and the cold steel of his sword's blade under his hand. It laid in the grass point closest to him and the cross guard away, between Belvarre's feet.

In an adrenaline-fuelled burst, he grabbed the blade in both hands and tugged desperately. The sharp edges bit into his flesh, but the guard caught Belvarre's ankle and, as he shifted his weight, pulled his leg out from under him. Bel toppled, his own sword flying from his grasp up into the air. Geoffrey surged to his feet as Belvarre fell, dropping his own blade and reaching for the tumbling sword as it span in the air and started to descend, point first, toward Bel's chest.

His slick fingers grabbed for the heavy blade and stopped it, barely an inch, from impaling the fallen Belvarre. They shared a brief look, understanding of what had passed. Bel gave the barest of nods; his point was made. Geoffrey winked at him then let the blade slip the last inch. He barely nicked the skin; the official had to lift Belvarre's shirt and swab the spot before he awarded the point, but the shallow cut bled and therefore counted. Calling for the on hand medics, the official awarded the duel.

"It is found in this contest of honour that Sir Geoffrey Mayland of Stafford is in the right. The honour of M'lady Dame Rosalyn Taunton-Savant is upheld."

The duel itself concluded, the cameras switched to their attendant reporters for comments and interviews with the crowd. Geoffrey was being

360

tended by a stern looking medic as Ros came over to him.

"Are you going to tell me what that was about?" she asked softly.

"Oh, y'know." Geoffrey winced at the medics less-than-gentle ministrations. "Beat the bad guy, save the world," He laid a hand on hers, "Get the girl."

She smiled, despite her concern, and took his hand. "And are you ever going to tell me what it was really about?"

He smiled back. "One day. One day I'll tell you everything."

Chapter 28

Launde, Morgana's Black Knight, once Sebastian Crown, watched as his lady stirred her wine with a finger. Amid the debauchery taking place in her throne room, amid the sights and smells of death, decay and unbridled passion, she moved it languidly around and around in the scarlet liquid and then around the rim of the chalice. A clear, sweet note rang out and filled the great hall, cutting through the cheering and singing of drunken warriors, and through the screaming.

The Norse pirates had dared claim they were stronger warriors than her own orc soldiers, and the Queen had heard of it. She had called for their strongest warrior and pitted him against her weakest creation. The contest was a simple one. The orc was to rip the arms off the pirate; all the pirate had to do was keep them.

The misshapen beast had the human's wrists held in each hand, and was simply pulling its arms wide. The Viking screamed and pulled against the monster's great strength, but he was losing. With a sickening crack, one of his arms dislocated, and the screaming took on a high-pitched, desperate quality.

Launde's bloodlust was screaming at him to watch the spectacle, to revel in the pain and the inevitable rending of flesh but, in his cracked and broken mind, every void in his psyche was filled with Her. His Lady, his Queen, and his gaze remained firmly upon her. He saw the glimmer of malicious glee in her eyes, heard the soft and wanton mewling noises she made in anticipation, felt the quickening of her breath as the end drew near.

He watched the light perspiration, brought forth by her twisted desire, as it graced the pale skin between her breasts. She dipped her finger into her wine once more then sucked the ruby liquid languidly from it.

Finally, there was a wet ripping sound, and the desperate screaming became hoarse as the throat it issued from tore itself apart in desperation and fear. The hulking orc tore the pirate's left arm off and dropped the spasming limb to the floor. Morgana shuddered, her eyelids fluttering and waved a hand. Launde glanced quickly at the 'entertainment,' as the man-monster placed its free hand on the screaming Norseman's shoulder and, with barely an effort, tore the right arm off too. A great keening wail arose from the assembled pirates as they fell to their knees, each pledging their loyalty once more to Morgana.

Only Launde witnessed her shiver of release before, all too quickly, a pout of displeasure replaced the smile of her sated passion.

"Well that was over all too quickly," she complained, petulantly.

"M'lady," a sinuous voice crept from the shadows, carrying a tone of disapproval and diminishing patience. "Perhaps it would be wise not to dismember our allies one by one in front of their kin." Launde growled, unreasoning jealousy threatening to overwhelm his senses. A tall, pale figure detached itself from the shadows.

"You forget yourself, Jerome," Morgana reprimanded, playfully. "I do what I will. My servants will know their place, even you." She stretched out across her throne, one leg draping over the arm as she reached out a soft hand toward Duke Grayson. "For what I have given you, you ought to be grateful; like my precious Launde, he knows how to thank me," she giggled and straightened up on her throne. "Besides," she said casually, feigning disinterest, "once they've finished their keening, they shall go and drink and fight, and by morning there will be a new champion. Such wonderfully predictable creatures."

Jerome bowed his head. "As you say m'lady."

"And now I have a task for you. Go with Launde and a few of the others, take a jaunt over to that prissy island and cause some trouble, will you?"

Jerome raised an eyebrow. "To what end m'lady?"

"Now, now," Morgana reprimanded him, softly. "Where would be the fun if I told you all the rules to the game?"

Rosalyn visited Geoffrey and Belvarre every day while they convalesced. With the augmentations to their bodies, it only took a short time for the wounds to heal to the point where physiotherapy could begin. Ros stepped in to help with that too. She tried to pry the truth behind the duel out of them both, but neither one would reveal the details. She was sitting in the corridor one evening, nodding off in her chair, when she fancied she saw Merlin duck into Belvarre's room in the infirmary, but she fell asleep before she could investigate.

As well as her assumed duties in the infirmary, she looked to her own training, and occasionally had sessions with Dame Seraphine, who kept her abreast of developments at 'the front'. That was somewhat of a joke. Without the ability to teleport to and from their targets, the insurgent attacks had tailed off. Now there were only a few attacks, most likely executed by long established terrorist cells, Seraphine said. Scotland Yard's anti-terror unit was hunting them down. That, along with occasional raids by Norse warships (easily turned away by coastal defences) seemed to be all there was to it. In the wider world, things were more desperate.

Extremist cells supported by these ghostly insurgents were striking targets all over Europe and, without the power to do anything about them, the various governments were suffering at the hands of the scared citizenry. Riots had broken out in many major cities and, in more than a few places, martial law was in effect. Their enemy was fighting a guerrilla war using terror, mistrust and chaos as its weapons, and it used them well. Ros had questioned why they didn't strike back. Seraphine had answered her question with one of her own, strike where? All they had was suspicions about their enemy's whereabouts. Without definitive Intel, they couldn't move for fear of making the situation worse. So for now they consolidated their position, restructuring to fill the vacant posts and training in preparation for the moment they could strike. Rosalyn was hardly satisfied by the answer, but she couldn't argue the point either.

The 'consolidation' was the worst part. With Phillip dead and, without any issue of his own, control of the military assets of the House of Essex and its seat at the Round Table fell to Ros. She had spoken with Phillip's wife, Samantha, about the arrangement. It had been an uncomfortable and stilted conversation via video link. The two women had not spoken since Phillip's death, and even before that, Ros had never had much of a relationship with Lady Dubois. She had always felt that there was a touch of jealousy in her, perhaps because of the amount of time Phillip spent personally teaching her.

As the titled Lady of Essex, Samantha Dubois retained the house and civic powers of her title. She also inherited Phillip's business interests; Ros had no claim on them, of course. What she did have claim on were the military assets. As the remaining representative of Camelot in the House of Essex, Ros automatically assumed command upon Phillip's death, until the Table saw fit to replace her.

It was during one of these training exercises that Seraphine asked the question she'd been dreading.

"Have you chosen what to wear?"

"I, uh, I hadn't thought about it," she lied.

Seraphine gave her a piercing glare. "Really?" she said suspiciously. "Your knighting ceremony, to be attended by the King, members of the senior council and the government. You really hadn't thought about it?"

Rosalyn sighed. Of course she'd thought about it. She'd taken Seraphine's offer of mentorship and, although technically a knight in her own right, she was now sworn to the senior knight, so she would be expected to wear Seraphine's colours for the first part of the ceremony.

"But..." Rosalyn took a deep breath. Seraphine's temper was legendary. "I know some use the event

368

of their knighting to dress lavishly and make an impression." Ros cursed herself inwardly, her mouth was running away trying to delay the inevitable, and she had completely forgotten that Seraphine had worn an elaborate recreation of a ball gown from the renaissance period at her own ceremony. Swallowing her embarrassment, she continued. "Given the situation, I had thought to wear my dress uniform, with the House of Essex colours." She braced herself for the tirade.

Instead, Seraphine simply smiled one of her rare smiles, barely there before it was gone, but beautiful nonetheless.

"In honour of Phillip. I approve, though you might have asked me sooner. Have you asked his wife?"

Ros nodded.

"And how did that go?"

"Lady Dubois was most... accommodating." Ros spoke slowly, each word carefully picked.

Seraphine pursed her lips thoughtfully, reading the unspoken meaning behind Rosalyn's statement.

"I'm sure she doesn't really blame you, any more than she blames Camelot for Phillip's death." She spoke softly. "But right now, she wants to blame someone. Someone she can punish, and, unfortunately, right now that's you."

"I understand that," Ros smiled sadly, "I'm that tangible link between him and the Table; I was the

369

thing about Camelot that cost her the most time with him. Training me, educating me, all at the behest of the Table."

"No, not you," Seraphine said. "Duty. Duty often costs us that which we hold most dear."

"What do you mean?" Ros asked, she felt she knew the answer, but right now the conversation was reassuring and she was in need of that.

Seraphine smiled "That young man of yours, Geoffrey. What are your plans there?"

Startled by the sudden change of subject, Ros grasped for an answer. "I hadn't, I don't... well, we have... um. Look on the boat back, I thought we could... but it was just us, and it was so simple but now, with everyone around? And there's a war on... I don't really know what I want." She finished, embarrassed.

Seraphine smiled gently. "It seems complicated, doesn't it? There are a million things to strategize and prepare for, contingencies to be planned in the case of any eventuality, yes?"

Ros let out a great sigh, finally somebody understood!

"Yes, yes that's it exactly!"

Seraphine shook her head. "No."

Ros was confused. "No?"

"No," repeated Seraphine. "If you have feelings for him, go to him, and if he has feelings for you, let that be enough."

Ros was dumbfounded. Words had completely escaped her in the face of such simple advice. The Lady rolled her eyes and tried to explain. "I know it must be hard Rosalyn, harder for you than most. Your emotions were suppressed for so long, you're still learning to deal with them; it's only natural to be wary of their influence." She caught Ros' expression at that, and immediately regretted referring to the girl's suppressed development. "But you have come on wonderfully, and shown yourself more than capable in any arena. Why should love be any different?"

Ros tried to look away. "I'm scared," she whispered, and then quickly, "and I don't have time."

Lady Seraphine took her hand, stood to her full height and looked Ros square in the eye. "And yet, this might be all the time you have," she said seriously. "Your duty to the Table might take you far from him for a time, a long time. It will lead you both into danger, and there is no telling if either of you will survive, so make the most of what you have. You cannot fear to lose what you have never had."

Rosalyn took in her earnestness, her conviction, and made a great leap. "What did you lose?"

Seraphine looked startled, but only for a moment before she concealed it again.

"You are very perceptive, Rosalyn." She was thoughtful for a while. "I lost... a chance. When I was about your age, I knew a young man and we might have..." she sighed. "But I yearned to excel, to prove myself, so I volunteered for every assignment, mission and quest that I could. I dedicated myself to doing my duty. Once I felt I had nothing left to prove, I returned with every intention to pick up where we had left off."

"But?" Ros prompted after a long moment of silence.

"He found someone else, married and moved on," she said, matter-of-factly.

"But didn't he..?" Ros let the question hang.

"Love me?" Seraphine finished for her. "Love isn't always true, and it isn't always exclusive. Sometimes it's convenience, and sometimes it isn't love at all, just infatuation. Yes, we might have had something, but I made my choice. I chose duty."

Ros thought about that for a long time. "Who was he?" she asked finally.

Seraphine shook her head. "I'm not sure I should tell you that."

Ros chuckled, cynically. "Yeah, because there haven't been enough secrets kept from me to date."

Seraphine bridled, and her voice was cold as she replied. "Those secrets were about you, kept from you to protect you. That doesn't give you privileged access to everyone else's lives!"

Ros hung her head "I'm sorry," she said. "You didn't deserve that."

Seraphine turned away and her rigid shoulders sank as she let out a sigh.

"It was Phillip," she almost whispered the words.

"What?" Ros said aghast.

"It was Phillip," Seraphine repeated. "I had a chance at a life with Phillip, but swore myself to my duty. After him, no other man seemed good enough, you know?"

Ros nodded in stunned silence. Seraphine ran a hand through her hair, and suddenly all the angst was gone, her vulnerability cast away with that simple motion and her unshakable calm restored.

"So, shall we talk about what you're going to do with your hair?"

Chapter 29

The knighting ceremony took place in the grand hall, presided over by the King. Banners and bunting dressed the hall, and seats were lined for the guests. The King had personally arranged for a number of well-positioned figures to attend. The Archbishop of Canterbury presided over the oath to King and Country. The Secretary of Defence gave thanks to the new knights on behalf of the people's parliament. But ever conscious of public image, the King had managed the attendees so that the calibre of their station was noticed by anyone watching, but their number was small enough so that the security personnel attending wouldn't draw criticism as a 'misuse of resources in a time of crisis'. Admittedly, the whole ceremony was little more than an exercise. Ros and the others had all been confirmed knights (with the exception of Belvarre) after their return with Merlin, it was just a matter of holding the ceremony for the nation to witness. Everything seemed to move along so quickly, there was little time for the new knights to do much besides smile, shake hands and receive the congratulations of the assembly. The day was an exhausting one, and Ros was glad to get to her bed that night.

The next morning, she was woken by a knocking on her door. Rubbing her head, and muttering bleary curses, she shuffled across the room and opened it. Standing there with a steaming cup in one hand and Eric the raven on her shoulder, Cassie beamed up at the bleary eyed knight. "I'm not a morning person either, but you look horrible," she chirped, cheerfully.

Ros grimaced and gestured to the cup. "That better be for me or I am going to hurt you." Cassie held out the steaming cup with a snicker, Ros took it and stepped back from the door so that her friend could step inside.

"So, I've been dragging up everything I can on the process. Kind of strange they should ask me, but hey, it's all hands on deck at this point." Cassie walked around the room waving her hands as she spoke, her excitement an almost tangible thing. "The defected mages tried to corrupt as much data as they could before they left, but that kind of file retrieval is something of a speciality of mine," she said proudly.

"Along with data encryption, decryption, security infiltration and all the other forms of data-heresy," Ros teased, and took a sip of her coffee. Cassie punched her on the arm, sending Eric flapping to the window ledge. Ros spluttered in protest. "Make me spill this and they'll never find the body."

Cassie pouted theatrically but went on, "So, anyway, after a lot of very complicated processes involving algorithms, data fragment correlations and cross-database referencing, we're ready, and they would like to begin as soon as possible."

Ros sat down with a sigh. "Cassie, what do you make of all this?"

The little hacker frowned, "What do you mean?"

Ros gestured vaguely, "Of this... everything."

Cassie frowned. "You mean the lull? It hasn't been that quiet really. Eric?"

The raven ruffled his feathers. "Insurgent attacks continue on the continent in nearly every major city, and suspected sleeper cells are operating throughout the British Isles. At this point, it seems the enemy wish to destabilise and demoralise without presenting a cohesive target themselves."

"But Sidney said there was word of Morgana in Russia," Ros protested.

"And?" Eric chirped. "Those are legends. Look at it logically, my dear. That nation has kept largely to itself since the last Great War over one hundred years ago, and during which it aided in the defeat of the axis powers. For any country to cross its borders with a military strength on the suspicion that it is secretly ruled by a sorceress who has been alive for more than fifteen centuries is sheer folly. No, the logical thing to do is to bide our time, gather intelligence, and prepare for the true attack."

"Which also means that we should use the time effectively and continue with your programme, Ros," Cassie chipped in.

"It wasn't that long ago that I was, what was it? Oh yes, a 'genetically modified super-freak.' Now you can't wait to see the next step?"

Cassie blushed. "Well, you have to admit, the circumstances at that moment were less than ideal." She closed her eyes briefly. When she opened them Ros was staring at her intently.

"Radio-telepathy," she supplied, sheepishly. "Nicholaeos wanted to know how soon you'd be arriving for your treatment."

"Alright, I give in!" Ros raised her hands in mock surrender. "Just let me get dressed and we'll go."

As they walked, Cassie excitedly explained the procedure Ros was to undergo. "I mean, it's not even invasive," she said, clearly astounded. "Injections every six hours for the next two days, then electro muscular stimulation for another five days, and you're back on your feet!"

"If I come out of the induced coma," Ros observed. Cassie looked momentarily shocked. "I'm just teasing," she reassured. "Remember, I've done this before, so have all the knights."

"Oh, I know the process is thoroughly tested." Cassie didn't sound reassured. "It's the people doing it that I'm concerned about."

Ros stopped and sighed. "Look," she said, laying a hand on Cassie's shoulder. "Nicholaeos is perfectly capable. I know he's never done this as such, but he had some training, and at least a couple of the older masters stayed with us to teach him how." She tried not to let her face betray her thoughts on 'the masters'. In the weeks following the initial attacks, it had been thought that every senior Mage had defected to Morgana's side, leaving only acolytes and apprentices too new to have been turned or without skill enough to make them valuable. More recently, those acolytes and apprentices, in their efforts to rebuild and repurpose what was left of the cult, had located a mere handful of masters still loyal to Camelot. The Mages were ancient, the oldest individual had seen better than three hundred years, or would have seen them if he hadn't dedicated the last half century to some obscure research project deep in the vaults of the Cult's Institute of Learning. The same seemed to apply to each of them; each had devoted themselves to a project they had felt sure would 'revolutionise' something or other, and had stuck at it fanatically for twenty years or more (a lot more, in some cases). Ros didn't want to think of them as senile old crackpots, but they lent themselves to the label very well indeed.

Shaking off the thought, she turned back to Cassie. "And I'm sure the data you reconstructed is accurate, they have that to go on, and Sidney will be assisting. It'll all be fine."

Cassie still looked uncertain.

"Look, I'm going through with this. So are the others. We need to know we can still perform the process, and I'm not taking two days' worth of intramuscular and intra skeletal stimulant injections, not to mention the five days of constant electric shocks to grow my muscles while I'm *conscious*, Thank you so very much."

"Well, when you put it like that..." Cassie sighed.

"If you're going to worry about anyone, worry about Geoffrey. They have to re-lace his bionics during the procedure."

"None of this worries you, does it?" Cassie's question was more of a statement.

"Why should it? I've been having major surgeries and gene-therapy's all my life. By the time I was your age, I'd had most of my cranial implants, my skeleton had been strengthened with stims and titanium lacings, my nervous and immune systems had both been ramped up..." Ros stopped to think of the catalogue of 'improvements' she had submitted to without question. "I guess at least some of those so-called 'treatments' were just monitoring my development. Being a clone and all." She smiled sadly.

"I don't think there's anything wrong with being a clone, Ros." Cassie smiled up at her. "You're a better person that most of the people I've met to date."

"Well, you are a heretic," Ros observed dryly, "so that's not saying much."

Cassie placed a hand melodramatically over her heart, "Me?" she protested, radiating offended innocence, "But I'm a good girl I am."

"You're good, but they still caught you, eventually," Ros sniggered.

With a pout of mock indignation, Cassie folded her arms and strutted down the corridor, but only as far as it took Ros to catch her and set about tickling her. Laughing hard, the two friends chased each other all the way to the surgical suites.

Geoffrey wasn't quite so happy. He stood in one of the prep chambers, dressed only in his boxer shorts, looking at his bionics in the mirror. Baron Dominic leant against the far wall watching his squire.

"I don't know what you're so worried about, we've been doing this for decades now," he growled.

"I know, my Lord," Geoffrey sighed. "But I've had them for a long time."

"And?" Dominic shrugged. "You'll have new ones."

"But how do I know they will work as well? It took me months to get used to these."

"Well then it's a good thing we're not replacing the model, isn't it? You'll just need a bigger set by the time we're done. I'm afraid I don't see where your anxiety is coming from boy. I went through four different frames while I was undergoing enhancement, and each time they had to re-attach it to my skeleton. With screws, mind you. None of that fancy calcamite epoxy, screwed it right to my bones."

"Yes sir," Geoffrey said sullenly.

"Oh, what is it boy? You can't be sentimental about these things, it breeds melancholy, and you know my feelings about melancholy."

"Yes sir, 'Melancholy is only good for poets, and the only appreciated poets are dead poets' sir." Geoffrey thought for a moment. "Everything's changing, Sir. I guess these old Ulysses frames are just the last link to how things were."

The Baron came and laid a heavy hand on Geoffrey's shoulder. "We all feel trepidation in moving on, m'boy," he said reassuringly.

"How do you deal with it?" Geoffrey asked. "The demands on me grow, and I just don't have the confidence I used to. People are relying on me, and I can't say if I think that they should."

"Crisis of faith?" Dominic raised an eyebrow, "After that little display on the duelling field? Now don't tell me that was simply over a girl's honour? Don't tell me at all, I don't want to know. What I do know is you played that situation with all the skill, cunning and bravado I'd have expected of you, and no small amount of guts. It was a proud victory, whatever the cause, and I think you would do well to remember the lessons you learned from it. So, if all else fails my boy, in like Flynn and the devil with the consequences." Dominic's fierce grin was infectious. "So, do we go ahead? Or do we throw caution to the wind, hack off your legs and go fully prosthetic? Your friend John might approve."

Geoffrey stared at his knight a moment before the twinkle in his eyes betrayed the joke.

"I think I shall proceed as planned, my lord," he said.

"Fine, fine." Dominic ushered him on. "Plenty of time to hack 'em off later if you change your mind," he chortled at Geoffrey's outraged protests.

Chapter 30

Very much later, after fever dreams full of shadows, pain and death, the knights awoke to the steady pulse of cardiograms. Ros opened her eyes carefully. The room was hazy, but soon things started to form themselves into recognizable shapes. Royston, John and Geoffrey each lay in beds much like hers. Royston turned to her, already awake, and she saw that much of his face was bandaged. Of course, his cranial targeting array would have had to be replaced. John was still asleep, and he looked strangely uneven with his bionic arm removed. She thought about that for a moment. Her own implants would have been isolated while she was in the induced coma, to protect them from the power surges used to constantly flex and relax her musculature. With his arm, they would have to disconnect it entirely in case the pulses triggered an unforeseen reaction. The limb could lash out and, with its power, injure one of the med staff, or John himself. So there it was, detached and waiting on a trolley nearby. Geoffrey's bed was surrounded by metalwork. He was in full traction, legs swathed in bandages with improbable looking weights keeping them both raised and extended. Despite that, he looked well as he chatted with Royston. When he saw her awake, he waved.

"How are you feeling, Ros?" he called.

She rubbed at her temples. "A little fuzzy, pretty sore, but I'm okay, I think." She reached out for a glass of water on her bedside table. As her hand wrapped around it, she noticed something. She recognised the design. It was a standard medical-bay tumbler, she'd held similar many times before but now... now her hand almost encased the glass as it had never done before. Carefully, she put the object down and inspected her hands. They looked no different, but as she clenched them into fists, she could feel the increased power trembling through her tendons. Throwing back her blankets she swung her legs off the bed.

"I wouldn't do that," Geoffrey cautioned. "The doctor advised we stay in bed."

"That's okay for you," Ros licked her lips and gripped the side of the bed. "You can't get up."

"Oh, that's not fair," Geoff chuckled.

Tall as the medical bed was, her feet now touched the ground quite easily. Steeling herself, she braced her legs and stood. It was a strange feeling. She had been a rangy six feet tall just moments before (in her own perception, thanks to the induced coma). Now, shaky though she was, she was standing an easy seven feet tall, maybe more. There was resistance, so she straightened her back and legs with an effort, too late remembering she was still holding the bed frame for support. The heavy medical bed went over with a crash as she let it go and she staggered forward, legs too long, steps out of sync with what she was expecting. She reached out to the wall, but her hand reached it before she'd expected and glanced across it. With an unladylike curse, she fell to the floor in an ungainly heap. At that moment, the door opened and in walked Nicholaeos. He looked down disapprovingly at Ros and clucked his tongue. "Impatience," he muttered, and shook his head. Rosalyn struggled back to her feet as small hands helped her to sit on a chair. "Well?" she said, "This could take a while to get used to, I was eager to begin."

"Au contraire," Cassie piped up from beside her. She looked to Nicholaeos for a moment until he nodded almost imperceptibly. "This is exactly what we have come to fix."

"There was a problem?" Ros asked, suddenly anxious.

"No problems," Nicholaeos cut in smoothly. "We simply had to wait for the growth enhancers to finish their work, take your final measurements of height, weight and reach, and now we shall upload the corrected data to your cerebral implants and they shall help you adjust to your new... stature. Your armour will help you compensate too."

John was just waking, but all four of them perked to this statement. "Armour?" Royston queried eagerly.

"Of course," Nicholaeos grinned. "Once we had an idea of your final sizes, we assembled the basic frames and began tailoring to suit your individual strengths. You'll have the rest of today to recoup, your individual surgeries are healing well. Tomorrow, once you have assimilated the biometric data updates, there will be some light physical training, and then you will be fitted with your armours." With his part said, Nicholaeos led Cassie around each bed and (with some help from Eric and a data tablet) he made the brief connection with each of them. It was a strange sensation, Ros thought later, as if the world contracted while she grew beyond her skin just for a moment. At first it was dizzying, then the moment passed and her perception snapped back to itself. A couple of orderlies had entered and put right the bed she had overturned. They helped her back into it, but she already felt a greater surety in her movements.

"Excuse me?" Geoffrey motioned Nicholaeos. "When are you going to extract me from this contraption, Nick?"

The junior mage pondered a moment (and Ros noted that he actually did ponder, he stroked his goatee and everything).

"Given your proclivity for japes and shenanigans, I believe it safer for all if we just leave you there," he finally announced in a sombre tone.

Everyone stared, gobsmacked.

"However, given the current situation, I think we can unlimber you in the morning," he grinned.

"What, was that a joke?" Geoff questioned and then beamed. "That WAS a joke! Good on you Nick, you've been far and away too serious lately."

"Someone has to be," the mage quipped and, gesturing for Cassie to follow, they left.

That evening, the group had little to do besides talk. They excitedly discussed the possibilities of what their armours might be capable of, what they hoped would be included, and joked over what ridiculous features would suit each other. Soon enough, however, the discussion turned to more serious topics.

"So why wasn't Bel with us?" Geoffrey asked. "The King gave that whole speech about 'trusting us all until we gave him cause not to' and all that."

"I heard it was Bel's own choice," Royston chimed in. "Declined the King, politely, to his face."

"You're not wrong," John rumbled, "I got the whole story from one of the guards who was there. Bel declined the knighthood, said 'the public wouldn't trust the decision' and he might not be too far from the truth at that. Seems a couple of the tabloid rags have made the Graysons the public face of all the trouble that's been going on. One even claims Duke Jerome is behind it all, vying for the throne."

"That's ludicrous!" Geoffrey spat. "Bel fought as hard as any of us on that quest, he deserves the honour too."

"Aye he does," John said calmly. "But he shows good sense in holding back from it. Looks like he wants to earn it in the public's eyes."

"Well, it's his choice," Royston threw in. "He's changed a lot these past weeks."

"Haven't we all," Ros grinned sadly. In her mind she saw the faces of those she'd lost and the violence she'd witnessed since, but she also thought of the bravery of the friends around her and the sacrifices made. Her sadness was tinged with pride, and she let herself dwell on that a moment.

"They say you can't choose your family," John mused. "I never agreed with that."

"What do you mean?" Geoff asked.

"I never had much of a family, blood and that." John stretched and leaned back with his one arm behind his head. "There were some in the militia who I was close to, but it wasn't until Sir Andrew took me up that I felt I had somethin' even close to family, and now I have you shower to look after. It's almost like havin' kids in a way." He grinned.

"Oh cheers," Geoff chortled, throwing a pillow at the big man.

"My point is," John continued as the laughter died down, "that you can choose, and Jerome chose to keep everything from Bel and leave him behind."

They all thought about that for a moment before Royston chipped in. "Well I'm glad to be back, but I'd like to go home at some point, see my parents... um..." he tailed off as he realized what he'd said, and who he'd said it in front of. "I'm sorry Ros, I didn't..."

"It's okay Royston, I don't begrudge you for having family. It's not like I don't."

"But," Royston began uncomfortably, "But you're a..."

"A clone?" Ros asked and smiled. "Like John said, you can choose your family." She gestured to them all. "I chose you."

"And on that heart-warming revelation, I'm turning in," John announced. "Big day tomorrow."

Royston was staring at her intently. "Thank you," he said quietly, before turning in himself.

Ros sighed and, getting out of her bed, went to sit by Geoffrey.

"So, what happens next?" she asked him.

"We fight, I suppose," he replied and, affecting a jowly monotone went on, "We shall fight them on the beaches, in the fields and in the streets. We shall never surrender!"

Ros chuckled and punched him lightly on the arm. "That's not what I meant, genius. What happens next, y'know... with us?"

Geoffrey's eyes widened in surprise. "Oh, um, well I guess we ought to follow the protocol." He paused, trying to recall the 'Relationship Registration Guidelines' for members of the table.

"There's a few forms to fill in, and we should notify our knights and... our... parents," he tailed off sadly. "I'm sorry Ros," he breathed and raised a hand to her downcast face, cupping her chin and brushing his thumb across her cheek.

Ros shook her head and took a deep breath. "Don't be sorry," she half smiled. "It's a bit of a sticky wicket for sure. Phillip is dead and officially I'm a ward of his house, it's all I can remember. Lady Dubois hasn't responded to my attempts to contact her since we got back from Avalon, and I don't know that I'm ready to approach Seraphine with something this... personal." Even after the Dame's admission about her feelings for Phillip, Ros couldn't help but feel that she would be betraying her former liege. It was ridiculous, she knew that objectively, but it was how she felt. Her loyalty to Phillip remained strong.

"There is another choice," Geoffrey offered quietly. Ros looked at him quizzically.

"It's a little unorthodox... I mean, he has the authority, and technically he's your great to the power of I-don't-know how many great-nephew but, given his position... I don't think anyone would argue." Geoffrey grinned playfully.

"You don't mean..?" Ros hadn't even considered it. "The King?"

"He's a blood relative, and your ultimate liege lord." Geoffrey shrugged. "I kinda think Phillip would approve."

"Maybe," Ros conceded, "maybe..." she rested her head on Geoffrey's chest and fell into an exhausted slumber.

Chapter 31

Launde stalked the corridors of the Norse pirate hulk. The hulking warrior bared his teeth and growled at any knots of the barbarian warriors who stood in his path. It pleased him that they scurried out of his way, bowing their obeisance. The ship stank of blood, sweat and effluence but the reeking corridors didn't trouble him; in fact they sang to him of the impending battle. He licked his lips in anticipation even though they had barely left dock. Soon, he thought to himself; soon he would wet his blades in the flesh of men, those simpering weaklings of Camelot, and they would see how superior he had become. His grin took on a wolfish nature as he recalled Morgana's final words to him and his 'fellow' knights of the Purple Dragon.

"Just cross the water, draw them into a little battle then make it appear as if you are retreating." She had grinned, playfully.

"But my Lady," Lord Grayson had chimed in, solicitously; "if we can take a beach-head then why not press our advantage?"

Irritation had flickered briefly in the sorceress's eyes before she smiled sweetly and took the tall, pale knight's hand. Launde had growled with jealousy.

"My poor, short-sighted Jerome," she had fawned. "Why stretch ourselves logistically by invading them when we can trick them into chasing our warriors back across the seas to a place of our choosing? Once we have their advance force in the trap, we can cut them off, demoralise them, hunt them at our leisure, and destroy them utterly. Won't that be fun?" she pouted impishly.

"But still, my Lady" Jerome had begun. Morgana had struck him with a swiftness and strength that belied her slight, sensuous frame. The warrior was fully twice her height but, for an instant she had towered over him and her hand had struck like a thunderclap, dashing him from his arrogant feet. Then the instant was passed and she was the tiny, playful girl in her simple, pearl-white shift again. Launde had felt his pulse leap in desire for her, for her body, for her power, as Jerome raised a hand to his mouth where blood now trickled from his lips. He had touched the back of his pale hand to the dark fluid and looked at it, then licked it from his hand and run his tongue over his split lip, trembling slightly as one indulging in some forbidden narcotic.

Morgana stepped lightly over to the fallen man and knelt by him. "My poor Jerome, so self-assured, so hungry for power." She took his face in her tiny hand. "So don't forget who gave you your power, and who can take it away so easily," she purred.

"Tossing her head so that her hair flowed like silk over her shoulder, she addressed Launde. "Oh, and take the beast with you. I find its noisome stench displeasing. Try and lose it somewhere along the way will you, my Black Knight?"

Shaking himself from the memory, Launde approached the bow compartment that had been converted to serve as a landing ramp for the hulk. Once civilians had parked their cars on this deck. The hulk was a converted ferry rather than a pleasure liner, but now it was where the barbarians would muster before pouring out onto the beaches once they reached their destination. To the very front, just before the disembarking ramp, was a huge box of crudely-welded steel, and inside something crashed about with tremendous force and wailed with a strange ululating cry as if from many throats at once. Launde strode past the Norse guards who huddled away from the cage, whispering primitive prayers and making dark protective signs each time the sides shuddered from an impact. Placing a hand upon the cool steel wall, Launde murmured softly. "Soon, my brothers, soon."

To the astonishment of the cringing guards, the wailing and shuddering stopped and the creature inside the box subsided.

Ultimately any plans to progress their relationship soon proved moot, as Ros, Geoffrey and their friends were awakened very early the next morning. The lights flickered on without warning as meds and techs flooded the room.

"What time is it?" grumbled Ros as she was shaken awake.

"Time to go, I'm afraid." came a clear, clipped response.

"Nick?" Geoffrey called. Ros was ushered gently away from his bedside as a swarm of staff descended babbling to each other as they worked to disassemble the frames that surrounded his legs. Rosalyn detected an air of urgency to their movements and discussion, as tools were passed back and forth and scans were run and read aloud. A couple of techs had John sitting up and were calibrating his arm before reattachment (the limb could apparently resize itself due a series of interlocking plates built into it by the Master at Arms in anticipation of this day).

"Time to go to work," Nicholaeos spoke crisply. "A pirate fleet has appeared on our long range alert systems. It appears it has put out from Grimstad and, if it continues on course, will reach somewhere near Great Yarmouth in approximately twelve hours."

"Why so long?" Ros questioned, suspiciously.

"You haven't heard the shipping forecast." The acolyte half smiled. "The weather out there is awful, they must be mad."

"Or hoping that the conditions interfere with our detection systems," Royston chimed in, as his head poked up out of the shirt he was wriggling into.

"Indeed," Nicholaeos agreed. "Whatever the reason, it is all hands on deck. The King has commanded all able-bodied knights to arms and, at my recommendation, that includes you lot."

With a clatter of discarded metalwork, Geoffrey sat up and swung his legs over the side of his bed. "So, you think we're ready?"

"The enemy is finally on our doorstep, Sir Geoffrey. Would you ever have forgiven me had I not vouched your readiness to his majesty?"

Geoff winked at him, "Probably not, and Nick... thanks." he said.

"What for?" queried the mage.

"For calling me 'Sir Geoffrey'. You're the first person to call me that since the ceremony," he grinned. After that, there wasn't much time for words as the newest knights of Camelot were dragged out of their recovery beds and marched through the corridors of the castle, headed once more for the technical bays. This time they knew they weren't going to be the ones fitting the armour, but the ones to be fitted.

Dominic was waiting for Geoffrey in the armoury halls as he was led by the techs, still trailing wires that connected him to their handheld biometric data readers. It was strange for the young knight; the last time he'd seen his liege-lord, the red-haired giant had towered above him. Dominic was still broad, and there was no doubt in Geoff's mind that his erstwhile knight could still snap him in two given the inclination but... now? Geoffrey almost stared the Baron in the eye.

"I always knew you'd be tall," Dominic chortled before vigorously shoo-ing most of the attending technicians away. "So, today's the day," he mused aloud, as he led Geoffrey toward one of two arming stations marked with the red upon yellow chevron of Stafford. The curtains were drawn over the opening and the arched entrance was etched with the motto "The Knot Unites." Geoffrey was given pause to think of all the ties he'd made recently, ties that had been tested and forged and strengthened, and the ties that had been broken or severed. Dominic must have caught his maudlin expression because he elbowed the younger man in the ribs conspiratorially and winked at him.

"Do you want to see it?" the big man growled jovially. Geoff's breath caught in his throat. He'd helped Dominic don his own armour many times, and the battered and cumbersome result looked more suited to loading crates in a warehouse or working on a construction site, except for the fact that it bristled with weaponry and bore the scars and honour markings of combat over nearly every inch of its armoured hide. On the assumption that Geoffrey wouldn't attain knighthood for at least another two years, any discussions about his own suit had been passing and purely hypothetical. Geoff knew for a fact that Dominic always favoured function over form, and that's why his armour more closely resembled a forklift or a tank than anything else. He closed his eyes and breathed, not wanting to show his inevitable disappointment to the man who had essentially raised him from an early age.

"Surprise!" Dominic bellowed as the young knight tentatively opened his eyes.

Dame Seraphine was standing at parade-ground rest outside the bay marked 'Essex' as Ros approached and adopted a similar stance. Without a word, Rosalyn snapped to attention, head high and chest out. Seraphine walked a slow circle around her, studying her like a prized stud horse, occasionally muttering to herself. When she'd passed a full circle she stood in front of Ros and once again they looked each other straight in the eye.

"You've turned out beautifully, Savant," she beamed genuinely. "Much like your armour."

Ros moved to draw the curtain, but the Dame held out a hand to stop her. "First, read this," she said, and with her other hand, gave Ros an envelope marked with the Essex crest. Not really understanding, Ros opened the envelope and drew out the note inside and read;

Dear Rosalyn,

I know we have not ever been much to each other, less so since Phillip was killed, and I know now that was my fault alone.

Phillip left a suggestion in his will (in the case should he pass prematurely to your graduating to knighthood) and it is this that has caused me to think deeply about what I have, and what more I may have had, had I but been open to the possibility, and so I choose to agree with this option of his will.

Rather than have his arms and armour interred in memoriam here at the hall of Essex, I have had them sent to Camelot to be refitted for your personal use. Phillip wished, and so now do I, that they honour his memory by serving and protecting you.

You came to us a ward, but I never allowed you to become that which we could not have; a daughter.

Once this service is over I beseech you, Rosalyn, to come home to Essex and to forgive me my follies. I know I cannot undo the past but I hope we can reconcile to some extent in the future.

Wear our colours well.

402

Yours in hope
        Lady Samantha Christian-Dubois,
        Countess of Exeter

Rosalyn choked back a tear as she finished the letter before closing her eyes, smiling, and pressing the paper to her chest. Seraphine was pointedly looking away, but cleared her throat when she noted that Ros had finished reading. "Let's get on with this, shall we?" The senior knight beckoned in a pair of techs to draw back the curtains, revealing the red colossus that Ros recalled so well. Although, looking at it critically, she noted the changes to its form. The plate's still gleamed ruby red with the emblazoned gold seaxes across the chest, but the suit was trimmer, more slender.

"All the original systems are still in place," the techs notified her. "The command grade sensors and comms unit are still fitted, but we've added a number of new systems in light of recent events." A screen on the wall showed a wire-frame schematic of the suit, and the technician manipulated this to indicate the new additions and how they were accessed from within the suit. "We have integrated a standard assault rifle to the forearm, a 7.62 Enfield carbine, magazine fed, so you still have to change those, but it avoids problems with complicated feed-systems jamming, and it won't compromise your mobility. A kill-cam under the barrel feeds into your helmets visual display for the purposes of aiming." A few taps, and a new area of the armour schematic came up. "We mounted grenade tubes in the shoulders for concussion and fragmentation grenades. You also have red and green smoke should you need it, and one last thing." An exploded diagram of the helmet flashed up. "After what your team reported of the 'Techno-shaman' on the Norse hulk, we've developed this." He indicated a small collection of components on the diagram. "This system links to and buffers your cranial comms unit. Should you feel any interference or adverse effects, this unit can be activated to isolate the frequency, whether it's microwave, radio or any common wave-form transmission, and quickly transmit a disruption signal to disperse the culprit."

"Disperse the culprit?" Ros questioned, "Odd choice of words."

"Not really," the tech offered. "If the origin source is within transmitting range of your suits emitter, then the disruption wave will naturally create sympathetic vibrations in whatever is creating the signal, and then that equipment will overload or shake itself apart as a consequence."

Rosalyn grinned, "Serves them right 'eh?"

"Indeed," the tech commented.

Rosalyn spared a moment to take in the soft lines of the construct before her. "She's beautiful," she said finally. "Okay boys, strap me in!"

Geoffrey gasped in astonishment. The golden yellow armour standing before him was... amazing. He walked around it in stunned silence, noting the graceful appearance and shining paintwork. The shoulder plates sported two sleek fins. "Stabilisers," Dominic commented, "for controlling your jump trajectory."

"Lift jets?" Geoffrey questioned in astonishment, letting his eyes drop to the ever-so-slightly flared lower leg armours. On each limb, the red chevron of the house crest had been reworked so that stylish lightning flashes followed the contours of the armour.

"Aye," rumbled the baron. "And the compensators built into the legwork will compliment your new Ulysses frames for unaided jumps." The older man stepped forward, indicating different features built into the suit. "Nine millimetre submachine guns in each forearm to keep it balanced and reduce weight. Grenades deploy from the chest and upper arms, so you can drop them at the apex. You even have limited counter measures for dealing with RPG's and guided missiles. The operating system is a work of art in itself, ramped up to complement your increased processing ability. The duralloy shell hasn't reduced the speed at all. The micro servo's should to allow you to add twenty five percent on your top speed." For the first time ever, Geoffrey saw Dominic look pensive. "I had the design work done by one of those sports car boys, works for Jaguar, I think. Do you like it?" the baron asked, wringing his massive hands.

Geoffrey regarded the man carefully, thinking back on John's words about 'choosing your family'. Dominic had never denied Geoffrey a visit to or from his own parents, in fact, they were close friends, and it was part of why Geoff had come to squire in the house of Stafford. Dominic was not just his mentor; he had become a surrogate father figure, like a favourite uncle. Sometimes stern and occasionally critical, but always encouraging him to do better, to be better. 'Yes' thought Geoffrey, Dominic was family. He turned to his Knight with a huge and genuine grin. "It's fantastic," he offered, near dumbstruck. "I can't wait to see how she drives."

Dominic grinned briefly, his eyes glittering at the approval, but quickly hid the expression with his usual good-natured bluster. "Well, you won't find a better chance. There's some bastards coming looking for a good hiding. Are you ready to give it to them, boy?"

"Ready, willing and able Sir!" Geoffrey snapped to attention and saluted, "Willing and able."

Chapter 32

Belvarre waited just out of sight of the main garage. He waited with his motorcycle as he'd been instructed. From here, though he himself was mostly hidden, he could watch his friends as they emerged on their new transports. He recognised each of them by their house colours. Rosalyn with the Golden Seaxes on red mounted atop Earl Phillip's own fifth generation C.T.E.E.D. if Belvarre wasn't very much mistaken. Inwardly, he was pleased. Phillip had been rich enough to afford the best from Bellerophon Cybernetics Industries 'Alpha line', and generous enough to make arrangements to pass it on in the event of his untimely death; good. In Bel's opinion, no-one deserved the gen five 'Stalwart' model more than Ros. If memory served, the creature was designated 'Ajax', after the hero of legend. Geoffrey followed her, riding next to Baron Dominic who escorted the new knights, both in the yellow and red heraldic colours of Stafford. It was an education in opposites. Dominic's' armour and mount were bulky, hard lines and angles of thick armour on frames as broad as they were tall gave him a passable resemblance to a battle tank, a resemblance affirmed by the battle scars his armour and mount wore as badges of honour. In complete contrast to the baron and his battered, yet sturdy third gen 'Draught Horse' mount, Geoffrey and his fourth gen looked almost prepared to take flight. The mount even sported a spoiler across its haunches, a rarity among C.T.E.E.D.s but a clear indicator of the speed the construct was capable of. The cybernetic beast skittered and Bel humoured himself considering the A.I.'s impatience to run fast and free. Geoffrey himself looked gleaming and resplendent with the stubby fins on his shoulders raised in preparation to account for just such a jaunt.

Behind them. Royston and John Loxley rode in their new armours. Glasbury was still dwarfed by his fellows. From this distance he looked like a child riding a pony next to adults on horseback, but Bel wasn't fooled. Even before this last stage of the augmentation process, Royston had been strong for his size, the bows he'd used in competition had been fully two-hundred pounds at full draw. Bel eyed the compound bow attached to Royston's weapons harness; now maybe three-hundred, three hundred and fifty? His own augmetic sight (not so refined as the 'little' knights' but still respectable) shifted to the quiver hanging on the other side from the bow. At a guess, Bel would assume the arrows were a selection of flechette, high explosive and maybe depleted uranium tips, maybe combinations of the three. That

408

would give Royston varied options against personnel and lightly or even heavily armoured targets that would far exceed the capabilities of most anti-materiel rifles. His armour itself was quite basic, no turned edges or flamboyant touches which might catch the string of his bow. It was functional and smooth. If it wasn't for the blue, white and grey design of Tonbridge emblazoned across his chest, Bel would have postulated that the armour itself was designed to encourage anonymity. Looking over him at the hulking form of John Loxley, Bel stifled a smirk. As a play on his nickname, his C.T.E.E.D resembled not a horse, but some kind of oxen with hunched shoulders a short, low hung neck and even horns on either side of its head. Belvarre was sure it was a custom job from top to bottom and worth a great deal of money at that. His smirk turned to a rueful sigh as, looking to John himself he spotted the cannon gracing his friends shoulder. The barrel turned in tandem with John's head, it's targeting systems slaved to his helmet movements and, Bel allowed, it wasn't a cannon as such but one of Durham Munitions Systems latest 40mm automatic grenade launchers. There were many among the table who would question the 'honour' of such a weapon but few, saving the oldest current knights, had seen anything like real warfare, and with his own experiences Bel was certain they would soon adopt

409

such weapons themselves. The 'launcher had been left black so it stood out against the George Cross motif of the Yorkish coat of arms. The gold lions that adorned the cross itself were raised reliefs on the design that repeated over the larger areas like the chest and shins, but not on Johns prosthetic arm. That copper bound and cream coloured limb, rather than be fully encased was supplemented with ablative plates that mag-locked directly to his bionic limb.

Watching them pass him by and head toward the muster for the task force, he smiled sadly. He longed to accompany them, but he also stood by what he'd told the King. The public still held him responsible for the actions of his father and the traitorous element at large, guilty by association. He cast his gaze once more over the suits of armour, the symbol of everything he had hoped to achieve and then down at his own garments. He wasn't wearing armour of any sort, not even a surcoat with the Oxford coat of arms on it. He was dressed in a simple black suit. Reaching into his pocket he pulled out his sunglasses and put them on. He looked like the bored bodyguard of some up and coming celebrity which, to be fair, he was. Shortly after his 'discussion' with Merlin and the duel with Geoffrey, he had been notified of his new appointment as 'liaison' to the great wizard. He was to aid and, should it be called for, protect Merlin whenever the need should arise. In reality the whole situation had been engineered to free him from any other duties and put him at the beck and call of the irascible old man. No sooner had he thought about the wizard, Merlin himself hove into view. As a stark reminder of the wizard's erratic mental state Bel noted that, despite the somewhat murky weather, he had dressed not unlike one of the rebellious up and coming celebri-brats Belvarre had just been considering. With a gaudy sports jersey, striped flat-cap and various gold chains, bracelets and a chunky jewel-studded watch, the bearded old mage strode jauntily up to Bel where he waited with his motorbike.

"Try not to draw too much attention," the young squire muttered sarcastically.

"You underestimate the amount of freedom an egotistical drama-queen persona can allow a fellow," the wizard shot back.

"Just remember that you said that, not me," Belvarre returned smugly. "Still, Merlin. Those clothes," he sneered disdainfully. The grand wizard affected an offended air and flicked his wrist dismissively "Hellooo, you weren't locked in a cave for near two thousand years. How do you expect me to appreciate modern culture if I don't experience it properly?" Belvarre just gawped, completely at a loss for words. "Well, I'm glad we sorted that out." Merlin smiled condescendingly. "Now, to the matter at hand." Reaching into the pocket of his eye-searingly bright tracksuit bottoms he pulled out a leather pouch on a neck thong, opening the pouch he tipped two small, ebony amulets into his hand. "Take good care of these," he spoke seriously now. "One is for you, the other for your bike, just slap it onto the tank to activate that one and place the other around your neck."

Belvarre nodded, "And they will do just what you claim?"

Merlin smiled evilly. "You'll have to take my word for it."

"How?" Bel questioned casually.

The wizard raised his hands, fingers spread wide. "Magic!" he replied, "Once you are in position observe what occurs. If you feel it necessary, then you may intervene. Who knows, before we are done you may restore your honour."

"Or die trying," Belvarre finished.

Merlin closed his hand over the amulets. "I do hope not, such heroics are so tiresome." At Belvarre's shocked expression, Merlin sighed deeply and explained. "Do what you can but you can always do more if you are alive. No matter how noble the death, a dead hero is of no use to anyone. Unless you have no other recourse, of course." The wizard proffered the items again, "Understood?"

"I understand," Belvarre replied, then his brow wrinkled thoughtfully. "Why aren't you coming again?"

Merlin made a show of inspecting his fingernails, "Oh, this is just Morgana letting her dogs off the leash a bit, she won't be there so why should I?"

Belvarre looked sceptical, "Really?"

The wizard sighed theatrically. "It is as I explained in the cave. What I can do should be considered a tool, not a crutch. I have every confidence that Camelot will repulse this attack, and the confidence that will grant them has a value in and of itself, so long as that confidence is tempered with the proper wisdom," he concluded, indicating himself with a sweeping gesture. "Now, off with you. You must make it to the landing area in good time and bypass the security checkpoints. Go!"

Belvarre nodded, pocketed the pouch and leapt onto his motorcycle, speeding off with a screech of tires and a roar of its powerful engine.

Merlin sighed. "Drama queen," he grinned to himself.

By the time the task force reached Great Yarmouth preparations were already well underway. Ever since the early warning systems picked up the pirate armada and the analysts had plotted their course, minelayers had been out seeding the waters north of Caister and south of Gorleston up to a mile out to sea. The ships left a strategically viable channel to funnel their enemies toward Yarmouth, but then laid a heavy net of the floating explosives to cover the last few hundred metres to the shore. The Navy had recalled all the ships still in territorial waters and assigned them to battlegroups approaching from the English Channel to the south. The beach itself was mined to the north and south of the intended landing zone for several hundred metres. Mobile gun and missile emplacements had taken station over several kilometres on either side to further discourage attempted landings outside of the trap, and the open stretch between was laced with tank traps. Earth movers had raised a bulwark for the defenders at points along the ten kilometre stretch, and concrete road dividers were being laid to hold the sand in place and provide a fire-step for the soldiers at the top of the beach. Behind them, no more than a few hundred metres through the evacuated buildings of the resort towns and residents homes, the rivers Yale and Bure acted as a natural barrier for two thirds of the 'front' and the second line, reserves and main artillery waited beyond them.

The King's forward command centre had been set up in a supermarket near to the city's train station. Tables had been brought and arranged in a rough square to the front of the shop floor, and an array of comms equipment and military monitoring equipment now occupied them. Within this, a map table had been lain out, and the King himself stood there with his senior knights and the commanding officers and liaisons from the army and navy. As Ros strode in with her friends, the sight of the stacked shelves laden with produce surrounding them lent the whole scene a comedic or surreal quality as messengers and sub-officers came and went with the latest news of the enemy's progress and dispatches for the knights and battalion commanders already in place.

Once they had arrived, John Loxley had gone to find Sir Andrew and the York muster, leaving Rosalyn with Geoffrey, Royston and Baron Dominic. The baron's armour barely let him enter the sliding double doors of the place, but he managed to slip in and strode toward the King with his little group in tow.

"Stafford, Essex and Tonbridge reporting for orders, my liege," he intoned gravely. Ros was amazed by how calm the King seemed, a never-ending stream of papers and messages seemed to pass into and out of his hands. He gave each one a brief scan then passed them back or onward with a brief instruction and maybe a word of encouragement or a quick, reassuring grasp of the messenger's shoulder. He turned to Dominic, and Ros felt he was assessing each of them as he spoke.

"Dominic, your message indicated you had one hundred men at arms with you, is that correct?"

"Yes my liege," the big baron nodded curtly.

"Take them to the front, central position with the athletics track to your rear. You'll have regulars on either flank along with armoured support. We're expecting the main landing there."

Dominic grunted his 'affirmative' and left with Geoffrey, glancing over his shoulder at Rosalyn, trailing in his massive wake.

"Tonbridge!" the King barked, and Royston stepped forward. "What do you have, Sir Royston?" the King inquired. Not long ago Ros would have pictured Royston all aquiver at being addressed personally by the King, but here, now, he was all business.

"Sharpshooters, my liege, six of the best," he announced, his voice clear of any tremors.

"Are you sure of that?" the King raised an eyebrow at the claim.

"Your majesty, I have trained alongside these men my whole life. They taught me." Ros was struck with how much her young friend had changed in such a short space of time. Gone was the goofy youth he had been, and here before her stood a resolute and assured young man.

The King clapped a golden, gauntleted hand on Royston's shoulder. "Glad to hear it. There's little in the way of high ground out there, but there's the tower and roof of the marine parade. Watch yourself though, they may have heavy ordinance, and if they suspect you're up there, they'll shell that place to buggery, so pick your targets and make them count."

"Yes, my liege!" Royston snapped off a salute and flashed Ros a wink as he turned to return to the small cluster of snipers who had joined their column en-route.

Rosalyn was still watching him, leave so she missed when the King called her name.

"Essex!" he thundered.

Ros started and put out one of the flimsy, foam roof tiles of the ceiling with her head. 'Too tall' she chided herself and stepped toward her monarch.

"Here, my liege," she announced.

"It says here you also have a hundred men?" the King had scanned a troop report.

"Yes sire. I trained with them under Sir Phillip, I know them well."

"Did you ever command them?" the King's eyes were intently focused on her now.

"Once or twice, on exercise," she admitted.

The King thought a moment. "There's a small boatyard over the road," he said finally, "take them there and hold. If the centre falters, I'll need your men to bolster the line, and I need to know where you are so don't go anywhere," he concluded and waved her away. Ros waited just a moment before turning smartly on her heel and marching out to brief her men. It was just as she walked out the doors that her armour systems detected the first sounds of cannon fire rolling in off the coast.

Chapter 33

Launde stood on the bridge of his hulk. The Camelot fleet had managed to sink one of the monstrous vessels by sheer weight of fire. The captured cruise liners didn't sink easily once the Norse pirates had 'modified' them, and even now the burning bulk of it was still slipping into the water, spewing out smoke and survivors. He was losing ships. Luckily, his ragtag armada was comprised of so many smaller jigs, tugs and freighters that plenty would still make the coast, and frankly the pirates were expendable, so Launde didn't really mind using their vessels to shield his own. He was barely listening to Lord Jerome's irritating nasal voice as it snaked through the bridge from the radio. "Just follow the plan, or I'll kill you myself, Crown!"

Morgana's Black Knight snarled into the radio. "My name is Launde! You don't get to lord it anymore Jerome, you stuck-up bastard. One word from me and Morgana will have your head on a plate if I don't tear it off myself! You handle your side of things, and I'll handle mine."

Turning to his bridge crew, he rattled off a string of orders to change course, speed, and man the scavenged guns that bristled from the decks of the ship. To hell with Jerome's plan. He was going to edge out and send a few of those prissy Camelot yachts down into the ocean's depths before they made shore. As the crew leapt about his orders, the ship shuddered as its guns began to fire at will; Launde paced the deck, feeling his blood rise with the prospect of battle.

"Now," he muttered, "We spotted their minefield so they know we're not that dumb, but we're following the path they've left us, so they know we're really not that bright." He chortled to himself before turning dark eyes on the ship's Norse captain. "Captain, let's show them something they don't know."

Geoffrey had always heard that it was the waiting before the battle that was the worst, but now he wasn't sure. He could see the enemy ships ploughing through the waves five hundred meters out, belching smoke (whether from hits scored by the navy ships or from their own mutilated engines, he couldn't tell). With a brief thought, his helmet's visual systems magnified the images, and he saw something that didn't make sense. Activating his comm's link to Baron Dominic, he addressed his battalion commander.

"Sir, are you seeing this?"

"Be more specific, Geoffrey," Dominic replied tersely.

Their communication, shielded as it was by their helmets, was still interrupted by the deafening roar of the nearest artillery pieces as they let loose a punishing salvo toward the enemy ships. Water fountained among the vessels and fire blossomed on a few, rocking them in the water.

"The larger vessels: They're putting down lifeboats. But they don't look like they're in trouble." Geoffrey was still trying to work out what was going on as the small vessels touched the water. He focussed on one of the boats, thinking it was some kind of advanced landing force, but there was only a pilot. Confused, he widened his view. It soon became clear that even the smallest of the enemy armada was towing a small motorboat, and dozens of them were now careening through their bigger brethren toward the beach.

"What if..." Geoffrey spoke into the open comm. "What if they know about the mines nearer the shore?" he ventured.

"What?" Dominic was in the middle of calling targeting coordinates to the main batteries in the second line.

"The lifeboats," Geoffrey shouted, "They're going to clear the mines for the landing craft!"

"They'll never diffuse them in time, the artillery with tear them apart." Dominic shot back.

"I don't think they're going to stop." Geoffrey breathed, horrified.

Sure enough, the little flotilla barrelled out ahead of the main fleet, spreading into a thin line. It seemed to Geoffrey that some of the other regiments up and down the beach had come to the same conclusion he had, because heavy machine gun fire started ripping toward the boats in short, staccato bursts. He ordered the Stafford gun groups to target the boats too, and his men started rattling off shots, but firing at the little boats, bumping and racing over the choppy sea, was futile.

After no more than thirty seconds, the first racing boat found the start of the final screen of mines before the beach. A dull 'Whump!' and a geyser of spray signalled the detonation. One after another, the little boats disappeared in columns of spray, but the tide of them seemed endless. Those mines were meant to cripple the troopships, litter the ocean floor with dangerous debris and reduce the numbers that the enemy could bring to shore, but with the out-runners throwing themselves into it, the explosive screen was quickly being rendered useless.

"Dammit," Dominic hissed over the comm, "Looks like we're doing this the hard way."

From his perch high in the tower, Royston watched the various ships and boats stream toward the beach. The first to land were a couple of military assault craft; spitting automatic fire from gun turrets, they hosed the bulwark defences as their ramps dropped and they disembarked the ugliest armoured vehicles Royston had ever seen. Even as the armour roared onto the beach, the Camelot artillery zeroed the boats and they exploded in showers of twisted metal and salt water. The vehicles gained the beach, guns roaring, but were quickly immobilized by anti-tank rockets from the defensive lines. Fast moving speedboats ran themselves aground among the debris. They only carried half a dozen troops each, but the stranded vehicles provided sufficient cover for the men to start returning fire, targeting the defenders' machine gun emplacements and rocket teams. Heavier cruisers followed, converted tugs and scows, pleasure craft and captured military vessels. Each one ploughed into the shallows, disregarding the debris already starting to clog the beach, lending their own brand of jury-rigged fire-power to the building storm of lead in the air. Grenades had started flying from both sides, the 'Crump!' of explosive munitions adding smoke, sand and shrapnel to the mix.

Royston had his men hold fire: They had their orders. He glanced down at his men; six shooters with spotters attached in teams along the roof of the marine parade. Their uniforms may have been mis-matched and out of date, but their weapons were a selection of the finest rifles ever crafted. Turning his attention back to the battle, he saw the pirate hulk, one of several spaced up and down the landing zone, steaming toward the shore. 'It'll never make it,' he thought, 'the beach shelf is over a hundred meters out and the draft on that channel ferry is too deep!' True enough, the huge vessel cut engines, the black clouds belching from its smokestacks fading away in the stiff, coastal winds. The knight of Tonbridge watched confused as his helmet magnified the fore-deck. Men were swarming around the huge harpoon cannons the pirates used to capture their prey-craft out in the ocean. Even as he wondered what they were doing, the cannons fired, sending their deadly projectiles over the beach and into the buildings farther inshore. The roar of the mighty guns followed after like a physical thing; men staggered and windows shattered, the smog of battle roiled like tormented spirits as, first the soundwave, then the blast wave rolled over the beach. Royston gasped. Each harpoon had been the size of a truck, and towing what looked like anchor chain. The links themselves were wider across than his own, armoured torso! These weren't for trapping ships, they were going to haul the mammoth hulk ashore! With a groaning of stressed iron the chains started to go taut, and the vast ship started to inch toward the shore. Bullets and rockets sparked as they ricocheted off the massive links, causing little or no damage. Royston tried to call in artillery on the fore-deck of the ship, to weaken the structure and let the winches pry themselves loose from the armoured hull, but the lines were jammed with calls for targeted fire. As the hulk groaned and crawled its way closer, gun emplacements on the deck started spraying and belching down toward the defenders. That was bad; fire from such a raised position gave the invaders a clear advantage. Activating his squad-link comms, Royston gave his orders; first the machine gunners and loaders, the crews on the heavier guns weren't as likely to notice the lack of automatic fire as the machine gunners were to notice the absence of the constant 'Thud! Thud! Thud!' of the heavy guns, then the crews on the larger artillery. After that they would relocate to another site or join the line itself.

As his men calculated windage and distance, Royston's optics noticed a large figure on the ship's bridge. 'Crown!' thought the knight, snarling at the distant shape. Reaching into his quiver, he selected a single, very special arrow. Putting the knock to the string of his powerful bow he drew and sighted down the shaft. He was dimly aware of pirate gunners dropping in his peripheral vision, but most of his attention was focussed on the window of the hulk as it edged ever closer to the beach. One of the crew on the hulk must have realised what was happening, as he leapt onto one of the heavy machine guns and sent a stream of high-calibre rounds toward Royston's position. Letting his breath ease out even as rounds impacted the tower, Royston released the arrow. The pirate gunner's shouts of defiance were cut short when a bullet popped his cranium and the inbound rounds ceased. The arrow arched through the air and struck the bridge window dead centre. It's depleted uranium tip shattered the window, and it's special payload ignited.

"How do you like white phosphorus, you black-hearted bastard?!" Royston whooped as the windows blazed with bright light before all was obscured by thick smoke.

Launde spat curses as the foul smoke filled his lungs. He reeled back from the window, bumping against console tables and howling, burning bridge crew. He shouldered them aside; it wasn't like he needed them anymore. Flecks of the searing incendiary had lodged in the joints and seams of his armour, and burned despite the mystic properties that infused the black iron. Someone was going to pay for his discomfort, he thought as he barged through the doorway, slamming and sealing the bulkhead behind him. Some of the bridge crew hammered on the steel as Launde stormed down the stairway headed for the lower decks. Still furious and smouldering, he bulled his way through the troops assembled in the hold, making his way toward the steel box that now rattled and shook as the thing within sensed the press of bodies nearby. With a bellowed order, teams of muscular Norsemen hauled on the chains that would operate the mechanism to raise the bow like a gaping maw and disgorge his frothing, raging troops.

Geoffrey poked his head over the sand bulwark. The hulk was close, hauling itself in on the massive chains and gouging up the soft sand seabed like a gigantic plough. The entire front end of the ship was hinging upward, and a ramp as wide as a city street dropped into the surf. Camelot machine guns traced up the ramp as a tide of ragged, emaciated bodies surged out. Bullets ripped and tore at the emerging press but they didn't falter, didn't slow. Within the shadows of the hull, Geoff thought he could make out a faint electrical glow playing over the emerging troops. 'Servitors!' he cursed. The tide of bodies pressed on regardless of casualties. Those who were ripped up by bullets would stumble from the damage, but the press carried them forward regardless. The block fanned out as they hit the shallows. By the time they reached the sand itself, the entire front rank was a red mass of ruined meat being carried forward by those behind. In the wake of these mindless wretches, real Norse shock troops

427

were advancing, using the servitors as meat-shields. Artillery roared and spat death into the screen, opening ragged gaps of red sand and flying gibbets, but still they came.

It occurred to Geoff that, whatever the histories said about 'glorious battle,' even the most naive of his fellows would, by now, have realized that this was going to get very, very ugly.

Chapter 34

Rosalyn's hands itched as she waited with her men in the boat shed. She was horribly conscious that there were men and women dying just a few hundred metres away, doing the job she was meant for. They'd been waiting for nearly an hour, listening to gunfire and the rattle of the windows as the big guns kept up a steady barrage against the enemy. She had them running final kit and weapons checks when the command line in her comms chirruped open.

"Essex One, this is Camelot One. Savant, stand to, I need you. I'll be at your position in three minutes, over?"

Ros immediately recognised the King's voice. "Camelot One, this is Essex One. Received and understood, over and out." She surged to her feet and opened her battalion comms. "Stand to!" she barked, "Every one of you, up and ready and outside in two minutes! With a will, now!" The soldiers scrambled to their feet and were out the door in a minute forty-eight.

Outside, she could see the King approaching. What little light there was coming through the clouds shimmered along the contours of his golden armour, four of his personal bodyguard at his back. He strode purposefully into the boatyard and straight up to Rosalyn.

"The centre of the line is being hammered, Stafford is calling for reinforcement."

"Yes Sire!" Ros kept her responses clipped.

"I'm taking your battalion to bolster the line."

"Sire?" Ros responded tentatively.

Anthony edged closer, dropping his voice. "I'm not taking your command, Rosalyn," he reassured her. "I know you've seen action, but this is a real battle and I just want to be on hand if you need some support."

"Yes sire," Ros sighed. She knew he was trying to help her, but she couldn't help but feel that his uncertainty stemmed not from her inexperience but from a deeper question of whether her loyalty held true. She resolved, right there, to prove herself once and for all. Straightening her back and squaring her shoulders she looked him straight in the eye, "Is that all sire?""

He met her gaze unflinchingly, "Yes."

"Then let's go kick those bastards back into the sea," she growled.

The King grinned and stepped back. "Very well. Dame Savant, order your men."

Ros keyed up her battalion comm's and ordered the advance. She was going to war. They moved swiftly through the smoking ruins of buildings that had suffered under the incoming shells, moving with cautious swiftness as tracer-fire rattled overhead. They passed corpsmen carrying back the wounded and the dead on stretchers. Within minutes, they had reached the forward defensive position and dropped behind the fire-step with Baron Dominic and Geoffrey. Ros had been monitoring the radio reports of the battle and logging the progress in her tactical implants, but it was nothing compared to the scene over the bulwark. She popped her head up and took a moment to survey the scene. She took in the shell craters, the disciplined, sporadic incoming fire and the twitching, crawling remnants of the servitors dragging themselves up the beach. The sand bathed red for a hundred yards in either direction, the vaguely identifiable shapes of limbs sticking out of the sand and the patches of scorched viscera... she stopped. Suddenly her brain wouldn't process the smoke-swathed horror of the landing field. She tore her eyes from the sand and looked out over the incoming soldiers darting from cover to cover, shell hole to shell hole and firing as they came.

Something was wrong, something was badly wrong.

"Sire," she barked into her comms, switching to the channel the King was sharing with Baron Dominic. "What is it, Savant?" he replied, coolly.

"This is wrong; the capacity of those ships is far in excess of what we have seen, and the Norse don't rely on artillery and precision shooting. Why haven't

431

they launched a full assault? Why are they picking at this line and not rushing it?" Her implants dissected, charted and plotted the enemy's movements and projected the possibilities, and now they were screaming at her.

"Agreed," Dominic chimed in, "so what are they waiting for?"

Ros scanned the front and the line. She caught a glimmer out of her peripheral vision and turned toward it. The sun was coming through a little stronger; it caught the gold in the King's armour and reflected like it was announcing his presence to the world at large.

"The King," she announced. "They wanted to draw out the King." Even as she said it, the invaders let out a thunderous roar.

Launde laughed aloud. Jerome might be a stuck-up, snobbish bastard, but his plan was working. Of course the entire attack was a feint to draw Camelot into a ground assault on hostile terrain, but Jerome had reasoned that, without a clear objective for the raid, Camelot would question why Morgana had attacked and likely wait and draw more strength for their response. But, by weakening their forces and drawing in the reserves, they could make a run on the King himself. Camelot would never let such an act go unchallenged. His keen eyesight, made

432

sharper by Morgana's magic's, picked out the golden armour of the King, and a predatory grin appeared on his lips.

"Now, my warriors!" he cried, "Let slip the dogs of war! Give them hell!" The Norse, keyed up already on their own noxious mixture of combat stimulants roared in response, and charged out of the dark bowels of the hulk. The huge, misshapen leader of the orc detachment assigned to the attack moved up beside Launde.

"Now, Sire?" it slurred from between its uneven teeth.

Launde held up a hand. "Not yet. Let the berserkers drain away their ammunition first and draw them away from their defences. Then you shall have your turn, along with the beast."

The battle cry of the Norse was almost as loud as the ragged rain of lead they let fly as they hit the surf and rushed up the sand. "We must take the battle to them," growled Dominic, "while they are in the open. We can't let them gain significant cover."

The King nodded and turned to Ros. "Savant?"

Ros didn't stop to wonder why she was addressed. "Sire, I recommend a round of grenades at thirty feet to thin them out and stun them before engaging."

King Anthony grinned. "A wise choice." He gestured briefly, "Make it so."

Dominic and Ros both accessed their comms. "Grenades at range three, oh feet. Ready!" They waited a moment as the machine guns hammered outward of their position. "Mark..." another brief pause, "Throw!"

Grenades arced out as the men threw. A few dropped short, but most landed with the precision born of practice and discipline. Several men were wounded as they threw, bullets tugging them back off the fire-step. The bellowing of the pirates was momentarily eclipsed by a chain of explosions that would have deafened Rosalyn if not for the audio dampeners of her armour. Her men enjoyed similar systems in their comm-beads, but not all regiments could afford such things.

In the wake of the detonations, the King mounted the fire-step, drawing and raising his sword aloft, "Soldiers of Camelot! Charge!"

Rosalyn easily vaulted the bulwark ahead of her men (a knight's place was at the fore of the charge) and ploughed into the invaders' ranks. She picked a tight knot of staggering Vikings and went in with her shield held before her. For this engagement she'd been outfitted with an electro-feedback unit that passed a hefty electrical current through the shield; a useful weapon in close-combat against mobs, but with its own inherent risks. As she bull-rushed the enemy, blue lightning crackled through them and anyone they touched. As they reeled, she thumbed the control on her tech-sword and swung it in a wide arc. The blade blazed as it generated a field of thermal energy, burning its way through flesh, bone and steel. Near half a dozen heads rolled to the ground from the blackened stumps of their necks. A brief visual check showed her that her soldiers had fallen upon the dazed and confused Vikings with a will, and were dispatching the easy targets quite efficiently, but there were more to come, and they were not so staggered. The lines clashed and warriors died. Rosalyn's troops had long knives, tonfas, and high calibre pistols for side-arms, plus long hours of rigorous hand-to-hand training. The invaders responded with wicked looking clubs, spiked maces, an assortment of small arms and a lifetime of savagery.

Rosalyn laid about her with her increased strength and powerful weapons, holding her own against the tide of ragged warriors. Even as she did so, her own troops were forced steadily back, and suddenly she realised she was being surrounded and overwhelmed. Her attackers pressed in close, regardless of the ruin she wrought upon them; they were stifling her mobility, suffocating her ability to fight back until her comm-line crackled open. "Essex one! This is Stafford two, coming in hard. Brace! Brace! Brace!"

435

Ros pulled her arms in close as blows rained in on her, and then Geoffrey came crashing down into the thick of the fight. From there, they fought back to back, edging back to the safety of their own lines.

"You didn't have to do that," grunted Ros over the comm.

Geoffrey tossed a Norsemen back into his comrades, buying a second or two, "Do what?" he replied.

"Rescue me," she shot back.

"It wasn't that." Geoffrey broke off and swept his chattering submachine guns in a wide arc. "Just didn't want you to get all the fun."

"Oh really?" Ros grinned within her helmet and swatted a particularly persistent warrior away with her shield. He shrieked as he spasmed and flew back into the throng. Sparing a moment for her tactical readout, she could see that the Norse were steadily pushing the line back, but only here. They were holding to the north and south, making a concerted effort to tie up any possible support, but with every passing second Rosalyn was more certain of their goal.

"We need support," she called on the comm. "They're making a push for the King!"

"Then let's not disappoint them," came Anthony's unmistakable, measured tone in response.

Looking back at her readout, Ros noticed a cluster of ident markers with the King. He had pulled in the new

436

knights, knight errants (those without troops of their own) and a few senior squires to bolster his honour guard for a counter push. She had the worrying feeling that this was what the enemy was waiting for.

Launde watched the frothing, screaming warriors rush up the beach. He watched them engage the disciplined troops of Camelot and, despite the casualties, saw them push the line back. Then came the moment he had been waiting for; the moment when the King of Camelot gathered a group of knights to him and made to break the line. His expression became grim. Now was the time. Time for revenge, time to show them all what power his lady possessed, and time to show them what became of those who did not entertain her favour. He reached out and pulled the lever on the side of the great steel crate. A rusty groan of protest announced the many thick locking bolts drawing out of their sockets. For a moment there was silence, before whatever was inside barrelled through the open door, rending the metal, such was the violence of its passage.

'Go my brothers,' he thought 'visit upon them the wrath of the lady Morgana'.

Turning almost absentmindedly back to the orc commander, he growled "And why are you still here?"

The orc raised a mighty fist; his troops let out a rolling battle cry from their misshapen throats and charged after the beast.

'Now is the time,' he thought with satisfaction. 'My time.' And with that, he strode into the surf toward the battle.

Chapter 35

Rosalyn shouldered her way through friendly troops to the King's position. He was fighting a particularly muscular brute until Rosalyn stepped in front of him, punching the warrior with all her strength; his head snapped back with an audible 'Crack!' and he fell. The King's men took the hint and pushed forward, creating an island of calm in the melee.

"Sire!" Ros snapped.

"Savant," the King acknowledged. He seemed amused by her savage entrance.

"Something is amiss here my lord, something is wrong."

"Aye," the king nodded, "this pagan filth have set foot upon our blessed isle. Now we must rebuke them."

Ros swore. "That is exactly what I mean, what can they hope to gain from this futile attack?"

"You said it yourself," the King glanced about and gestured with his sword. "They wish to draw me out and make attempt on my life, am I to stand idle while my soldier's fight for me?"

"That is not what I mean, my liege," Ros started but was cut off by a horrendous roar. She turned and craned her head about to see the source through the fog of battle, and here it came. For a moment she was shocked, sickened, and dismayed by the sight of the aberration thundering up the beach. Hunched and barrel-chested, it loped forward on a mismatched collection of limbs. Its right arm was huge, fully the width of her torso and as long as she was tall. From its left shoulder sprouted a nest of arms of different sizes. Its legs were bowed and crooked and equally uneven, with a number of shrivelled, wasted appendages hanging or dragging along behind it. The body was covered in splints and shards of armoured plate, overlapping and grinding together in a grotesque mockery of the fine suits they must once have been. She could see the coats of arms on some of the pieces; a number of the knights who had defected when first this conflict began. Atop its massive shoulders, heads were melted and mashed together, all screaming or bellowing in both anguish and rage, but even at this distance she could recognise some features, mutilated though they were. Even as her mind railed at the image, she recognised Raoul Folkestone and Sir Hector Tonbridge, Royston's knight, melded and screaming in torment. It was as if half a dozen knights had been mashed together into this monster with little care, giving it the size and power of a cargo van and the ferocity of a tank. The creature ploughed into the

440

Norse line from the rear with no heed paid to friend or foe, it simply smashed through all who stood in front of it making a bloody bee-line for King Anthony, and Ros stood between it and him. Shaking off the paralyzing revulsion she felt, she gritted her teeth, squared her shoulders and set her blade at guard.

Before she could engage, another giant barged past her. Baron Dominic, in his chipped and scored yellow armour loomed over her as he strode toward the beast. He set his feet and Ros saw the metal plates on his back shudder. Dominic was well known as a siege engineer and his armour reflected this. With a loud grating and protesting of worn mechanisms, the bulky rear section of his armour unfolded and stretched out into two great arms. Into these, his own already fearsome limbs slotted neatly, and he took on the colossal appearance of something caught between a gorilla and an earthmover, capable of tearing down reinforced walls with ease. He flexed the massive hands once, then balled them into fists and pounded his further augmented arms on the ground in challenge, causing tremors to shake those who stood nearby. Creature and Colossus came together with a resounding crash that drew the attention of every warrior in the vicinity. The aberration came in with its various arms raised high to smash its would-be opponent. Dominic caught the massive right arm by the wrist with a howling of hydraulics, gears and servo-motors, but the writhing mass of arms snaked out almost bonelessly and snared his other arm, clawing at it and his chest and face-plate. They struggled to and fro, knocking the lesser combatants aside as they fought for some advantage. Ros' gaze drifted away for a moment as her peripheral vision caught sight of large, black clad shapes now moving through the enemy throng. She was about to cry an alarm when a metallic roar of pain and rage drew her back to the titanic clash nearby. The monster had freed some of its multiple arms, the rest still entwined around Dominic, and was ripping shards of metal from its own body and jamming them into the joints in Dominic's powered plate. In return, Dominic pulled the creature forward and drove his armoured helm into the midst of its multiple heads. They staggered apart, blood ichor flowed from the aberration and its mighty chest heaved with effort, but it seemed otherwise unaffected. Dominic was bleeding too, oil and hydraulic fluid stained the yellow of his armour, and one of his augmented arms twitched fitfully as the shards embedded in the joints interrupted its functions. His monstrous opponent threw itself forward and the titans joined battle once more.

Dragging herself away from the spectacle, Ros grabbed at Anthony's armoured shoulder. "Sire!" she snapped. "This beast has opened the way for

442

Morgana's shock troops!" And she pointed to where the black clad orcs rushed forward in the void left by the ferocious charge of the creature. Anthony scowled and cast his gaze about. To either side of Dominic and his opponent, the soldiers of Camelot struggled against the Norse Raiders, holding the line but barely. The Knights he had gathered lent their fearsome might to the combat, but even they were struggling, the foe was too many. He looked about to speak, when there was a great sound of tortured metal and both looked to see the beast tearing one of Dominic's augmetic arms away in a shower of sparks and shrapnel. The great knight dropped to a knee, his cry of anguish amplified but stuttering as his suit protested this abuse. The creature swung its prize like a club, and battered Dominic clear off his feet and onto his back.

"My Lord!" cried Geoffrey and raised both arms to spew automatic fire at his knight's tormentor. He might as well have spat into the face of a storm for all the apparent effect it had on the beast, which turned toward the hail of fire and lurched toward Geoff, Ros and the King.

"I've had enough of this brute," spat Anthony, and before anyone could stop him, he surged forward.

Rosalyn had seen her liege lord Phillip fight, in sport and in earnest. She had often thought that no man could truly be so swift, graceful and powerful all at

443

once. She was wrong. As Anthony raced to meet the foe, his golden armour blazed, and his movements flowed like water as he ducked the swinging wreckage of knightly armour meant to strike him. He danced inside the monster's flailing arms, and drove the sword Excalibur into the horror's chest. Black blood spewed forth like an unholy geyser but, where it should have drenched the monarch in its foulness, it simply burned on his energy shield. The creature howled and reeled, clutching at the King and the sword impaled within its body. It turned its many heads downward and glared death at the golden warrior now held by its many jointed cluster of arms, and raised the still sparking club high.

Ros was shifting her weight and starting her charge to the King's aid, when her suit registered the passage of a supersonic object close by her. The head that had once been Tonbridge exploded in a shower of gore, and Ros' comm link stuttered to life.

"Take that you traitorous bastard!" came Royston's voice, full of rage and triumph. More high calibre rounds impacted the creature as Glasbury's sharpshooters came to the aid of their monarch. Its grip on the King loosened as it staggered under the punishment. Another roared challenge echoed out over the scene, this one from Geoffrey.

The appearance of the gross abomination had shaken Geoff. He recognised a few of the misshapen heads and bastardised faces scattered across its horrendous shoulders. He had expected Dominic to fell the monstrous creature but, when it had rent the knight's armour asunder, the young knight had felt a chill of fear. He could only watch as Anthony charged to meet the threat and looked to suffer under the beast's unkind attentions. Then the bullets struck, and he heard Royston's challenge on the radio, and his fear turned to anger. How could he allow this mismatched and ill-conceived homunculus to put him in fear? How dare it, how dare it strike down the brave Sir Dominic and lay its traitorous, contemptible hands on the King of Camelot himself! Geoffrey leapt, activating his jet assists, not to give him additional height but additional velocity, as he landed a two-footed kick on the staggered monster. He dropped lightly to the ground in a full crouch as it flailed above him, letting both his sword and shield fall from his grasp, as he leapt upward once more. He grabbed the largest head as he passed, a conjoined mess of features atop a twin neck, and brought his body up straight atop the beast's shoulders. For a fraction of a second he stayed in a hand-stand atop the vile creature before, with a shout of rage, he savagely twisted his body around. There was a sickening grinding and popping of bone and gristle as

445

the heads turned with him, necks winding around each other in gross distortion. Geoffrey longed to release his grip, the visceral sensation sending waves of revulsion through his body, but still he grasped the heads as he swung down behind the abomination and planted his feet in the small of its broad back. With a tremendous heave of furious strength, he folded the body with him, snapping the spine as the remaining heads took up an agonised keening. The mutilated monster fell as its legs ceased to function, and flopped about in the bloodied sand, just so much dying meat. Geoffrey rolled away from his victory, the nearest Norse pirates taking up the keening as their great beast died. He just had time to regain his feet and take a deep breath before a resounding blow robbed him of consciousness.

Belvarre flinched as the blow landed, it rattled his teeth, and he was watching from a concealed position some ways away. He watched Geoffrey's armoured body sail through the air and come to rest, unmoving in the sand. Still, he thought, the helmet ought to have soaked up most of the blow, it didn't seem to have caved too much, he reasoned. He couldn't justify joining the battle at this point, not for personal reasons. "Only if the need is great," Merlin had said, sternly. Well it wasn't great yet, he would hold, no matter the risk to his friends.

Launde had risen up behind Geoffrey like a nightmare and simply backhanded him with all the force of a cannon shot. Rosalyn saw this and cried out. She threw her arm out toward the orc she was currently fighting, and its miserable face disappeared in a spray of dark blood and 7.62 ammunition. The assault rifle mounted on her arm chattered, stuttered and went silent. She didn't stop to reload it. She leapt forward and raced to where Geoffrey had landed beside the hulking form of Dominic. Other armoured figures streamed past her to clash with the raiders and orc monsters, but she paid them no heed. Her fingers fumbled to remove her helmet which she cast aside. She hesitated for a moment as she cradled Geoff's head in her lap, and then activated the visor release on his armour. With a hiss the faceplate opened and she stared down into his face. He looked almost tranquil, as if asleep, except for the thin trickles of blood across his temple. Ros leaned down and brought her cheek toward his mouth to check for breath. She trembled, and it seemed like she waited so long, but then there was a faint whisper against her skin. She raised her face to the sky in silent thanks to the powers of heaven before screaming "Medic!" as loud as her bio-augmented lungs would allow. She only flinched slightly as a hand came to rest on her armoured shoulder.

"Get up Ros!" urged John Loxley. "Best way to help him now is to kill every godless sonuvabitch on this beach!"

Ros looked at her friend. His helmet was gone, his head bloodied and hair matted with gore. There were burns around the now tarnished silver electrode connections that made a line down his temple. Ros supposed they had suffered some power discharge when his helmet came off, but the damage couldn't be too serious, because the grenade launcher on his shoulder still scanned lazily around as he moved his head. Wherever he had come from, it hadn't been an easy journey.

Ros allowed Geoffrey to lay back on the sand, and accepted Loxley's grip to drag her to her feet. "Alright," she took a deep, steadying breath and hefted her sword "Let's gut the bastard."

John grinned and looked toward the combat, he spat a vicious curse.

"We better do it fuckin' quick," he snarled.

Ros followed his gaze. Launde was fighting Anthony, hammering away at Excalibur with furious blows that sent the King reeling. Every so often, other warriors would step in to assist on one side or the other. Anthony had struck a few of the invaders down, but Launde just swatted any warrior away from his fight to leave them awkward and broken on the bloodied sand, laughing contemptuously as he did it.

Even as they watched, another tall black form was surging down the beach toward the King, impossibly fast. A couple of times, Ros thought she saw the streak of darkness lift men to its mouth, and then cast them away, arterial blood gushing from their necks.

"We need to do something, fast!" she gasped.

"Don't need to tell me twice," John growled, and looked toward their reeling monarch. The grey barrel of the cannon on his shoulder panned to follow his gaze as John closed one eye, for all the world as if he were sighting along an arrow shaft. "Get in there!" he ordered as the launcher coughed out a string of grenades, Ros watched them for a split second, calculating their trajectory, and then, with a savage grin, she dashed toward Launde, Sebastian Crown, the Black Knight, everything in this world that she currently hated and she laughed as she did.

Chapter 36

Belvarre watched. He saw the King engaged by Launde and the desperate battle that ensued. He watched Loxley hasten Ros back to her feet and back to the fight. He was also watching the path of the approaching 'combatant', if that was what it was. He had scant seconds to decide before it reached Anthony, and then, suddenly, he got what he needed. Someone, some soldier, stepped in front of the running figure holding a sword, and it slowed to meet the challenge. The armour was a deep red, not black as he had thought. He was taller than Belvarre remembered, and paler too. But his eyes, those cold pink eyes were now red and held more arrogance, more contempt and cruelty than ever they had before. Belvarre gritted his teeth, 'Father'.

Now was the time, now was the tipping point Merlin had spoken of in their quiet discussions together. Now was his chance, not only to make amends for the wrong his father had done, but to prove to himself that he was worthy to be a part of Camelot's future... and the revenge, the revenge was good too. Lifting the soft leather pouch out of his pocket, he drew out the matching amulets, and held one in each hand. Closing his eyes he drew a deep breath, steadying himself against the creeping unease at what he was about to do.

"Urgh, superstitious mumbo-jumbo!" he cursed himself for his hesitation and dropped the first pendant over his neck like a young drinker taking their first shot of whisky.

The chain burned cold on the back of his neck as it touched his skin, a sensation that spread through his body like a rush of adrenaline. He gasped in shock as his muscles started to quiver and spasm forcing him to his knees. Gripping the second amulet he gasped "In for a penny!" through gritted teeth and slapped his hand against his motorcycle.

Jon's grenades stitched a line of detonations in the sand, forcing Launde back and allowing Anthony to roll clear. Ros followed through the fire and smoke, and hunkered down to hide her attack. She briefly noted loyal knights moving toward Anthony, before Morgana's Black Knight himself was before her. She ploughed into his midsection with both arms crossed in front of her, so she could drag her sword and parrying dagger across his stomach as he staggered back. The powered blades could rip through most materials, yet they drew mere sparks as they gouged the black plate. Growling in frustration, Ros span and landed a ferocious round-house kick on the chin of the massive horned helmet.

452

"God damn you, Sebastian!" she yelled, "Was it not enough? To be of Camelot, to be a knight? Why, tell me why!"

Launde rumbled with laughter as he turned and stared down at her. "You will not understand, it could never be enough. There is never enough, enough power, enough wealth, enough of anything!" he roared. "My lady promised me power like you could never imagine, power without limit or restraint, and that is what I wanted, that it what I hungered for. My thirst cannot be slaked by mere mortal influence! I want everything, and Morgana has promised me this!" He brought his great black sword around in a sweeping arc. Rosalyn didn't even try to block, but vaulted backward out of range.

"You are insane! Damn you, damn your inadequacy and damn your mad bitch mistress!" she yelled as she thumbed the control rings on her sword and dagger. Instantly, the wavering translucent kinetic blades that gave the weapons their cutting edge burst into incandescence, as the thermal laser field engaged, focusing light with the power of a plasma cutter along the length of both.

Launde howled with rage at the insult to his lady and came steaming forward, swinging wildly. Ros danced and spun away from his attacks, her swords trailing flames as she created a curtain of laser edged steel around her. She knew she was going to have to do

453

something soon, or the avalanche of black fury was going to roll right over her.

Though his knights made great effort to bring the King away from the fighting, they were hampered in their efforts by Anthony himself. Bloodied but unbowed, he pushed them away as they tried to drag him from harm's way. He raised his sword aloft and called his men to rally, but before the words had left his lips, a shadow was sweeping among them. The dark blur struck out with flashes of green edged steel, and men and knights were sent reeling; some spouting blood, others knocked from their feet. When all about him was chaos, and the King stood alone among his battered and bleeding troops, the darkness stilled and revealed itself. Duke Jerome Grayson sneered at the King and raised his bloodied blade to his lips, savouring the fresh, red liquid as he touched it to his tongue. Anthony was struck by the difference in the Duke. He was taller, but no less lean than he had been. Always pale, his skin now seemed to drink the light from around him, a halo of darkness surrounding his mane of white hair, and he moved with an unnatural grace that no mortal known possessed.

Looking down at the golden-haired monarch, Jerome smiled coldly.

"Don't do that," growled Anthony. "I know that condescending look you get before you talk down to someone, Jerome, and I won't let you play that game with me!" he bellowed. "I don't want to hear anything you have to say, you traitor!"

Jerome's face blanked for a moment, still and cold and dead, before he leapt forward with a snarl. Anthony raised his sword but he knew it wouldn't be enough. Jerome was too fast and his own movements seemed impossibly slow. The sword struck like a hammer blow, its force completely disproportionate to its apparent heft. Anthony reeled from the blow as another struck him across the stomach and he stumbled, raising a hand to ward off another. The fog of battle, smoke from explosions and gunfire wreathed about them, obscuring them from view, as Jerome glared down at the King.

"Surrounded by your warriors, you die alone, your majesty," he spat, venomously.

"Everyone dies alone, Jerome," Anthony gasped, as the Duke's shadow fell across him.

His Majesty, King Anthony Pendragon, was never sure what happened next. There was a thundering sound that pounded rhythmically from behind him. Jerome's eyes widened in surprise, and there was a sensation of something big moving at speed, and then the pale warrior was gone with only a swirling pattern in the gathered fog to mark his passing. From what some of the survivors of the battle could tell him, a knight, all in black on a great black stallion, had ridden into the smoke cloud alone and ridden out of it dragging a howling apparition with long white hair.

Ros parried and ducked and rolled with Launde's repeated attacks, looking for an opening and lashing out when she could. Blood oozed from minor cuts she had landed around the joints of her opponent's armour, though her own suit was faring little better. The glancing blows had dented and scratched it, and her mobility was dropping moment by moment as the servos strained against the punished plates. It was no small relief when Loxley waded in. Shield high and mace swinging, he battered the so-called Black Knight.

"What's this, Ox?" bellowed Launde taking a few steps clear of the assault. "Not going to take me hand to hand like old times? What's the matter, scared?"

"Not this time, you bastard!" Loxley shot back. "I may be slow on the uptake, but I do learn!"

Ros stepped up beside her friend. "What do you say, John?" she asked grimly. "No prisoners," he growled back.

Ros leapt forward and Launde swung his great blade at her, but she didn't engage immediately. Instead she vaulted over his swing and landed behind him. Reflexively he turned to follow her movements, which was when John attacked, forcing Launde to move again, keeping him off balance. Around them, the beach was in chaos. Gunfire, combat and the screams of the wounded and dying turned the scene into a collage of overlapping violence. The three combatants danced through the flying bullets, constantly deflecting blows aimed at them by other warriors, occasionally stumbling on fallen bodies or pieces of them.

A rumbling chuckle escaped the Black Knight. "So, you can't take me with all of your friends behind you, but you think you stand a chance here? When I have an army behind me!"

Ros swung her sword in a blazing arc, driving back or dismembering the Norse raiders who came too close. "You don't get to run this time, you coward! You don't get to just pop out when it gets too dangerous for you! This time you and your inferiority complex are dead! You hear me, Crown! You're dead!"

"Inferior?" Launde raged, his faceplate withdrew and Ros could see the blood-flecked foam on his lips. "I'll show you inferior!" he screamed in fury, and brought his sword down on Loxley's shield. The kinetic repulsion engine squealed and blew out as the sword curved around again, and ripped it right off it's grips to send it spinning away through the confusion of battle. He turned and kicked out, catching Ros in the stomach before reaching out and lifting her by the throat. She dropped her sword as she was raised high, and grabbed at his arm to stop her head being ripped off. As John came at Launde again, he swung his greatsword in a low arc and slapped the big knight's legs out from beneath him. He crashed to the ground were Launde planted a foot on his chest.

"You see?" he crowed, "I was playing with you, you could never beat me."

Ros tried to speak, but the hand was crushing her throat and all that came out were strangled noises.

"What? What did you say, bitch!" he pulled her close and relaxed his grip just enough to let her speak.

"We... never had to... beat you," she gasped. "You always... beat... yourself!" and she swung her free arm, with the dagger still in it, pommel first into his jaw. As Launde was rocked by the blow, John hammered the side of his knee with his artificial fist. The joint shattered and Launde screamed in pain as he dropped to his knees, releasing Ros in the process. He swung his sword like a giant scythe, but Rosalyn braced her dagger with her forearms crossed and caught the sloppy blow. She reached out and grabbed the hilt of the great black sword, and wrenched it loose from the fallen monster's fist.

"You betrayed us, you betrayed all of us!" she spat. "We didn't like you, we never 'liked' you. You were a bully, but..." she paused, "You were Camelot, and we would have fought beside you against anyone. Why couldn't you see that?"

Launde spat blood and reached for her with a feral snarl. It took most of her augmented strength, but she brought the great black blade up and took his arm off at the elbow.

"Enough!" she yelled, "You're done! No more! No more innocents will die by your hand, can't you see that?"

John loomed over Launde's shoulder. "You want me to do it?" he asked coolly. Ros shook her head, her eyes never leaving Launde's face

"Because she can't?" Launde grimaced. "My men will kill you, you'll never make it off this beach," he spat again.

A great roar rose up around them, but this wasn't feral, not the bestial cries of the invaders. It was a roar from the army of Camelot as, with Anthony at the lead, they smashed into the mismatched hoard.

"Not this time. This is for Brandon." Ros spoke almost to herself, before ramming the sword through her enemy. His expression was briefly quizzical, the name of his victim unfamiliar to him. Then disbelieving, as if this wasn't the ending he'd imagined.

The shock as it pierced his breastplate ran up her arm as it encountered his spine and back plate. She fancied it passed all the way up her arm and through her body, into her consciousness and back through

459

her memories. In that split second she felt the eyes of her past, of her younger self, her teachers and mentors, of Phillip and of her friends watching her, judging her. So this was cold killing was it? She thought, as she watched the light go out of Launde's eyes and his lifeblood drain away into the dirty sand. The body slumped to the ground, the sword still through it.

John moved to her side, "Are you okay?" he asked.

"I don't know," Ros murmured.

"Well, the enemy are falling back, but there's still work to be done, c'mon," he grunted.

The fire that had filled her during the battle had become a heavy, hollow sensation in her gut. After a last look at the fallen body of Sebastian Crown she followed, eager to replace the weight with fire, but sure that it would soon return when the hot killing was done.

Some distance away, the Black Knight cast his howling burden to the ground and, when Duke Jerome looked up, it was to see the point of a blade as clear and bright as polished silver. Hovering, unwaveringly, a hairsbreadth from his face.

"You are beaten," the knight declared in a voice like distant thunder, "but death shall not find you this day. It is more than you deserve. So go. Return to your mistress and suffer her wrath before you finally suffer mine."

Jerome pawed at the sand and hissed despite himself. He was alone in the smoke with this knight and, though he'd never admit it, he was afraid and not fully in control. His animalistic movements caused the Knight, with a flick of his wrist, to place a deep cut along Jerome's cheek. "Go!" the knight thundered again.

Jerome's rational mind knew the army was in full rout. He knew Launde, the brutish enforcer of Morgan le Fay, was dead, and that he would suffer her displeasure for that failure, and he knew, much as it galled him to accept it, that the very attack itself was a baited hook to provoke reprisal. With that thought, he regained enough self to see that flight was still a preferable choice to facing down this unknown foe, and so he fled.

Bel watched him go from beneath his black helm, his jaw clenched, and shook his head sadly.

Chapter 37

The day after the battle, those that could gathered back at Camelot. Rosalyn and her comrades had spent a long evening of seeing to their troops in terms of transport and casualties, before undergoing a longer night of diagnostics after receiving medical treatment for their wounds. Nicholaeos and Cassie 'Ummed' and 'Ahhed' over the results, before declaring the augmentation processes a complete success.

After a few hours' sleep, they were roused and brought to the round table for a council meeting. The knights around the table all looked weary, most sported bandages and some had their augmetic limbs detached for repairs. Sir Dominic's beard bristled from a swathe of bandages around his head but (and he was almost alone in this) his eyes gleamed bright with triumph. The council chamber itself reminded Ros of how it had been when she had first seen it after the initial attacks; quiet and downcast, with empty seats here and there. Looking around, Ros wondered why victory looked so close to how she had imagined defeat. She locked eyes with each of her friends in turn; Cassie, Nicholaeos, Royston, John and Geoffrey. Belvarre was conspicuous by his absence. She guessed he was still with Merlin.

Anthony strode into the council room and took his appointed seat. He looked troubled, and somehow older. There was a nervous energy to his movements. No, not nervous, Ros realised; angry. He laid a sheaf of papers down on the table in front of him and laid his hands, palms down upon its ancient surface.

"Knights of the table, brothers and sisters all, our enemy has handed us our opening. The fleet they sent to our shores is being tracked by our navy as it flees back to its home port. We are mobilising all military forces and reserves and co-ordinating with our allies on the continent. We will trace the enemy back to their own shore, and repay them their 'kindness' a thousand fold. I will not beat around the bush, this will be war on a scale that will beggar the last Great War. There will be hardship, pain and loss." He paused and locked eyes with every knight present, "But there will also be glory, honour to be won, and justice for every life, wrongfully taken, to be delivered."

Another knight that Ros knew as Sir Hector banged a fist on the table. "Aye! Now is the time to get to grips with this threat, we cannot allow their attempt upon your life to stand, my liege!"

The other knights at the table rose in agreement, giving voice to their own feelings of anger over the attack. Anthony raised his hands to bring the outraged knights to order once more.

"My knights, much as I appreciate your sentiment in this, were it simply an attack on me, I would not bring war upon us. This is about our enemies' ruthless and indiscriminate persecution of those we are sworn to protect. This table exists not to further its own power, but to stand in defence of those that cannot protect themselves. This war must not be based upon revenge, that is not our way, but to the purpose of seeing an end to the threat that hangs over the people of this nation, and those of its allies."

As he spoke, Rosalyn saw the vigour returning to him, heard the conviction in his words, and was reassured as to why she owed allegiance to him as King. The meeting went on with plans outlined, some knights assigned to national defence, but most divided into battalions for the upcoming counter-offensive. After a time, the meeting concluded, and the knights filed swiftly from the council room to see about preparations for their forces. Rosalyn stayed behind, nodding to those knights of her acquaintance as they left. Finally, it was just her and Anthony sat at the table. He was reading some of the reports he'd brought with him, and seemed oblivious of her presence. After watching him awhile, she cleared her throat.

465

"Essex," he said, without raising his head. "Something I can do for you?"

Ros hesitated for a moment, his manner seemed contrary to that he had just presented to the table as a whole.

"Er, I did have a matter I wanted to raise with you my liege," she began.

"If it is the matter of your relationship with Sir Geoffrey, then I must admit to some trepidation in the matter. How is he?" the question took a moment to reach Ros.

"Ah... a severe concussion, but he should recover," she replied briskly.

"Good," the king nodded absently. He finally set aside the papers and looked at her. "But I am also confused as to why you feel you need to speak to me about it. You are both knighted, are you not? Simply submit the paperwork to the records keepers," he said dismissively.

"That is part of it, your majesty." Ros took a deep breath, "however both sides must have the approval of their liege lords and families." She let the statement hang in the air.

Anthony looked bemused. "Surely there could be no issue from Stafford or Essex?" he began.

"But I am not Essex!" Ros bridled, suddenly angry with the monarch's obtuse response. "Without Phillip, I have no true tie to that house anymore, and am I really on the house Savant? They raised me only until I was old enough to begin my training!"

"According to official records they are your parents," the King replied, sternly.

"But they aren't my parents!" she snapped. "The only responsibility they have for me is that which you commanded of them, my liege." She knew she was hurt and angry. Listening to him speak of the war for his subject's safety, she had felt the sincerity of his feelings over what was to come. Where was that feeling now? She existed because of his command, his desire, and yet he brushed her aside and palmed her off the moment she was... she even hesitated to think of herself as 'born'.

"If any owns that responsibility, it is you!" She rose and leaned across the table. "You 'commissioned' me like a new frigate, except that you never bothered to show up for *my* christening!" She pushed away from the table and started to pace. "Your plan! Your guilt! Your responsibility!" She paused just a moment before adding, "And your *blood!*" she finished, panting with the emotion.

The King stared at her, levelly. "You overstep yourself," he said quietly. "I am older than my appearance betrays," he paused, "though perhaps not so much today... But I was a young king when I conceived the romantic notion of trying to redeem your off-shoot bloodline." He closed his eyes, and Ros sensed he was staring into the mists of memory.

"I admit I had little idea of what it would achieve, even with the rumours of Morgana or her cultists flying around, I just... felt that it had to be done." He sighed and opened his eyes. "Then there you were, and I had to do something with you. I couldn't keep you close, because I was unmarried, and even if I could have claimed you as my own, I couldn't guarantee to give you the attention you needed, or that those who feared what you might become felt you needed, in any case." The last seemed bitter in his mouth before he carried on. "So what was I to do but have you 'adopted' to a trustworthy family until you were of age to be trained by Phillip?" he sighed. "Jerome hated that, he felt it proved I trusted Phillip over him and... maybe I did. Perhaps that is what drove him to betray us," he finished thoughtfully. He ran his fingers through his long, golden hair, taking a deep steadying breath. "So, what would you have of me? What do you feel is owed?"

Rosalyn's hands hung at her side, her anger, her indignation had cooled, and now it felt like a pressure inside her. The past months her emotions had risen past the barriers that had been raised in her head and still she struggled to manage them. She knew that Anthony had been intimately involved in every step of the process, every decision about her

468

development. For the vast majority of her life, none of her choices had been her own, and she could see it now as she looked back. Quiet words, softly spoken over her young head, hushed voices in closed rooms, and meaningful glances exchanged when other thought she wasn't looking. She saw it all, the doubt, and the suspicion... the fear. Fingers of doubt creeping at the edge of her thoughts pushed some forward, and held others back. What did she owe Camelot? What of their promises? What of their values? What. Of. Their. Lies?

She shook her head. These thoughts couldn't be hers, she knew better. She owed it to Phillip who, despite all of what must have been going on beyond her notice, had been like a father to her. The enemy was insidious. It used your ambition, your greed, your fear and your doubt. That was how they'd gotten to Crown and Duke Grayson and all the others and she knew, she knew in her heart that none of them had half the reason she did to turn. Those traitors had doubted her conviction, her loyalty since before she was born, and she was damned if she'd let those weak, avaricious and envious turn coats be right, but... she needed something, one gesture to hold on to. Her emotions welled up from the pit of her stomach, pressure from her chest welling up in her throat, threatening to rob her of her voice.

"I want..." it came as a strangled whisper so she clenched her jaw and reached deep for her courage. "I want family, I want my name."

Anthony tilted his head at that, "Your name?"

The tears that had threatened to flow forestalled, Rosalyn drew herself up to her full height and stood square, and then she dared it all. "Yes, cousin. My hearts beats as yours with the blood of the Pendragons. I want no claim to title or throne but please, give me my name. Rosalyn Pendragon, knight of the Round Table."

"An ultimatum?" the King ventured.

"Never that, my lord." Rosalyn held her tone and stance.

King Anthony of Camelot smiled then, and Rosalyn swore that some of the worry lines and shadows eased from his face, if not returning him to the fresh-faced monarch he once was, but certainly there was once more a youthfulness, tempered by maturity. He stood and moved around the table to stand before her. He seemed to be weighing her, trying to get her measure. He hadn't put her under such scrutiny since those moments before the battle on the beach. Finally, he laid his hands gently on her shoulders. "Are you sure you want this? Even bearing the name is..." he shook his head, "I have not words for the privilege, nor the burden."

Ros took a deep breath, "I understand."

470

"No you don't," he smiled sadly. "But if I know anything of you, it is that you are willing to at least try to shoulder the burden."

They stood that way for what seemed like an age.

"Very well," Anthony said quietly. "Not so long ago, I recognised you as worthy to be a knight of Camelot, amidst what pomp and ceremony we could raise in the circumstances. Here, now, at this time, with nothing between us, no formality and no ceremony, I recognise you as my cousin in name, and in oath, Rosalyn Pendragon."

Someone in the doorway started slow clapping. Whether it was for emphasis or some cynical sarcasm was unsure, but there, pacing slowly into the room was Merlin. They stood silent as he approached them, wary until, from within his close cropped beard emerged a warm, genuine smile. He threw his arms around them both as best he could and drew them together. "Well done! Now, there is much to discuss and little time to do it in, there is a war on y'know."

Jerome Grayson screamed. Stripped of his armour, he lay tied across a curved rack, dragging his arms and legs not only out but down too, as his back was arched outward. He gritted his teeth as Morgana paced around the device, lovingly trailing her finger across the dark wood. Even as his muscles and joints screamed at him, there was a part of his brain disapproving of the simple white shift that was all she wore. Alive for god alone knew how many thousand years, and yet she couldn't grasp a simple concept like decorum. What made it worse was the way she perspired lightly when aroused, as she was now, and how that made the light material cling more, leaving nothing to the imagination. One of the side effects of his more recent transformation was that he now sweated blood, and his torso was dripping with it. Morgana left off caressing the rack and trailed her finger across his chest.

"So you let my beloved Black Knight die," she stated simply, her lips caressing each syllable.

"He... Wouldn't... be told!" Jerome grunted, "Under... estimated his foe!"

She licked her blood smeared finger, again with that gauche gesture, his inner voice commented.

"And you handed those fools at Camelot a victory," she went on.

"It... was the... plan!" he flinched as she leaned on the lever of the torture device. It had taken two burly men to put the last turns on that wheel, and yet, as she daintily pressed her hand against it, it turned another notch.

"Yes, yes it was," she smiled demurely. "Draw them out, offend their honour and bring them to us that we might embrace them in our loving arms," she giggled at her own dark wit. Once more, he was reminded how deranged she was.

"Then why!" he tossed his head, indicating the rack. She laughed at that. "This? This for Launde, and for my amusement." She steepled her long, delicate fingers and raised them to her lips giving the impression of deep thought. 'Did she ever give that much thought to anything?' he wondered.

"You think you are better than me, Jerome," she stated simply. "You think I'm mad." There was an all too sane expression on her face. "I will not allow you to keep questioning me, and I am wise to your attempts to weaken my position by letting my strongest assets fall in battle." She grinned at him. "If you think that is a new trick, you're not nearly as intelligent as others give you credit for." She climbed gracefully onto the rack, moving her lithe body atop him with little effort. Even amidst the pain, he was aware of the heat of her pressed against him. She placed both hands on his chest and scratched her nails down his bare skin. She tossed her head and sighed, "You know what I like about you, Jerome?" He grunted as the pressure of her body strained his joints. She continued, "You remind me of me from long, long ago. Ambitious, cunning, and devoid of any loyalty save to yourself." She leaned down and wrapped her fingers in his long, white hair, whispering breathlessly into his ear. "I used all the

473

tricks you're trying to play against me, Jerome. Questioning my decisions in public, removing my most loyal assets. I wouldn't be surprised if you were sending feelers out with the Norse to try and turn them to your cause..." she caressed his face. "But I'll give you some advice. Just this once, because I..." she squeezed her thighs against his flanks making him rise under her. "Like you."

She laid her head against his heaving chest, speaking to him as a lover might in the most intimate moment. "You can take my allies, Jerome. You can kill my champions." She raised herself atop him, the room grew dark around her and the temperature dropped. Jerome felt primal fear stirring within as Morgana pressed herself against him with each breathy word "Because I. Don't. Need. Them." She let out a climactic groan as she finished, and Jerome cried out in pain. She dismounted him and the rack, her dress stained with his blood. Turning her attention to the torturers stood just out of the dim light, she said, "Leave him on there another hour, then release him." Turning back to Jerome, she purred "Camelot will come against us and they will burn, and if you try to undermine my authority again? You will burn too."

The End

Coming Soon from David Cartwright:

Camelot 2050: Dragon Fire

Lightning Source UK Ltd.
Milton Keynes UK
UKOW01f2216230218
318411UK00001B/1/P